THE
SECRET STITCH

UNRAVELING: BOOK ONE

C. JANE REID

Helen,

Enjoy the adventure!

C. Jane Reid

SPINNING TALES PRESS

FIRST EDITION
ISBN: 0692660127
ISBN-13: 978-0692660126

For

Mom, who encouraged me to do it,

Dad, who believed I could do it,

Laurinda, for making me.

CHAPTER ONE

September 11th, 1720
Londonderry, Ireland

Of all the places I thought I might one day find myself, a wharf in Londonderry had never crossed my mind. I belonged nowhere near a ship. Yet here I stood dressed in my second-best skirt and bodice amidst the rank stench of the docks, all my worldly belongings packed in crates about me. And not many crates, either. No, I'd given away as many things as I'd been allowed to bring.

Still, I smiled to myself. I'd hidden the shawl my mother had given me on my wedding day. Grahame thought I'd given it to the Karney girl, but I couldn't bring myself to do it. I gave the girl my nicest stays instead. They were only good to wear to church, as the boning pinched too much for everyday work. She wouldn't find any use for it, except to reuse the linen and boning, but at least she could do that much. I was still learning my stitches.

I shifted on my feet, holding my canvas bag closer. A couple of men ambled by, sailors by the look of them, with rough shorn hair and patched clothes and a strange swagger in their walk. I half-expected them to say something, or at least to look at me, a young woman standing alone in the early morning amid crates, but they passed without a glance. Was it so common to see a young woman waiting on the pier?

I wasn't the only woman at the dockside, though—just the only one standing alone. The other passengers were gathered several paces

1

away. The women were keeping an eye on a handful of children while the men stood nearby, watchful.

Grahame was speaking with two other men by the pier in the shadow of a tall, three-masted ship. One of the men was the captain. The second man looked to be the leader of the nearby group. I couldn't hear them speaking, and I didn't know the man I'd married well enough to read his stance. The other two men looked relaxed, though, and welcoming.

The other passengers clearly knew one another. I tried not to stare but stole quick glances instead to examine them. I didn't recognize any of the women. That was a blessing at least. I couldn't bear to spend however long we were going to be on a ship pretending not to hear remarks made about me.

Perhaps Mother had been right and this was the chance at a new beginning. I had a new husband taking me to a new land for a start at a new life without the mistakes of the past dogging my steps. I stood straighter and lifted my chin. I could pretend this was good and try to ignore the sinking feeling in my stomach.

Grahame looked in my direction, and I was pleased to think that I might look confident and ready for whatever the future held. I wished I could read his expression better, but his dark eyes kept his secrets too well. It gave me pause to realize how untamed he looked. Grahame was presentable, his coat and trousers clean and well-mended, his black hair drawn back, and his beard trimmed. The other men, however, wore powdered wigs that were the current fashion, and coats and knee breeches of good quality, if not the finest I'd seen. The captain had a weathered, controlled look to him, and the leader of the passengers was shorter than Grahame by at least a hand-span and a bit portly around the middle. Grahame was long and lean, and when he moved, it was like watching a wolfhound on the prowl.

The captain turned for his ship, and Grahame and the second man came towards me. I tried to keep my expression polite, but my heart was hammering.

"Mr. Vance," Grahame said by way of introduction. "My wife, Ailee." His tone was neutral, as though he wasn't certain how to feel yet about having a wife.

"Mrs. Donaghue," the man said politely. I inclined my head, not sure if I should bend a knee or not.

"What fortune to have taken such a young wife, Mr. Donaghue,"

Mr. Vance said to Grahame. I struggled to keep my own expression smooth. Of course that was what Mr. Vance would see—a young woman not yet twenty wooed and won by a man ten years her senior. I should have been thankful that's all he saw and not the truth behind it.

I hid my thoughts behind as calm an expression as I could manage, thankful that I did when Grahame glanced at me. His own look was still unreadable.

"Shall we settle the terms with Captain Dawson while the crates are loaded?" Mr. Vance gestured toward the ship. "Your young wife can stay with our women. She'll be made welcome."

"Fine." A typical one-word answer from Grahame.

Mr. Vance raised his hand toward the women, and one broke free of the group to join us. "My wife, Tavey Vance," he told me. "She'll help you see to what you need."

The men left us to glance over each other. The older woman was dressed in clothing that had been mended a few times, with touches of lace on her mobcap and on the kerchief around her neck. Her shawl was knitted wool. She was neither stout nor frail, and I guessed her age at a couple decades above my own. Her face had fine lines that suggested she smiled often, though at the moment she was appraising me with a solemn expression. Despite my finer clothing, I felt sized up and found lacking.

"Have you a name, child?"

"Ailee."

"And your family?"

"Only my husband," I answered, feeling a pang at the lie. But it was also the truth. I'd left home and family behind.

A new beginning, Mother had said. Mother wasn't the one leaving everything she'd ever known.

"Well then, let's see if you're prepared." The woman held out her hand. With a start, I realized Mrs. Vance wanted to see what I carried. I considered refusing, but then I wasn't entirely certain what I did need. Grahame had seen to all of our supplies except for my own possessions, and he'd merely limited me in the number of items with a few curt suggestions I hadn't dared refuse, except for the shawl, which I'd hidden in my bag. The bag Mrs. Vance held out her hand to take.

"Oh, come now, child," Mrs. Vance said in a tone my mother

used with the serving girl. "Once you're on the ship, there'll be no chance to fetch what you might be missing."

Suppressing a sigh, I handed over the bag. Mrs. Vance untied the knots with deft fingers. "Let's see then," she said, and she laid out my possessions across the top of the nearest crate, saying each item as though ticking them off a list. "Your huswife and apron, stockings and kerchief, comb and brush, a mirror—my, that is fancy now, isn't it—wool and needles—haven't gotten far on this knitting, have you—gloves, not sure you'll be needing these, but they're small enough, and—what's this?"

Mrs. Vance held up the shawl. It was a triangle of finely woven ivory linen with cheyne lace in pale thread worked around the edges and three large lace flowers attached at the mid-points. Mrs. Vance gave me a long look. Wordlessly, she folded the shawl and put it back in the bag, replacing all the rest with it except the wool and needles. She pulled the needles free of the ball of wool and stretched them out to see the strip of knitting I had managed.

I heard the woman tsk under her breath. "We'll need to work on this," she said in a kinder tone. "You've dropped stitches, I can see, but there's a trick to picking them up. We've plenty of time to have it finished before we make land."

I nodded, my throat thick.

Mrs. Vance eyed me. "How long since you wed?"

"Just last month."

"Do you think you are with child?"

I felt my face burn and shook my head.

"Sure, are you? Good, that's good. Two of our women are carrying, God help them, and it'll make the crossing all the worse. Been aboard ship before?"

I shook my head again.

"'Tisn't so bad if you've the stomach for it, I'm told," Mrs. Vance said sagely. "Jacky," she called to the group, her voice piercing through the noise of the wharf. One of the men hurried over to her. He was tall, nearly as tall as Grahame, but gangly, like he hadn't quite finished growing. He looked around my age or maybe in his early twenties, and he wore a friendly smile. He moved as though he wasn't quite comfortable in his short breeches and buckled shoes, as if he'd have been more at ease in a kilt and boots.

"Fetch some of those boys," Mrs. Vance instructed him, "and

have them move these crates over to ours. Mrs. Donaghue and her husband will be joining us for the crossing. You come with me, Ailee, and meet the others."

Swept up in the woman's wake, I could do nothing but follow, uncertain what had just happened. I'd gone from suspicious to pitiable in the space of a moment. What had Mrs. Vance thought of the shawl? It was a useless thing, I knew. All lace and frail linen, meant for show and splendor. I'd been so proud of myself, hiding a bit of culture from my old life to carry into my new, a piece of my old identity to remind myself that once I'd been well-to-do and admired.

Now I was simply ashamed of it. I should have given it to the Karney girl.

At least I had my everyday shawl. It was warm and sturdy and everything a women like Mrs. Vance must admire. Mother had tutted at it, and I had worn it each day with a sense of dismay ever since the Karney girl had given it to me, but now I was happy to have it. Especially when Mrs. Vance introduced me to another young woman who wore a similarly worked shawl.

"Elsie, this is Ailee. She and her husband will be crossing with us."

Elsie, a fair girl with warm brown eyes and a ready smile, looked close to my age, too. Her dress was plainer than Mrs. Vance's, though she wore a bit of cheyne lace on the kerchief at her throat. I had the impression that everyone in the group was dressed in their finest clothing. Which put them a bit richer than Grahame, but not by much, and certainly nowhere near my parents' standing.

"Elsie MacClayne," she introduced herself. "So pleased to meet you, Ailee. Did you travel far?"

"Two days," I said.

"Are those your livestock?" another woman asked, gesturing toward the small, fenced yard across the road. "I saw your man with them earlier."

"We should have brought livestock," a second woman said.

"Patrick says there'll be plenty for purchase after we cross," answered the first woman.

"From where?" I asked before I thought better of it.

"The town, naturally." The first woman answered as though speaking to a young, rather slow-witted child. My cheeks burned.

"Be kind, Iona," Elsie said. "We've all wondered, too, what might be there."

I couldn't picture a town, such as where I stood, existing across the sea in a wilderness of untamed land. I wasn't well-traveled, not like some of the folks my parents had entertained, but I'd spent my younger years in Letterkenny before we moved to Lifford. I recalled being overwhelmed by the number of buildings and people the city held. Londonderry was probably as large, or larger, and I'd been a bit overwhelmed entering it yesterday. These cities had been founded generations ago. The new world wasn't even a proper country, so how could it have towns?

"Fine looking sheep," Mrs. Vance said. "I hope we won't have to eat them."

I started at the comment. Why would we want to eat the sheep? That's what the chickens were for.

"How many hens have you?" Elsie asked as if reading my thoughts. "We brought about thirty between us all, but a handful stopped laying."

"Ten," I answered. I had no idea which were laying or not. I'd only recently learned how to care for them and had the peck marks to show it.

"I wonder where they'll put all this stuff," the second woman said. "And the animals. They won't like being in the ship's belly."

"Better than in ours." The woman, Iona, laughed at her own jest. She was a large woman with lace around her mob cap and a mole like a lump of dirt on her chin. She had a coarse voice, like she'd been yelling at the children.

Elsie pulled me a few steps away from the others. "Don't mind Iona. She doesn't like the thought of sea travel, and she's loud when she's nervous. She's a wonderful cook and so handy with a needle. Not as good as Tavey, though. How are your stitches?"

"Sturdy," I answered. "According to my husband." Truly, though, it is the only kind thing one could say about my needlework. I'd never had a fair hand for it. And I wondered why Elsie asked it of me. It was a strange way to start a friendship. The Karney girl had done much the same, as though all wives and wives-to-be should talk of needlework.

"I do so like stitching, though I'm better at knitting," Elsie said.

"I'm hopeless at knitting," I admitted.

"This is very finely done," Elsie told me, touching the shawl I wore.

"It was a neighbor's work. She was trying to teach me, but I can't get the needles to work the way I wish."

"Only just learning?" Elsie sounded surprised.

I avoided answering. "I'm fair at spinning, though. I packed my wheel."

"Did you? Jacky promised to make me a new one when we arrived. I gave mine to one of the local girls."

"You couldn't bring it?"

"We're so limited on what we could pack—Jacky had tools he needed to bring instead."

"Why though?" I asked, finally giving voice to thoughts that had nagged at me since leaving the village. "It's a big enough ship. Seems as though we could have a bit more room for our things."

"I think it is something to do with the weight. Jacky tried to explain it. He's in love with the idea of sailing. The only thing I could liken it to was over-filling a cart."

"But a ship has no axle. And it can't bog in the mud."

"But it can sink," Iona interrupted loudly. "And it could founder."

"Let's not be having talk of sinking," Tavey told her. "Not before we're to board."

There wasn't much to do on the pier. I stayed near Elsie, and we helped watch the children. There were eight, ranging in age from a couple of years to ten or so. There was a babe, too, tied by a shawl to a nervous-looking mother with red-rimmed eyes. I learned through a few questions to Elsie and listening to the talk around me that the members of the group were all from the same cluster of villages. There were nearly ninety of them, and this voyage had been over a year in the planning. A couple of families had already made the crossing, and the news from them had been good. They all hoped to meet again in the new world.

"Have you family there?" Elsie asked.

"My husband does. His brother. And an uncle, I think, or an aunt. But I don't, myself."

"My cousin went," Elsie told me. "I had a letter from him last spring. He says it is amazing there. A little frightening at times, but like a paradise."

I smiled but kept my thoughts to myself. Grahame didn't act like it was paradise. He'd crated his musket and powder and sword while I'd watched, wide-eyed and chilled. I heard him tell the Karney girl's father that it was an opportunity for the brave.

I was raised to be confident, perhaps even bold, and my nature was far more daring than a young lady's should be, or so my mother had often commented. I'd been daring once, against all propriety. It had cost me everything. I didn't intend to make that mistake again, but I thought I could be brave.

The men joined us, Grahame among them. He came over and gave me that questioning look I'd finally interpreted as his way of asking if all was well. I gave him a brief nod, which seemed to please him. He wasn't one for words, my husband.

"We'll board as soon as the supplies are settled," Mr. Vance told everyone. "It shouldn't take too long. Keep close to the ship, though. The captain means to leave on time, and I doubt he'll wait for anyone who strays."

I looked to Grahame, not sure where to go.

"The livestock," Grahame told me in that quiet way of his. I suppressed a sigh, knowing I wouldn't be of much use, but I followed him across the road to the stockyard.

I was surprised when, after he closed the gate and we were among the flock, he spoke. "Were they friendly?"

The women, he meant. With a start I realized that he'd sent me among them to sound out the group. Clever, though I wished he'd warned me. I suppose he might have feared I'd give myself away, though I'd think he'd have learned I could keep a secret when needed.

"Yes. They're all of the same area, following a few families who've already crossed. Elsie said the rents had gone up again across the villages, and their flax crop failed for the second year. Several of their flocks got the rot, too."

Grahame was going from sheep to sheep, checking them over. "I heard the same. Vance is a minister."

With that bit of news, I understood Mrs. Vance's direct questions.

"They admired your flock," I told Grahame. My voice went all quiet and breathy for some reason.

He glanced over at me. I thought I saw the shadow of a smile cross his face, but it might have been a trick of the light. "Have they any livestock?"

"Chickens. A few milk cows. They plan to purchase once we arrive." I was surprised by how much I'd learned listening to the women talk. "I brought the shawl," I added impulsively.

Grahame straightened, a questioning look crossing his eyes.

"The lace shawl," I told him. "The one I said I gave to the Karney girl. I kept it. I am sorry." I didn't know why I felt compelled to apologize. It was my shawl.

It wasn't about the shawl, I realized. I didn't want falsehoods between us. Grahame and I had enough between us as it was, and I'd had enough of lies to last a lifetime.

Grahame was silent for a moment. "It's fine," he said at last.

I drew a shuddering breath. "It is?"

This time the smile wasn't a shadow. "Yes."

He'd known all along. He'd been waiting for me to tell him. "I'm sorry," I said again, but not for the shawl.

He touched my cheek, gently, something he hadn't done before. "Thank you."

I wanted to step into the circle of his arms, but I didn't dare. He was still a stranger, no matter that we'd shared a bed. So I offered him a smile instead.

"How can I help?" I asked.

"The chickens."

That, at least, I'd learned how to do.

CHAPTER TWO

The *Resolution* was a tall ship with three masts and two raised decks, fore and aft. "That's the forecastle," Jacky told Elsie as the last of the crates was being loaded. I stood nearby, watching the couple but trying not to be obvious. Jacky was dripping sweat from hauling crates, and his lank brown hair was sodden and clung to the sides of his face where it had come loose from the binding. Elsie's whole bearing had changed when he'd joined her, becoming relaxed and content, like a cat curled before a fire.

"And that's the quarter deck," Jacky continued. "And the fore and main and mizzen masts. They'll have gun decks, too, I expect."

"And a kitchen, I hope," Elsie said with a fond grin for her husband.

"Galley," he corrected. "Yes, but small."

"And rooms for us all?"

Jacky gave her a smile. "No rooms. Berths."

"Oh dear, that doesn't sound pleasant."

"It'll be fine," he told her. "You'll see. Close, but we're all friends and family." His easy grin took in me as well. "Your man knows his way about a ship, I noticed. Done much sailing, has he?"

"I couldn't say," I admitted, a bit startled. Grahame had not spoken of any time at sea. Then again, he'd not spoken much of his life before I came into it. I'd have never taken him for a sailor, though.

"He won't care for his height below decks," Jacky said. "I walloped my head twice now." He rivaled Grahame in height, though he was as slender as a reed.

"Mind yourself," Elsie told him. "You can't afford to be shaking loose any of the sense that remains to you."

They chuckled, and I joined in. I was growing fond of the couple. We were close in age, if not experience. Jacky looked as though he'd never said a cross word in his life, and Elsie had such a gentle and welcoming manner that I couldn't help but want to spend time with her. They were unlike anyone I'd called friend before. That was a small blessing.

Grahame joined us, looking none the worse for having helped load. "It's time," he told me.

"What about the animals?"

"They load after the women and children."

"The captain will want the ship ready to sail," Jacky added, "before the decks are crowded with beasts."

"They'll stay on the decks?" I was shocked at the thought.

"There's a place in the hold for the chickens," Jacky assured me. "The rest will shelter near the forecastle, I understand."

"They'll be fine," Grahame said. "Come."

I picked up my bag and followed my husband toward the ship, Elsie and Jacky trailing after. The hull of the ship towered overhead as I approached the plank that led up to its deck. The ship heaved with the warp and weave of the water, dipping down and then riding high. The plank was wide, but without rails or even ropes to grasp, nothing would keep me from pitching into the water between the pier and the ship should I misstep.

Grahame must have noticed my hesitation. "I'll be right behind you," he said, bending low to speak in my ear. His nearness was both foreign and comforting.

Grasping my bag close, I stepped onto the plank. It felt stable and stout, so I took another step. I could sense Grahame and his steadying presence behind me. The ship raised, and the plank with it. For a moment I thought I would fall, but I kept my balance. The ship settled and butterflies chased around in my belly. I laughed louder than I should have, but the sensation was so thrilling, a mixture of fear and excitement that left me breathless.

"See, Elsie," I heard Jacky say from the pier, "there's nothing to it. No need for nerves, my lass."

I crossed the rest of the plank and stepped down onto the deck. I nearly skipped with pride. I found Grahame watching me and was surprised to see a gleam of pleasure in his eyes.

Jacky guided Elsie across, holding her hand until they reached the ship and then lifting her down to the deck. Elsie was pale, but she tried for a wan smile to her husband.

The deck was thick with sailors and passengers. Men were leading the women and children through a narrow doorway set in the wall of the quarter deck as sailors scurried up masts and across yardarms, working with the ropes tying down the sails. Jacky was caught up watching the sailors, but Grahame ignored the bustle and led me to the entryway, gesturing inside.

The passage was narrow with a low ceiling and smelt of sweat, tar, and dampness with a pungent under scent I couldn't place. We had to wait for the line of passengers to file down a sturdy but steep set of stairs. The children seemed thrilled and called out with shrieks and laughter. The women muttered about the closeness.

Two decks down, a long, low-ceilinged hallway spanned half the length of the ship. On one side hung cots one above another—not proper beds but sheets of canvas hanging between the beams with rope. No bedding, either. Oil lamps hung along the other wall, carefully shielded to keep the flames protected. Their light managed to cast more gloom than true illumination. It was like entering a wooden cavern, and the place felt confining and depressing. I heard one woman liken it to moving into a root cellar.

"We're at the far end," Grahame told me, his voice low in my ear. His breath across my neck chased an unexpected thrill up my spine, and I could feel the warmth of him against my back. We'd spent the last month alone together on his farm with only our wedding night shared between us. Why was I having these sensations now?

The last two cots hung at the far end of the berths near the opening to another passage. Steps branched from the passage, but where the steps led, I couldn't say. The rank stench was worse at this end. It seemed that being made welcome by the group didn't give us the option for a better position in the berths, but the worst of it.

"What is that smell?" I finally asked.

"Fish," Grahame answered. "A shipment went bad. It will pass."

Please, God, let it be so, I prayed, but I was dubious. My stomach knotted from the overpowering stench.

Grahame had been busy as a few of our boxes and bags were

waiting for us. The boxes were tied to the beams and the bags hung from pegs. He had already assembled one of the small wooden stools he had dismantled and packed before our journey from the farm, a thoughtful gesture towards my comfort as there were no other seats in sight.

Grahame moved to one of the boxes, pulling out blankets for us both. "You have the top cot. The stool will help you. I'll help, too, if it's needed," he added as a look of doubt crossed my face.

I glanced around. "Are there no rooms? For changing and the like?"

"We'll hang a blanket," he said.

The truth about what this voyage would be like began to dawn on me. The farmhouse had been small, much smaller than I was accustomed to, but Grahame had respected my privacy. On the ship, however, I would be cramped with over ninety strangers, including a husband I was only beginning to get to know, on decks that reeked of fish, with all my worldly possessions tied in a bag to the wall, for several weeks while we journeyed across the sea. Desperation hit me with such force, I had to grasp the cot to steady myself. The material was rough and unforgiving. Like this ship. Like my new life.

"Ailee—" Grahame reached for me, his tone odd. He took gentle hold of my arm.

I forced myself upright and took a deep breath, but the stench choked my efforts.

"We can go on the deck, can't we?" I asked with a note of pleading I couldn't suppress. "During the voyage?"

"When it's safe." He looked uncertain, as if wondering if I were going to faint. I tried to gather myself once more.

"Good. That's good." I struggled to regain some semblance of composure.

"Ailee," he said again, stepping closer. He took hold of my other arm. With gentle pressure, he pulled me against his chest. My heart thudded, and with a swift burning of tears, I buried my face against him. I blinked furiously to keep from crying.

He didn't offer me a word, simply held me until I had control. I pushed against him and he released me.

"I need to check the livestock," he told me, uncertainty in his voice.

"Of course." I raised my face to show him that I was recovered. I didn't try to smile. I knew it would look sick and pathetic. He waited another moment, as if to give me a chance to change my mind, then left through the passage next to us.

I busied myself to keep the anxiety at bay, poking through the boxes and bags. Clothes, soap, eating and cooking utensils, stores of food, a few extra blankets, and, oddly, my spinning wheel.

"It's dreadful, isn't it," I heard Elsie say. I stood to see my new friend poking at the cots. "I don't know how I'll sleep in such things."

"I don't know how to even get into it," I said, trying to keep my tone light. Elsie made a small laugh, but it sounded forced. "I suspect we'll adjust," I told her. "Maybe in a few weeks, it'll be like we've always slept this way."

"Weeks." Elsie wrapped her arms around herself. "I don't think I can do it."

I moved over to her and put an arm around her after a moment's hesitation. "I'll help you," I said, wondering how I intended to do such a thing. "We'll help each other."

Elsie leaned her head on my shoulder in a way no other person had done before. A fierce protectiveness swelled in me.

"We can do this," I whispered, for both our sakes.

I wanted to be on deck when the ship left port, but Grahame told me it would be too crowded. So Elsie and I sat together on Grahame's cot, our feet planted on the worn wood decking to keep the cot from swinging. The air was still pungent, with oil lamps adding a haziness to the atmosphere and casting deep shadows. Women and children filled the passageway and berths. I'd have rather been crowded out on deck. At least on deck the sky would have been open to us.

The motion of the ship changed slightly as we left dock, but not extremely so. The cot tried to swing out a couple of times, but Elsie and I held it still. We glanced upwards from time to time, as though we might be able to tell what was happening by the look of the planks above our heads. We didn't speak to one another, both pretending to work on our knitting, though our needles lay mostly quiet. It was the only quiet to be found in the berths.

"I don't see why the men should be topside," Iona was

complaining not far from us. "It's not like they have a lick of sense about sailing. What one of them has ever been on a ship before? And what if they catch chill? We'll be the ones caring for them."

"You know how the men get about these things," Mrs. Vance told her. "They'll come down after we've set off."

I didn't hear Iona's reply. What were we going to do for weeks stuck aboard a ship? Knitting for the women, I imagined. Or sewing. And the men might get to learn a thing or two about sailing if the captain put them to work topside. Wouldn't the sailors be angry if the men sat around while there was work to be done? Or would they prefer strangers to keep below and out of the way?

Questions I'd never thought to ask danced around my head. Who were these people I'd surrounded myself with? They weren't the sorts I'd grown accustomed to when I lived in my parents' home. The women were more boisterous, settling in as though making new homes for themselves. The children ran in feral packs, being chastised by whichever mother was within reach when they grew too bold. And the men, before they went topside, had been noisy, quick with a jest and quicker with a coarse word when it suited them.

Weeks. In here. With these people. Listening to Iona scoff and Mrs. Vance placate and the children shriek and—

"Those must be dark thoughts you're thinking," Elsie said.

I had to laugh to shake off the gloom. "Yes, I guess they were."

"What shall we do instead?"

"I don't know. I do wish we could be on deck." I glanced upwards again, but the wood planks told me nothing.

"Jacky says they'll let us up once we're in the lough. You have your knitting." Elsie nodded toward the ladies nearby who were occupying themselves with their needles. Mine lay forgotten in my lap.

I let out a long sigh. "Yes."

"You don't care much for it, do you?"

"No, not too much," I answered. "I'm just so awful at it all."

"I'm surprised your mother did not force you to practice. Mine was strict about it."

I thought about shying away from the comment, but I wanted to trust Elsie. "Mother thought embroidery more suitable for a young lady," I told her.

Elsie's mouth opened in surprise, but she closed it quickly.

"I am trying to learn, though," I continued. "If you might have any suggestions?"

"Practice," Elsie said firmly.

I was at it for some while, working on the shawl I had begun under the Karney girl's instruction. Elsie made suggestions and showed me when I'd dropped a stitch or added an extra. I was relieved when Jacky came for us. My eyes were strained from trying to see the stitches in the gloomy light, and my jaw ached from clenching it in concentration.

"Do you want to go topside?" Jacky asked. "Your man said it was fine," he added with a look to me.

I nodded eagerly. Elsie seemed less inclined, but she let Jacky convince her. I shoved my knitting back into my bag, hung it on a peg, and followed Elsie and Jacky up the narrow steps.

The sunlight was bright enough to blind after spending time in the dark berths. The deck was busy with sailors, and there was a rhythm to their work that nearly matched the rhythmic swelling of the ship through the waters of Lough Foyle. Jacky led us around the sailors to where Grahame and Mr. Vance stood at the rail.

My husband offered me a slight smile as I joined him. He gestured to a place by him at the rail, and I stepped up. The breeze tugged at my mob cap, pulling a few locks of my auburn hair free to whip across my face and neck. The breeze felt glorious, clean and crisp and carrying the scent of damp earth and green growing things. The water splashed against the hull below me and the lough spread out around us until it spilled onto the rocky shore of Donegal county.

Sudden tears blurred my sight. This might be the last time I looked upon my homeland. Would I ever see Ireland again? What would the new land look like where we traveled? Could it ever be so green, so wild, so rich with history and tradition? Green, perhaps, and certainly wild, but how could a place so newly settled ever feel rich? I hadn't realized the intangible things I was losing.

I was clutching the rail, the polished wood strong and solid beneath my grip.

"'Tis a lovely way to say farewell," I heard Jacky say to Elsie.

I felt Grahame's hand on my shoulder. I looked up at him, but he was looking out over the waters of the lough, at the shore sliding past. His expression was closed, his gaze far away, as if he were seeing something beyond the shores. I wanted to ask him what he saw, but I hesitated to break into his reverie.

"This isn't so bad," Mr. Vance was saying to his wife, who had come topside with most of the other women. They were standing on the other side of Jacky and Elsie, staring out at the shore. "If the crossing is like this, we'll have an easy one."

I glanced at Jacky. Elsie was standing with her back against his chest, leaning into him, a hopeful smile on her face. Jacky, however, was looking down at her with apprehension.

What did he know that Mr. Vance didn't?

Grahame's hand tightened on my shoulder, drawing my attention. I found him also watching Elsie. He had the same look in his eye as Jacky.

Worry unsettled my stomach and I drew a step closer to him. His arm went around my shoulders, and I welcomed his warmth and his closeness, foreign as it was. I wasn't alone. I might not know the people around me, but I wasn't alone.

CHAPTER THREE

I remained on the deck as the other women went below. Standing by the rail out of the way of the crew, I tried to ignore the worry gnawing at me. Grahame left to help the sailors, and Jacky shadowed him, watching what he did. It was surprising to see how much Grahame understood ships and sailing. The captain commented on it as well, and I was close enough to overhear.

"You've seen a few ships in your day," Captain Dawson said.

"A few," Grahame agreed.

"Ever been across the Atlantic?"

"No, sir, nothing so grand."

"Even so," the captain said, "another steady hand is always welcome."

Where had he traveled, I wondered. I'd never asked him about his past. I hadn't the right given my own. But now I wished I knew. What little I had learned from the Karney girl was that Grahame had left home at a young age after a disagreement with his father and had been gone ten years at least. He'd come home in time to make peace with the old man before he'd died and had then taken over the farming and the flocks.

He seemed at ease on the ship, and he didn't seem to mind Jacky's attention. He didn't say much to the younger man, but he slowed his knot-tying to give Jacky a chance to see how it was done. I was less uneasy seeing how confident he was on a ship.

Before going below, Elsie had wandered over to see the animals in their rope enclosure by the forecastle. Altogether, there were a dozen sheep, most of them Grahame's long sheep, four milk cows, one of them Grahame's, and a bull, also Grahame's. The bull was gentle as a babe, something for which I was thankful, for he was a thick-horned, sturdy beast as black as pitch, just like the cow. The chickens were housed below. I wanted to see to them, but I hadn't been able to force myself back into the belly of the ship quite yet. It was so pleasant on the deck.

The ship itself had seemed large from the pier, but now aboard with easily the same number of sailors as passengers, it felt not nearly large enough. The masts, however, were as thick as tree trunks, wider around than I could circle my arms. The sails overhead were like canopies, flapping and billowing with the winds. But what was more amazing was how clean it all was. The decks were scrubbed, the brass polished, the inside of the railing was even painted a lovely shade of blue. This was a ship to be proud of and she was treated as such.

If only below-decks could be as clean.

Not that they were dirty, I reminded myself. They had been clean, just dark and smelly. But Grahame had said the smell would fade.

I joined Elsie by the sheep. The wind was still strong, even in the lee of the forecastle, and I had to clutch at my shawl to keep it from tugging free.

Elsie was stroking one of the sheep along its smooth nose. The touch seemed to bring both her and the animal comfort, but Elsie's expression was tight. The wind tugged at her mob cap and her shawl, but a clever curve of beaten copper wire kept her shawl in place.

"Is that a shawl pin?" I asked her.

Elsie put her hand to the pin and smiled. "Of a sort. Jacky made it for me when we were courting. He was always teasing me for losing my shawl pins. The pins would work loose and fall before I knew it, and I never could find them again. So he made me this."

The pin was curled into a flattened spiral, with a sharpened end to slide into and around the stitches, gathering the layers together and holding them in place. It was very clever, and I could see how useful it would be.

"Does it leave holes?"

"Not too badly," Elsie said. Her expression grew pensive again. "We should go below," she said, glancing around the deck.

"I think Grahame would tell us if we needed to. Stay out a bit longer."

Elsie took a long breath, as though weighing the chance of taking ill from the outside versus the discomfort of the cramped, stinking berths below.

I understood how she felt. For most of my life I'd been warned against staying outside for too long and the dangers of catching a chill. Grahame insisted on being outside as much as possible, though. We had even taken meals at a table he'd set under the eaves of the farmhouse. He must have picked up the habit during his travels.

After a month with him, I had begun to understand why. I felt so much more freedom being outside. So much more alive. The stench of chamber pots and smoke and old meals was oppressive when I went back inside. And here it was worse. "Do you think there's a way to air out the berths?"

Elsie laughed. "Wouldn't that be handy? But I suppose we could ask. Jacky might know. He's been learning all he can from whoever would speak to him of ships and sailing. We'll ask him at supper."

I frowned, stymied by another problem I hadn't considered. "What will supper be? Are we to cook it? Where would we cook it?"

"I'm not sure," Elsie admitted. "Let's find Tavey. She'll know, I'm certain."

Mrs. Vance had gone below, and I was loath to do so. But if I would be expected to supply a meal for Grahame and myself, I needed to figure out how and soon. The sun was riding high in the sky. It was well past time for the noon meal.

Reluctantly, I followed Elsie back into the ship. The smell was as bad as before, but now the odor of too many bodies in too close of space mingled with the stench of rotting fish.

We found Mrs. Vance helping hang blankets between cots to serve for a bit of privacy.

"All settled?" the older woman asked us.

"For now," Elsie answered. "We were wondering what to do about meals?"

"Bruce says there is a cook aboard," Mrs. Vance told us. A cook? Of course, that made sense. Someone would have to feed all those sailors. "No doubt he'll be of help. And we've plenty of fresh supplies to be used for the next few days. The captain has said cook fires are not to be lit outside the kitchen."

Galley, I corrected, but silently.

"So we'll need to arrange the use of the hearth, or what passes for one," Mrs. Vance continued. "I was going to ask Iona to speak with the cook. Mr. Beacham is his name. He'll be a bit coarse, but I expect he'll mind his manners around ladies. Why don't you go with her?"

"Are you certain we should be the ones to go, Mrs. Vance?" I asked. I wasn't so sure how welcoming Iona would be of my company.

"I don't see why not," she told me. "And please, call me Tavey. It's a long voyage for such formality."

Tavey went back to her work, leaving us to find Iona.

"Let me speak with her," Elsie said. "She can be a bit harsh."

I'd already taken note of Iona's manner and had no trouble letting Elsie handle her.

We found her at the other end of the berths, chastising a pair of boys for going topside without their parents.

"And if I catch you at it again, I'll take a switch to your backsides," she finished. The boys were cowering. I figured them between eight and ten, brothers or cousins by the look of them. They scurried off to their cots when Iona turned away.

"Tavey thought we might accompany you to the galley," Elsie said in a sweet, placating tone.

Iona bristled. "I'll not set another foot into that man's kitchen, God save me. Have a go at me, will he? He'll be wishing he had our help when the time comes to feed us all."

Elsie and I exchanged looks.

"Does Tavey know—" Elsie began, but Iona cut her off.

"Tavey can go speak with him herself. I've other work to tend."

"And where," I ventured before the bitter woman could leave, "might Tavey find the cook?"

Iona waved toward the passageway we had first entered. "Up those stairs, through the first passage, and go to the end of the hall."

She turned away then.

Elsie bit her lip in chagrin as I stood staring the direction Iona had gestured. Going by ourselves hadn't been exactly what Tavey had meant, but Iona had given us little choice unless we wished to return to Tavey in failure.

Failing at my first requested task did not sit well with me.

"It can't be hard to find," I said. "We might have better luck than she."

Elsie hesitated.

I straightened my shoulders, determined to manage some part of this voyage on my own. "Shall we be at it?"

I thought Elsie might refuse, but apparently the idea of letting me go alone was too much. She nodded, though reluctantly.

We wended our way past the last few berths and mounted the stairs. The first passage was narrow and the lintel came close to touching the tops of our caps. The entrance at the end of the hall opened to a narrow space crowded with a closed-in hearth, a board set along one angled wall with pots hanging from hooks over it, and shelves fronted with a plank to keep their contents from spilling free.

The thin man filling the narrow space turned to cast a fierce gaze upon us. He was an unkempt little man with an evil cast to his eye, his lank hair bound back by a stained kerchief, his clothing equally stained, though, I noted with dismay, well stitched.

"What do ye what?" His tone was hard, and he spoke in a Londoner's accent.

"We've come to offer a hand at meals," I offered.

The man glared at me. "If I wanted women in my galley," he growled, "I'd have married and taken a house. Get out, the both of ye. I've no use fer the either of ye. 'Tis my duty to feed those souls aboard ship, and do that I will." His growl had twisted into a hissing lisp, as though he hadn't all his teeth.

Elsie backed away, frightened, but a stab of anger drove me to speak even when I knew it would be best to keep silent.

"You've nearly ninety extra bodies to feed, sir, and only a single pair of hands. You'll excuse us if we'd rather not wait until the end of the day for a single meal. Mistress Tavey sent us to help, and help you we shall. Now," I said, giving the place another glance, "what needs doing?"

The man gaped at me, and Elsie was wide-eyed with astonishment. I felt a blush threatening to burn across my cheeks, but I tipped my chin up and looked the man in the eye, refusing to back down.

A rusty chuckle shook through him, startling me. "Well, now, aren't ye all spit and fire, just like I hear all Irish lasses are."

"Scots-Irish, if you please," I corrected. My father wouldn't have wanted me to let that point slide past.

"Oh, Scottish and Irish are ye? Well, now, don't that beat all. Fine, then, my fiery miss. Come with me."

He brushed past us, smelling of cabbage, fish, and sweat. Elsie looked at me. I couldn't very well refuse now. I gave her an encouraging smile that may have looked more like a grimace before following the cook.

He led us down two decks and into a hold stacked with boxes and barrels, with piles of canvas bags filling every available crevice and others hanging from hooks set in the beams.

"The freshest of it all won't last, so we'll have at it first," the cook told us, picking through the bags closest to him. "Some fine meals, fer a bit. But later—" He turned to cast a dark-eyed gaze over us. "Later it'll be all salt meat and beans and hard tack. And potatoes and peas."

"Peas?" Elsie looked surprised.

"So it isn't all potatoes, my fine lady" he told her with a grin full of missing teeth, which accounted for his lisp. "There's butter and rum and beer and water, but that last will go sparingly. Cap'n is careful about the water. We've chickens, aside from those ones ye brought. Biscuits to break yer fast, and peas and butter fer dinner, and beans and meat fer suppers, with a measure of beer or rum, depending on the day. There's salt beef and fish, and a thankful thing the fish isn't from that last shipment." Again that gaping grin, this time with a rusty chuckle that shook his narrow body. "Foul lot that was, and Cap'n fouler still from the trouble it caused."

"What happened?" I asked without thinking.

"Supposing to be salt fish," he answered while hefting bags aside. He was much stronger than he looked. "But weren't all. Had some fresh mutted in. Didn't realize it 'til a two-day from port. Went from Amsterdam to Aberdeen with that stench coming up at us, and then finally pitched the whole of it over the side. Washed the whole place down and still it reeks, but it'll clear in a few weeks yet. Cap'n was fast fer the devil in his ire, rightly so, and took the whole business to the magistrate. Didn't see any pay of it, but no loss, either, so there's that."

The man was becoming chatty as we lingered. I suspected he didn't have much in the way of company, alone in his galley, and women or not, we'd do for conversation.

"So these here," he said, gesturing to the bags. "I've fresh beef to go with these cabbages and onions, and fresh bread, too, and eggs and milk. These'll need tending." He pulled out a head of cabbage.

"Quartered, thusly." He made a couple of slashing motions. "And the onions the same and the eggs cracked." He patted a small crate. "But fer the noon meal, first, there's butter and bread and a good hard cheese." Lifting the top of another crate, he pulled out a large wheel. "So send them women to me and I'll dole it all out, and then later ye both can have at the cabbage and onions fer the supper."

He eyed us, and I saw a challenge in his gaze.

I nodded. "Of course."

"Fine, then, off with ye. And no women in my galley," he called after us. "I have the charge of it. I won't be sharing the cook fire. I told that woman what came asking already. 'Tis in my trust, and I don't take it lightly."

I held up my hand in supplication. "Of course not, Mr. Beacham. It is your kitchen."

We found our way back to the berths. I wasn't sure whether to laugh or not. Whatever had I been thinking? I was only a few months learning how to cook. How could I possibly do anything but add to Mr. Beacham's work?

"I can't believe you were so bold," Elsie told me. "I'm not ashamed to say he frightened me badly."

"I'm a bit surprised myself," I admitted. I decided not to share my doubts, at least for the moment. "Let's find Tavey and give her the word."

Grahame didn't come below for his dinner, so I carried it up to him. I found him helping to secure one of the sails. It was mesmerizing to watch the men work together, and I was impressed by how seamlessly Grahame had fit in with the crew.

I moved to the rail, not wanting to be in the way, and saw a large cliff, like a flat-topped mountain, jutting out into the lough. It was looming ahead of the ship, like a guardian of a castle entrance.

"That be Magilligan Point." The cook's rough voice came from behind me. He stood a few paces back, carrying a large pail of peas mixed with butter in one hand and a pail of wooden bowls in the other. He had wrapped a discolored length of knitting a couple times around his neck, as though afraid to take chill. The strange scarf hung down his chest in a loop. It had grown chillier out, with a bite in the wind. I wished I'd thought to wear something warmer.

"Ye shouldn't be standing on the rail," he told me. "'Tisn't safe."

"I'll take care not to fall," I said, a bit dismayed that he would think me so careless.

"'Tisn't falling that I'd fear," he said ominously and went on about his duties.

I was staring after him as Grahame approached.

"Did he offer you a wrong word?" Grahame asked darkly.

"No, nothing like that." I shook off the feeling. "I brought your dinner. The others are eating in the berths."

"Let's sit over here." Grahame led me to a sheltered place near the livestock and accepted the bowl of buttered peas, a wedge of cheese, and hunk of bread. "What do you think of Mr. Beacham?"

His question surprised me, more because he asked it than what he asked.

"The cook? He isn't a pleasant fellow, but he was helpful enough."

"Has everyone settled in?"

"Yes. We're hanging blankets for privacy. I saw Jacky came below."

Grahame merely nodded.

"Will you be working for the whole voyage?" I asked, encouraged by finding him so talkative.

"The captain lost a couple hands in Aberdeen. We've struck a bargain." Grahame didn't say more, and I was uncertain how to press him, so I let it go.

"Will you come below soon?"

"For supper."

That ended my attempts at conversation. I stared toward land as Grahame finished his meal. The coastline was still green and lush, dotted with boulders as if cast about by a giant, like from my nanny's tales.

Watching the shore slide by, I could still believe I would see home again. A long sigh escaped me, and I glanced at Grahame to find him watching me with those dark eyes.

He looked away, then held his bowl out.

"My thanks."

"Of course," I answered, for the lack of any better response.

"I'll see you below."

It was as much of a dismissal as he would give. I gave him as cheerful a smile as I could manage, collected his empty bowl, and returned to the berths.

I fetched my own meal and found Elsie and Jacky eating near their cots.

Jacky offered me his stool, and I sat, grateful for the company. The rest of the berths were lively with conversation.

"I was just telling Elsie how we'd reach Magilligan Point," Jacky told me. "Once we pass it, it isn't long to round Inishowen Head and be out on open water." He was buzzing with excitement and coming close to hitting his head on the planked ceiling with each gesture.

Elsie was smiling patiently at her husband with a look of amusement and adoration. It was sweet to see, but after the uncomfortable meeting with Grahame, it also reminded me of what was lacking in my own marriage.

"The cook said something strange," I said, trying to shake off my malaise. "He told me that I shouldn't stand close to the rail."

"It would be awful if you were to fall over," Elsie said.

"I thought that was his point," I told her, "but he said that it wasn't falling that worried him. What else might it be?"

I looked to Jacky, but the young man shrugged. "I couldn't say. But I can tell you that sailors are ripe with superstitions. They're worse than spinsters." He laughed.

Jacky returned to the deck to try his hand again at helping Grahame. Elsie and I found where to wash the dishes. The cook had set up a barrel of sea water through the passage leading out of the berths next to my cot. We saw to the dishes, drying them on towels I had brought. I was glad that Grahame had known what to prepare, but as he seemed to have sailed before, I knew I shouldn't be surprised. Some of the others had no dishes at all and had to borrow, or had no suitable dishtowels and had to share. Others were dismayed by sharing a single barrel of wash water. I hoped it would be emptied each day, at least. And that we wouldn't be expected to bathe with the same water.

I pushed the thoughts out of my head.

Elsie and I returned to the stools by Elsie's cots to work on stitching again. We spoke mainly of needles and knitting, and Elsie was a wealth of knowledge. I knew embroidery, it being the lady's work that my mother most enjoyed, and I knew enough stitchwork to sew a seam or a button. Elsie knew stitches by the score, and she recommended them, shyly at first, and then more emboldened as I readily accepted. I wanted to be better at the work and knew I had a long ways to go. Plus, it did help pass the time.

CHAPTER FOUR

By the time Tavey found us, I was ready to set aside stitchwork for kitchen work, a thought that would never have crossed my mind two months ago.

"Can you two see to helping the cook? We've got others preparing what we've brought for supper, but I'm sure he could use an extra pairs of hands."

I readily agreed. Elsie was reluctant but nevertheless joined me. We found Beacham in the galley, muttering to himself. He didn't notice us until I cleared my throat.

"Blast ye, er—" Beacham caught himself quickly and ducked his head. "Beg pardon, miss. Thought you were the first mate."

"Does he often come to the galley?" I asked, curious.

"Only when the cap'n says. Now, what might I be doing fer ye, miss?"

"We've come to help with the evening meal, as we said we would."

He looked surprised. "I figured ye'd have found better occupation by now than quartering cabbages and onions."

"As it turns out, there seems very little for women to do."

He chuckled, a sinister edge to the sound. "We aren't too much accustomed to women folk aboard, 'tis true indeed. But I'll not say no to help, since ye insisted in it so ably afore. Remember ye where the storage hold stands?"

I nodded.

"Then take this," he said, handing me a large cleaver. The handle

28

was smooth with use, and the blade gleamed sharply along its length. "And take ye this," he said, handing a thick, square board to Elsie. "And this." He handed me a bucket. "Fill it and bring it back. We'll do that a handful of times and see where we stand."

I had hoped to ask the cook about his strange warning, but he gave me no chance, turning instead back to his kettle and cutting board.

"Shall we?" I asked Elsie. She looked uncomfortable carrying the board, but she wrangled it into a better hold and nodded.

In the storage hold, we set the board over a barrel and began. Elsie fetched out a cabbage and I had at it with the cleaver. It took me several tries, and the cabbage was less quartered than hacked into oddly shaped bits. The second one was no better. It didn't help that the ship's movements made the thing roll on the board.

"Try taking a slice off the end first," Elsie suggested.

I did that, setting the cleaver against the cabbage and then sinking my weight onto it. The flatter end helped to keep the cabbage from rolling and the work went faster.

We filled the bucket, and I offered to run it up. Elsie was happy to let me face the cook, though she was set to accompany me.

"There's no reason for both of us to make the climb," I told her. "I won't be a moment."

The cook was muttering again, and this time I caught a few words. They actually sounded like prayers.

"Excuse me," I called. He faced me, and his expression curled into a sideways grin to see the bucket of cabbage.

"They may not be perfectly quartered," I admitted.

"They'll do, miss," Beacham assured me. He dumped the bucket load into the large kettle.

"If I might ask," I began, then continued when the cook raised his brow encouragingly, "for what were you praying?"

"A smooth sailing," he told me. "Every voyage be different, miss, but each and every one, I pray fer a smooth one."

"Does it work?"

He gave a half-shrug. "Cannot hurt. Once we're past the point, the sea will turn on us. The North Sea is always unhappy this time of the year."

"What does that mean?"

"We'll be tossed about a bit," he said. "Naught to fear, mind ye.

The cap'n knows these waters. We'll stay within sight of land fer a day or so, but then we'll be at the mercy of the sea."

I wasn't sure I liked the sound of that.

That evening, the passengers gathered in the hold before supper was served. Mr. Vance led us in worship. I was surprised to find that all of the passengers not only knew each other, they were all of the same congregation. It made sense, I realized, but it only served to make me feel even more the outsider.

At least Grahame had come below to join us. I had never learned how faithful he was, having only sat with him in service before our wedding day. He made all the correct responses, however, and whispered in prayer to himself when the time came. I had to hurry mine, so captivated was I in watching him.

We sat with Jacky and Elsie for this first supper. The stew was passable, though I took more pride in the cabbages than I knew was strictly necessary. The passengers shared other food between them that they had brought, such as apples and bread, meat pies, greens and carrots. It was a hearty meal eaten with laughter and anticipation.

Jacky described passing Magilligan Point, and I realized that was when the cabbages were rolling so badly. We were rounding Inishowen Head now, Jacky told us, and he seemed sorely pressed to be missing it. Elsie took pity on him and sent him upward as soon as he'd finished his meal. He gave his wife a kiss and dashed off.

Grahame thanked both me and Elsie for the meal, touched my shoulder, and followed the younger man to the deck. I stared after him. He'd touched me more in the last day than in the whole of the last month.

Elsie and I returned to the wash barrel and were dismayed to see the same water in the same barrel.

"I'll ask Mr. Beacham about it," I said.

"Oh, I don't want you to get scolded," Elsie told me. "I'm sure it'll sort itself out."

"Nonsense," I said with a lift of my chin.

But then we heard a fuss coming from the berths. We both hurried down the narrow steps to find Iona dressing down Mr. Beacham about the state of the water.

"We won't tolerate your slovenly manners," Iona was saying. She gestured grandly as she spoke. Her back was to us, so I couldn't see her expression, but indignation stiffened her back and punctuated her gestures.

Beacham was staring at the gesticulating woman with narrowed, dangerous-looking eyes, but he didn't move. Nor did he answer. When she wound down, she stood huffing in his path, awaiting his response. Beacham said nothing for a long moment, and people in the passage were silent with anticipation.

Suddenly, he tugged his forelock, ducked his head, and I heard his murmured, "Madam." He pushed past her, and she stared after him, stunned. The handful of passengers between him and the exit moved out of his way as he stomped through, hunched with the weight of the two buckets in his hands. Elsie and I stepped out of the passageway to let him by.

He glanced at me, and I saw a twinkle of mischief in his eyes. I also saw the slop he was carrying in each bucket.

"Don't you walk away from us!" Iona's husband was calling after the cook, following him while Iona urged him onward with little taps on his shoulder. Beacham didn't stop but went up the steps toward where the barrel stood on the landing above. I followed Iona as they passed me, and I felt Elsie pressing close behind.

As soon as we reached the landing, we saw Beacham dump a bucket into the water. The slop was brown and nasty and full of bits, both vegetable and animal.

Iona gagged. Her husband went silent. The contents of the second bucket followed the first.

Beacham wiped his hands on his trousers, picked up both buckets with one hand, and went back up the stairs. Everyone hurried to make room for him. Silence followed him through the hold until he passed out the other side.

I wanted to cheer for him, and I couldn't say exactly why.

Conversation buzzed around us after Beacham left.

"Are you going to let him get away with that, Patrick?" one man asked.

"Call him out, Pat!" cried another, followed by a round of hearty encouragement.

"Patrick, don't you dare," Iona scolded. Her husband looked torn between doing his wife's bidding or keeping pride among his fellows.

"We'll just see what the captain has to say about all this," he announced. I watched as he and a handful of men stomped off toward the exit.

"Why did the cook do such a thing?" Elsie wondered aloud.

"Maybe to put us in our place," I said. I considered a moment. "It's his ship, after all. We're guests here. We may not like everything that happens on board, but that's no reason to go demanding our own way."

"He let you demand it, though," Elsie said.

She had a point. "Maybe because I was demanding to help."

"What do you think will happen now?"

"I really couldn't say." But I feared the cook would get a talking to from the captain. Or worse.

I stole to the deck as the rest of the passengers made ready for our first night at sea. The sky overhead was quickening into night, but in the brilliant sunset, I could still see land off the rail of the ship. The waves were stronger, though, than they had been in the lough, and to one side of the ship stretched open water. We were sailing past Ireland's northernmost point. By morning, I thought, we will have left home behind.

I swallowed against a rush of emotion. Sorrow and grief, but something more primal, a sense of loss that went deeper than I had the words to describe. I was sailing from my past into an unknown future. I'd felt similarly after my wedding when I'd climbed aboard the wagon that Grahame had brought to take me home with him, but this was more profound. Then, I could have found a way to return to see my parents and the home where I'd been raised and all the familiar places. How I could do that now, I couldn't begin to imagine.

I felt someone approach and turned to find Grahame joining me. I was several paces off the rail, deciding to take the cook's strange warning to heart. Grahame stood with me, watching Ireland slide by into the gloom of the gathering night.

"I heard of trouble below," he said, speaking low.

"Mr. Beacham and Iona, one of the women," I told him. "Is he in trouble?"

"I suspect so."

"Did you see the men speaking with the captain? Several came up to the deck afterwards."

"I caught the end."

I waited, but Grahame said nothing more. I clenched my fist with frustration.

"And the water barrel?" I asked at last.

"It's dumped each night."

It was something, at least.

"I wonder why he didn't just say so?" I didn't expect Grahame to answer. It surprised me when he did.

"Sailors aren't accustomed to women aboard. They won't take kindly to demands."

"Oh." Beacham had mentioned as much, at least the first part.

"Careful how you speak to them," Grahame warned me, reaching down to take hold of my hand. "Best to avoid them." His hand, large and calloused and strong, threaded into mine.

"I can't avoid the cook," I told him. "We have to make meals and need his help."

"Let one of the others."

I stared up at him, puzzled, but his expression was inscrutable.

"I offered to help him," I said at last.

Grahame looked startled. "Why?"

"Because it needs doing," I answered, startled in return. "And I've the time to spare."

Grahame's expression smoothed into consideration. I watched his jaw work back and forth under his beard before an echo of a smile curved his mouth.

"I need help with the chickens," he told me. "If you have time."

My own smile was wry. "Well, that is certainly something I've learned to do."

Grahame escorted me below as night closed in around the ship. He held up a blanket without word so I could undress. I got out of my bodice and skirts, hanging them on pegs along with my jumps and pockets. I wrapped in the blanket before Grahame helped me into the upper cot. It swayed alarmingly, and I clung to the canvas edges until Grahame steadied it.

"You'll get used to it," he assured me.

I was still dubious.

"I need to check the animals," he told me. "And finish my duties."

I nodded, drawing another blanket up around me. The chill had followed us below.

He hesitated, then gave me a quick kiss on the forehead before disappearing through the passageway.

I stared after him, stunned.

Eventually, all the lamps but a few were extinguished, casting the berths into nearly total darkness. I felt the weariness in my very bones. The day had been the longest one I'd lived through since, well, since first going to Grahame's farm. But even still, it took a long while to fall asleep. The cot swayed oddly, the cold seeped in through the canvas, and the sound of ninety others trying to get comfortable enough to fall asleep, and then the snoring that followed, filled the berths for quite a while.

When I finally did drift off, I was plagued by dreams of clinging to the rail as the ship tossed upon the waves while something dark and ominous lurked deep under the roiling surface of the sea, waiting for me to fall.

CHAPTER FIVE

Morning found me unrested and unsettled. The ship lurched and rolled, trying to toss me off my feet once I found a way out of the cot. The lamps had been lit, but the persistent gloom did not help give me any sense of the time, though it was well past morning, as Grahame was already gone and had left his blanket folded neatly in the middle of his cot.

Dressing was an act of athletic ability that I did not possess. I actually hit my head on the plank wall. I finally sat on my stool to regain a sense of stability. What was going on around us to make the ship move so?

I heard others in the berths moving around and decided to find Jacky to ask him. Or go on deck for a look. Gathering myself, I got to my feet, using the walls and the beams to keep upright. The others weren't having any better luck.

I made my way down the berths. Elsie was up and dressed but had planted herself on her own stool, bracing against the wall when she needed support.

"Has Jacky gone up?" I asked her, clinging to the beam.

"Yes." Elsie's voice was pinched. "I asked him not to, but he insisted."

"I'm sure he'll be fine."

"But all this tossing about—what if he's swept overboard?"

"Grahame will watch him," I told her with certainty.

Elsie seemed reassured, if only just.

"I thought I'd go have a look myself," I told her.

"Oh, please don't," Elsie begged me.

"I won't go on deck," I assured her. "I just want to see what is going on outside." And I needed to breathe fresh air.

Elsie was not going to be convinced, but I was insistent. I knew she wouldn't go, so I told her I'd return with news soon. And that I'd take care. A few of the other passengers had heard me and watched with trepidation as I made my way through the passage topside.

Outside the skies were gray and ominous with thick clouds. Rain splattered intermittently and the deck was wet. The waves rolled around us, some breaching into whitecaps that sprayed into the air, but the sailors were at their work even so, most wearing sturdy coats and a few with hats. I saw Grahame wearing his leather coat, the wide collar turned up against the wind. His head was bare, however, his hair plastered back into its knot. Jacky was nearby, frozen by the middle mast with a look of doubt and fear.

Grahame noticed me and came over to the doorway.

"Stay below," he told me. "See to the chickens."

"I will."

He hesitated, as if he wished to say more but thought better of it. With a final nod, he returned to his work.

I went below, bracing myself against each swell as I walked. Rather than returning to the berths, I found my way to the galley.

Beacham was in there. He stood with the confidence of a man used to riding waves, swaying with the ship's motion, only catching himself on the deepest lurches. He turned to reach for a ladle and saw me braced in the entrance.

"Goodness me, miss—ye gave me a fright."

"I do apologize."

He waved it away. "It'll be a hot meal to break the fast," he told me. "Porridge and milk and whatever the likes of ye have brought. So I'll not be needing the use of ye now."

"That's fine. I need to take care of the chickens."

"If you see any eggs, ye bring them to me, miss, and we'll see what we can make with them. But I'm doubting you'll find any this day. And mind yer step. They've got the run of their little cranny. Ye know the way?"

"Yes, I think so."

"Ye'll be needing this," he said, and he drew up a lantern from a storage place under his work counter. He lit it from his own, closed the glass, and held it out. "Bring her back when you've finished. I'll have yer meal ready by then."

I took the lantern with gratitude. He nodded and returned to his work.

I found the small room where the chickens had been cooped. It was past the storage hold, and I'd stopped there for a bag of feed. The hold housing the chickens was small and low ceilinged but with a beam for roosting. Straw was piled on the floor around the slatted crates that had carried the chickens to the ship, and the crates were left open for nesting. The place reeked of chicken droppings. I closed the door quickly behind me to keep them cooped, but when I held the lantern out, I realized I needn't have bothered. They were all roosted, the game hens were clinging tightly to the beam and the Scots Dumpies were nesting along the walls in the curve of the outer hull or in the crates. None of them looked eager to move. I checked their water and scattered feed for them. Not a one of them stirred.

Concerned, I let myself out again and returned to the galley.

"'Tis the tossing," Beacham told me when I described what I'd seen. "It'll pass." He hoisted two buckets filled with porridge by their rope handles. I hoped they weren't the same buckets from last night, but I had a feeling they were. "If ye wouldn't mind, miss, helping me with seeing these to the others?" He asked it with such a strange tone that I wondered once more what the captain had done to him.

It was on my tongue to ask, but he gave me a long look, his eyes glimmering with that dangerous light I'd seen before, so I swallowed the words and merely gave him a nod. I picked up the wooden ladle he'd left on the counter.

We passed through the berths, distributing the meal. Beacham said nothing to the others, though he gave Elsie a nod. I noticed the cook getting dark looks, but no one spoke to him, for which I was thankful. He had to return to the galley twice to refill his buckets. When we reached the far end, he set down a bucket to tug his forelock in thanks.

"I'll see to the men now, miss," he told me.

"Shall I help?"

"Goodness me, no, miss. Cap'n would flay—er, cap'n wouldn't like it, you coming topside with this weather. Thank ye, though." He ducked his head towards me and retreated.

I took my breakfast and rejoined Elsie as prayers began.

"I hope it isn't like this the entire voyage," Elsie said after we had eaten.

"I'm sure we'll get used to it," I answered. I noticed that the odor of fish wasn't as pervasive. Either it was passing or I was growing accustomed to it. So I had hopes for the rest.

I told Elsie about the chickens, trying to make light of how I'd found them. We shared a laugh, but it was a nervous sound that soon died.

For lack of anything better, I pulled out my knitting. Elsie tried to help me, but between my lack of skill and the ship's motion, I made little progress. Still, it passed the time. Somewhere farther up the berths, a woman began singing. A boy joined in, his voice bright and clear. Others joined in, too, and the song cheered us.

Near dinnertime, I retreated back to my cot to see what provisions Grahame had brought that we could share. I found hazelnuts and apples, dried meat, carrots, leeks, potatoes, and more cabbage. I wasn't sure what to offer, though. Would he want me sharing with the others? Uncertain, I debated going on deck to ask but recalled Beacham's warning about the captain.

Captain Dawson hadn't seen me on deck earlier, but Grahame had been quick to send me back below. I doubted he'd be pleased to see me topside again so soon.

I returned to Elsie and found that Jacky had come below and was sitting on his cot. He had changed clothes, though his hair was still wet. His damp clothing was hanging from pegs, dripping water onto the wood planks. Elsie was trying to coax bread into him.

"No, lass, take it away. I've eaten all I can stomach." Jacky looked a bit green and laid back on his cot, a hand over his stomach. Elsie covered him with a wool blanket and looked down at him with concern. I came closer.

"What is it?" I whispered to her.

Elsie shook her head. She pulled a stool over to the head of the cot to sit and reached out to smooth Jacky's hair.

"Shall I sit with you?" I asked, uncertain.

"If you like," Elsie answered, but her gaze never left Jacky.

I fetched my own stool and returned. As I did, I heard a few others comment on feeling unwell.

Was it a sickness? The porridge hadn't been wonderful, but then if it were the food, wouldn't we all be coming down ill? Maybe it was the rough seas, and, like the chickens, we needed to keep still and rest until it passed.

Jacky slept, and we took up our knitting again. I remembered my provisions when Beacham came through with a share of butter, more bread, and peas that had been boiled nearly into mush. Jacky refused any of it. I excused myself and trailed after the cook to collect my own share of food.

"Seasick, that's what it is," Beacham told me as he handed over my shares. "Seen it afore. Usually passes after a time. 'Tisn't good it's hitting so early, though," he said with a glance back down the berths.

"Will Jacky get better?"

"Hard to say. Strikes everyone different, it does. Most likely get ye all in the end. 'Cepting yer man, of course. He's seen a ship or two in his day, I'll wager."

I didn't say anything, and Beacham returned to his work. I ate what I could, stowed the rest away, thankful to find a crock to put the butter in, and returned to Elsie and Jacky.

Jacky was still asleep. Elsie was watching him furtively

"He's never ill," she whispered. "I've seen him soaked to the bone out in the cold and not even a wisp of a fever the next day."

"Mr. Beacham said it's a sea sickness and that it usually passes."

Elsie looked a bit relieved.

Grahame joined us not long afterward. His hair was wet, but he'd put off his coat. He looked Jacky over, his expression closed. "Did he eat?"

"Only bread," Elsie answered, "when he first came down."

"Get him to drink," Grahame told her. "Not water. Anything but."

Elsie nodded.

I followed Grahame to our cots. "Will he recover?"

Grahame didn't answer. "How are you feeling?"

"A bit unsteady," I admitted. I was regretting the peas and butter for dinner. "Why are we moving like this? Is it the rain?"

"A storm's passing. It makes the seas wild."

"How long will it last?"

"Not long."

I took hope and sat quietly as Grahame ate. I tried to find a subject of conversation but failed. Grahame didn't seem interested in talk. He ate quickly, thanked me, and returned topside.

The seas calmed by afternoon, much to everyone's relief. I checked on Jacky to find him awake and taking bread with beer. Elsie looked relieved.

I returned to the galley and Beacham helped set me up in the storage hold with a cleaver and cabbages.

"I'll be back for them in a bit," he told me. "And mind," he said, pausing at the entrance to the hold, "if the weather turns, ye put down that knife and come up."

"I will."

"And don't go out on deck. Wild seas stir up the deep."

I blinked, but before I could think to ask what he meant, he had gone.

I spent the next hour taking my worry out on heads of cabbage.

By supper time, the motion of the ship had grown stronger, and Jacky had gotten worse. He'd been sick once when the swells began anew, and now anything he tried to swallow came up again. Several others began to complain of sickness, too, and panic would have struck through the group if the captain hadn't spoken with Mr. Vance and the other men. I tried to listen in but couldn't get close enough. Mr. Vance, however, came through the berths afterwards, asking that we stay calm and rest.

Could it be that simple? Stay calm, rest in the berths, and the sickness would pass us by. I wished it were so easy to cure the sores on my hands. I'd discovered blisters on my palms after handling the cleaver again so soon, and a few had opened. I didn't want to bother Elsie with it, as she had her hands full tending Jacky, and I wasn't sure who else to ask. Fortunately, I ran into Tavey.

"How are you feeling?" the older woman asked kindly. I knew the question was to see if I was coming down ill, but I choose the opportunity to show Tavey my hand.

"It's a small thing," I lied as the woman tsked over the sores on my palm, "but if you could recommend something?"

"I've just the thing that might help." Tavey took my arm to lead me. We stopped along the berths while Tavey checked on a few of the other passengers before ending up at her cot.

She took out her bag and rummaged through it. "Whatever have you been doing, child?" she asked, glancing over at me.

"Chopping cabbages for the cook."

Tavey paused, her expression one of surprise. "Chopping cabbages gave you those?"

"There were an awful lot of cabbages," I defended, "over the last two days."

Tavey pursed her lips. "Not used to this sort of work, are you?"

I looked down, biting my lip, wondering how to answer. Tavey saved me the need.

"I'd wondered," she said, "when I first met you."

Was it the shawl that had given me away? Or my finer clothing?

Tavey found what she was looking for. It was a small jar that smelled rich of rosemary and lavender when she opened it.

"It's a salve," Tavey told me. "It won't take much. Rub it on and cover it with a cloth overnight. Do it for the next several nights, and you should heal up without taking infection."

I accepted the jar. "Thank you. That's very kind of you."

Tavey gave me a warm smile. "You take care now, lass. Wear gloves if you can. That'll help."

I promised I would try and returned to my own cot. I put the salve on at once, delighting in the smell even though my palms stung from the touch. I found my gloves, pretty things not made for hard work, and slid one on carefully.

I was about to close up my bag when I saw the edge of the shawl. I drew it out, careful to look around first to see if anyone was watching. I ran my fingers across the linen and over one of the lace flowers. My throat caught at the beauty of it, and how out of place it was.

Had it only been two days since we had left port? And only a month since leaving home?

A month and a lifetime.

I folded the shawl and buried it deep in my bag, along with the memories.

I fixed Grahame's trencher as Beacham passed with the stew. The cook eyed me but said nothing. I took some stew for myself but ate little of it. My stomach clenched at the thought of food.

Grahame joined me after I'd given up trying to eat.

"How are you?" Grahame looked concerned for me, though he'd left me on my own for most of the day.

"Fine," I said, then at his piercing look, added "not completely well, but I'll manage."

"Have you eaten?"

I nodded. I had eaten. Just not very much.

"Good. You need your strength."

"Will it be like this for the entire journey?" I asked, worried.

Grahame looked down the berths where more passengers had taken to their cots early. "It might."

Something in his tone suggested it might even be worse.

The second night was awful. I didn't get sick, thankfully, but others did. The motion of the cot was of no comfort at all, though Tavey had tried to tell us it would be like we were babes again in the cradle. The smell was horrid, sweat mingling with vomit. And the sounds of so many people packed too close together were just as unsettling. There was no hiding from the fact when a passenger became sick. There was no closing out the noise of snoring from those lucky few who could sleep, or the weeping from those who could not. Below me, Grahame was a reassuring presence, but there seemed to be nothing he could do for the others.

The next day it was better. Jacky kept down broth, and a few of the others were eating by suppertime. I was helping Beacham full-time since so many of the other women were either too sick or too busy helping those who were ill to prepare meals. I tried to spend time with Elsie and Jacky, but it wasn't for long, for Beacham had endless amounts of work for me, from washing up the trenchers and bowls in seawater to cutting and peeling and scrubbing vegetables. How did I wonder what I would do to pass the time?

I would at least know how to put together a stew when it was all over, I thought.

I took frequent trips to the deck to breathe in clear air and to see how Grahame was fairing, sneaking out when no one was watching. He worked as hard as the other sailors and seemed content in the work, even under the gray skies. The rain came and went, but the sailors worked on, heedless.

Grahame did seek me out once or twice during the day for meals, and Elsie told me that he came to look in on Jacky as well. It was something to know he was watching out for them.

Mostly, though, I felt helpless and alone. I wasn't a part of the group of passengers like Elsie and Jacky, and I wasn't a part of the ship's crew like Grahame. I had no true place, unless I counted the supply hold.

The fourth day saw heavier rain. The waves lashed the ship. It was enough to put those who had weathered the trip so far into their cots, moaning and shivering. By mid-day, I finally took to mine, my stomach roiling with each toss of the ship. My life narrowed into a thin attempt not to vomit, clutching the chamber pot close with my eyes squeezed shut and my teeth clenched. In the end, I lost the battle.

"Ah, miss, ye poor thing, ye just hang on."

I came out of a bout to find Beacham standing at my cot, holding the chamber pot steady for me.

"'Tisn't so bad," he soothed in his rusty voice. "Ye just take deep breaths. Just keep the breaths coming, there's a fine girl. Here's yer man to see ye through it."

Grahame took Beacham's place, taking the chamber pot away to hold a pewter mug to my lips.

"Drink," he urged in a gentle voice.

The liquid smelt of spice, and I drank hesitantly. It was water but mixed with something warm and earthy with a bite to it that erased the traces of vomit as I swallowed. Grahame didn't let me drink too much, pulling the mug away after only a few sips and urging me to lie back.

Time passed in a blur of sleep and sickness. Grahame stayed with me, coaxing bread soaked in broth and sips of the strange water down me. My sleep was haunted by visions of seas boiling over with black-bodied creatures, their mouths filled with needled teeth and their eyes glowing yellow in the hazy fog. My waking hours were a torment of sickness, my stomach heaving and my body shaking and sweating in turns.

I tried to fight Grahame as he urged more of the spicy drink into me along with broth and bread, but he was relentless. Much of it came back up, but not always, until more and more stayed down. My sweating chills subsided. The nightmares retreated.

I came to myself to find Grahame smoothing my hair back from my face, a gesture my mother used to make when I was ill as a child. It was comforting as nothing else had been, and I fell asleep, this time into a true sleep, and did not wake again until morning.

CHAPTER SIX

Grahame wasn't there when I woke. I felt weak and sticky, but I managed to swing out of the cot. I stumbled upon landing, hanging on to the swinging edge of the cot to keep from falling. The ship spun around me, but after a few moments it settled into its usual rocking motion.

I eased onto Grahame's cot. My head felt light but my limbs were heavy. I was tempted to curl up and let sleep reclaim me. It was unusually quiet in the berths, with only hushed murmurs and a few moans breaking the muffled creaking of the ship's decks and hull, with the occasional thump from above.

A woman made her way slowly past the berths, stopping to check at every pair of cots. When she drew closer, I realized I recognized her but didn't know her name.

"How are you feeling?" the woman asked. She was older, around Tavey's age, with a careworn look but kind eyes.

"Better," I answered.

"That is good to hear. You rest. You need to get a bit of food in you, quick as you can. I'll send the man with it."

She began to move away, but I raised my hand to stop her.

"How long have I been ill?"

"I couldn't say," the woman admitted.

"Please, can you tell me how Jacky is?"

The woman's face grew shadowed. "Not well, I'm afraid. Elsie seems a wee bit better, but Jacky is weak as a lamb." She gave me a long look. "When you're feeling stronger, maybe you could give us a

44

hand?"

I quickly agreed. I wanted to stand up then and try to make my way to them, but I knew that would be foolish.

Beacham came through carrying a pail of broth that smelt richly of onions. He grinned a gaping smile when he saw me.

"Bless me, but it does me good to see ye roused, miss. Stand a cup of broth, could ye?"

"I think I could, yes." I was surprised to find myself growing hungry from the smell of the broth.

Beacham ladled out a cupful for me and handed me the mug. The scent of broth set my stomach to rumbling.

"Ye sit easy," Beacham told me, "and I'll fetch yer man."

He was off before I could stop him. Rather than call him back, I sipped at the broth. It was cool and watery, but it was a welcome sensation that helped chase the sour taste from my mouth. I sipped slowly, unwilling to force too much upon my stomach for fear of setting the sickness off again, but the broth settled well inside me, coaxing me back towards sleep.

Grahame found me clutching the mug, feet braced by my stockinged toes against the decking to keep the cot from swinging, fighting the urge to collapse upon the blanket. I was startled by the relief blatant on his face.

He knelt down before me. "How do you feel?"

"Tired," I admitted, "but better."

Beacham hovered nearby, his pail in hand. Grahame took the mug from me and handed it back to the cook. "Is there bread left?"

"No, sir, 'tis gone. But I've been soaking the hardtack and could fetch a bit of that."

"If you will."

Beacham scurried off.

"How long was I sick?" I asked.

"Three days."

I stared at him in disbelief. It didn't seem possible.

"Will you eat?" he asked me.

"Yes. A woman said that Elsie fell ill. And that Jacky was worse."

Grahame's expression tightened. "Everything that can be done will be," he assured me.

"I want to help."

"Of course. When we know you're stronger."

"How long will that be?"

"It takes longer to mend than to fall ill," he said patiently. "You mustn't rush."

"It wouldn't do me harm to sit with them, would it?"

Something in my tone must have carried my worry across to him. He sat back on his heels, considering.

"No, it wouldn't. Eat first, then we'll see."

I didn't push any further.

The hardtack that Beacham brought was a sort of biscuit that had been soaked in broth. It sat in a doughy sludge in the bowl, as unappetizing as anything I had eaten before. Still, with both men looking on, I picked up the spoon and forced down a bite. It was tasteless but oddly filling. I took another, which pleased Beacham to no end.

"I'd best be about me duties," the cook said reluctantly. "You take care, miss."

I thanked him, which seemed to please him even more.

Grahame sat with me while I finished the strange meal, watching every bite as though waiting for me to relapse back into sickness. When I finished eating without signs of the illness returning, he insisted that I lay down. I didn't argue. Sleep tugged at me. He pulled the blanket over me and smoothed back my hair with a gentle hand. I wanted to thank him, but I fell asleep before the words would come.

The next two days I spent with Jacky and Elsie, seated on a stool by their cots. The shadows around us were deep, the nimbus of light from the lanterns small and ineffective, as if the flames were afraid to fall ill by touching us. Elsie was improving, taking sips of broth and bites of soaked hardtack, but she had gotten very weak, even more so than I. Jacky, however, refused nearly everything I tried to give him, and when I could coax it down him, it came back up within the hour.

Beacham gave me all the advice he could, from holding Jacky's nose to get him to swallow, which seemed cruel but did actually work a little, to pulping moistened hardtack into a mash to slide into his mouth. I wanted to try water, but Beacham told me it was the worst thing for him.

"Trust me, miss, I seen it afore. Ye try some of that grog afore ye try water, but broth's the best fer him now. The grog won't work when they've gone this long. We got a bit into his little wife, though, and it did her a world of good, just as it did ye."

"You helped her?"

"Me and yer man, sure."

I was profoundly thankful for that, which surprised me. The idea of these two different men helping complete strangers was oddly reassuring. If they could come together to save Jacky, surely he would live.

But though I tried everything Beacham offered, very little of it worked for Jacky. He was pale and feverish under his blanket, and there were times when I worried that his breath had stopped.

Elsie finally came back to herself on the evening of the second night. She was weak and wan, but she offered me a thin smile.

"You're so kind to help us," she murmured, her voice the barest whisper.

I didn't know what to say. I hadn't felt like I was doing much good at all as I watched Jacky grow weaker. But seeing Elsie awake and alert gave me hope.

"Try to drink this," I told her, helping her to sit up a little so that she could sip from the mug. "And then we'll see about something more solid."

"Is Jacky up?" Elsie asked after she'd finished the broth.

I hesitated, and Elsie must have read the worry on me.

"He's not better, is he?"

"No," I answered. "I'm sorry. I've been trying everything I can."

"Help me up."

"Elsie—"

"I need to see him."

I didn't think I was strong enough to help Elsie alone. "Let me fetch help. Please," I added, pleading, when Elsie struggled to move herself. She settled reluctantly.

I hurried down the berths, looking for someone who might help. More passengers were up and about, but they were all still weak or helping those who hadn't recovered. Beacham was nowhere in sight, and I suspected that Grahame was on deck at his duties.

I finally found Iona standing near the entrance. The older woman looked worn out and carried a hard expression on her face. Still, I approached her.

"Can you help me, please? With Elsie and Jacky?"

Iona's expression tightened. "Not now, girl."

"But Jacky—"

"I said not now." Her voice was hushed but sharp as a knife. I fell into a stunned silence and only then realized I was hearing muffled sobs coming from the berths behind me.

One of the men was cradling a woman close to him. He shook as each sob wrenched him. The woman was limp, her arms dangling and her head lolling with each of his shudders. Her skin was pale and her eyes were staring upwards, unseeing.

Dead. The woman was dead.

I stumbled back, horrified. I retreated as quickly as I could and fled to Elsie. The shadows seemed to reach out as I rushed down the narrow hall, each berth holding horrors within their cots.

I stopped beside the blanket dividing the berths next to Jacky and Elsie. I tried to gather myself, but my heart was hammering and my stomach roiled once more. A cold sweat broke out over me.

People were dying.

I clung to the wooden beam as the edges of my vision blackened. I fought against the urge to faint, taking long, deep breaths despite the stench permeating the air. I didn't look at the people in the cots behind me. I was terrified I'd find open, lifeless eyes staring upward out of slack faces.

Movement from the other side of the curtain finally cut through my panic. Fearful of what I'd find, I stepped around it.

Elsie had worked herself into a sitting position but was leaning heavily back towards the cot. I rushed forward to help support her.

"You need to rest," I told her. My voice was trembling. "Please, Elsie. Please." Crooning the words over and over again, I coaxed Elsie back under the blanket.

"Jacky—" Elsie breathed out his name.

"Just rest," I told her, pleading. "He's here. He's right below you. Please, rest."

When Elsie was settled and her eyelids drooped closed, I busied myself straightening her blanket. I knew I was letting fear take over, but I couldn't help myself. I could not bear to look down at Jacky.

It was Beacham who saved me. He came upon me fussing with Elsie's blanket, tucking it in around her feet.

"He's stopped the shaking, then," Beacham said, his tone sober.

I froze, unwilling to look below.

"'Tis peaceful, this part," he continued. "But lets us keep to trying. Might be we could bring him around yet."

"Do you think so?" I wanted so much to believe him.

Beacham gave me a little shrug. "I seen it once or twice. No harm in the trying, miss."

He offered me a mug of broth and a spoon. I took it and, finally, looked down at Jacky.

He did look peaceful. And still alive.

Pursing my lips, I sat down on the stool next to his cot and began once more to coax dribbles of broth into him.

The next day Elsie was stronger. And insistent. I found that I could help her from the cot unassisted, but she was still frail. I propped her on the stool next to Jacky's cot and stood close at hand.

"He's still very weak," I whispered to Elsie. "I can't get much down him. Beacham has been all sorts of help, though."

"I'll get him to eat," Elsie said, weary but determined.

So for the next few days, I watched Elsie coax, urge, and demand Jacky into eating. At first, he responded to her. He drank more broth. He took small bites of the mushy hardtack. He even opened his eyes and once reached out toward his wife. I went to sleep that night with the first real hope in days.

By morning, however, he was worse. He'd been sick again in the night, so much so that now he refused anything Elsie tried to press on him.

And another person had died in the night, this time one of the children. The wails of grief tore my heart in two, and I couldn't hold back my own sobs.

Elsie still tried to get Jacky to take anything. She was up at all hours, resting only in bits. I took on the task of keeping Elsie strong, seeing that she ate and rested. It was nearly as hard as getting Jacky to eat, but reminding her that she needed to rebuild her own strength to help her husband often worked.

I wanted to help the others, but I couldn't bring myself to leave the sphere of Elsie and Jacky. The others faded to noises and smells, a backdrop of misery too great for me to consider. Elsie and Jacky became my entire focus, my world narrowing to the space around their cots, and only when someone came into that small circle did they become real. Grahame came by at least once a day but never for long. Beacham came by more often, carrying his ever-present pail of broth and a face filled with hard-edged sorrow. Tavey came by once, herself weak and wan, and she did not linger. She offered Elsie a few encouraging words that none of us believed before continuing down the berths.

At the end of the second week of our voyage, Jacky died.

I was sitting on my stool by the wooden beam, watching Elsie in prayer. I wanted to pray with her, but I was so tired that I couldn't form the words.

"Jacky?" Elsie said her husband's name with a tinge of panic.

I stood, fear taking hold of me.

"Jacky, love, please." He lay far too still. My heart began to pound.

"Jacky? Can you hear me? Won't you wake, just for a moment?" Her voice was choked. "Jacky, please." She shook him, trying to get a response.

His head lolled

I pulled back in horror. Elsie's cry filled the air around us.

"Jacky!"

Others came into the space, pressing around Elsie and the cot. I let myself be pushed farther from her side as Mr. Vance, Tavey, Iona, and a handful of others came together. Elsie's cry turned to a sob, stabbing me with grief.

I fled.

I hated myself for doing so, but I couldn't face it. It was too big for me, the pressing grief, the horror, the hopelessness. I fled, finding myself halted in the supply hold. I fell upon the hard, uncaring planks and sobbed.

I didn't know how long I knelt there, sorrow and fear tearing at me, before large, gentle hands urged me to rise. I let myself be raised from the deck and folded into Grahame's embrace. I clutched him as sobs racked my body. He weathered the worst of it until I was too exhausted to continue. Then he picked up me and carried me out of the hold.

The fear of returning to the berths where death lay in wait made me fight against him, but he hushed me and kept going past the entrance to the berths. He didn't stop until we were out on the deck of the ship.

The sky was a brilliant blue, like nothing I had ever seen. The wind was cold and crisp and chased the stench of sickness away. Surrounding the ship was nothing but water, an ocean of blue-green like I had never imagined. Waves lulled around us, swells like gentle ripples in supple cloth. The sails snapped overhead, and the beams and ropes creaked with the strain of the wind.

It was like coming out of hell and into paradise. How could two such different places exist on one vessel? Below was death and sickness and darkness, but on deck was sunshine and wind and the occasional bluster of male laughter.

Grahame set me down on my feet near the rail. He released me, but he stayed close by, his arm around my waist. The wind carried a damp spray with it, just enough to feel the moisture from the sea, to taste the salt, so similar to my own tears. The peacefulness soothed my battered soul, cleansed my tired and aching body, and, surprisingly, let loose an anger I had never felt before.

"Jacky is dead," I said, my voice barely loud enough to be heard. "Jacky is dead," I said again, putting force behind the words. I wanted the world to know it.

"I know," Grahame answered, solemn.

I looked up at my husband, a man I barely knew. Elsie knew Jacky, knew him like long-time friends and lovers should know one another. Knew him and had lost him and now would face a strange new land alone.

I had a husband I didn't know and would also face a strange new land alone.

"Why?" I demanded. "Why are we doing this? What was so wrong with Donegal? With your home? With our country? Is all this worth it? All this death and illness and hardship?"

Grahame stared at me, silent, his dark eyes unreadable.

"Why are we doing this?"

When Grahame still didn't answer, I fought the urge to slap him. Anything to get a response from him.

"Why me?" The whine in my voice was unmistakable.

Grahame's lips parted, as though he might answer, but then closed again. He looked away, out over the ocean, the wind tugging at his hair. He struck me as such a sober, solitary person, much like he had when I first met him. Why would such a man want a wife like me? Why would he want a woman like me for a voyage like this? Of course, any man would have wanted my dowry, but to claim it and still take me along? It made no sense. None of it made any sense.

"Will you please talk to me?" I pleaded.

He bowed his head. "I'm sorry for Jacky," he said at last.

I blinked against a quickening of tears, waiting for more.

Grahame turned away.

I stared at him, watching as he walked down the length of the ship. I felt hollow inside and bruised and battered on the outside. And alone. So alone.

What must Elsie be feeling?

Guilt filled the hollow place inside of me. Without another glance for my husband, I left the deck, returning to the berths and the hell they held to seek out Elsie and offer her whatever comfort I could.

CHAPTER SEVEN

I didn't understand how they would hold a funeral on the ship, but as they had already held four, there must be a way. I'd missed the others, busy as I'd been with Elsie and Jacky, but the reminders of loss were ever-present.

Mrs. Wurthing, the mother of the child who had died, still sobbed late into the night, and I found that I missed the fair-haired boy running up and down the passage with his fellows, his laughter light and inviting everyone to join in. He'd had such a lovely voice, too, when he sang with his mother.

Clancy O'Leagh wandered the berths in a daze since his wife's death. I thought of Mrs. O'Leagh often, unable to shake the image of those sightless eyes. I wished I'd known the woman when she had been alive and could bring up other memories of her. Mrs. O'Leagh haunted my nights as an unshakeable presence of staring eyes and slack features in the background of even pleasant dreams.

Mr. Finn had no family aboard to mourn his passing, but plenty of the passengers had called him friend and spoke of his generosity and faithfulness. Mr. Bell, however, was unchanged after his wife's death. I heard Tavey tell Iona that it had been the third wife he'd buried.

But how does one bury at sea? I had never found the nerve to ask. Today I'd see for myself.

The morning after Jacky's death, I gathered with the rest of the men and women who were able to walk to the top deck. Elsie and I walked arm in arm, as much for comfort as for support, following Mr. Vance and Tavey. Mr. Vance recited passages from his Book of

Common Prayer as we walked. Elsie moved in a fog, her face pale and her eyes unfocused. I murmured the responses, too focused on Elsie to pay heed to Mr. Vance's recitations. She had sat up all night with Jacky's corpse in silent prayer. I'd have sat up, too, except Tavey had called me away.

"Give her the last hours alone," she'd urged me gently. I had retreated to my own cot, but I hadn't slept.

On deck, the air was cold. The sun was still low in the east, risen just above the water, and the sky was streaked with banners of clouds whose undersides shone gold above the blue-green waters. The wind didn't blow as briskly and the sails sagged, as though bowing in respect for the man who had been so keen to know their ways.

Jacky's body lay swathed in sail cloth on two stacks of crates near the rail of the ship. The mourners gathered near, and Mr. Vance came forward, solemn and sorrowful, to read from his book.

"Man that is born of a woman is of few days and is full of trouble. He cometh forth like a flower and is cut down. He fleeth also as a shadow and continueth not . . ."

Elsie clutched my hands. All I could think was how Jacky would never see flowers again, or a shadow, or another morning like this, so bright and full of hope. Trouble or not, how much better would it have been to live? I knew I would never voice such thoughts, but I couldn't stop them from swimming through my thoughts. They circled around and around in an endless spiral of sorrow until tears were streaking down my face.

When the singing began, I forced myself to focus on the words, searching for a bit of solace, but the only comfort I had was Elsie's nearness.

Mr. Vance closed his book at last and stepped aside. I looked at Elsie and found her dry-eyed and calm, almost beatific in the way she was staring out toward the sea. I wondered what she had heard in the words to give her such repose.

Elsie released me and stepped forward. She placed her hands over where Jacky's own were folded under the sail cloth. She lowered her head, but she didn't speak or sob. She stood quietly with only the sound of the waves and the wind and the creaking ship filling the air. And then she stepped back. I took her hand, heedless of the tears rolling down my cheeks.

Captain Dawson stepped forward. He gestured and three sailors came up to the crates. One of the men was Grahame. The three took hold of Jacky's shrouded body, and as Mr. Vance said a few last parting words, they cast Jacky over the side of the ship.

I was stunned with horror. I might have cried out if Elsie hadn't sagged next to me. Instead, I caught her as others hurried forward to help. Together we guided Elsie back to the berths and the darkness that awaited us.

Elsie had finally fallen asleep. I had helped tuck her into Jacky's cot and sat with her. Tavey came by often, giving me a sad smile as she paused to check on Elsie, and then she'd be off once more. Beacham came by as well, offering a mug of something hot to drink. I tried to coax a bit of it into Elsie when she woke, but she turned her head without word. The drink was bitter, but not unpleasant, and warmed me until I felt my head nodding toward sleep.

Quiet voices drifted through the berths, lulling me deeper, until I started out of rest.

"It's the child I'd be afraid for." It was Iona, who didn't seem to know how to whisper. Her voice carried full and clear down the berths. "Coming into the world in a new land with no father. What will Elsie do?"

"She'll manage," Tavey answered. "Just as we all would."

Startled, I studied Elsie at her sleep. Elsie with child. Of course, I remembered now. Tavey had mentioned a couple of women were carrying when I'd first met the group on the pier, but I had never thought to ask who.

With horrible realization, I understood the depths of Elsie's grief. She hadn't merely lost her husband, she'd lost the father of her unborn child.

What would she do? I couldn't bear to think on it. It was tragic and heart-breaking.

Determination stirred inside of me. This was my friend. I would do what I could to help. Elsie didn't have to face it alone.

"You're a quiet one," Beacham observed.

I was sitting in the passage outside the galley door, cutting the bad spots off potatoes. Beacham had the fires lit to cook what would pass as our supper—potatoes and salt beef with dried peas brought up with a bit of water. He'd put me outside the galley so that he could put the potatoes in the kettle as soon as I'd finished with them. "To keep them from browning," he'd told me, but given how they looked to begin with, I didn't see what the difference would be.

I didn't feel much like talking. There was constant noise in the berths, and the silence was a welcome respite. It was one of the reasons I kept coming back to help Beacham.

"Shouldn't you be with your friend?" he asked, not unkindly.

"She's resting."

Elsie wasn't resting. She lay in her cot, staring at the wall without seeing. Tavey said it was grief and shock, and that it would pass. It had been over a week, though, since Jacky's death, and I was beginning to doubt she'd ever come out of it. I managed to coax food and drink into her, and once got her to wash and change from her stained clothing, but little else.

I sat on a hard stool with a large wooden bowl perched on my lap filling with peels. To one side of me stood a bag of potatoes, on the other a bucket filling far too slowly with those I'd peeled. I was beginning to think that I would be better at knitting than peeling. I'd nicked my thumb several times and had a strip of cloth wound around it.

"Most everyone's back on the mend," Beacham said, breaking the silence with his rusty voice. "The cap'n be pleased."

"Is he?" I said it to make noise, not really caring what the captain thought. He was a figurehead, like a lord in a tower or a distant king. I only saw him rarely and had never spoken with him.

"Oh, surely. It pains him to see folks ill. And to lose one—"

"Five," I interrupted, a catch in my voice. "We've lost five."

"I know it, miss."

Silence pervaded. I found I didn't like the silence so much after all. It left me too much alone with my thoughts, which always seemed dark.

"You never did say why I shouldn't stand at the rail on deck," I told Beacham. "And I saw a few of the other sailors keep away. Why is that? Is it because you fear falling overboard?"

"In a gale there's that fear," Beacham said, turning away from the kettle to look down at me. He was still an unsavory-looking fellow, with stained clothes and lank hair and a glimmer to his eyes that wasn't entirely welcoming, but there was intelligence there, too, and a measure of care in the lines of his face. I couldn't begin to guess his age. "But there are other fears, too."

"Such as?"

He sniffed. "You don't want to be hearing no sailor's tales, miss. You'd never sleep at night."

"I already don't sleep at night."

He eyed me, as though trying to read the heart of me. He set aside his ladle and hooked a stool with his leg, pulling it out to sit down in the galley entrance.

"There's places in this world, miss, what are still wild. Wild in ways the likes you've never seen."

"Ireland can be wild—"

"Oh, and England, too, in places," he interrupted me. "But not like this. In a place what has never seen the touch of man, there be creatures what'll open a body from—" He stopped himself. "Well, they be deadly, these creatures."

"Have you seen one?"

He looked down for a moment. "Not with me own eyes, no. But I've spoken to those what have. I recall a fellow, German he was— we met in an alehouse in Calais. He had a tale, he did, of something in the water what rose where they lay anchored off the port of Tunis. Grabbed a man right off the ship, it did, and dove back into the sea, taking the poor blighter with it."

"Grabbed him?"

"That it did. The German saw it happen."

"What did it look like?"

"He couldn't see it clearly. T'were dark, he said," Beacham defended. "Said it were man height with arms of a sort, but it had no head, or at least no neck, as I understood him. Head and body all were of a one."

"Did it have legs?" I was curiously fascinated by the tale.

"He didn't think so."

"How did it stand?"

"Gracious, miss, you should be a magistrate with all them questions."

I blushed lightly, but I still pressed him. "Have you ever heard of anything else like it?"

"Not like that, no, but I know other tales. The German, he was right full of them. Said where he came from, the woods still howled with wolves what would eat the children. And then there was a fellow from Venice what spoke of some things coming into the house from the canals."

"Canals?"

"Venice be full of them. Waterways running all through the city. They use them like roads, with boats instead of wagons."

I grinned. "Now I know you are jesting."

"On my honor, miss." Beacham covered his heart with his hand. "And by the grace of God, I swear it be true."

"You've been there?"

"No, but I knew a man what had."

I laughed, not harshly, but with the first real pleasure I'd felt in weeks. "What else did the German tell you?"

"Of flying fish and dolphins what saved a man and a whale eating an octopus."

I laughed, and Beacham chuckled his rusty laughter with me. He sobered then, standing, and reached for the odd scarf he wore when on deck that he otherwise kept hanging just inside the galley entrance.

"He gave me this, though, the German did." He held the scarf out. "Said it would keep me safe."

"Does it?"

"I'm still here, ain't I?"

I took the scarf. It was all of one piece, the ends connected to make a large circle, and made of raw wool that once was white but had turned dingy with wearing. The knitting was finely done, made with better skill than I possessed. No, not knitted. I pulled at it, stretching the stitches to see how they were done, but they made no sense.

"I've never seen its like," I admitted.

"His mother made one for him, the German told me, when he went from home. All the men of his village wear them when they travel, he said, to protect from the wolves."

"How?"

"Maybe it keeps them off their neck," Beacham said. He took the scarf back. "I couldn't say. All I know is that he swore by it and gave me this one."

"That was kind of him."

"He had it extra, from a friend what had died. And since he

couldn't pay fer his beer, I offered to," Beacham said, his eyes narrowing shrewdly, "if he give me the scarf. So it were a trade of sorts."

I understood at once. I could picture Beacham listening to the frightening stories the German sailor told, growing more and more pale, and finally seeing his chance for a source of protection. After hearing only a few stories, I wished I had such a scarf, too, or the skills to make one.

"Well, I shall stay off the rail," I assured him. "Unless I am wearing one of those scarfs."

"You do that, miss." Beacham looked relieved.

When I returned to Elsie's side, I found her still awake and still staring.

"Beacham just told me the most marvelous tales," I whispered to her. I pulled out my stool to sit next to the cot and began repeating the story to Elsie about the scarf. I didn't talk about the man being pulled overboard—it was too reminiscent of Jacky's loss—but I embellished the story of Beacham at the alehouse in Calais with the German sailor, making a tale out of it like my nanny used to do when I wouldn't settle for sleep. She would tell tales of giants and the fair folk and St. Patrick driving out the snakes.

"And so that is why he wears that awful scarf," I finished. "He thinks it will keep him safe."

"Does it?" Elsie's voice was weak and far away, but it was the first she had spoken in days.

"He says he's still alive, so it must."

Elsie sat up, stiff and slow, to face me. "Do you think something like that would have helped Jacky?"

I bit my lip, uncertain how to respond.

Elsie let out a long breath. "No, no, I suppose not. If prayer and broth and everything we tried didn't, how would a scarf?"

"Elsie—"

But Elsie laid back down and turned over toward the wall.

I looked down at her, uncertain what to do, and decided to let her rest. I pulled my bag over and took out my knitting. I had worked on it, a few rows at a time, as I sat with Elsie, but never for long. The shawl it was supposed to be looked awful.

I tried to loop the wool a different way, to see if I could make it look like Beacham's scarf, but the loops merely fell off or came apart.

Of course I'd not be able to recreate it. I couldn't even finish a simple shawl. But something in the way Beacham spoke of the scarf had me wanting to try. I knew it wouldn't have saved Jacky, but it held some power over Beacham. Or held power for him, like a relic or a blessing. Foolish thoughts, I knew, but then given all we had suffered, what could it hurt?

Besides, it was different work to try and kept my hands and my mind busy, so that I didn't dwell on death and discomfort and my hurting thumb.

CHAPTER EIGHT

After a harrowing first few weeks, we all improved in health if not completely in spirit, and life on the ship settled into a routine. While I never came to feel completely accepted by the others, I at least had found a place onboard helping Beacham and spending as much time as I could with Elsie. I was able to coax Elsie to sit with me outside the galley while I peeled potatoes or chopped onions or salt beef and we'd listen to Beacham tell stories he had gathered during his travels. We learned that the *Resolution* was the third ship he had served aboard, that he had started out as a deck hand, repairing and keeping the ship's tackle in good order. He'd been to nearly every port in Europe, many along the Mediterranean, and had been to the New World once when the *Resolution* had traveled to the West Indies. He had stories ranging from pirates and ghost ships to storms and shipwrecks to strange customs in far off lands.

I was transfixed by his tales. I didn't know how Elsie felt about them, for she spent most of the time silent and withdrawn, but I was captivated. The stories drew me out of my own fears and worries, giving me something other to think about than my discomforts and the uncertainty of the future. They reminded me of my nanny's tales, usually dark and deadly stories, and often with a purpose—be it as simple as 'keep off the rail.' That advice seemed to serve Beacham on numerous occasions, from storms to pirates to walking the wharf at night.

Though I asked to see it several times, I had no luck knitting anything that resembled Beacham's strange German scarf. I kept at it, as it was more enjoyable than muddling along on a shawl I knew would turn out horribly. It became a quest of sorts to try to master it.

The days got colder and the nights bitter as we traveled. I saw Grahame only once or twice a day, and while I exchanged a civil word with him, I was beginning to realize that instead of bringing us closer together, this voyage had drawn us apart. We spoke little during the brief times we spent together, and though I could see the hint of deep thoughts within his gaze, he never voiced them. He was even more reserved than before, standoffish and aloof.

Back in Ireland, we spent our evenings alone together, quietly finishing the day's work. While the quiet had been awkward, I knew it had stemmed from the newness of our relationship. I had hoped it would pass with time

On the ship, I felt suspended in a purgatory of doubt. Grahame was my husband, but now it was only in name. He was courteous but distant, staying to the decks or to other duties and leaving me to my own keeping. I watched the other men among the passengers, and most of them stayed below decks with their families, helping topside only when the need arose. Grahame's bargain with the captain seemed to be one he alone had made, and he was using it to keep away from me. I couldn't imagine what I had done to earn this distance. Was he having doubts of our marriage? Did he regret it? The thought plagued me, but I had no way to relieve my anxiety when Grahame was only around long enough to bid me a good day.

On a clear but cold afternoon, I coaxed Elsie to the deck to walk in the fresh air. We wore several layers of clothing and had wrapped in blankets to help ward off the chill. We walked on the forecastle deck to stay out of the way of the work below. I had no better idea of how the sailors worked the ship than I had when we first boarded, but they were always busy at some task. I often came on deck for the fresh air and watched them at their work. Inevitably, my gaze would seek out Grahame.

"There's Grahame," Elsie said. I had already found him seated amongst a few other sailors, working with rope. The other sailors were talking, laughing at one another, but Grahame sat quietly, mindful of his work.

"He was very kind to help us," Elsie said. "Like you were."

I gave her a sad smile.

"He is of a sober turn, isn't he?" Elsie continued. She hadn't spoken much since Jacky's death, so it was good to hear, but I wasn't sure I wanted to speak of Grahame when my thoughts were so tossed about on the subject of him.

"Yes, he seems so," I answered cautiously.

Elsie glanced at me. "Did you not know him well before you wed?"

"I didn't know him at all."

Elsie didn't look as though she knew what to say to that. "I didn't mean to pry."

"No, you aren't." I turned away to walk toward the prow of the ship. The wind tugged at my cap and pulled tendrils of hair free to whip across my face. The cold numbed my nose and cheeks, but the air felt fresh, and I drew in deep breaths of it.

"Is he kind to you?" Elsie asked.

"In his way, I suppose." I tugged the blanket tighter around my shoulders. "He is still such a stranger."

"How did you meet?"

"Through my father." I studied Elsie. "You don't want to hear all this, do you?"

"It helps," Elsie answered. "It takes my mind off of things."

"Beacham's stories do that for me."

"His stories are too dark for my tastes. I want to hear something of life. Real life, not a sailor's tale. But if you'd rather not—"

"No, it's fine. I've not spoken of it, that's all." I glanced around, taking note of how close anyone might be. The sailors nearby were at their work and not paying us any attention.

"My father met him first during a trip to Letterkenny. They did business together, or did business with someone they both knew, I'm not clear on that. They got to talking, though, and made an arrangement for Grahame to bring a flock of sheep to my father to sell. Father does all sorts of business," I added. "Running tenant farms and bartering livestock and goods and the like. When Grahame came, I guess he took a liking to me and asked about marriage. That was about three months ago."

"Did he not court you first?"

"He lived a fair distance," I told her. "He was kind enough, if quiet. And he seemed truly interested in me."

"Was it a fine wedding?" Elsie sounded a bit wistful.

"I don't know about that. We went to Letterkenny, to the church there for the ceremony. Mostly family attended. Grahame had a neighbor stand up for him, he and his wife and daughter. The daughter was kind. She helped me that first month."

And I still can't remember her name, I thought. Just the look of her, all elbows and chin and the strange way of laughing she had. But she had been kind, I realized, not mocking as I'd first thought. But then, I'd expected to be mocked or cut or disregarded completely. That had become my social life. It had been refreshing to have even a poor farmer's daughter offer me attention. I shook my head, ashamed with myself.

Elsie was watching me, as if she knew that I was holding back important pieces of the story.

"Why did you decide to leave Donegal?" she asked at last.

"Grahame had already decided it before we wed. He'd been making plans for the last year, or so I understand. He has a brother," I added, "at the colonies already. We're to meet him. There might be other family, too, I think, but I'm not sure on that."

Elsie gave me a thin smile. "You're not too sure on a lot of things to be making such a long journey."

I flushed. "I know." My voice was small.

Elsie paled. "Forgive me, Ailee, that was cruel. I didn't mean to sound so harsh."

"It's nothing but the truth," I told her. "And I know it."

"You didn't ask him for all the details?"

"I didn't know about it until a week before we made the trip to Londonderry. Oh, I see it now, when I think back on it. Selling off livestock and goods, and the visits from the farm's owner. But I've never lived on a farm, so I didn't know that wasn't usual. And then I was so . . . ." Shocked? Surprised? Scared? I didn't have a word for the emotions that had overwhelmed me when Grahame had finally shared his plans.

"That wasn't fair of him," Elsie said, looking darkly towards where Grahame sat with the other sailors. "He should have made it clear from the beginning."

"He did, to my father at least," I said quickly. "I just didn't understand."

"He should have made sure you did. Did you even want to come? You could have stayed and married another—" Elsie stopped talking. I had blanched and turned away to try to hide my reaction.

"Ailee, is there something else?"

"No, it's fine. I would have come regardless. Truly." I tried to smile, but I could feel how sickly it must look. I wanted to blurt it all out then and there, all the mistakes and hopes and dashed dreams and the disgrace that followed.

"There is something you aren't saying," Elsie said unexpectedly.

I hesitated, trying to think of anything to dissuade her and failing.

Elsie's gaze softened. She took my hand. "I'm your friend," she told me quietly. "Please know you can tell me anything, and it won't change what I feel for you."

A wrench of pain had me suck in my breath. "You don't know what it is," I managed to say. I didn't know what I would do if I lost Elsie's friendship.

"Did someone die from your carelessness?"

"What?" I was taken aback. "No. No, of course not."

"Was another life ruined?"

"No—well, not another's."

"Then," Elsie said solemnly, "you have nothing to fear. You cannot possibly lose my friendship for anything less than those."

I hesitated again, and Elsie put her arm around my shoulders. "You can tell me anything," she said gently. "I already know something has happened to you, something you fear to speak of. I don't want you to be afraid to speak to me. I'll respect your wishes if it is too difficult to put into words, but I need you to know that I'll be free to imagine the very worst. So if you can speak of it, please do."

It was a masterful bit of logic. I had to admire Elsie's skills. They rivaled my mother's when it came to ferreting out secrets. Only Elsie did so kindly, offering a way out but adding just a touch of guilt. It wasn't a threat but the honest truth, and I appreciated honesty, more now than ever before.

I drew a deep breath. Elsie must have realized she'd convinced me because she embraced me tighter for a moment in encouragement.

"At the harvest dance last year, I had several turns," I began. "I usually did. There wasn't a man I fancied yet, though a couple had come courting in the last year. That night, I danced with a man who was new to town. He and his wife had moved from Dublin that spring. I had seen Mrs. Kerk around, of course, and my mother had her to call not long after, but she wasn't a very pleasant woman.

Hard," I said, trying to explain. "Iona reminds me of her a little, but without the moments of kindness."

Elsie nodded that she understood.

"That night at the dance, Mrs. Kerk wasn't there. She'd gone visiting family, I was told."

"Told by who?"

My cheeks reddened. "Her husband. He asked me to dance. He was a gentleman about it. He was such a gentleman." I sighed, then stopped myself. "Wallace was his name. Wallace Kerk. He didn't flirt like the other men did. He simply spoke with me like I was worth speaking to, not just being seen with. It was nice."

It had been more than nice. It had been eye-opening. I couldn't recall a time before when anyone had treated me as more than a pretty face or a dowry to be won.

"I saw him at the market the next week and we walked together. He was funny," I said with a smile. "He could make me laugh."

I paused, trapped in the memory of his laughter and how his cheeks wrinkled and his eyes lit up. How he seemed only to see me.

"You fell in love," Elsie said quietly.

I bit my lip and nodded.

"How did your parents find out?"

Elsie had a remarkable grasp of the situation. I was glad for it. I wasn't sure I could relive it all while trying to explain and not fall apart on the deck. As it were, I was glad Grahame had moved out of sight.

"Mother saw us out together one day. We'd met on the edge of town, and he'd taken me driving in his carriage. He had a fine carriage," I added, but then I felt silly. "That's a ridiculous reason to go out with a married man, but none of the men who courted me kept a carriage."

"It was exciting," Elsie guessed.

"Yes, it was. But we drove too close to town and Mother saw us. I didn't know she'd gone out to visit Mrs. Dunnelly. And I didn't see her, so when I got home, I pretended that I'd been visiting with a friend. It was awful." The way Mother had turned on me, the betrayal and outrage on her face. The hushed way she spoke, as though not wanting to be overheard talking to a ruined girl.

"Did you and Mr. Kerk—" Even Elsie couldn't bring herself to voice the question. Mother had sounded the same.

I responded the same way I had to Mother, with a single, devastating nod.

Elsie took a long breath. "He was no gentleman."

"I know."

I recalled bitterly how he'd disappeared from town, packing up Mrs. Kerk to visit family in the south. He abandoned me, leaving me to face my mother's wrath, and my father's disappointment, and the glances and gossip of the townsfolk. He hadn't returned by the time I'd married. I'd been glad of it. By then, all I wanted to do was flee and put it all behind me.

Silence fell over us. I longed for Elsie to speak but feared what she might say.

"How did you meet Grahame?" Elsie's question was once more unexpected, and her tone was curious without a hint of judgment or reserve. I breathed a sigh of relief.

"He did come to do business with Father. By then, the rumors circling me had been accepted as fact. Father and Mother were desperate to make a match for me, and Father increased my dowry. A few men were willing, but they were . . ." I struggled to find the right word. They had been older widowers or reckless, indebted young men. No one I would have chosen in normal circumstances. I had known my father was going to make a match for me soon. He had no choice if he hoped to salvage any reputation for my younger brothers. But I couldn't face a life with a man such as would want me then.

"Not right?" Elsie completed the sentence delicately.

I nodded. "Not that I should have argued," I admitted, "but they were all so . . . not right." There had been a horrible row with Mother about it, and we had said hurtful words to each other that I knew we'd never be able to forget, even though we'd forgiven.

"I don't think Father even considered Grahame a possibility," I continued. "I'm not even sure how Grahame learned of me. Father didn't say anything, I know, in case the rumors had gotten to Grahame that might spoil the deal. Father had plans to sell the flocks in the north where the rot had been so bad. Father was always looking to make deals like that."

Like the one he hoped to make for me, I thought.

"When they met to finish the deal, Grahame asked after me. Father arranged for him to meet me. And that was that, really." I tried to play it off, but Elsie gave me a long, steady look that told me she wasn't buying it.

"Well, not entirely," I admitted. "Mother was opposed to it. She wanted me married to someone in town, not to a . . ." I couldn't find a delicate way to put it.

"A common farmer?" Elsie supplied knowingly.

I nodded, a bit ashamed. I'd shared Mother's feelings about the common part, but I hadn't wanted to remain in town.

"I couldn't stay. I knew the rumors would follow me my entire life. Grahame was a chance to escape all of that. And he was kind. I told Father I was interested, but only if Grahame knew the truth. I didn't want to go into a marriage with a falsehood hanging between us. But when he'd been told and still asked for my hand, I accepted."

"You made the decision? Not your father." Elsie looked surprised.

"I don't think Father expected me to accept. I admit I didn't know what I was getting into," I told her with a wan smile. "I had no true idea how much work it was, being wed to a farmer. But I knew I had to leave town. I couldn't live under such a shadow, no matter that I'd earned it. And he's . . . handsome," I added with a blush.

"He is that," Elsie agreed.

We exchanged looks, and then we both laughed. It felt good to laugh. It was freeing. I had shared the worst thing about myself, and Elsie accepted me anyway. I'd never known a friendship like this before. I couldn't imagine it ever ending.

CHAPTER NINE

"Grahame—" I hesitated, uncertain he'd heard me. There was still time to back away, leave him to his work, talk to Tavey or Mr. Vance instead.

No, he was my husband. I should be able to take my concerns to him.

He had heard me. He stopped on the stairs, turning to face me, his expression guarded.

I mounted the steps to come close enough to talk low.

"I've been thinking about Elsie," I began, "and what she'll do now without Jacky and—"

"I've spoken to Vance," Grahame interrupted. "Family is waiting for her. A cousin."

I remembered then that Elsie had spoken of a letter from a cousin. "Of course. And he'll be there for her?"

Grahame stepped down, his gaze boring into mine. I didn't back away, though I wanted to, and I didn't look away, though it was with an effort.

"She's your friend and you're worried, but Vance will see she's safe."

I wasn't completely satisfied with that.

Grahame laid his hand on my shoulder, and the weight was foreign and startling, but not unwelcomed. An urge to curl up against him made me lean forward, but I stopped myself. He turned away to continue up the stairs, taking his hand off my shoulder and leaving a hollow chill where the warmth had been.

That was it, then, I realized. I hadn't gotten the chance to plead for Elsie to come with us. Grahame had already worked it out with Vance. It meant something that Grahame had looked into the matter, though. It showed a kindness in him, or at least a care for me or for Elsie.

Why was it so easy to see a rough, unapproachable side to him? He'd done nothing against me. He was quiet, yes, and kept his thoughts to himself, but he'd taken care of me when I was sick, and he'd helped Jacky and Elsie, too. He'd never offered a harsh word or hand to me. He'd even been gentle.

And he'd dragged me across the ocean away from my family and everything I'd ever known without so much as an apology or explanation. He'd looked into Elsie's future, but he wouldn't help her. He spent as much time away from me and the others as he could.

I sighed. He was a puzzle, and I still wasn't certain where I stood with him. I wondered if I ever would be.

I chose this, I reminded myself. Not this exactly, I thought, but I'd chosen Grahame and all that came with him. Even if that included a new world. And if I wanted things to be different between us, maybe I needed to be the one to change them.

Determined, I followed after my husband.

The morning was bright and clear, as fine a day as any I'd hoped to see. The sea was blue, the wind cold, but the sunlight felt good on my face. I looked for Grahame but didn't see him from my place by the passageway. I eased out and worked towards the rail, only to see the captain turning my direction.

Quickly, I hurried to the lee of the quarter deck where the captain wouldn't spy me. There was still no sign of Grahame. The rail was close, but not quite within reach. I followed the wall of the quarter deck to the stern of the ship.

"It's the natives I'd fear," I heard a gruff, thickly accented voice saying. I froze. The voice came from around the corner of the quarter deck where the deck thinned to a narrow passage between the deck and the rail of the ship. "I've not forgot those tales of Roanoke."

"'Tis a hunnert and fifty years past," another voice admonished. "We've towns now, and men. Men with guns. I fear no native."

"'Tisn't man to be a'feared of," a third voice said, speaking low in an ominous tone.

"Not that again, Rakes," the first scoffed.

"Yer gettin' to be as bad as Beacham," the second said.

"Ye mark me," Rakes told them. "Ye leave the ship when we make port, ye'll stay to the town and to the lamplight."

"Or what?" the first challenged.

There was no reply, and the first two sailors laughed.

A man rounded the corner suddenly before I could flee. He was small and wiry with dark hair and a scraggly beard. He paused to see me there and gave me a hard, long look full of menace. Scars ran down the side of his face, tearing through the corner of his mouth, leaving him with a permanent scowl.

I was frozen under that penetrating look.

"Ye be Beacham's lady," he said suddenly.

I couldn't begin to form an answer.

"Ye list'n to him. Ye stay off the rail. And ye list'n to me. Ye stay in the light."

I nodded, stunned and terrified.

"Ailee?"

I turned to see Grahame hurrying towards me. The gruff sailor pushed past me and didn't look at Grahame as he went.

"Why are you here?" Grahame asked, his voice tense.

I stared at him, my mind blank.

"Come." He took my arm and guided me more brusquely than was his manner. He released me at the passageway. "Go below."

I finally recalled why I'd come to find him, but the look he gave me was not encouraging. I hurried below.

Unsettled and shaking, I made my way to where the chickens were cooped. I couldn't bear the berths where it was too crowded to hear my own thoughts. There were fewer chickens than when we'd set out. Many had gone into the broth Beacham made when we were all so ill. The others clucked softly when I entered, hoping for grain.

I overturned the bucket I used for carrying feed and sat, my thoughts stumbling over themselves.

What if Beacham's tales weren't just stories? What if they were true?

I never considered it possible. After all, Nanny's stories had been just tales.

But what if they weren't?

Fear and excitement buzzed through me in turns. I saw a new world stretch out before me, a world filled with giants and fair folk and creatures rising from the waters to steal unsuspecting sailors. A world where old scarfs held power.

It was nonsense, but for a moment, recalling the look in Rakes's eyes, I could believe it was true.

On the day the first ship was sighted, Elsie and I went on deck with the men to see. It was far away and looked so small.

"Brigantine," I heard one of the men say.

"Can you see whose?"

"Need a glass for that."

"Don't need no glass," Beacham said from behind me. "That be pirates."

A cold silence fell over the group. Elsie raised a hand to her mouth in horror. I, however, felt a small thrill run up my back. I'd spent the last few days retelling Beacham's and Nanny's stories to myself, and here was one come to life.

Pirates.

"They sail these waters," Beacham continued, "looking fer treasure ships."

"Then they'll leave us alone," one of the men said, though not entirely certain.

"They have to make sure first," Beacham said. "They'll follow us a time, decide whether to come closer. They've got more sail than we, so they'd catch us up if they wanted."

"What would happen if they did?" I asked. A couple of the men gave me hard looks, and I realized I probably shouldn't be speaking to the cook in open company.

"Depends on their cap'n. They might sail us past, having a look. They might call out to us. They might fire upon us or try to board us."

"They never would!" another man said, indignant.

"Oh, they can, trust in me," Beacham said with his gap-toothed grin. "We'd have seventy men to their hundred and more, unless the lot of you know how to fight. We've four guns to their twenty or more. We're loaded down and riding low and maneuver like a full cart pulled by a lame draft. Oh, they can take us, if they wanted."

"Mr. Beacham!"

The captain's voice pierced the whispers of fear and dread. Captain Dawson had come up to the group, and by the look on his face, he'd heard Beacham's speech.

Beacham's face went pale, and he turned toward his captain. He tugged his forelock. "Cap'n, sir."

"Stow that talk and return below."

Beacham gave his forelock another tug and scurried away. By the way Captain Dawson watched him go, I had the feeling that Beacham wasn't out of trouble yet.

"He likes to tell stories," I said to Elsie to calm her, but I also said it loud enough that maybe the captain would not be so hard on the cook. "I'm sure we'll be fine."

"That we will, madam," Captain Dawson answered. "There is nothing to be concerned with. These waters see quite a bit of travel."

"Does that mean we are close?" Mr. Vance asked.

"It does," the captain answered. "With good weather and a fair wind, we shall see land by the week's end."

The attitude in the group changed from fear to hope, and they broke away into twos and threes to discuss plans for arrival.

"You should be below," the captain told Elsie and me in a tone that brooked no refusal.

"Of course," I said with a curtsy. I took Elsie's arm in mine and steered her toward the hatch. I glanced behind, though, to see the captain giving quiet orders to his first mate. Grahame was standing nearby, and his face was set with determination that held a shadow of danger.

Another thrill ran up my back, but I didn't know if it was from the danger of the pirates or the threat my husband promised should they attempt to take the ship or the fact that one of Beacham's stories had actually come to life.

The pirate ship loomed on the horizon for the rest of the day. Talk in the berths bounced between fear of the pirates and joy that our journey was nearing an end. I sat with Elsie, both of us at our knitting. I was still trying to work out the stitches for Beacham's strange scarf while Elsie worked on what might become a shawl or a small blanket. We sat in silence, listening to the talk around us. I was careful in what conversation I began with Elsie. So many topics were charged with emotion, like the landing and our future, or the past and where we came from. Shipboard life was safe enough, if I kept it to the day's trials, but there was only so much one could say about living on the ship before the topic was exhausted.

I wanted to ask about her knitting, but if it was a blanket for a baby, that might cause Elsie grief to think about having a child without Jacky.

Elsie solved the problem for me.

"What is it you are working on?" Elsie asked, finally taking notice of my knitting.

I held it up and watched it unravel again. I'd long given up on the shawl and had spent the better part of a day pulling it out and rewinding the wool into a ball. Considering the weeks I'd been working on something to resemble the strange scarf, I had absolutely nothing to show for it, but I'd never been happier knitting.

"I'm trying to figure out Beacham's scarf," I admitted.

"His scarf?"

"That loop he wears out on deck. The one the German sailor gave him for protection."

Elsie nodded politely, but I could tell that she didn't recall the story.

"Come, I'll show you."

It gave me an excuse to check on Beacham. We set aside our needles and wool, and I led the way to the galley.

The galley was empty. It was strange not to find Beacham in it. I wondered if the captain had called him to his study or room or whatever a captain used to chastise his men.

I wondered if it might be worse than just a talking to.

To hide my fear for Beacham, I found the scarf where it hung near the doorway. "This is it," I said. I didn't want to touch it while Beacham was gone.

Elsie peered closer at it. "It is a strange stitch." She pulled at it, gently, to spread the garment. "I don't think I've ever seen its like."

I was a bit disappointed. It would have been nice to find someone who recognized it and could teach me.

"I don't think it's knitting, though," Elsie told me.

"How can you tell?"

"It doesn't look it. The stitches are too . . . different. I wonder,

74

though."

I was about to press her when Beacham stepped to the doorway.

"What's this then? Having at my things?" His tone was hard, and there was a dark light in his eyes.

"I was hoping Elsie might know the stitch," I said quickly as Elsie stepped back from the scarf. "That I could make you another."

Beacham's hard look grew guilty. "I'm sorry, miss. That is kind of ye. I were just—"

"I am sorry we intruded," I interrupted him. "Is there something we can do to help prepare for supper?"

Beacham looked uncertain, then drew himself up. "Well, if ye be offering, I can't see no harm in that."

He set us to the potatoes again, but I didn't protest. I hoped Beacham would speak of what happened with the captain, but he was oddly quiet and reserved as we worked. Elsie seemed no more inclined to speak, which left me to my thoughts, and they naturally turned toward pirates. Were they still following us? How would we know if they chose to attack? What would Grahame look like with a musket at his shoulder? Could I learn to work one, too?

The talk during supper was of the pirates. Most of the men stayed topside, which concerned many of their wives.

"There's naught to be done," Iona said loudly. "Why they think they'll be of any use is beyond me."

"It gives them a sense of duty to be watchful," Tavey told her. "In case something does occur."

"It gives me a headache how much they look to their 'duty' and leave us to clearing up," Iona grumbled.

"Do you think we should be afraid?" Elsie asked me quietly.

"I can't say," I admitted. Beacham hadn't spoken more than a handful of words to us, and I hadn't been able to tell if his reticence was from concern of the pirates or whatever had happened between him and the captain.

"I can't seem to bring myself to fear," Elsie admitted quietly. "I know I should be afraid. The others are, even Iona, though she hides it under anger. But I'm not." She looked at me with wide eyes. "Is there something wrong with me?"

I hesitated, uncertain what to say. I wanted to wave off Elsie's concern, but I recalled that time before marrying Grahame when fear lived so close at hand it became a part of me.

"No, I don't think there's anything wrong with you," I said. "You've lost something irreplaceable. Not just Jacky, though I know that is awful enough. You have a future you can't see into yet." I took Elsie's hand. "But you'll see it again. It can't lie empty forever."

"Do you see yours now?"

I gripped harder. Elsie understood my own struggle, and it meant the world that she did.

"Not yet. But I know it will come."

By morning, the pirate ship had gone. I was somewhat disappointed, but the relief in the berths was palpable. The fear that colored yesterday's talk changed to hope as we drew closer and closer to land. I crept out to the deck often throughout the day to see if land or more pirates had been sighted. Once, Grahame caught me, but he merely gave me that long look of his that had me turning back into the passageway.

As the time for making port came closer, I found that I was beginning to think about leaving the ship. I realized with a shock that I hadn't let myself think about life after landing. My entire focus had been on the ship, surviving the passage, peeling yet another wizened old potato, making another stitch. I'd considered Elsie's future, worried over it and tried to imagine what it might be like for her once we arrived, but I'd never given much thought to my own.

Now that I was, I found that I couldn't imagine what it would be like at all. I wanted to talk to Elsie about it, but I was afraid that would only bring up dark thoughts for her. Tavey was too busy for more than a passing exchange. Iona was too good at seeing only the bad that could happen. And I hadn't gotten to know most of the other women.

So I asked Beacham.

"You said you've been to the new world before," I began, leaning in the galley doorway.

"To the West Indies, that I have." He glanced over at me from where he was chopping yet more salt beef. "But that weren't nothing like where we be heading, miss, if ye're wanting to know."

"Have you spoken to anyone who has been where we're heading?" I thought the port was called Fillydelfy, but I wasn't certain. I'd heard the name bantered back and forth in the berths several times, but the pronunciation kept changing.

"Oh, a few. One of the crew has been afore he joined this ship."

"Truly!"

"But don't you go running off to find him," Beacham warned. "I'm sure your man has already spoken with him."

"Was it Mr. Rakes?"

Beacham froze, then he slowly looked at me, the light in his eyes a dangerous glimmer.

"What know ye of Rakes?" he asked in a hushed tone.

"I . . . I overheard him on deck," I stammered, taken aback.

"Ye keep away from Rakes," Beacham told me. "That man be scarred by more than what mars his face."

"What do you mean?"

"Just keep away from him."

"He told me—" I hesitated under Beacham's glare. "He told me to listen to you. To stay off the rail."

Beacham turned back to his chopping board. "Ye should be back in the berths, miss." His voice was still hushed.

"Mr. Beacham—"

"Good day, miss."

I held back a sigh, dismayed. Returning to the berths, I found Elsie at my cot.

"I was looking for you," she said.

"I was seeing if Mr. Beacham needed help." What had I done to put him off so? What was it about Rakes that fretted him?

"I had a thought," Elsie told me. "Do you know this?" She held out the kerchief she had first worn to board the ship. "This lace, here."

I nodded. "Cheyne lace. I have a shawl worked with it."

Elsie looked impressed. "Truly? Well, my thought was that something like this made Mr. Beacham's scarf. But in wool, not thread. I've never seen it done quite that way, it might be a stitch I wasn't taught."

"Do you think it possible?"

"It might be. Though I'm not sure what tool you would use. When I do cheyne lace, I use a needle of sorts."

"You know how to make cheyne lace?"

Elsie nodded, looking embarrassed. "My mother taught me. She used to make it to sell, before she wed my father."

"Could you teach me?"

Elsie frowned with a pained expression. "My tools are in the hold. But perhaps when we make land . . ." Her words trailed off.

When we make land, neither of us knew what to expect.

I wasn't going to think about it. "That would be wonderful," I told her, smiling. My answer pleased her, easing the pain from her face. We sat and looked over the lace on her kerchief and she spoke of her mother's work. All I could think about was my shawl nestled in the bottom of my bag and, though I knew it unlikely, wonder if Elsie's mother had made it.

That evening, Grahame took his supper in the berths. It was an odd sight, him sitting on a stool in the narrow space, bent over like a giant in a child's room. I'd stopped taking him his meals after my illness since I'd been so busy helping with Elsie and the others. I'd offered once, but he'd gestured to where Beacham was handing out the crew member's meals and that had been that. Usually I took my meals with Elsie.

This evening, though, he sat with me. I felt as nervous as when we'd taken our first meal together as husband and wife. I didn't know what to say or where to look. The food had gotten plainer and more predictable, but I ate it because there was nothing else. I was sick to death of potatoes and peas and salt beef and those hard little biscuits.

"When we make land, we'll take a room," Grahame said, surprising me.

"Where?"

"In town."

I watched him, no longer interested in my own meal, hoping he would speak more of his plans. He cleaned off his plate with the appetite of a working man.

"We'll see land soon," he told me. " But it'll be days yet to make port."

He was offering me that information to warn me, I realized. I nodded, to show I understood.

He handed me his empty trencher. Before he left, though, he leaned towards me.

"You've done well," he said in a hushed tone. It was as though he was surprised by the fact.

I didn't know how to feel about that, and he didn't give me time to respond as I watched him disappear up the passage.

CHAPTER TEN

The next day we sighted land.

Everyone went topside to see it. The green was a solid strip along the horizon cutting the ocean and sky in two. It had been so long since I'd seen land, or seen such green, that I cried. I wasn't alone in my tears. Elsie clung to me, holding in sobs, and I knew she was weeping for more than the sight of land.

The passengers remained on deck for a long while, watching that strip of land. Some of the joyful murmurings began to sour as the strip grew no larger after some time has passed.

"Grahame says it'll be a few days before we make port," I told Elsie.

"How many?"

"I'm not sure."

A few others overheard me and the news spread quickly. Most of the passengers returned below, but Elsie and I remained on deck, standing on the forecastle clutching one another in the cold wind, staring landward.

With a sudden impulse, I asked Elsie to wait while I dashed below deck. I returned with the wedding shawl folded in my arms.

"I want you to have this," I told her, pressing the shawl into Elsie's hands.

Elsie breathed out in wonder. "I can't take this," she argued.

"Yes, you can." I stepped back, crossing my arms. "You need something lovely to look on, something of beauty and home and friendship. You keep that and maybe it'll help remind you that you aren't alone. Then you give it to your baby, if it's a girl, and tell her of our homeland and her father and of me. And if it's a boy, do the same. He'll have a fine gift for a future wife.

"But if things go wrong, you sell it," I insisted. My eyes were brimming with tears, and Elsie was weeping quietly. "You use it to keep yourself and your babe. It's my gift to you, and don't you hesitate to use it, Elsie MacClayne."

Elsie embraced me, clutching me tightly. The grief struck me like a blow that I would be parted from my dearest friend. I tried for a moment to contain it, but I hadn't the strength. We wept, the shawl pressed between us.

I wasn't sure how long we huddled together, overcome, but when I finally regained control, my eyes were sore and puffy. I found my handkerchief and dabbed at my nose.

"We can do this," Elsie told me. Her face was resolute, even with tears still gleaming in the sunlight. She gripped my hand.

I took a steadying breath. "We can do this."

The *Resolution* sailed through a wide bay before entering into the mouth of a river. After so many days at sea, the sight of land so close had me in tears. Trees bordered each bank of the river, stout trunks with leaves already turned the brilliant golds and reds of autumn. The colors were breath-taking. Had trees ever looked so regal? Had land ever looked so gentle? I could smell the damp, earthy scent of soil and the fragrant crispness of fallen leaves. The ocean fell behind us like a wrong-doing we'd rather forget, and the river opened into a watery road leading us to our future.

Occasional breaks where land had been cleared revealed farmland or pasture. The signs of civilization were shockingly exposed between the stretches of wilderness. We passed other ships moving swiftly with the current towards the sea, and the sailors called out to one another, sometimes using crude language that left me blushing. But new voices were welcomed after so many weeks with only our own, and the sight of other people, alive and so close, was uplifting. The mood on the ship turned towards celebration.

Elsie and I stayed close together, watching for the port as our time together grew shorter. We didn't speak. Anything we said would have been bittersweet. The other passengers were excited and eager to make land. The worst was behind us, they reckoned.

I looked to Grahame when I thought he wouldn't notice. He wasn't watching the land eagerly, looking for the first signs of the town. He was at his work with the sailors, keeping his bargain even amid the excitement on deck. I might have felt proud if I weren't so unsettled and uncertain about what lay ahead.

Wilderness slowly gave way to farmland. The fields showed signs of the late harvest, the soil turned into dark runnels across the clear cut earth. A few houses dotted the area, most wooden, some squat, others tall, several surrounded by cross-rail fences. Cows of various hues, oxen both shaggy and sleek, and white-fleeced sheep grazed in yellowing pastures.

Then we came to the town. It started gradually, with houses closer together and a few narrow piers for small boats. The piers grew larger, as did the buildings, until we were entering the port itself. Ships abounded, and buildings, people, and trees filled every available space. It was crowded and noisy and unexpectedly civilized. Elsie and I watched, stunned into silence at the sight. It was one of the largest cities I'd seen, but it looked out of place after the wilderness we'd passed. So many people, already come to this new land, and here we were yet another batch to spill out across the town. The town would suck us up, and we'd disappear amid the streets and buildings, never to find one another again.

Elsie grasped for my hand.

It took the better part of an hour to make port. While we were still approaching the wharf, a boat rowed up to the ship and a man dressed in breeches and a long coat climbed a rope ladder aboard to speak with Captain Dawson.

"He's come to see that none of us are ill," Tavey said as Mr. Vance and the captain met the man on the deck.

"And if we were?" Iona challenged.

"I expect they'd keep us from docking," Tavey answered. "To keep sickness out of the town."

"They can't do that." Iona stiffened with outrage and the other ladies murmured in concern, looking fretful.

"I'm sure they can, if they wished it. But there's no need to fear," Tavey assured us quickly. "None of us is ill."

Mr. Vance sent the women and children back down to the berth. Iona and several other women grumbled, tired of the confining space. I didn't try to stay on deck but went with Elsie, figuring that Grahame would wish it, but I wasn't any happier to go back below.

Elsie and I stayed together by her cot as Mr. Vance escorted the stranger through the berths. The stranger looked over each of us, holding a lantern aloft to see our faces. His own clean-shaven face was expressionless. It was a curious sensation, rather like we were sheep at the market up for sale.

When he reached where Elsie and I stood, I stared back at him, not dropping my gaze, giving him as impertinent a look as he was giving us. I saw a flicker of emotion in his eyes, but then he was moving past us to the next berth.

Mr. Vance and the stranger finally left for the top deck and word passed through that we would be allowed to dock. The women were speaking excitedly and gathering their belongings. Tavey was cautioning everyone not to be too hasty.

"These things take time," she said. "They'll dock us first and take a tally. Then the menfolk will have to make declarations, and those still needing to pay passage will be noted. Then there's the unloading and whatnot."

Iona scoffed. "We'll be lucky to be off the ship by nightfall. We might even need to spend another night aboard."

No one wanted to believe her.

"I can't stay here another night," Elsie said to me in a quiet voice.

"I'm sure it won't come to that," I told her. Now that the time was upon us, I didn't know how I felt about leaving the ship. It would mean leaving Elsie, who had become as dear to me as a sister, but remaining aboard wasn't a choice I'd pick, either.

Determined, I returned to my berth to pack up my meager belongings.

I felt when the ship made dock. It was a subtle change to the ship's movement, like a gasp turning into a sigh. I tied my last bag closed and went down the passageway to Elsie's cot. I was surprised to see her sitting, bags and belongings still unpacked. Elsie was staring across at the wall, her look distant and closed. For all she wanted to leave the ship, she hadn't made any progress towards packing.

I sat down next to her. "Can I help you pack?"

Elsie blinked and came back to herself.

"I can help you," I repeated, unsure whether she had heard me.

"I—I don't know what to do with Jacky's things." Elsie stammered over the words, her grief as raw as the day she'd lost him.

With a pang of sorrow, I took Elsie's hand. "Pack them," I encouraged her. "They might be useful."

Elsie looked uncertain.

"I'll help," I told her again, and I stood and began to pull the bags out from behind the lowest cot. Elsie watched me for a moment before standing to reach for another bag.

It was quick work and sadly done, but I had the last bag tied before Elsie could linger long enough for her grief to deepen. I spoke as we worked, just to make talk. How hard would it be to get the animals off the ship, what a meal off the ship would be like after so long, how I hoped never to peel a potato again.

"Beacham said the other day how strange we would find it to walk on dry land again," I told Elsie.

"Do you think we'll see each other again?" She asked it quietly, as though she hadn't wanted to voice to the fact that we were parting.

I paused in tying the last bag. I knelt down on the wooden planks, thinking how best to answer. A platitude would be kind and give us both hope, but it would be a false hope. "I don't think so," I admitted slowly, and it hurt to say it. "Grahame says we'll leave town for some place outside of it. But—" I said, making a sudden connection, "he had a letter from his brother who lives there. Surely we can write to one another."

Elsie's pale face grew somber, and she looked away. I'd forgotten my place yet again. "I'm sure you could find someone to write for you," I suggested hesitantly. "Your cousin, perhaps?"

Elsie brightened. "Yes, Connor could do that." She looked relieved. "It will be nice to know I'm not alone here."

I took her hands again. "You aren't alone, Elsie." I hoped with all my heart it would be true.

An hour later, we were still sitting in the shadowy berth. The excitement had died down and boredom settled in. Elsie had fetched her knitting, and I soon got my own to continue trying to make a scarf like Beacham's. I wasn't able to concentrate on it, though it did keep my hands busy. Grahame came down at one point, but he only gave me a nod before continuing to our berth. I rose and followed only to see him disappearing through the other passageway with one of our boxes.

"Grahame's carrying out our things," I told Elsie. "It must be near time."

Fear and excitement turned my stomach into knots, with sorrow and relief warring in my chest until I couldn't draw a full breath. I settled next to Elsie again and tried to work on my knitting, but in the end, all I did was stare at it, my thoughts in a jumble.

After an indeterminable passage of time, women at the far end of the passage began speaking over each other and rising, filling the narrow passage. I took to my feet to try to see, but I couldn't get a clear view, and the jumble of voices made no sense until they finally quieted down into one.

Mr. Vance was speaking at the other end. I couldn't make out what he was saying, but I could guess.

"What is it?" Elsie had gotten to her feet next to me.

"I think he's saying it's time to leave."

Excitement buzzed through the air once more.

"We're leaving the ship," Iona told us, taking the news down the passageway. "Get what you can carry and make for the pier. The men will bring up the rest of it."

Despite my worries, I was swept away by the eagerness to be off the ship, and I could see by the bright gleam in her eyes that Elsie was, too. I went for my bags and found just two left. Grahame had cleared the rest out of our berth. It looked strangely empty and forlorn, as though all the weeks of fear and sickness and boredom had been swept clean, leaving only a faint trace behind. I hefted my two bags and returned to help Elsie with hers. I took as much as I could so she wouldn't have to burden herself. I felt ladened down like an ox as we maneuvered up the narrow stairs to the deck.

Evening was falling across the town, and the lamplighters had been to their work already, setting the candles aflame in the town's lamps. The sky overhead was darkening, the orange and reds of a clear sunset running to midnight blue where stars were already dotting the eastern sky. The air was crisp with the promise of frost, and I could see my breath in the air.

The men came to help the women with their bags as the children scurried around the ship, getting underfoot. Iona's husband and Mr. Vance offered to help Elsie. I looked around, but Grahame was nowhere in sight.

Confused, I circled the deck of the ship, thinking I had missed seeing him at some final bit of work. But no, he was nowhere on the deck.

"Yer man went off ship." Beacham approached me, sidling up as though he didn't want to be caught out by the captain.

"What do you mean?"

"Yer man," Beacham repeated. "He left the ship."

Fear tore into me. "He left the ship?" The panic must have come through in my voice, because Beacham hurriedly raised his hands.

"To make arrangements, he said," the cook told me quickly. "I heard him speaking to that man Vance. He'll be back, sure as anything. Ye just wait."

I glanced over to where the passengers were already walking the wide wooden plank down to the pier. Elsie was standing with Mr. Vance and Tavey, waiting her turn anxiously.

"I'm to wait here," I repeated numbly.

"It can't be long," Beacham told me. "He's come back and fetched the animals already. No doubt getting them settled afore he comes for you."

I saw that the rope enclosure that had held the animals was indeed empty, the rope pulled away and coiled to one side of the forecastle.

"Ailee?" Elsie called over to me.

I had no idea what to do.

"Ye wait on the ship," Beacham repeated, a look of warning in his eyes. "Tisn't safe to be alone on the wharf come dark."

Elsie hurried over to me. "Aren't you coming?"

"Grahame said to wait for him," I repeated weakly.

"He isn't here?" Elsie looked around sharply. "Where did he go?"

"I—I'm not sure."

"He had some arrangements to make," Mr. Vance said as he came up to us, Tavey with him. "Forgive me, Mrs. Donaghue. In all the excitement, I forgot to pass on his message. It shouldn't be too long. I'm certain the captain will watch over you. Come now, Elsie. There's much to do yet."

"Wait," Elsie said as he began to move away. "If you could say where we're staying, so Ailee and I might correspond."

Mr. Vance smiled kindly. "Mrs. Royce's Boarding House, near Fifth and Pine, was recommended to us." he added. He gave me a low bow. "Mrs. Donaghue, much luck to you and your husband."

Tavey gave me a motherly embrace. "You take care of yourself," she told me with a knowing look.

I gave her the warmest smile I could manage. Mr. Vance and Tavey crossed to the plank to descend. Elsie and I exchanged long looks, and I realized this was it.

"I'll send a note to you," I told her. "As soon as I can."

"I'm sure I can have one sent in return," Elsie answered.

We looked at each other, neither certain what to say. I finally gave up trying to find words and embraced my friend. Elsie returned it, and we stood together for long moments, comforting one another, until Elsie reluctantly pulled away.

She reached up to her shawl. "I want you to have this." She twisted her spiral shawl pin free of the stitches and pressed it into my hand.

"I couldn't—"

"Yes, you can. I want you to have it. Please, Ailee, take it. Remember us by it."

I blinked against a swift burning of tears. "I don't need this to remember you. Or Jacky. I could never forget either of you."

Elsie was blinking against her own tears. "Then take it because it will make me happy to know you have it."

I closed my fingers around the shawl pin. "I hope—" But I wasn't certain what I hoped.

Elsie gave me another embrace. "I know."

She turned away quickly and joined Mr. Vance at the plank. With his help, Elsie left the ship.

I rushed to the rail. Elsie turned when she reached the pier and waved up at me. I waved back. And then Elsie was lost in the crowd of passengers and bags and crates filling the pier.

I fought against the sob that wanted to tear loose from me. I clutched the rail and remembered the shawl pin. Carefully, I threaded it through the scratchy layers of my own shawl.

"They won't live the year out," I heard a dark voice mutter. Not far from me stood Rakes staring after the departing passengers with an odd light in his eyes, his scarred lip curled from a scowl to a grimace. A chill fell over me. I thought I would step away, find another place to wait for Grahame, but Rakes turned and fixed his gaze on me.

"Dead, all ye. Soft ignorant things ye be." He drew closer before I realized he'd moved. "Hunted like lambs, yer throats tore out, nothing but bones scattered in the woods."

His breath reeked of grog and rotted teeth. He reached up with a grimy hand to touch my face, and I was too terrified to pull back.

"Pity. Such a pretty little thing."

"Mr. Rakes!" Beacham's voice shot across the deck. Rakes drew back as though bitten. He cast a dark glance toward the cook, who stood solid and resolute only a few feet away.

Rakes slunk away, muttering dark words I couldn't make out. Shivers rippled through me, and I clutched my shawl tighter, knowing it wouldn't help.

"Ye all right then, miss?" Beacham asked, his expression twisted with concern.

"Yes, thank you. He—he only wished to frighten me."

Beacham's look suggested that Rakes would have done more than just frighten me had he been given the chance. I swallowed, fervently wishing Grahame would return.

"Step back, miss, I beg ye," Beacham said, coming close enough to grasp me should the need arise. I glanced at him and saw real fear on his face. Startled, I came away from the rail.

"Thank ye, miss."

"No, I want to thank you, Mr. Beacham," I told him, trying to regain control of myself. "Thank you for everything you did for me and for Elsie while we were aboard. You can't know what it meant to us."

He looked uncomfortably at the deck, shuffling his feet like a nervous boy. "Tweren't anything another wouldn't do, miss."

"I doubt that very much. You're a good man, Mr. Beacham."

He flushed and looked uncomfortable with so much praise.

"I'm only sorry I couldn't figure out how to make another one of those scarves," I said, gesturing to the loop of knotted wool doubled around his neck. "I had hoped to repay you with it."

"No, miss, I wouldn't have taken it. If ye figure it out, ye keep it for yerself. Trust me, miss. Don't let this town fool ye. There be dangers in old, untouched places."

He looked as though he wanted to say more, but the captain spied him and called him over. Beacham tugged his forelock in farewell and retreated. I was sorry to see him leave, both because it left me alone and because I wasn't sure I'd have a chance to speak with him again before I left.

Chapter Eleven

I stood watch on the forecastle as night settled over the town, figuring that there I was in plain sight to everyone on the deck and not so easy a target for drunken sailors. The few lamps were no longer enough to keep the gloom at bay, and dark shadows claimed the town, stealing through the streets until the town looked like huddled buildings crouching close to the light to get away from the dark.

I repeated over and over that Grahame would not leave me. I wanted to believe it, to truly believe my importance to him, but aside from the fact that we had married, I couldn't think of anything I had added to his life. He'd spent the many weeks at sea apart from me, except for when he'd cared for me while I was ill. Before our time on the ship, he'd spent much of his time afield while I struggled to learn to keep house. I knew how little I brought to our union. A pretty face could only carry me so far in a working man's life. I had never been raised to marry beneath my rank.

The thought struck me oddly. Grahame was so self-possessed and confident, even in his silence, that I'd never thought him of a lower status. Even when he'd taken me home, I'd thought of how large the dwelling was, not how rough, and how big the flocks were, not that he had to tend them himself. But there was no denying that his life was primed for a wife bred for the keeping of home and gardens, of raising children and chickens. I'd been able to put aside my concerns while cloistered aboard the ship, but they all returned as I stared over the city, watching the last of the dock workers at their trade.

When I recognized Grahame approaching where the ship was tied, my heart quickened. He hadn't left me.

He crossed the plank and stopped on the deck, looking around. I raised my hand, then lowered it, feeling like a fool, but he'd seen me.

"I kept you," he said in apology as he joined me. "I've seen the crates and livestock housed."

"I understand," I answered quickly, perhaps too quickly, for he raised an eyebrow in question. "I hoped to give word to Elsie before she left of where we'd be living."

He nodded with understanding and, I thought, with a trace of guilt.

"I'll send a note tomorrow."

"You know how to find her?"

"I had it from Vance."

I was surprised he had taken the time to learn. It must have shown, for he gave me a rare smile. "I did promise," he reminded me.

"Of course, yes. Thank you," I added weakly.

"Are you ready?"

I thought there'd be no happier moment than leaving this ship, but I hesitated. The future was still a fog, and I hadn't a clue where we were going.

"We've a room waiting," Grahame continued at my hesitation. "And a warm meal."

The meal won me over. I nodded, clutching my bags tighter. Wordlessly, Grahame held out his hand, offering to take them, and I accepted.

· Captain Dawson came to have a few parting words with Grahame. I overheard where we were staying, an inn called the Renfern Place, and I did my best to thank the captain for the fine voyage, though I still couldn't entirely chase the thoughts away of Jacky's body being dumped over the rail. Then Grahame was helping me down the plank and off the ship. I paused for a moment to look for Beacham, but the cook was nowhere in sight. I hoped he was having his fine meal and learning new stories.

It was strange to stand on solid ground. Even docked, the ship was constantly moving. On dry land, the ground was firm, but I still felt as though I were swaying. Unthinking, I grasped Grahame's arm to keep my balance.

Grahame tucked my arm around his, something he'd not done since the moment after we were wed. He swung the bags onto his other shoulder and escorted me from the wharf.

The dirt road was still damp from either recent rain or the nearby river. I thought rain more likely as we turned down a crossroad and found it just as damp. It wasn't quite muddy, but it might have been earlier. The night had turned cold and I thought the mud might freeze during the night. As it was, I wished I'd pulled out another layer of clothing to wear or had another wool shawl to wrap over my head and neck. I should have finished one by now instead of ripping out my work and wasting my time in fruitless pursuit of an impossible stitch.

The town streets were still busy, though by no means crowded. We passed many taverns doing brisk business, and noise poured out onto the street each time the doors opened. The buildings looked surprisingly sound, many with glass windows and brickwork.

The building Grahame escorted me into was a couple stories high with glass in the windows, and of wood and stone construction. Inside, the place was warm and dry and better lit than the berth of the ship had been. I had to blink at the brightness, so accustomed had I become to the dark.

A hall ran from the entrance, broken by a stair on one side and a doorway across from it. A stout matronly looking woman paused in the doorway, which must have been a parlor. I heard a smattering of voices coming from within. I blinked again, overcome by an overwhelming homesickness.

"Mr. Donaghue," the woman greeted Grahame. Her accent was firmly English, which helped ease some of my homesickness. "And this must be your wife."

"Yes, Mrs. Renfern."

"Dinner will be served shortly," Mrs. Renfern told us. "I don't hold it back for no one."

"We understand."

Satisfied, the matron continued on her errand and made a similar announcement inside the parlor. The scent of a meal cooking was overpowering and my stomach grumbled to remind me how long it had been since I'd eaten.

"Come," Grahame told me. From a narrow table by the wall he took up a taper from a pewter box and lit it from the lamp.

I followed him upstairs, the steps creaking amiably underfoot. A worn rug ran the length of the hallway, and the papered walls were set with a couple of burning lamps. Several doors lined the hall. Grahame led me to the third to the left and held the door for me.

It was a tidy room with a carpet over the floorboards and a small window already shuttered and sashed for the night. A wash stand stood against one wall, and a bed large enough for two stood against the opposite wall. A couple of chairs and a lamp on the wall, already lit, completed the homey atmosphere.

I almost missed the details of the rest of the room when I saw the bed. A bed. A real, honest bed. I hurried to it and pressed my hand against the quilt. The fabric was stout and well made. The bed was thick and blessedly solid. And there were pillows, true pillows that sunk under my hand. I was surprised to find tears in my eyes, but I had spent so many weeks sleeping on a canvas cot that swayed and left a crick in my neck and never allowed me to be fully warm, no matter how I swathed myself in blankets. I could have skipped supper and climbed straight into bed just to remember what it felt like to sleep comfortably once more.

Grahame was waiting patiently at the door, and it came to me all in a rush that there was but one bed. Naturally I'd lain with him in his bed after our marriage, but after boarding the ship, we'd spent more nights apart than together since we'd wed. My breathing quickened when I realized that tonight we'd share a bed once more.

"Do you want to change for dinner?" he asked, as subtle an offer to freshen up as he would make. He was watching me with a trace of bemusement in his dark eyes.

He must have already availed himself of the wash stand when he'd taken the room, for his beard and hair were combed, his clothing fresh, and his hands clean. I could smell a ripe odor in the tight confines of the room, and without ninety other bodies to contend with, I knew that smell was coming from me. I nodded to him.

"I'll be downstairs," he told me. He left the room, closing the door firmly behind him.

I hesitated a moment, then crossed to throw the bolt on the door. I slipped off my shawl, making certain Elsie's shawl pin was secure as I hung the shawl on a peg set in the wall. I pried off my shoes, peeled out of bodice and skirts, untied my pockets, pulled off my shift and stockings. The clothes I left in a pile, knowing they needed a good washing and mending. Two of my bags were stacked near the window, and the top one held a few clothes I'd packed in Ireland. From it I pulled out a fresh shift, stockings, and skirts, a nice bodice, my second set of pockets, and my laced mobcap. My everyday shawl stank of the ship, so I'd have to go without it, but I did find my linen kerchief among the other spare clothing. It was thin, but the house wasn't too chill. It would serve.

There was water in the bowl on the stand and a towel. I wiped off the worst of the stink, the water chilly and raising goose flesh across my skin. I pulled on the fresh shift and tied it, then fixed the pockets around my waist before letting my hair down my back. It stank of the ship, too, but I didn't have time to wash it, and it could be dangerous this late at night with no fire and with water so cold. Instead, I ran my brush through it, trying to get the worst of the snags out, then wrapped it back up and tucked it under the fresh mobcap. The cap smelt of the heather twigs that I'd tucked into the folds of my clothing before packing them. It helped mask the smell.

I finished dressing and put my shoes back on. I considered pulling out my hand mirror but decided against it. I hadn't used it the entire voyage, cautious of the curiosity it might arouse in the ladies from the berths around me, and tonight didn't seem like the best time to have a look. I knew I'd lost weight on the voyage, as my bodice stays were looser than ever, and I didn't need the added uncertainty of my appearance to cloud my doubts further.

Satisfied as much as I could be, I left the room, fastening the door behind me, and took the stairs to the downstairs hall.

Grahame wasn't waiting in the hall.

I tried not to be surprised, or hurt, but both emotions crept over me. I wasn't certain what I should do.

Then I heard Grahame's voice. At least, I thought it sounded like Grahame. It was louder than I was accustomed to hearing him speak. I followed the sound into the parlor.

The room was set with tidy groupings of chairs and small tables, like a tea house, I realized. And there was Grahame at the table closest to the doorway, sitting with another man whose back was to me. His hair was as dark as Grahame's and ringed from where he'd worn a hat. It didn't fall as long as Grahame's, though, settling just past the collar of his coat.

Grahame was watching the man, who was speaking, and I realized it was this strange man that I had heard. Grahame looked intent and, I marveled, somewhat guilty. The man was asking him how he'd let the matter go so far, and that was when Grahame noticed me. His expression smoothed into placid unreadability and he stood. The other man stopped speaking mid query and turned to see me standing there before rising from his seat. He shared Grahame's look in eyes and nose, though he wasn't as tall nor as untamed. His face was clean-shaven, and he looked civilized in a way I wondered if Grahame could ever match. He looked me over as if reckoning all my skills and faults to weigh them against a balance sheet and see my worth. I had the feeling he found me lacking.

Grahame came over to escort me the few steps to the table. "Niall, I am pleased to introduce you to my wife, Ailee."

Niall, whose name I now recalled as that of Grahame's brother, gave me another long look before sweeping into a short bow. I bobbed in curtsy, ducking my head to avoid that weighty stare.

"This is a surprise indeed," Niall answered, and from his tone, I could tell it wasn't a happy one.

"We're taking supper," Grahame told his brother. "Would you join us?"

"No, I've business elsewhere. But I'll return by morning. Are your belongings stored?"

"And the animals."

"How many have you?"

Grahame didn't answer, and Niall took only a moment to comprehend his brother's meaning. It took me a few beats longer.

"Of course," Niall said. "Time enough to talk later. I'll leave you to your supper." He bowed stiffly before sweeping his tricorn hat onto his head and leaving us.

I found I was out of breath and trembling after the swift reunion. Did all families greet one another so formally after so long apart? It had been so guarded, as though the brothers had been saying more to each other than words could carry. And I had been swept into that silent conversation and judged in that short time.

"Come," Grahame told me, offering me a thin smile. I tried to smile back, but I failed and nodded instead to cover it. I couldn't shake the feeling that Grahame's brother hadn't approved of me.

Grahame led me into a dimly lit dining room. The long table was seated for twelve, and all but four chairs were filled. All the other diners were men, two of them gentlemen in tailored clothing. A few of the men dressed more moderately, like Grahame, and a couple looked as though they'd just come in from a hunt. It was the oddest gathering I'd seen. I got a fair share of curious glances as Grahame held the chair for me by the end of the table, but no one spoke and only the two gentlemen and one of the others stood as I sat.

The scents of roast meat, bread, and sauces had my mouth watering, and my worries over Grahame's brother faded away. Grahame took the seat next to me before helping to fill my plate. He didn't ask what I wanted but gave me helpings of everything. Roasted beef, bread, vegetables in a rich sauce, fish pie, a pudding, and other foods I didn't recognize. I tried them all, and kept trying them long past the point of fullness. A rich beer chased down the food, and soon I could barely keep my eyes open.

One by one the other diners retired from the table, the gentlemen leaving together in quiet conversation. Grahame and I were not the last to leave, but close to, and I leaned on his arm, weary to my bones.

Grahame escorted me back to our room, and I didn't care that he was there as I disrobed down to my shift and stockings. After weeks of sharing a berth with so many strangers and never having a true moment alone with my husband, I was too tired to be nervous of the quiet silence and intimacy of the room. I could only think of the bed and the pillow and of being warm. I tucked into the bed with a groan of pleasure that elicited a rare laugh from Grahame.

"I'm sorry," I said, uncertain.

"Don't apologize," he chastened me. "It was all I could do not to fall into it myself."

I grinned, struggling to imagine my stalwart, staid husband collapsing crosswise on the bed like an errant boy. A warmth filled the room that had nothing to do with heat, and suddenly I was flushing as I watched him hang up his coat and pull the tie from his hair. His back to me, his long, dark locks fell in lazy curls past his muscular shoulders. He kicked off his boots with a sigh that must have been pleasure, and I hastily turned away as he began removing his breeches.

The room went suddenly dark as he blew out the lamp and the bed sagged under his weight as he slid under the blankets. His long frame heated the bed more than mine ever could. I found myself inching closer to him and was surprised when he wrapped his arms around me and pulled me against him. I could barely remember the last time when he'd held me thus, but I remembered what had followed it, and a heady anticipation quivered inside of me.

He seemed content just to hold me. I tucked my head against him on the pillow and closed my eyes. I had no memory of my last thoughts as sleep claimed me.

Chapter Twelve

The next morning dawned cold and bright. I was shivering by the time I had dressed. I dragged out as many layers as I could, pulling on an extra pair of stockings and tucking my dainty kerchief around my neck and into my bodice before wrapping my shawl around me. I found my gloves, too, and folded them in my pocket, knowing they would be meager protection against the chill but better than nothing. Truly, why had I not added more warm clothing to my trousseau? My single cloak was buried in a crate with the few linens we'd brought. How could I have failed to keep that at hand?

We broke our fast at the same table, and it was just as filling as supper had been, with porridge and ham and, I saw with a slight uneasy turn of my stomach, potatoes. The tea was hot and savory, and by the time I'd eaten my fill, avoiding the potatoes, I felt ready to face the day.

Though I didn't know what I'd be facing.

Mrs. Renfern came in just as we were standing from the table. "A gentleman's come to call for you," she told Grahame.

He thanked her and escorted me to the parlor. Niall was waiting for us, dressed much as he had been the night before, but with a heavier woolen coat that I tried not to look at with envy.

Niall and Grahame exchanged greetings by mere head nods, and Niall offered me a brief bow. I could feel his disapproval, but if Grahame noticed it, he said nothing. Instead, Grahame left me to sit with his brother as he brought down our baggage.

"'Tis cold today," I said just to break the uncomfortable silence.

Niall merely made a curt nod that he'd heard me. I gave up. I never thought I'd meet a man as sternly quiet as my husband. Of course it would take his brother to prove me wrong.

Thankfully, Grahame wasn't long, and we were soon leaving Mrs. Renfern's inn. Outside, taking up half the street, stood a wagon drawn by two oxen. A thin man in a worn tweed coat stood at the head of the oxen, looking somber.

"Our man, Thom," Niall said to Grahame. "He'll help with the loading and driving the animals. Can she herd a flock, at least?"

Niall was looking at me, but he obviously meant the question for Grahame.

"She can," Grahame answered, and there was a note of warning in his voice. For that, at least, I was grateful. Niall let the matter drop.

The dirt roads of the town were still damp and occasionally sucked at my shoes. Grahame led the way, tucking my arm in his. I was thankful for the extra hand. I tried to walk matter-of-factly down the road and not mince ladylike around frosted puddles or muddy sections, but it was difficult. The oxen squelched their way down the road, driven forward by Thom as Niall trailed after.

"I sent a note on for Elsie," Grahame told me in an undertone. I breathed a sigh of relief. "She'll know how to reach us."

"Thank you."

Grahame nodded in reply.

We walked several blocks back in the direction of the wharf, halting a road away from the river where a stout-looking building dominated the block.

It proved to be the warehouse where Grahame had stored our belongings. After a bit of negotiation with the man supervising, the men were hauling the crates to the wagon. Well, Grahame and Thom were hauling crates. Niall hung back, ostensibly to mind the oxen, but he struck up a conversation with the supervisor instead.

I stood out of the way, listening. They were speaking names I'd never heard of, some talk of the politics of the town, I figured. Niall's accent was strange, foreign at times with words I'd never heard before. The supervisor sounded as though he'd started English but had been too long away to keep the accent as his speech was peppered with odd, foreign words. Perhaps that was the speech of the town, whose name I finally overheard in the course of their talk.

Philadelphia. What a fancy name for such an unusual town. I still couldn't shake the sense of youthfulness laid over the place, a newness that was unlike anything I'd experienced in Donegal, where century-old ruins might overlook a town only slightly younger. Any stone building there would be rounded at the edges from the years of exposure to wind and rain. Here, the stones were still sharp from the chisel and the brickwork stout and freshly mortared.

Once the wagon was loaded, the oxen put more effort against their yoke, leaning against the weight to get the wagon rolling. Grahame led the way to the stockyards, where he went through much the same procedure of negotiating and then herding out our livestock. The beasts were all thinner, but we had only lost two sheep and a couple of chickens. The bull was looking curiously at the oxen, the cow was looking for fodder, and the sheep wanted to roam at once. I tried to live up to Grahame's claim that I could herd by heading them off and was pleased to see it actually worked.

After the chicken crates were loaded on the wagon and the bull and cow tied to the back, Niall took the lead, walking alongside the oxen to guide the way, though Thom clearly knew it. Grahame had me help herd the sheep behind the wagon, and we trailed after, keeping them together. He did most of the work. I had the feeling Grahame asked me to help to prove a point to Niall, but his brother didn't bother to pay us much heed. I thought Niall understood how new I was to this work and had already discounted any chance of my being truly useful.

It angered me, but it was a helpless rage because I knew he was right. Still, I did my best, looking to Grahame for his occasional nods of encouragement or guidance.

We took a road north. The sun was higher in the sky, bringing a weak sort of warmth between the cold shadows of the town's buildings until those began to thin and spread out.

"Are we not staying in the town?" I chanced to ask Grahame.

"No."

I bit my lip, thinking of Elsie. I had still held onto hope of see her again, but those hopes kept dwindling.

Grahame must have known where my thoughts lay. "The farm is less than a day's travel." he told me.

I nodded but kept silent. A day's walk. I'd not be able to return often, then, if Elsie remained there herself.

The roads were decent, if rutted. There was a surprising amount of traffic, mostly on foot with a few men on saddle horses. I saw several types of dress that I hadn't seen before, from long pants to thin skirts to half cloaks with puffy hats. The traffic thinned as we got farther from town, and the land became less clear cut, with more forests bulging to the edge of the road. Those trees were thick and tall, more so than anything I'd ever seen before, and the shadows swallowed the midmorning light breaking through the canopy where the leaves had fallen.

I wished Elsie were here. I wished I dared talk to Grahame, but he was concentrating on the animals to keep them from straying. I tried to focus on my work, too, but after a couple of hours, I realized how out of practice I had gotten at walking for long stretches. My feet ached in shoes not meant for such distances, my legs ached after too long spent aboard ship, and my shoulders ached from waving at the beasts to keep them together. My neck had a crick from craning to look into the depth of the forest until even that was too much work.

We stopped at midday. Grahame offered me a seat on the wagon, and I ignored Niall's pestering stare and accepted gratefully. We shared a meal Grahame had bought from Mrs. Renfern of smoked fish, cheese, apples, and a flagon of beer. Grahame and Niall talked of the road, and I heard mention of a place called Germantown. Thom said nothing, but I noted with alarm that he was priming a pistol. He slid it back under the wagon seat and caught me watching. He gave me a nod, as though acknowledging that I'd witnessed him and he was fine with that.

I wondered if we were in danger. The land had become less cultivated the farther we'd traveled from town, with more forest and wild country than farms. Were there dangers in the forests? Beacham had alluded to such, something about dangers in untouched places. Did he mean untouched by men? That would certainly describe the forests around us. They were rugged, deep, and shadowed, even with much of their leaves fallen.

A chill that had nothing to do with the air rushed through me, and I was suddenly glad that Thom had a pistol ready. When we began walking once more, I stayed away from the edges of the road but kept watching the forest. I'm afraid I was less help to Grahame by doing so, but the sheep were following more docilely as they tired from the journey, so I don't think he minded my abrupt caution. At least he said nothing of it.

We reached Germantown in late afternoon. The sun was already westering, casting a golden orange glow across the farmland surrounding the town. I had never met a German and had no idea what to expect, but I found the town to be quaint and amiable. The houses had a different look to anything I had seen before, with cross beams and white washing and interesting stonework. The roofs were thatched and most had chimneys. The road ran through the center of town, with a few rough side streets coming from it. We passed a smithy and a small market area, and a public house that smelled richly of pungent odors I'd never encountered before. It wasn't at all unpleasant. I hoped we might stop to take a meal, but Niall led us through the town without pause.

Of the townsfolk, they were dressed differently as well, in thick clothing suited to the climate and oddly shaped hats. The aprons and shawls the women wore were of a different cut than I was used to, the shawls wrapping round the women's torsos to tie in back. A few of the men wore scarves. It wasn't until we were out of the town and in the surrounding farmland that I began wondering if those scarves had been like the one Beacham wore. Would there be someone there who could teach me the stitch? If the farm Grahame spoke of was a day's travel from Philadelphia, surely we were nearly there.

The shadows closed around us as the forest returned along the roadside, which narrowed into a lane. The sky overhead was darkening as well, but around us it was already night as the forest boughs closed overhead. Niall paused long enough to light lanterns to hang off the wagon poles and carried one himself. Grahame took another, which helped to keep the animals clustered between us and the wagon.

I felt eyes watching us from the forest, and the skin crawled along my neck. I couldn't help but hear the sailor, Rakes, cautioning in his gruff voice: "Stay in the light." I kept close to Grahame and the lantern light, feeling as timid as the sheep. It served only to make the evening seem darker and more ominous outside that ruddy glow.

We crossed a bridge only barely wide enough to accommodate the wagon. The animals' hooves beat a tattoo of sound across the wooden planks, heavy and even-stepped for the oxen and cattle, quick and light for the sheep. It wasn't a long bridge, spanning a creek rather than a river. A few hundred paces past the bridge, Niall guided us off the lane and onto a rutted path through the woods.

The trees hovered around us, dark and forbidding. I crept even closer to Grahame. I was weary and frightened but also curious, sensing we were close to our destination by the way the oxen picked up their pace.

When the trees broke, the sight of the house dominating the open space filled me with relief. In the gloom, I could only tell that the house was tall, it's narrow end pointed toward us, had a candle lit in a the single front window, and that the door stood nearly at the corner. This side of the house had a neglected air to it, the clearing before it more of a meadow, with no signs of fields or pasture or even a garden.

Thom brought the wagon to a halt. Niall went to the door and knocked three sturdy raps. After not very long, the door opened to a woman holding aloft a lamp. She was older and dressed against the chill in the air with a thick wool shawl over her aproned skirts. She eyed Niall, then looked past him to Thom before laying sight on where I stood next to Grahame. No one spoke, held silent by the commanding look of this stout woman.

"Thom," she said suddenly, "you drive those sheep to the back and put them in the field." The woman's tone was forceful, direct, and Scottish. "Niall, you start hauling in the baggage. Stack it in the parlor for now." She stepped out of the doorway as Thom turned away from the oxen and Niall turned toward the cart. I was surprised at Niall's ready acceptance of this woman's demands.

The woman approached, and Grahame straightened with either apprehension or respect, or perhaps both.

"Grahame," the woman greeted, turning his name from one syllable to two. "You have your father's look about you. Have you found something of his spirit, too, then?" She was very firmly Scottish, in look and in accent.

Grahame didn't answer but bowed instead. "Mistress Cadha."

"Who is this, then?" the woman asked abruptly, turning on me.

"My wife, Ailee. Ailee, it is my honor to present you to my aunt, Cadha Donaghue."

I curtsied. The woman's eyebrow arched, and her quick gaze swept me with a judging glance. I couldn't tell if I passed muster or was found lacking. I was growing rather tired of being judged at a glance, however, and I stood straighter, raising my chin. The woman's eyes widened slightly, and I thought I saw the beginning of a smile cross her narrow mouth.

"Get her inside out of the chill. Second room at the top of the stairs is yours. Bed's a tad small, but it'll suit for now."

Grahame bowed again, and I curtsied and allowed him to escort me inside. The house was dark, with only a single candle lit on a table under the window. Grahame's lantern revealed plain walls and wooden floors and stairs facing the window next to a darkened doorway. The wood creaked underfoot as we climbed the stairs, the boards bare.

The hall above sloped with the slanting roof to the left, making it difficult for Grahame to walk without bending his head. The doors all stood along the right. Grahame opened the second door into a small, plain room that was almost as cold as the outside had been. A bed nearly half the size as the one at Mrs. Redfern's dominated the space. A chair had been placed next to a small stand in one corner. A window broke the far wall, shuttered but uncurtained. I saw it only when the lantern light reflected off the heavy glass.

I was not disappointed, though. I was tired, my feet and legs ached from the walk, my arms were sore from herding sheep, and my nose had gone numb with the cold. The room didn't offer much in warmth or welcome, but it was solid, sheltering, and I felt the fears that had been gnawing at my insides for the past half day ebb away.

"I'll return shortly," Grahame told me, setting the lantern on the stand. He closed the door as he left.

The room was emptier without his presence, but I tried not to fret. I didn't wait for my bags but stripped out of my muddy shoes and loosened my stays before sliding into the cold bed. The quilt upon it was happily thick, the mattress firm enough, and the pillow downy. I pulled the covers up to my chin and as the first bit of warmth crept across me, I fell asleep.

CHAPTER THIRTEEN

I slept fitfully, unable to fall into a deeper sleep with the cold picking at me and the multiple aches pushing into my awareness. It wasn't until Grahame slid into the bed with me, his warmth chasing out the worst of the cold, that I fell into a restful sleep. It ended far too soon, however, with a knocking upon the door.

"Up and about, my lady," Grahame's aunt called to me roughly through the wood. "We don't sleep the morning away here."

I sat up, shocked into wakefulness by embarrassment. Grahame was already gone. Light streamed in thin slants from around the shuttered window, giving the room a gloomy light not unlike the berth under full lamplight.

I pulled the covers back and instantly regretted it. The cold hit me as soon as the blankets were gone, and I had nothing in which to dress for more warmth. I was still wearing my clothing from yesterday, though they were tangled and askew from sleep. I did what I could to straighten myself, my fingers chill and my hands shaking as I tightened my stays, tucked my hair under my mobcap, and pulled on the muddy shoes. I wished I had cleaned them off before entering the house.

When I was finished, I was thankful for the lack of a mirror. I had no wish to see how bedraggled I truly was.

I opened the door. The hall was quiet and dark. Two shadowed recesses spoke of doors, one to either side of my own. I went down the stairs, finding the steps by an ambient light coming up from below, hoping I would run into Grahame before anyone else. The front door was closed, the candle in the window before the stairway cold and dark. The shutters were opened, and I was looking through real, if incredibly thick, glass. A wan light filled the window, but the glass was too thick to make out any details of the yard beyond.

A doorway stood between the stairs and the window. I looked through it and found our crates and luggage piled in what must usually serve as the parlor. I couldn't tell much from the room except that it had a small stone hearth set in the wall that served as the front of the house and a window to either side of the stone chimney. The room above, the one at the top of the stairs, must get a measure of warmth from the chimney, at least. I wondered if that was Cadha's room or if Niall had laid claim to it.

No one was in the parlor, so I circled the stairs to the next doorway, which opened into a small dining room, filled with a stout wooden table with four rough chairs around it. A single window broke the wall opposite the door. Like the parlor, it was empty.

I had one more door to try, and I approached it. I paused, expecting to hear voices, but the room beyond was silent. I pushed the door open to find a wood room. A few tools hung on the wall on pegs, along with a couple of heavy-looking coats, a battered wool cloak, and knitted scarf with a few pairs of well-worn leather gloves; otherwise, the room was full of split lumber.

And not one person.

The back door of the house was shut and latched. I considered borrowing one of the coats from the wood room, decided against it, and then realized I had already been scolded for sleeping late. What would another scolding cost me but more embarrassment? At least I'd be warm.

I took down the smaller of the two coats and found it to be thick wool. Gratefully, I shrugged into it and wrapped my arms around myself. It smelt of sweat and animals, but I felt warmer almost at once.

I unlatched the back door. The cleared space behind the house was dotted with several out-buildings. I recognized a bake house, which was stone, and saw a wooden building with partially slatted walls that held chickens, but the rest of the buildings were unfamiliar. Aside from the bake house, only one other had a chimney.

Between the small buildings stood garden plots—not just a single one, but several. The soil had been turned over and winter wheat sown in many, but a few still grew herbs and winter greens. Beyond the out-buildings stood a barn that was as long as the house, if not quite as tall. The roof was pitched high on one side, then ran off the building to form a porch of sorts for the animals to gather under. A cross-rail fence ran from the shorter corners, encircling a paddock were I saw our sheep intermingling with a larger flock of stranger looking sheep, and our cow with a handful of brown cows grazing on hay that had been tossed into the muddy enclosure. The bull stood forlornly in another section, fenced off with the oxen.

Suddenly, a pair of mastiffs came racing around the farthest outbuilding, barking with deep-throated alarm. I froze. The dogs were thick and stocky with heavy jowls and small ears. They were fawn colored with dark eyes and they charged forward on stout legs, barreling toward me.

A fierce shout halted them. Thom stood just outside the barn, some short tool in his hand. He called the dogs back. They hesitated, looking between Thom and where I stood, until he called again. Together, they turned in a lumbering sort of way and loped to him.

Thom walked back inside the barn, the dogs on his heels. The two of them came up to the man's waist. I saw no sign of Niall or Grahame. As I stood pinioned against the back door waiting for my heart to stop racing, I heard a woman singing in a throaty alto.

The sound led to the bake house. I opened the door to luscious warmth and the heady scent of bread. Grahame's aunt was throwing dough and singing a song in a language I partially recognized.

I approached her cautiously, not wishing to startle her. Cadha glanced at me but stopped neither her song nor her kneading, giving me time to examine her.

She was older still in the cloudy light of day, probably in her late forties. What hair showed under her cap was black going to gray. She was stout but not heavy and had the look of strength about her. She wore several thick skirts and a couple layers of wool shirts, a well-made apron, and over that a knitted shawl that wrapped across her front and around her waist to tie in the back. A set of keys jangled from her apron ties. Her boots were thick leather and looked warm.

Her song ended. My attention snapped back to Cadha's face.

"Have a lie in, did we? You'll find we keep long hours here, my lady. And if you miss breaking the fast, you'll suffer without until dinner." Her tone was mocking, made more so with the Scottish cadence, but as much as it rubbed at me, it wasn't entirely unkind, either. And there was a glimmer of amusement in her blue eyes.

"I am sorry," I said with a curtsy. "The walk from the town must have tired me more than I realized."

"Or that husband of yours is soft and let you sleep," she added knowingly. "We'll break him of that, quick enough. You mustn't let him coddle you, girl, or you'll be no worth to any of us."

I nodded, my cheeks burning. "There were dogs—"

Cadha scowled. "Those empty-headed beasts. We'll get you acquainted with them. They're Niall's, though why he thought they'd be of any use to us, I'll never understand. Now then," she told me, "let's see how you are with bread."

I already knew how I was with bread, which was why Grahame had continued to buy it from a neighbor before we left Ireland. But I came over at his aunt's bidding and took the dough up carefully.

"Ack, girl, it isn't a newborn kitten. Handle it with some certainty or it'll get away from you."

The next hour I spent kneading dough under Cadha's instruction. There were several balls of it to work, and as I worked and made corrections, Grahame's aunt told me that today was bread-making day, that every seventh day was, and that we'd either make enough to last until the next bread-making or go without. "And those men are not happy to go without," she added, correcting my kneading once more with a couple of prods of her finger.

When I was finished, my arms and shoulders ached, my stomach was growling, my mouth was dry, and I had twelve round loaves to slide into the oven. The fires were already lit, but Cadha called out to Thom before I'd finished, and he came to tend the coals laid under the stone oven.

"There's more of us now," she said, "but I do believe these will suit. We'll leave them to rise and return to put them in. Thom, you mind those coals stay lit."

Thom ducked his head in acknowledgment, but not in a deferential way. More like he couldn't be bothered to make a full nod of it.

"Come with me, girl, and I'll show you about. Your man and his brother are walking the field, but they'll return soon enough. Let me show you the stream."

As Cadha led me out of the bake house with a bucket in each

hand, I hesitated, looking for the dogs. When they didn't appear bounding around some building, I dared to ask a question.

"I do beg your pardon," I began, feeling out the words. "But how should I address you?"

Cadha made a sound that might have been a scoff. She turned on her heels. I realized I was an inch or two taller than she when I wasn't hunched over a table. "So that's how it is. Cadha will do, if you like, or Mistress Cadha if you feel the urge to be formal." Cadha moved on through the yard. She led the way to a well-trod path into the woods.

The woods were shadowy even with mostly bare branches, though the trees had been thinned out nearest the yard. "The stream passes from here to the pastures, so the water is clear," she told me. The stream was just a little wider across than I could jump. The water ran deepest at the center, and it was as clear as Cadha said. I could see the silty bottom, punctuated with rounded stones fuzzy with moss. The stream bank sloped until the ground was just a few fingerspans above the water. More stones dotted the river bank, making a nice stepping stone for reaching the water. I realized that was probably on purpose and the stones may have been placed there for that reason. The area around the path opening to the stream had been cleared back, leaving plenty of room to work.

Cadha handed me a bucket. "Never leave here empty-handed," she warned with that stern voice she used with Thom. Deftly, she stood on the flat stones and bent down to dip the bucket into the water. She let the flowing stream fill the bucket, then hefted it easily and set it on the bank. The bucket was nearly full and dripping. Cadha wasn't even damp.

"Now you," Cadha told me, stepping back to gesture at the stone.

It took me three tries to fill the bucket enough to her liking, and by then I'd managed to splash water across my skirts and into my shoes. It was as cold as it was clear. Cadha was shaking her head by the time I'd finished and clicking her tongue.

"Well, girl, you have a lot to learn. Goodness knows why Grahame married you, knowing he was bringing you out here. You belong in a fine dress in a parlor serving tea, you do." Still shaking her head, Cadha picked up her bucket and trekked back toward the house. My cheeks burning, I picked up my bucket, having to use both hands, and trailed after.

The rest of the day went much the same, with me trailing after Cadha, learning some new bit of work that I quickly proved clumsy with, then listening to Cadha talk about how unprepared I was while my cheeks burned. Dinner was a welcome respite, since I'd slept through breakfast. We took a hearty meal of pudding followed by meat pies, pickles, and roasted root vegetables. Grahame and Niall joined us at the table, though Thom filled his trencher and took it outside. Neither Niall nor Cadha commented, so Thom must have taken most of his meals away from the family. It was another sign that he was the farm servant. I wondered that a farm like this could afford to keep one.

Cadha asked Grahame questions about the livestock he'd brought, and tools, and bits of news. Niall had a plan to breed the new livestock with those already on the farm that apparently he and Grahame had already discussed, and to which Cadha readily approved.

I wasn't used to such talk at the table. At home, my family spoke of the goings on in town and news of friends and family, but my father never spoke of business. And at Grahame's table, neither of us had spoken much at all. At Cadha's table, it seemed dining was the time for such talk.

Cadha walked out with Niall when they finished their meal. She cast a glance to me and told me to take the dishes to the wash house for cleaning. Grahame hung back as I rose to begin gathering the dishes. He seemed to want to speak to me but didn't know what to say. I wished he would say anything. Instead, he touched my shoulder and offered me a nod, then left the room.

I sighed, long and heavy and weary. Homesickness bit at me, and I tried to push it away by thinking of something that might be familiar here, but nothing was. I refused to weep, though, and blinked against the tears.

Cadha and Niall both thought I was worthless. Grahame seemed to think so as well. Maybe I was. But I didn't have to stay that way. I'd been learning before leaving Ireland, I'd learned on the ship, and I could learn here. Not all at once, no, but I could pick something and make it my own.

I decided on water. That would be my first chore. It was simple and necessary and would make me stronger hauling it to the house. Yes, I decided with a nod to myself. I would become the best water carrier any of them had ever seen.

It was ridiculous to think they'd even notice, but it still made me feel better. I had a focus, something to strive for, and I was going to give it my all.

And after I got the hang of carrying the water, I'd pick something else. Like lighting the hearth or chopping something or stitching.

I found myself grinning. Perhaps stitching would be a bit of a stretch. I'd have more luck at bread-making.

Maybe Grahame would notice how hard I was trying. But then I wondered if that should be the reason I was trying. Cadha was doing fine making a life on her own. I assumed her husband, Grahame's uncle, had died, though no one had mentioned it. I don't know how Cadha kept control of the place, for it was obvious she was in charge and not just of the household. She had spoken with authority about all aspects of the farm during dinner.

It was the first time I'd met a woman so in charge of her own destiny. She wasn't entirely on her own. She had Niall and Thom, and now Grahame and me. I might not be of much use, but Cadha seemed willing to instruct me. I should embrace that and learn all I could, regardless of what Niall thought of me. Cadha was a woman worth more than just respect. I found that I admired her.

After helping Cadha prepare dinner, I had at least proved I could peel and chop. Supper was simpler fare which took less time, so I was relieved of my duties and free to go up to the room I would share with Grahame. Someone, probably Grahame, had moved my crates and bags to the room so I had access to all my clothes again. I sorted them and packed what I wouldn't need back in the crates, those items that wouldn't be useful working on the farm. That sadly included my cloak, which was too long and too thin to be truly helpful against the chill. When I was finished, I had three skirts and underskirts, two bodices, my shifts, stockings, kerchiefs, apron, and pockets. It was a paltry collection, but perhaps more than many wives in my position would own. And the room smelt pleasantly of dried heather afterwards, which brought a trace of home.

I stood over the crates, breathing in the scents of home, and an ache so profound sucked away my breath. How had I come to be so far away in such a short time? Only the time didn't feel short. It felt as though years had passed since I'd last seen my home and my parents. I wondered how my three brothers faired, if Elgin had begun courting, if Father had finally allowed Coy and Bryant to accompany him on his travels. I remembered Cook and her wonderful seedcakes, and the way Nanny had smelled of honey. I missed my room at the end of the hall, with its twin windows and my four-posted bed. I missed rugs and having help with my hair. I missed ribbons and linen.

Overcome, I wiped tears away. I could miss them all. It was right to miss those people and things I'd lost, but it didn't do to dwell on it. This was my life now. I had to make the most of it. I had to look ahead, not behind.

I gathered myself to change into fresh clothing, having worn what I had on for two days already and wanting to be somewhat fresh for supper. I was under no illusions that after supper I'd be able to lounge about and relax. I thought that Cadha would have enough work to keep us going well after the tapers were lit, though that time was drawing quickly near. I did miss retiring after supper for reading aloud and singing. Maybe those were things that happened here. Cadha had a full voice. I wondered if she had any books.

Tidied, if not entirely cleaned, I returned downstairs. As I neared the dining room, I heard Niall speaking. I was already in the doorway when his words registered.

"I can understand wanting the dowry to help with the crossing, but did you have to actually bring her?"

I froze, stunned. Niall's back was to me, but Grahame saw me. The look that crossed his face was both pained and shameful. Niall turned, and he had the decency to also look embarrassed.

I wanted to disappear. I wanted to flee. I wished I'd stayed in the room a few moments longer.

"Now what's this?" Cadha boomed from behind me. "Don't stand a staring, girl. Help me fetch in supper."

I whirled and fled for the kitchen house. I heard voices behind me, one of them sounding like Grahame calling my name, but I ignored him and didn't stop until I was in the heated stone building.

Thom was tending the fire. He looked at me with the first real emotion I'd seen in him since meeting him, curiosity in his usually sober expression. But he didn't speak, and I couldn't. Instead, I went to the trestle table and braced against it, taking deep breaths.

My dowry. That had been Grahame's purpose all along. I'd suspected it. My dowry hadn't been small. My father had seen to that as soon as he decided I needed to be wed and wed quickly. A few townsmen had come sniffing because of the size of it, but they'd all backed away, scared off by scandal, or sent away as the wrong sort. Even with a scandal hanging over me, my father wouldn't wed me to just anyone. And then Grahame had come into town and had seemed so taken with me.

Not with me. With my dowry.

Now it all made sense. The comments from the Karney girl about leaving so late in the season. The haste of preparing for the voyage, but Grahame's knowledge in what was needed and the swiftness with which he'd sold his goods and settled his accounts. Grahame had been planning on coming to the colonies, but he had been waiting until he could afford the voyage. My dowry had made it possible for him to leave sooner than he'd expected.

Or had it? How had Niall and Thom known to meet us if Grahame had only decided to leave sooner after meeting me? And he had already begun selling his flocks before he knew who I was, for that was how he met my father.

But the dowry must have been helpful, in ways I could not be.

I must be such an inconvenience to him. I'd proved I was a worthless helpmeet, with little skills at keeping a home outside of tasking a servant. Oh, my embroidery was neat enough, but what was that to a working man keeping a farm? I didn't have time to embroider.

No wonder Niall thought me beneath him and Cadha thought me hopeless. I must seem the worst choice in a wife that Grahame could have made.

I realized I was crying. I glanced behind me, but Thom had disappeared. It was a small blessing.

What could I do? I was wed, was weeks by ship from my home, and had only one friend in this new land, and she could be of no help to me. I had nowhere else to go, no other family to take me in. This was my life now.

My tears stopped as quickly as they'd begun. I'd prove I could be useful. That, at least, I could do. I might not have a husband's love, but I'd earn his respect. I already had a plan, so I'd keep at it.

And in the meantime, I'd just do the best I could, pay attention, and stay out of Niall and Grahame's way.

Calmed, if not heartened, I wiped my face with a damp rag, straightened my apron and skirts, and picked up the bowl of corn porridge. I placed it on a platter along with the bread and cheese Cadha had set out. Lifting my chin, I carried the platter to the house.

Thom was standing just outside the back door, the dogs seated to either side of him. I hesitated.

"Naught to fear, miss," he said, the most words I'd had from him. "This be Horace and this Edgar." The dogs and I stared at each other. I had the feeling they'd be after the food on the tray if Thom wasn't there. "I'll keep them out of your way, miss, whilst you settle in." He stepped aside for me, shooing the dogs back, and held the door open. I thanked him with a nod, and he returned it. It was the first acknowledgment he'd given of my presence, and I was grateful for it and for his control of the dogs.

I continued to the dining room. Niall and Cadha were standing in front of Grahame, and if they had been talking, which I was certain they had, they were silent when I entered. I set the platter on the table.

"Ailee helped with the pies for supper," Cadha said matter-of-factly as I moved to a seat. "She'll have a fair hand at turning dough soon enough. Thom, fetch the pitcher and mugs."

We all sat. Thom didn't join us but left the pitcher and mugs, took his trencher and one mug after Cadha filled it, and left the room. Talk turned non-committal, with observances on the weather, the roads from town, whether they needed to chop more wood tomorrow or the day after. Cadha thought the rains would return in a day or so, and that it would frost again by the first of next week. Niall wanted to go hunting at the end of the week and take Grahame out with him. Niall had bows instead of snares in mind. Grahame actually stopped glancing at me when he thought I wasn't looking to give Niall his full attention, so I could tell he liked the idea of a hunt. I had no idea he could work a bow.

I didn't try to join in the talk. I keenly felt more than ever that I was an outsider. I doubted I'd ever truly be one of them, but I held on to my resolve to at least earn their respect.

From the looks I caught Grahame giving me, I thought he, at least, was hoping I would try.

CHAPTER FOURTEEN

That evening after helping Cadha bank the fires in the kitchen house and checking that the chickens were all in the hen house, I returned to my room to find Grahame waiting for me. I was honestly surprised to see him there. He stood up from the single chair as I entered. He made the room feel smaller, simply from his height and his presence.

He'd taken the tie out of his hair, and it fell past his shoulders in black waves that wanted to curl. He was watching me with those unreadable brown eyes. I got the sense he was abashed, but I wasn't sure what told me that. His expression was inscrutable. Perhaps it was how he was hunching his shoulders, or the way he stood, as though ready for me to lash out at him.

He couldn't possibly be afraid of what I thought, could he? It was a strange sensation to feel like I might hold some power over him.

"Niall shouldn't have said what he did," Grahame said as soon as I'd closed the door behind me. I froze, uncertain where this might lead. But I didn't want to remain a passive observer in my own life anymore.

"Was it true?"

Grahame looked away, and that was all I needed to know.

"You wanted the dowry." The words breathed out of me, almost like a sigh of relief. But it tore me up inside to know it was the truth.

"I wanted the dowry," he repeated softly. He took a step toward me, just a single step. "But I wanted you, too."

My heart quickened. "Why?"

113

A smile crept across his face. "You're young and pretty."

"And not much good for anything." I'd been told I was pretty for most of my life. So far, being so had only brought me grief.

"You'll learn."

"Will I?" I focused on him, trying to read him like I would a page in a book. "After all this time, can you honestly believe I'll be of any true help to you out here?"

He hesitated.

"I want to be," I continued. "I do. I hate feeling helpless and useless. I want you to trust that I can be of use." And I'd like to show up Niall, I thought, but I didn't say it aloud.

"Then I brought you to the right place," he said at last. "Cadha can teach you."

I couldn't argue with that. "I don't want to hamper her, either," I admitted.

"You won't. Just do your best, that's all I ask."

I bristled, but I bit back my anger. I wasn't entirely sure why I was so angry. At the way he sounded like my father, or that I needed to live up to his expectations, or just because I felt like I'd been brought without warning into an impossible situation and now had to defend myself.

Grahame must have seen something of my anger, for he held up a hand to me. "I meant that I will help you as much as I can, when I am free to do so."

"Like on the ship?"

The words came out more bitter than I meant.

Grahame's expression darkened, and I saw him swallow. Fear jolted through me. What was I doing speaking back to this man?

"The ship was . . . bad," he said at last, his words thick with emotion. He took another step toward me. "And I'm sorry for that, Ailee. I truly am. It won't be like that again."

He had been scared, too, I realized suddenly. But scared of what? The ship? The death? Losing me?

By God, I wished I was brave enough to ask.

He took a final step, and it brought him within arm's reach of me. I fought against the urge to both slide up into his embrace and back away out of reach.

"We're both new to this," he said to me in his quiet, thoughtful tone. "To marriage," he added, and I wondered why he felt the need to say it. "We can take this slow. Winter is coming on. We have plenty of time to get to know each other better before the spring."

Spring was important, I knew that. Planting and lambing and all the other sorts of work that went into a farm in the springtime that I still had to learn about. It apparently held great importance to Grahame by the way he spoke of it.

But he was offering me something that went beyond mere awareness of changes in the seasons. I wasn't sure how a husband and wife could get to know each other any better than having taken to bed together.

So I dared to ask. "How do you mean?"

Grahame reached out and caught my hand in his. "I mean that I never had the chance to court you, as a man wanting a woman to wife should. I think now is as good a time as any."

I looked up at him, the first warmth of a blush crossing my cheeks. "That isn't necessary."

"I think it is." He grew serious. "I want you for my partner, Ailee. Not just for a dowry or a pretty girl at my side. I saw something in you that first day we met, and I see it more and more each day since. You fear not being useful. I say you will be. I say you will outshine Cadha in time when it comes to keeping a home. You've a fire beneath that easy upbringing. I want to see you bold enough to burn with it. And I want to be there when you realize it's there."

I gaped at him, stunned. He'd never spoken so much in one turn, and never in such a way about me.

He looked as if he wanted to say more, but he bent toward me instead and pressed a kiss upon my forehead under my mobcap. My blush deepened.

"Get some rest," he murmured, still bent close to me.

He straightened and stepped past me for the door.

"Cadha says I'm not to oversleep," I called to him, feeling meek but not wanting to withstand Cadha's dressing down again.

He hesitated, ducking his head slightly. "I know."

I had the impression that Cadha had chastised him already about letting me sleep too long.

He closed the door behind him, leaving me alone in the dim room. Loneliness settled over me like a shroud.

As the days passed by, the nights grew longer and the days shorter. A chill took hold in the air that turned to frost on clear evenings, but few evenings were given the chance to be clear. Rain settled over the area with a note of finality.

I was no stranger to rain. Donegal saw its fair share of it and at about the same time of year. But there the similarities ended. The chill was different, bleaker with the baleful gloom of the naked forest standing so close to the farm. The sound of running water was ever present, off the roofs and eaves, down the trees, through the stream where I gathered the water several times a day. I'd heard less water in the weeks living aboard a ship in the middle of an ocean. The irony was not lost on me.

My clothing wasn't quite up to keeping back the wet. My mobcap and shawl soaked through, my skirts dragged soddenly, and my feet were always wet and cold.

Grahame came through for me within a few days of our arrival, presenting me with a wide-brimmed leather hat. He presented it to me early in the morning before I left the house to fetch eggs. I had my egg basket in hand and was following Cadha, who was carrying the lantern, out into the pre-dawn gloom, when Grahame stepped from the dining room doorway. He gave me a shock, but I recovered quickly when he held the hat out to me.

I took it, and he bent in a half-bow before disappearing down the hall and through the back door. I had turned it over in my hands to examine before trying it on. It smelt of hide and tallow, but it was warm and kept my head dry. It had been treated with some substance to help repel the water. It was strange to keep off my mobcap after so long wearing it. I'd only just gotten used to it. Instead, I tied my hair back into a knot at the back of my neck to wear my hat.

The next day, Cadha caught me hanging my shawl near the kitchen fire in an attempt to dry it out.

"You need to treat that," the older woman told me briskly. "And make yourself something bigger."

"I'm not much of a knitter," I admitted. It still stung to admit my faults, though I'd gotten quite a bit of practice in over the last few weeks.

"How's your carding?"

"Not very nice," I admitted.

Cadha straightened to stare at me. "How's your spinning?"

"I've been told I have a fair hand at that."

Cadha cocked her head, considering. "Well, then, I can see you better practiced at carding. Then you can help me with the spinning, and I'll help you to make a better shawl. And stockings, too. No doubt yours need treating along with that shawl."

I wasn't sure what Cadha meant by treating, and I finally admitted as much.

"Tonight, then," Cadha told me. "I'll show you how. Go back to the house and fetch a coat for now. Leave that shawl there to dry."

That evening before supper, I gathered all my stockings as Cadha had instructed. As I did, I found the little jar of salve Tavey had given me on the ship. My hands were raw and aching from the daily strain of filling buckets, carrying platters and baskets, cutting and chopping in the kitchen house, and learning to churn cream for butter and cheese. I'd been thankful for the chill as an excuse to wear my gloves, but they'd been pretty things, meant to look fair not hold up to daily strain, and they were already sporting holes in the palms. I had blisters on my hands in those places, and I remembered how soothing Tavey's salve had been.

Grateful to the dear lady once more, I spread a bit of salve on the raw places. The fragrance of lemon balm and lavender filled the small room, carrying memories mixed with emotions. My home, playing in the kitchen garden while Cook snipped herbs. The ship, the constant roiling back and forth, and yet another potato to peel. I wondered how Elsie was faring, and Beacham, and my family in Ireland. Did they miss me?

Did he miss me?

I stood abruptly and turned a tight circle to chase the thought away. Those thoughts had no place inside me anymore. Stockings, I had them in hand. That's what I should be thinking of. I put the salve down on the little stand and left the room.

Cadha was waiting in the hall. "The kitchen," she told me, and she led the way.

My shawl was dry, finally. And the pleasant odor of supper had been replaced by something pungent and earthy that reminded me of melting wax, but not quite.

A kettle hung over the fire, and a jar of a dark yellowish substance sat open on the trestle table, giving off the scent.

"What is it?"

"Wool oil," Cadha told me. "Or wool grease, I've heard it called. Helps keep the sheep dry by coating their wool. I boil it off some of the wool we shear. Helps to keep us dry, too, among other things. Take that kettle and pour the water into that bucket, like I taught you."

I did as I was told while Cadha took a scoop of wool oil from the jar with a small wooden spoon. She handed the spoon to me. "Stir the water 'til it's all melted."

The room grew more fragrant with the scent of the pungent oil. It reminded me of something long ago, but I couldn't quite grasp the memory.

Cadha took a second bucket and poured about half the water into it. "To cool it," she said. "We don't want to bind the stitches. Now you'll want to put your shawl and stockings in and let them sit. Push them under the water, that's the way. While they soak, we'll bank the fire."

I banked the kitchen fire like Cadha had taught me while the older woman put away the clean cookware and stepped outside to dump the used wash water. I was finding that I hated to see the wash water dumped. It had taken an effort to haul it from the stream, and I was getting to where I didn't like to see water wasted. All those years I took it for granted, never caring how it got into the house or which of our family's three servants had hauled it in from the well house.

When we had the kitchen house ready for the night, Cadha showed me how to remove the shawl and stockings and wring them in a dry dish towel before hanging them to dry near the banked fire.

"They should be about dry come morning," Cadha told me, "and then do a better job of keeping the wet off of you. But mind, you'll have to treat them again after a while. The oil doesn't hold through washings and wearings."

I thanked her, looking forward to having dry stockings, at least. My feet were sore from the constant damp. It seemed they had just gotten dry by morning when it was time to go out into the wet again.

The next morning, I found a new pair of boots waiting for me by the bedroom door. They looked similar to the hat in construction and went nearly up to my knees. I dressed quickly, slid into the one pair of stockings I'd held back from treating, and then pulled on the boots. They were loose around the leg and ankle, but fit my feet well, with enough wiggle room in the toes not to pinch. The heel wasn't as tall as I was used to, but the boots felt good. And warm.

I left the room, carrying a taper to light my way through the dark house and yard. I met Cadha in the kitchen house, and the older woman was holding up one of the stockings.

"They're about ready," she told me. "Hang them out of the way, and let's get breakfast on. I'll fetch the eggs today."

My new boots and hat served me well throughout the day. The boots chafed a little at first, but by the end of the day, my foot was snug inside and took some prying to pull off. When I saw Grahame at breakfast, I gave him a shy smile and turned my heel out from under my skirts to show off the boot. His eyes lit up in pleasure, but he made no other notice. I was finding I enjoyed this quiet flirting we did during mealtimes. I rarely saw him the rest of the day.

Grahame and I had been on Cadha's farm for nearly a month when one evening, Cadha and Niall spoke of getting the work done first thing before leaving for the monthly service. It was somewhat of a shock to me to realize they had churches in the colonies, but given the size of the town, I felt foolish for my surprise. We had held them on the ship during travel, it hadn't had the same feel as attending with my family in Lifford where I knew everyone and had been attending since I was small. On the ship, it had been a comfort of familiarity, a balm to the grief of our losses. I had no idea what to expect out here.

Grahame said nothing of it that evening when he joined me in bed, and I wasn't sure what to ask. Instead, I decided the best thing would be to stay close to Cadha and watch what she did. I wondered if the Scottish worshiped the same way my family had? What if it were entirely different?

I fretted until I finally fell asleep.

There were no leisurely preparations like on worship days in Lifford. I was up before dawn and helping prepare breakfast while Niall, Grahame, and Thom saw to the animals. The only differences were that the animals were kept near the barn, we packed up baskets to carry with us, and after breakfast, Cadha had me bank the fire before we changed into something less muddy for the walk to the meeting house.

I came downstairs in my best dress. I hadn't worn it since leaving home. It was a little too fine for life on a farm, and it was probably too fine for a walk through the wilderness, but I had been wanting to wear it for so long now. The color, dark emerald green with cream hemming and ribbon, wasn't as showy as some of my old dresses had been, which is why I'd brought it from home. It suited a young married woman going to worship. I only wished I had a bonnet to wear with it. My laciest mobcap had to suffice.

Grahame surprised me at the bottom of the stairs with a cape. It was wool the same creamy color as his sheep. It was thick and warm and all it lacked was a hood to complete it. He held it out like an offering.

I ran my fingers over it. The wool was scratchy but dry and thick.

I looked up at him, and my question must have been plain on my face.

"I bought it in town," he said.

"While I was still on the ship?"

"I thought you might have need of it."

It was the closest thing to a whim I'd seen in him. It was a lovely cape, and completely useless on a farm. It was too long and too round and would have been nothing but in my way as I worked. But for a walk, it was perfect. And I loved it.

I smiled as he settled it around my shoulders and tied it in place.

Cadha joined us, and I was startled to see her dressed finely as well. After seeing her only in her working dresses, I hadn't realized how handsome she was. She must have been lovely in her youth. Her dress was primrose purple with a deep green trim close in color to my own skirts. She had no bonnet or mobcap, but instead had drawn a knitted capelet around her shoulders over her own cape and drawn the hood over her upswept graying hair. It buttoned under her chin with a simple hand-carved wooden button. The capelet was as rich of green as my skirts, too, and I noticed with some envy the fanciful Celtic knotwork stitched on the back. It looked warm, and I wished I had the skill to make one for myself. Perhaps she could teach me. Without the knotwork.

Cadha gave Thom a few final instructions before we set out. I was surprised he wasn't joining us, but then again, I had learned he was English and so maybe he went to another meeting house. I was a little hazy on just what religion the English were, though the ones my parents had entertained on occasion seemed to share my family's faith, at least in part.

I didn't know what to expect for the journey except that I remembered we were a day's walk from the town. And then I was shocked to see both Niall and Grahame swing muskets over their shoulders before we left the house. Just where was this church? My nervousness must have shown itself, for when Grahame took my arm, he gave me an encouraging smile.

"It's only a couple hours to the neighbor's house," he told me.

"We're not going to a church?"

Grahame shook his head. "We'll meet in houses. Each month, a neighbor hosts."

I nodded to show I understood. I was still wary, given the firearms, but a new excitement began to grow inside me. I grinned, and Grahame's echoing smile was as warm as my new cape.

CHAPTER FIFTEEN

The walk was easier than the last time I'd traveled this road because we didn't have to keep watch for any straying sheep, but it was harder for the muddy roads. Grahame helped me, easily carrying one of the baskets while keeping my arm twined in his to keep me from falling when my foot caught or slipped in a muddy patch. The forest was still as forbidding as the first time I'd traveled the road, except most of the leaves had dropped, which only made the creaking branches more ominous. Niall and Cadha led us. Niall's dogs, who had finally grown accustomed to me, paced with us, ranging ahead and then falling back, darting into the trees only to return once more.

The sun was warming, if not quite enough to chase away the chill in the air, and the walk brisk, and I soon forgot the musket over Grahame's shoulder. The woods were no less intimidating, but they were familiar. I entered them at least twice a day for water and had gained a grudging respect for them. I was free of chores today, with a gathering of new acquaintances to look forward to, and nearly a full day to spend in Grahame's company. I found that I was grinning as we walked.

I wanted to speak with him, to try to carry on a conversation that didn't involve sheep or fields or fence poles, but I didn't know what to say.

"Thank you for the cape," I offered. It was warm, and I was pleased not to have to wear one of the worn work coats or capes over my nicest dress.

"It suits you," he returned.

"I feel almost normal again," I admitted. He glanced down at me, his brow furrowed. "Like I was before. Out for a stroll before dinner, wearing something fine."

His expression sobered, and he looked away. I bit my lip, realizing what I was saying.

"You miss it." His tone was as sober as his expression.

"Sometimes. When I have a chance to think on it. I'm usually too busy learning what to do next to dwell on it. Yesterday, Cadha showed me how to pluck a chicken. I never had guessed there were that many feathers."

"Which chicken?"

"The rooster she didn't want. The one who kept getting out. She figured he'd be a better meal for us than for the beasts." She'd said 'dogs,' and then had gone on to explain how Niall's dogs occasionally caught a chicken that had strayed, but with Niall nearby, I didn't want to repeat her words.

Grahame's expression eased, and I spoke of a few other skills I had learned, hoping to smooth over the gaff I'd made. Wishing for my old life did no one any good. Did Grahame know who I was missing?

But no, I wouldn't let my thoughts go there. I'd left all that behind me.

The meeting house proved to be another farm on the far side of a river. The bridge we crossed had been newly built. I heard Cadha comment on it as we crossed. Apparently the old one had been washed away last spring.

The farm itself was about the same size as Cadha's, the house a little taller, with a sloping roof in the back and the door fronting on the length of the house rather than the shorter width. An ox cart stood in the front yard, the oxen pulling at the tall grass going yellow at the edge of the dirt drive. A saddle horse was tied near the cart, the horse watching the oxen warily. It snorted as Niall's dogs approached it, tossing its head and flattening its ears. Niall whistled them back. Cadha made for the front door while Niall slid along toward the back of the house.

"Stay with Cadha," Grahame told me. Since I had already made the decision, it wasn't difficult to agree until I realized that Grahame meant to follow Niall toward the back of the house. Still, I lifted my chin bravely and nodded.

A frail looking woman answered the door after Cadha's sturdy knocking. She greeted Cadha warmly, gesturing for us both to enter. Cadha introduced the woman as Mrs. Giverns. I followed them into the house, trailing as they shared complaints of a blight on the hens earlier in the fall, the current devilry of mud, and delighted in the new bridge.

Mrs. Giverns led us into a room that I supposed was meant to be the parlor. A fire burned in the rough stone hearth, heating a large kettle. A few wooden tables and chairs stood in the room on the wooden board floors. A rag rug covered the floor before the only elegant piece of furniture in the room, an upholstered couch of blue satin that once must have been lovely but now looked worn and out of place, much like Mrs. Giverns herself.

Two other women sat in the room near the fire. One was older, between me and Cadha in age, and she gave us a quick glance before turning back to her examination of the fire. She was of a slight build, too, but where Mrs. Giverns had an air of sickness about her, this woman had a wiry strength and barely contained energy. At first, I would have taken her position on the edge of the seat as social politeness, but after just a few minutes in the woman's presence, I realized she was poised to dart off at a moment's notice to tackle whatever might need doing.

The other woman was closer to my age with a smile that reminded me achingly of Elsie. The similarities ended there, however, as the woman was neither beautiful nor charming. She was friendly, however, and when she spoke she proved to be of English origins.

Mrs. Giverns introduced the ladies as Mrs. Monigal and Mrs. Bright. Mrs. Bright, the younger of the two, immediately encouraged me to call her Ruthie. The other woman only offered me a silent nod of acknowledgment.

I sat in one of the nearby chairs at Cadha's gesture and listened in as Mrs. Giverns and Cadha continued comparing woes and complaints since the last time they'd met. Apparently Mrs. Giverns was only now recovering from a bout of illness, which she described at great detail and with much relish. About halfway through a particularly gruesome event involving a chamber pot, Ruthie slid from her chair to join me.

"Have you just come to stay with Cadha?"

"A few weeks ago," I told her.

"Oh, you're Irish! So is Marjorie, but you won't know it for a while. She isn't much for talking."

I wondered about correcting her, as my parents were always very particular that we were of Scottish descent, but I let it slide. If Ruthie was here for worship, she must know that I wasn't Catholic.

"Was the voyage awful?" Ruthie asked. "I've heard such stories."

"I wouldn't care to make it again," I said, keeping my tone light. I wasn't ready to talk to someone I'd just met about the experience. "Was yours?"

"Oh, I never crossed. Born and raised here in Pennsylvania territory." Ruthie grinned proudly. "My parents crossed a few years before that. I had an elder brother, but he didn't survive the crossing. I've two younger ones now, though, so that worked out fine for them in the end."

I tried for an expression that was interested and sympathetic and hoped I hid my true reaction. All I could think of was the agony Mrs. Wurthing had suffered when her boy had died. Ruthie must never have lost anyone close to speak so casually of it. Or perhaps she had lost too many and it was the only way to keep sane, like Mr. Bell after losing his third wife and acting as though nothing had changed.

"How have you settled in? Cadha working you to the bones? My Clay has me doing all sorts of work that I didn't expect, coming from the city and all. Is it dreadful?"

Between Ruthie's questions and what I could overhear of Cadha and Mrs. Giverns's conversation, it seemed like the expectation was to share tales of misery and woe. I wasn't sure how best to respond.

"It's been hard," I finally admitted. "But I'm learning."

"Clay says he wonders if I'll ever be able to keep a decent home, but then he's Scottish, so he has some strange notions of what a good home is. I make a good loaf of bread and can brew beer, and that's the main reasons he married me, so what can he complain of, really?" Ruthie laughed. I smiled and had no idea what to say in response. Thankfully, Ruthie didn't give me a chance. "Just you wait for winter to settle in. The work gets all the tougher for it. Snow sometimes to your waist! And the melt afterwards, with all the mud, is just as bad. But you'll get used to it, I'm sure."

I kept the smile pasted onto my face, but inside my stomach was tightening with anxiety. Surely there couldn't be that much snow at one time?

The men came in then, and the women readjusted themselves to join their husbands. Grahame was looking bothered, but he covered it with a tight-lipped smile at me, and I knew I couldn't ask about it now. At least I had learned that seeing Grahame bothered was never good. I hoped he'd speak of it later.

Ruthie's husband was a thick-chested man nearly twice her age, all hair and beard and booming voice. They seemed oddly well-suited to one another. Marjorie's husband was thinner and just as wiry as she, with a soulful gaze. Mr. Giverns was older with a stern expression made more stern by his graying beard. Three other men joined us with Niall, all who looked to be unattached. We filled the small area, and it quickly grew overheated.

Thankfully, Mr. Giverns went straight into the worship. He led the service, and I was surprised to hear the celebration of St. Andrew. Was it already so late in the year? It wasn't the most inspired commemoration I'd heard. Instead, I felt even more disconnected, as though Mr. Giverns were speaking half the worship in a foreign tongue. I gave the responses and added in my voice during the singing, and when it was over, I went to help serve the simple meal from the collection of baskets the women had brought and the food Mrs. Giverns had prepared.

The meal was filling, and the talk was light as we ate. I listened in mostly, and at one point found myself standing next to Marjorie. The older woman gave me a slight nod but said nothing to me. I actually enjoyed the break of constant chatter. Ruthie talked to anyone and everyone who got within earshot, and I had found myself swept up in the girl's wake. I had missed conversation that didn't center around keeping the farm running, but I was used to being a part of the talking, not withstanding a barrage of words. I wanted to like Ruthie, but the girl was so much different than I expected, with none of the gentle language I was accustomed to. Cadha could be rough-spoken, but it was usually for a reason.

Still, I aimed to be friendly, and I was certainly made welcomed, which was a nice change. By the end of the afternoon, I felt a friendship forming and thought it would be nice to have someone else to speak with once in a while who was experiencing the same things as I was. Ruthie would never be as close to me as Elsie had been, I suspected, but she might become the sort of friend the

Karney girl would have been, had I stayed in Ireland at Grahame's farm instead of coming to the new world.

At least I remembered Ruthie's name. I still felt badly I couldn't think of the Karney girl's.

We said our goodbyes, and Ruthie and her husband walked with us past the new bridge to a fork in the road. The sun was low near the trees as we four made the walk back toward Cadha's farm. I was nervous of the shadows growing darker in the trees, and now I was thankful for Niall's dogs, who ranged the road to either side, keeping watch. Niall and Cadha led as before, and Grahame walked with me, my hand laid lightly on his arm, the empty basket in his other hand where bumped the musket hanging from his shoulder. He was watching Niall pensively, and I wondered what had happened but kept my thoughts to myself. Perhaps I could ask when we were alone that night.

But I could ask him another question that had been plaguing me.

"The girl back home," I said, and startled myself with how loud my voice carried. "Mr. Karney's daughter," I continued quieter. "What was her name?"

Grahame glanced down at me. I saw the question in his look but he didn't voice it, so I didn't explain. "Mary."

Mary, yes, that was it.

We were getting close to the farm when the dogs began to growl. Everyone stopped. Grahame let my hand fall off his arm to bring his musket to bear. I was startled to see Cadha take the basket Niall carried and pull a pistol from it. Niall unslung his own musket from his shoulder and began priming it. Cadha had drawn out a length of cord and was cutting it in two to hand one to Niall. Grahame held his musket easily, not bothering to load it. Rather, he held it as though he might fend someone off with it.

From the gloom up ahead, two figures approached. Niall whistled the growling dogs over to him and stepped aside to where Cadha had moved to the edge of the road. Grahame gestured me over with a nod of his head. I hurried to Cadha's side. The tension in the air was palpable, choking me with fear and uncertainty. The smoke from the cord attached to Cadha's pistol and Niall's musket didn't help.

The two men were like no one I had seen before. Their skin was the color of rust, their black hair cut strangely, and they wore leather clothing decorated with beads and bits of horn and shell. They were tall and lithe and moved like cautious, wild creatures. They stopped on the other side of the road several paces ahead. The two groups of men stared at each other as though trying to decide if the other meant harm.

Grahame held his musket loosely, cradled in his arms, one hand firm on the stock. Niall had pointed his upward, away from the approaching men. The two strange men carried weapons in their hands that I didn't recognize. I felt their gaze fall to me and shivered under the predatory looks.

Cadha took a step in front of me, her pistol raised but not aimed.

The tension grew thick and heavy. The dogs continued to growl, low and dangerous. The sounds of the forest receded.

One of the strange men called out a word I had never heard before.

Niall answered it with a second just as strange. He pulled the cord from his musket and held it aside. Cadha did the same.

The two men began walking again, edging past us with a cautious disregard. They continued past, not looking behind them. Grahame and Niall didn't move but stood watching until the two strange men disappeared around a bend in the road.

The tension eased back, but only slightly.

"Let's hurry," Cadha said quietly. She snuffed the cord on the heel of her shoe.

Neither man disagreed. Niall did not snuff his cord, I noticed, and Cadha handed hers to Grahame before picking up Niall's discarded basket and nodded for me to do the same with Grahame's.

We picked up our pace until I was huffing. Grahame had hold of my arm now, the musket in his other, and he swept me along. His grip was tight, but it helped keep me upright as I stumbled at the pace. The sun was low behind the trees, and I was out of breath when we finally reached the path to Cadha's farm.

My side in stitches of pain, I nevertheless followed Cadha around to the kitchen house where we left the baskets. Thom came out from the barn as the dogs ran past, barking.

"Go out front," Cadha told him. "Take the pistol."

Thom stiffened, but only for a moment before rushing back into the barn and returning with another musket, a powder horn, and a shot bag. He hurried around the house.

"You stay with me," Cadha told me.

And so I followed Cadha the rest of the evening, helping put together a cold supper of yesterday's meat pies and wedges of cheese before checking on the chickens and closing up the barn. I offered to go for water, though it was a shaky offer that I hoped Cadha would refuse. She did so, vehemently, and shooed me into the house to lay out supper.

Grahame came in as Cadha and I lit the tapers. He must have come into the house at some point, for he was wearing his leather jerkin and sword belt, something I had never seen him do before. He looked wild and dangerous standing in the shadows of the room with a sword sheathed on his waist and a pistol tucked into the belt. He took one of the platters, filled it with some of the meat pies and cheese, and left the room without a word.

"Might as well eat," Cadha told me. "Those three will be out for a time."

I pulled back a chair to sit, but I settled uneasily. "Why? What's happening?"

"Natives," Cadha told me, saying the word with a voice that mingled fear and respect. "They pass through often enough, but it isn't always without making trouble." Cadha gave me an odd look but said nothing more.

I forced myself to eat, but my stomach was roiling with nervousness. I couldn't shake the feeling that I was the cause of all this, but I had no idea how or why.

When we had finished, Cadha sent me upstairs instead of insisting that I help clean and ready the farm for the night. Alone in my room, I sat on the bed with the single lit taper casting dancing shadows across the walls. I pulled out my knitting, too uneasy to ready myself for bed, and bothered over the stitches for a while. I had stopped trying to recreate Beacham's scarf when I realized I'd never get it without help, so I'd gone back to knitting a shawl. I needed a second one, but it wasn't going well. My stitches were uneven and I'd dropped several and then clumsily added more on to make up for it.

A knocking on my door startled me, but it was only Cadha.

"Just seeing that you're settled," Cadha told me, but I sensed it was more than that. Cadha had never come into my room before.

"I'm just waiting up for Grahame," I answered.

"I wouldn't," Cadha said. "He might be late, and we've got a busy day's work before us since we lost most of today." Cadha cocked her head, then came over to me, setting her lantern down on the floor to pick up my needles.

"How long have you been working on this?" She turned the beginnings of the shawl over, stretching the needles to see it.

"A few weeks," I admitted with a wince.

Cadha huffed what sounded like a chuckle. "Goodness, girl, you weren't kidding when you said you weren't much for knitting. Your knitting looks like it's been pecked at by ducks." She handed back the needles. "Tomorrow evening, we'll have a go at it together. Get some sleep now."

I nodded, my cheeks burning, and Cadha left the room. The thought of facing Cadha's stern instruction while trying to knit made me nervous, but at least it helped take my mind off my other worries.

I packed up my knitting and undressed for bed. I kept the taper lit, though, and as I climbed into bed, I hoped Grahame wouldn't be too long. The room was cold and lonely without him.

CHAPTER SIXTEEN

I woke when Grahame settled into bed. He was cold and smelt of chilly air and pipe tobacco. He gathered me close, and I marveled at the strength in his embrace. He held me like I might be ripped away from him.

I snuggled close to him, taking in his scent, surprised by how the world felt right now that he was back with me. His silence was comforting, his presence more than making up for any words he might say. I had longed to ask him what was happening, but now that he was with me, I just wanted to lie in his arms and sleep, knowing he was near.

When had I begun to yearn for his nearness like this? I couldn't say. It had crept upon me unaware, stealing into my consciousness a little at a time until I could no longer imagine a bed empty of him without feeling his loss. I couldn't call it love; at least, it didn't feel like any love I'd known before. I wasn't sure what to call it, but names weren't important. He was here, and that was what mattered.

With a sigh, I settled against him, his heart beating strongly where I laid my head upon his chest. His undershirt smelt of wood smoke and tobacco smoke and man. He held me close, and his heartbeat didn't steady but raced as though he'd just run circles around the farm. I wanted to tell him that everything was fine, but I honestly didn't know if it was. Instead, I wrapped my arms around him, holding him as he held me. Twined together, I finally fell into a deep, peaceful sleep.

The next month passed in a blur of chores. The days grew shorter and colder, the rain settled in, often leaving ice behind at night. Mud was an ever-present obstacle, and I came to loath the sight of a water bucket. My hands and arms ached constantly from the carrying, kneading, stirring, mending, chopping, pulling, washing, and carding. But for all the hard work, I was more content than I remembered being in a long time.

Or maybe it was because of the hard work. I had never felt less at odds with life now that I was finally understanding all the effort that went into keeping a family warm, safe, fed, and dry. I found appreciation at each meal, mended stockings a blessing, a dry hat and coat a gift from above. The little details of a warm slice of bread or dry boots were more than a momentary pleasure. I looked forward to them. And I found myself becoming more and more taken by Cadha and her vast wealth of knowledge.

The evenings before bedtime, after the kitchen fire had been banked and the barn closed up, became moments I cherished. Cadha and I would sit near the hearth, a few tapers lit to add more light to the room, and spin or knit. My knitting still looked like it had been pecked at, but not nearly as badly under Cadha's instruction. The little rolls of carded wool for spinning—"roileags," Cadha called them—became smoother and less of a tangled mess. And my spinning grew finer each day. Cadha admitted that she could no longer spin fine enough wool for stockings, though she seemed spry enough to me, so I wondered if there was another reason.

I hadn't seen her spin since I arrived when I thought about it. Was this something I was actually better at than Cadha? It seemed unlikely, and I would never voice such a thing, but it gave me a chance to prove to her and the men that I was capable, even necessary. I made it my goal to spin all the fine wool she needed. I loved working the wheel, watching the spool of wool grow while my fingers worked of their own accord. I couldn't remember a time when anything came this easily to me.

Cadha finally spoke some of her life before the farm. I listened raptly, bent over my little spinning wheel as Cadha talked and knitted.

"My first husband, Durell, was a baker. That man could throw such bread. All the toffs would fetch bread from him. But he took ill and never recovered, and I couldn't keep the bakery going on my own. His brother came to take it and ran it into the ground the first year. Foolish man. So I ended up a waulker in Edinburgh."

"Walker?"

"Waulker," she repeated slower. "A fuller, I suppose you'd know it as."

I nodded. I'd heard of fullers, men and women who cleaned wool cloth. Father had considered going into the cloth business at one point, before the rot had started taking the sheep, which gave him a new enterprise.

"Grahame and Niall's uncle Morley and I met in Edinburgh," Cadha continued. "Morley was full of talk of adventure and new lands and the like. Edinburgh had never felt like a home to me, and waulking wasn't the sort of trade I'd planned to stay in, so it was easy to fall in with him. And he were handsome, Morley was," Cadha added, casting a sly wink at me. "When he asked for my hand, I was eager enough. And so we came here. Well, not straight away, but soon enough. And we had a good many years together 'til he died, I'll say that. And this time, I fought to keep what was mine." She said it in grim determination.

"Niall had already come, and I made it clear that the farm was mine, but he isn't eager to take it over. No, not Niall." She chuckled, and I could see what she meant. Niall worked hard enough when called for, but he took the easiest work he could.

"He's hoping to make a good match, he is," Cadha continued. "Come spring, he'll be going back and forth to Philadelphia so often it'll make you dizzy. Thank goodness Grahame's come. It was him I'd been wanting all along. Now that's a man who knows his work."

She spoke as though she knew something of his past, and I wanted to ask her of it, but then the men joined us. Niall lit up his long pipe while Grahame settled in with some small work to keep his hands busy. I was realizing how Grahame liked to keep busy, and how his hands were never empty of some occupation, either braiding rope or cutting leather or carving wood. Cadha wasn't happy about the last until Grahame swept the leavings into the fire, tidying after himself.

I had never quite forgiven Niall of his uncaring attitude toward me, but it didn't seem to matter, as he never seemed to relent of it. Cadha's news made me think that perhaps he was jealous that Grahame had married me when he was looking for a wife with a dowry of her own. For now, I was just another pair of hands at the work, and he didn't bother to speak or acknowledge me aside from any instruction he felt inclined to give. I felt closer to Thom, who spoke little enough to me but always doffed his hat and stepped aside respectfully.

I finally asked Cadha about Thom the next evening before the men had returned.

"Where did he come from?" I asked after Cadha made some comment about Thom and his work mending a hinge on the barn door that had come loose.

"Philadelphia," Cadha answered, "but London before that. He doesn't talk much of his past." She chuckled. "Doesn't talk much at all. Been working here come three years now, and I don't think I've had more than a handful of words at a time from the man in all those years. Rather like Grahame, come to think of it." Cadha held out her knitting to inspect it. She was working on a pair of stockings for Niall. "Not sure if I want to take on another man when his time is up. Been debating it for the last few months. There was no question of it before you and Grahame arrived, but now I'm not sure we need another."

I paused in my spinning to look over at Cadha. "What do you mean, 'when his time is up'?"

"Thom indentured with us."

I blinked, uncertain of Cadha's meaning.

"When he crossed," Cadha explained, seeing my confusion, "he crossed without the coin to pay passage. So when he landed, he had to go into service to pay. I paid his passage, and he's worked for me since. But his time is up at the start of the new year, and I expect he'll be setting off to start a place of his own."

"Three years to pay one passage?" I was shocked.

"Well, there's his keep, room and meals," Cadha said in her defense, "and we keep him clothed and shod. All of which costs."

"Did he know when he crossed that he'd have to go into service?"

"Sure. Many folks do. It's the rare ones who can afford it all at once. You and Grahame were fortunate." Cadha chuckled. "I should say, you were fortunate and Grahame was clever. He got his passage paid and you for a wife."

My cheeks burned. I returned to my spinning to hide the mixture of emotions that settled over me.

"Of course, I wasn't so sure he was clever at first," Cadha

admitted, "you being so untaught. But you're coming along fine. I expect in another few months, you could keep your own kitchen and no one would starve. But we do need to work on that knitting, girl, and your stitches."

Niall and Grahame joined us and talk turned to the monthly service coming up in a week. I kept my focus on spinning while I tried to soothe my embarrassment. I was proud that Cadha thought I was learning quickly. I wondered if the older woman had said much the same to Grahame about me. I knew he could see how hard I was working, but did he realize how much I was learning?

I wished I knew more about how he was spending his day.

I should ask him, I thought. Maybe he might actually speak to me about his work.

I realized then that Cadha was speaking about preparation for the monthly gathering at the farm.

"It's here this month?" I asked.

Cadha gave me a long look that told me I should have been paying attention. "Head in the clouds tonight? Yes, it's here. And I'll need you to take over some of the daily work to leave me to get ready. And I'll need your help tidying the place. We haven't turned this room out in an age. Not the best weather for it, but we'll make do."

I nodded readily. I could feel Niall's gaze boring into me, but I stoutly refused to return it.

It wasn't long after that Cadha sent me up to bed. I still felt like a child being allowed to sit up with the grown-ups the way Cadha would dismiss me. I tried to think of it as a kindness, that Cadha was concerned that I get enough rest, but it still rankled. If Grahame came up with me, it might be different.

Admit it, I told myself, you'll always be the child to them.

Unless I had a child.

I froze in the act of untying my stays. A child. What if I had a child? I couldn't even imagine a babe in this place, but surely it would happen sooner or later. I'd always assumed that I'd have my mother nearby when I was delivered of a child. Instead, I'd have a Scottish woman who had been a stranger just two months before.

It was a worry for another day. Hopefully a day quite a bit in the future.

The thought drew me along to Elsie, and I wondered where she was and how she was doing. I hadn't received any news, and while I tried not to fret, understanding that letters didn't move the same way in this new land as they did back home, I still couldn't help but worry. Had her cousin come for her? Where had she settled? How was she getting on?

Grahame came in, startling me out of my reverie. He paused when he saw me standing by the bed only half undressed.

"I was thinking of Elsie," I told him, answering the question in his expression.

"Ah." He crossed over to the bed and sat. "We'll go to Germantown in a fortnight. See if there's been word."

"Is that where we'd get it?"

"Yes."

I sank down to the bed with a sigh of relief. "I thought no one had written."

"We won't know until Germantown."

"And I can go?"

He looked surprised by the question. "Of course."

On a sudden whim, I slid across the bed and curled up next to him. He tensed, then relaxed and drew me closer. "Are you happy?" he asked in a hushed voice thick with emotion.

"No," I admitted. "But I'm not unhappy." I looked up at him, studying the lines of his jaw under his dark, close-cropped beard. "I like Cadha. And I think I'm starting to feel at home, in a way. But I miss Elsie. I miss my parents." Tears burned my eyes suddenly. "I miss Ireland."

He held me close to him. "I know."

"Don't you miss home?"

"I've always known I'd move on."

"Why is that?"

I felt him shrug. "I can't say. I've just always known it."

"Does that mean we'll move on again?"

He was silent, and I was startled by the anxiety that took hold of me. "You'll warn me, won't you," I asked, "well before it happens if we are to move?"

He didn't answer again, and I drew back from him. "I need to know that you will, Grahame. Please."

He studied me for a long moment, then reached out to touch my cheek, wiping away tears. "As soon as I know," he told me, "you'll know."

I took a shuddering breath, steadying myself. He drew me back to him.

"I care for you, Ailee," he murmured into my hair. "I won't let harm come to you."

It was the closest he'd come to admitting his feelings for me. A smile spread across my face, and I tilted my head upwards. He met my kiss with a strength he'd not shown before, pulling me tighter to him. Thrills chased along my back as he threaded his hand up under my mobcap and into my hair. He twisted me beneath him, laying me back onto the quilt, and his hands shook as he finished untying my stays. I couldn't tell if it was from nerves or passion until he kissed me again with a fierce want.

It was only the second time we'd lain together as husband and wife, and the power of it stole my breath from me. I had no idea a man could be both so gentle and yet so strong.

CHAPTER SEVENTEEN

The next week passed merrily despite the hard work. There was a sense of impending celebration in the air, and I couldn't remember the last time when I'd so looked forward to the future. I knew the monthly gathering wouldn't be the holiday party I was used to attending, with a dance and feasting, but it would be a celebration of sorts. Cadha was obviously eager to host it, because she bent her back to the work. Which meant the rest of us did too.

We baked all sorts of treats. We turned out the parlor and the dining room. We spent the evenings mending our finery. Thom surprised us with evergreen boughs cut to decorate the rooms, and Cadha brought out fresh candles to replace the used tapers. I was looking forward to seeing Ruthie again and perhaps getting to know Marjorie.

The rain eased late in the week, and the sky over the tall trees was blue and clear the morning of the gathering. I hummed a little tune as I went for water. Grahame had given me a pair of mittens the day before, and they were warm and protected my hands against the chafing bucket ropes. My other gloves had worn through a few weeks before, and I had been borrowing a pair from the work room, but they had been so large that they kept trying to slide off my hands, threatening to take the buckets with them.

My new mittens were supple leather with wool inside that snuggled between my fingers as I carried the buckets. It made the work less onerous, and anything that made work less like work was a welcomed change.

The dawn cast drifts of sunlight through the empty tree boughs and the frozen muddle of leaves across the narrow trail muffled my boot steps. I had been up for several hours already, but since returning from the last gathering, Cadha and Grahame refused to let me go to the stream in the dark. So I loaded the buckets late in the afternoon to get us through the next early morning, then went for fresh buckets after breakfast was cleared.

I knew the trail well by then. I'd walked it so often, I knew each bump and rut, each gnarled tree and thorny bush. I knew the sounds, too, of birds and owls and the occasional rustle of brush that meant a rabbit or raccoon had fled my presence. The first time I'd seen a raccoon, I'd been shocked. I'd never seen anything like their little masked faces and pointed noses, that look of intelligence and mischief in their black eyes. Cadha warned me about provoking them, so when I came across one, I'd stand and wait for it to lumber away. They didn't always at first. They liked to watch me, as though trying to figure me out. And I liked to watch them, too, foreign as they were.

The squirrels, however, were my favorites. They made death-defying leaps from bough to bough, chittered at me when I passed beneath their trees, and scurried up and down tree trunks faster than I could walk the trail. I'd taken to sneaking bits of food from breakfast to toss to them as I passed, and one began to follow me as soon as I was on the trail.

I'd never thought to take pleasure in watching wild beasts. It wasn't like tending chickens, which were tame and silly and not very smart about their own safety. Or sheep, which bustled and bleated like a gathering of ladies at tea, first seeking your approval, then turning their back on you at some slight you couldn't imagine making. Squirrels were clever and fast, curious and cautious, and I enjoyed them. Even the raccoons, with their sense of ownership and the look of mischief, were more interesting to watch than sheep.

The morning of the gathering, though, I had no time to admire the squirrels. I filled the buckets quickly, bending down at the stream first to crack the thin layer of ice along the bank with the bottom of the bucket. The water ran clear and cold, and muddied just a little as I dipped each bucket in to fill it.

As I stood, I realized the sounds around me had quieted. An eeriness fell over the woods, almost like shadows threading through the leafless trees, broken only by the running stream. My heart stuttered, then began to pound wildly.

I didn't see anything to fear. I couldn't hear anything that might give me a start. The eerie silence and the sense of being watched were all the warning I had, but it was enough. I grabbed the buckets, sloshing water across my legs and into my boots, soaking part of my skirt, and I fled.

I was breathless when I reached the clearing of the farm. My skirts tugged at me, twisting around my legs, and my feet squelched damply inside my boots. Behind me, the birds took up again and the forest noises returned slowly. As my fear abated, I chastised myself for a fool. I'd lost half a bucket of water, all told, was damp from the knee down, and had nothing to show for my fears.

But that was for the best, wasn't it? I didn't actually want something fearful chasing me down.

I debated telling Cadha or Grahame, but what would I say? I had nothing to tell them but a vague sense of threat. What would they do? Would they put off the gathering? Search the woods for natives? That is what I feared had lurked in the forest—natives waiting to do horrible things to me. I'm not sure what, but given how Cadha and Grahame had reacted before, it must be awful.

No, I didn't want to put them up in arms over my groundless fears. But I might ask someone to go with me if I had to fetch more water.

I left one bucket at the kitchen house, hoping I'd see Cadha inside, but it was empty. The crusty loaves of bread we'd baked earlier in the week sat on the trestle table next to the pan of bread and butter pudding we had made that morning. The fire was still going, though, banked deep in the hearth, and the chickens were hung on the spit. She must have only just stepped out.

I turned the spit before leaving with the second bucket. I took it to the house to fill the pitcher in the dining room and to wash down the table one final time.

Voices coming from the parlor. My work dress was still hanging damply around my legs, and though I had wiped my feet outside on the boot brushes, my feet still squelched inside the wet leather. I was curious enough to see who had arrived not to fret over my appearance, but I didn't want to shame Cadha. The steady work of the past several months had finally chased away nearly all concern over how I looked. I use to fret over mud on my skirts or ash on my hands when I'd first gone to live with Grahame, but after the ship and those awful water barrels that we used all day before dumping, and now the farm, where water was a commodity I had to work for, my sense of propriety in appearance was fairly lax. My mother would be aghast. Then again, my mother would never have traveled to a place like this.

Cadha would probably be less concerned over it, except she'd wonder how I'd gotten so wet. That was a story I wasn't ready to tell, but I was so eager to see who had arrived. I was looking forward to seeing Ruthie in a way I hadn't expected. She was the closest person to a friend I'd made, at least so far. I needed to change, but I might still have a look at who had arrived on my way up the stairs.

I set the bucket down in the dining room before continuing to the stairs. I slid around the banister, leaning just so far as to peer into the parlor before mounting the steps.

It was Marjorie, the quiet Scots-Irish woman. Cadha was setting her up in a chair near the fire that Thom had laid after breakfast. The room was pleasantly warm, and I caught a bit of its warmth. It was a respite after the chill from the wet clothing.

Marjorie saw me, her dark-eyed gaze meeting mine, her expression carefully schooled, and she neither spoke to nor gestured at me. I wasn't sure whether to be thankful or slighted. I decided on thankful and bounded up the stairs as quickly as my damp skirts would let me.

I changed into my finery, but settled my apron over my skirts and fixed my shawl across my shoulders. I'd take them off later, once all the preparations were finished, though I left off Elsie's shawl pin, setting it on the little table to keep safe. I put on my old shoes, which felt thin and fragile after the comfort of even soggy boots. I changed my hat for a mob cap, tucking my hair up quickly, and returned downstairs.

Cadha met me at the bottom of the stairs. Her quick gaze swept over me, and she gave me a nod. "Mind the spit," she told me.

I nodded to her as she went upstairs. I glanced into the parlor to see Marjorie sitting in a chair before the fire, her knitting in her hands but her needles unmoving. She was watching the flames as if they spoke in riddles to her. She looked serene, a far cry from the barely contained woman I'd seen at Mrs. Giverns. I wondered at the change.

I finished in the dining room as quickly as I could and took the bucket out with me to the kitchen house. Thom was there, turning the spit. He gave me an odd look when I entered, as though he hadn't seen me before.

I hesitated. "Cadha sent me to tend the chicken."

Thom gave a shake, as though trying to wake, and stepped back from the spit. I took his place, the fire and the scent of roasting chicken warming me.

Thom hovered for a moment, and I could feel him watching me. Had he seen me rush from the woods? Was he wondering what I'd seen out there and trying to find a polite way to ask. We hadn't exchanged more than a handful of words since I'd arrived. It might be kinder to spare him the trouble.

"I heard something in the woods," I told him, glancing at him. "It startled me."

He blinked, as though shocked by my words.

"I didn't see anything," I assured him quickly. "And I suppose I didn't actually hear anything. More like the woods went all quiet, and it was . . ." I didn't know how to describe it. "Eerie."

"Best not to go alone," he said after a lengthy pause. "Best keep to Mr. Dónaghue or Mistress Cadha. For today," he added.

There was something in the way he said it, like it was more warning than advice. The same way Beacham would say to keep off the rail. It made the hairs on the back of my neck stand up. But before I could ask him what he meant, he turned on his heels and left the kitchen house.

Was it the natives? Had they been seen again?

The thought worried at me until Cadha came through the door. She never merely entered a room. She took command of it, filling it with her presence as soon as she was through the doorway.

"Those are looking near to finished," she told me with a nod at the chickens. "Leave them for now and take that bread to the house. Don't forget the bread board and knife."

Keeping a knife close sounded like a wonderful idea. I laid it across the board and stacked three loaves of bread as well, as Cadha had taught me. She opened the door for me, a sign of her anxiety to have everything perfect for the gathering. In the past, she usually let me muddle with whatever I was carrying while trying to open a door, watching with a mixture of amusement and exasperation.

The door to the house was ajar, and I nudged it open with a flick of my foot. Another voice drifted down the hall from the parlor. Mrs. Giverns, I realized, recognizing her craggy, high-pitched complaint.

There was a woman I didn't wish to get to know better, but I rather thought I'd not have a choice in the matter. I could be a good hostess and listen politely and ask questions of her. Maybe I could learn more about how she'd come to live here and what it had been like for her to settle in a new land. I might receive a litany of illness and pains, but I might learn something, too.

I laid the bread out in the dining room on the sideboard. It was literally that, a board stretched between two stools. Thom had split the wood and planed the top and bottom flat but had left the sides rough yet with tree bark, so Cadha had draped a couple of embroidered cloths over it. I thought it had looked better without the cloths. It had suited the room. Clothed, it was a strange bit of elegance in an inelegant place, rather like Mrs. Giverns's blue satin couch. But I'd never tell Cadha that. She'd spread the cloth out with such pride, straightening the embroidery so that the purple thistles and blue primroses hung straight.

I wondered if I should go to the parlor to welcome Mrs. Giverns, but then thought better of it and returned to the kitchen house. Cadha was laying the last of the chickens out on a large wooden platter, another creation of Thom's over the past week. Grahame had helped with it one evening, carving thistles along the rim of the platter before waxing the wood.

Cadha sent me to the root cellar to bring up preserves and the cakes we'd made the day before. I laid them out on the sideboard, noticing after I finished the baskets lining the wall nearby. Marjorie's and Mrs. Giverns's additions to the gathering meal, I guessed. I wondered if I should lay it out, too. That, at least, gave me an excuse to go to the parlor to ask.

Mrs. Giverns was seated with her back to me by the fire, across from Marjorie. She was leaning in, speaking uncharacteristically low. Some new complaint, perhaps, or illness. I didn't want to intrude, so I stopped in the doorway and made a little sound. Marjorie looked at me, and Mrs. Giverns straightened but didn't turn.

"We're laying out the meal," I told them. "Shall I unpack the baskets so you can rest from the journey?"

I well recalled the walk it took to reach Mrs. Giverns farm. I had no idea if Marjorie lived closer or farther from us.

Marjorie glanced at Mrs. Giverns, who must not have heard me for she gave no sign. I made to move closer, but Marjorie rose suddenly. That peculiar explosive energy I'd noticed in her before was back.

"I'll see to it," she said, and the familiar lilt in her voice brought a stab of homesickness to me.

How long had it been since I'd heard a woman speak with my accent? I'd grown use to Cadha's Scottish cadence. I remembered clearly Ruthie's oddly punctuated English accent. But here was a woman who turned her words as I did, and it made me hungry to hear more.

I offered her a smile, hoping it was welcoming and not too eager. She didn't return it, but I thought I saw her eyes brighten slightly.

Perhaps my voice brought the same feelings of homesickness. Would she welcome it or shrink from the reminder of what we'd left behind? I wasn't even certain how long it had been since she left Ireland.

I wasn't sure what to do with myself. I could stay in the dining room, make some attempt at talk while Marjorie unpacked the baskets, and probably make a fool of myself. I could return to the kitchen house to see what Cadha needed doing. I wanted to find Grahame, to see if he and Niall had finished in the barn, though the men had probably joined them there, as they had at Mrs. Giverns, to look over the livestock and tools and talk fields and fences.

Cadha came in from the back, carrying the pudding. She frowned when she saw me standing in the hall.

"Go and put the kettle on," she told me sharply. "And fix up the tea tray."

I rushed for the door, glad to have something to occupy myself. When had I become so awkward? I used to be so good at all this-- hosting teas and attending dinners and dances, walking in the garden or the town market, making talk with my friends or with Mother and the ladies.

My definition of friend had changed, I realized. I used to know how to speak to those around me who shared my background and upbringing, my town and streets and language, my history. But ever since Grahame, I was no longer in familiar places with familiar people. I had no shared history or upbringing. I had no idea what to speak of.

Elsie had made it easy. We'd fallen in together with hardly a second thought. I didn't know much about where she'd come from or how she'd been raised. All I had known for certain was that she was kind and honest and generous and had seemed to genuinely like me.

She had been the first person, I realized, to take an interest in me for my own sake, not for societal obligations or expectations. She had been the first true friend I'd had. Now that she was gone, I was trying to find another. And I had no idea how to go about it.

I put the kettle on the hook over the fire and stood back, watching the flames sizzle as water dripped from it.

I already knew Ruthie wouldn't fill the hollow Elsie had left, but I wanted to like her. I wanted to be friendly and have someone to jest with and share stories with. Like I could have with Mary Karney, if I'd let her. I was still ashamed that I had spent most of our brief time together trying to ignore her and her common ways.

Marjorie might be a friend, if she would let me get to know her.

That fairly well summed up my options so far.

"That's a heavy sigh," Grahame said from the doorway.

I admit, my heart rose to see him standing there. He had changed into his finery. It was the same coat he'd worn for our wedding, and it fit him well, stretching across his wide shoulders and falling almost cape-like down his back. The black color suited him, giving him a dark and mysterious air. The look he gave me was concerned, and I hurried to reassure him.

"Just thinking on Elsie," I told him.

He came to me and surprised me by pulling me into his arms. He didn't try to offer any empty platitudes, telling me things that I'd know he couldn't know, like that she was doing well and was safe and sheltered. His embrace was comfort enough, however, and he seemed to know it.

"Ruthie arrived," he told me after a moment. He let me step back.

"Oh, good." And I was truly pleased for it. "I just need to fetch in the tea things."

"Do you need help?"

It was a kind offer and one I'd never accept. "No, though—" I hesitated, suddenly recalling what Thom had said. "If you wouldn't mind waiting for me?"

Grahame's rare smile lit the room.

CHAPTER EIGHTEEN

It didn't take long to fill the tea tray and pour the kettle. I was a bit anxious with Grahame watching me. He hadn't seen me work in the kitchen house very often, but I was pleased at how confident I felt at it. Cadha was right, I thought. I might be ready to run my own kitchen in another few months.

I didn't think that would actually happen for a long, long while. Not with Cadha here. Still, perhaps she'd let me make the bread on my own. I was ready to pass on water gathering to Thom.

But Thom would most likely be moving on soon, when his time was up.

I stifled another sigh and gathered up the tray. It was heavy but manageable. Grahame, thankfully, held the kitchen door and the door into the house open for me to pass through.

I heard Cadha and Mrs. Giverns speaking in the parlor, and Ruthie's interjections. Grahame followed me into the parlor and greeted the ladies as I laid out the tea things on Cadha's little table. It was the one polished piece of wood in the room, and it shone in the firelight and the bit of sunlight that made it past the newly washed curtains.

The room had grown curiously silent after Grahame's greetings. I turned to find the ladies looking from him to me in a strange way. Ruthie, dressed in a yellow gown that made her look a little sickly in the muted sunlight, had pursed her lips in a curious manner. Mrs. Giverns seemed to be trying to look down her nose at someone taller than her, and the effect was more comical than imposing. It was

Cadha, though, who gave me a start. She was looking at Grahame as if she was seeing him for the first time.

Grahame didn't seem to know what to make of it. I think it must have been what a bull feels like when walking suddenly into a flock of sheep. He made a slight bow, pulling it off with a grace and elegance that seemed strange in a man his size, gave me a puzzled look, and left the room.

The silence didn't follow him out. It hung over the room like a pall.

What was going on?

My upbringing kicked in. "Shall I pour—" I began to ask, but Ruthie cut me off.

"I'll pour, shall I," she said in a sickeningly sweet voice to Cadha. She crossed by me as if I weren't standing there.

Cadha was watching me now with that same look she'd given Grahame. Mrs. Giverns was pointedly not watching me. She seemed to be trying to look anywhere but.

Marjorie was knitting.

Cold apprehension crept up my back.

"Shall I bring in the bread and preserves?" I offered, wanting to do something, anything, to break the tension hanging over the room.

"That would be good," Cadha answered, and by her tone, she thought it was the first intelligent thing I'd said to her since I'd arrived.

Baffled and more than a little hurt, I left the parlor. Whispers started up behind me.

My hands trembled as I picked up the knife. I took a deep breath to steady myself, then began slicing bread. I focused on the bread, the crusty hardness opening into brown richness. I tried to push away the fear, tried not to acknowledge how familiar it felt.

My hands trembled still as I laid slices onto a tin plate. I picked up the plate and a jar of preserves.

Ruthie bustled into the room, her skirts sweeping across the floor. The lace on the dress was mended in places, as were the skirts, but she wore it as though dressed in cloth of gold.

Her expression was cold.

"I'll take those," she said, her tone just as cold as her expression. She grabbed the plate and jar from me.

"Ruthie—"

"Don't you go saying my name like we're friends," she snapped. "I would never be friends with someone like you. What do you think, just because we live in a wilderness, we don't have standards?"

I gaped at her, stunned.

She leaned closer, threat in every line of her stance.

"You stay away from my Clay. As a matter of fact, it might be best if you just stayed away altogether."

And with that, she turned on her heels and left the dining room, leaving me in a wake of hurt, fear, and betrayal so deep it ached.

She knew.

They all knew.

I couldn't take a breath. The room pressed in on me like the eyes of the world, watching me, judging me.

I fled.

Outside wasn't far enough. The buildings loomed over me, trapping me into a future I thought I'd escaped. My feet carried me down a familiar path, and my body took me onward, but in my head, I was still trapped, beating against the helplessness and the cruel jest my life was becoming. The trees mocked me, creaking with laughter, reaching out with roots to trip me as I tried to escape. I thought I heard them call my name, a distant shout driving me onward. Bramble caught at my skirts and tore across my hands. A chill bloomed from my center and spread until it numbed my fingers and toes. I could run forever and never be free of it. Not now. The loss and sacrifice and striving to learn and be more, none of it meant anything. I was back where I began, but this time in unfamiliar territory surrounded by people who knew or cared nothing about me.

Unfamiliar territory.

Shocked, I stopped cold. A space had opened around me, a clearing set amid the thick woods that I had never seen before. It was a secret space, a breath amid the tall trees and thick brush, quilted with yellow grass and fallen leaves. The sky opened above me like a prayer, clear and blue.

I stopped in the middle of the clearing, breathless, heart hammering, feet and legs shockingly cold and wet. I'd run through the stream, I remembered suddenly. My skirts were bedraggled with damp and torn in a place where it had caught on bramble.

What was I doing? Where was I going? Did I think to run all the way back to Ireland?

I sank to the ground, despair overcoming me. There was no place to go. I was trapped in a land I never wanted by people I didn't know and a marriage I'd not have made otherwise.

Grahame.

It pained me to think of him. It must have been Grahame. How else would anyone have learned of my past? I had never spoken of it, except to Elsie, and I knew, deep in my heart that she would never have shared that story.

But Grahame had known.

Who had he told? Why did he tell? Did he care so little for me? Did he think of me at all? Or was this how he would punish me for my mistakes, mistakes I had made before I'd even met him? He'd never once commented on my past, never given me any sense that he judged me for it. I'd thought him a paragon for not holding me accountable for the mistakes I'd made and that I'd already answered for.

How could I have been so wrong? People like that didn't exist. Even my own parents couldn't forgive me, not truly, not in their hearts. I'd wronged them. I'd wronged myself.

And now I would suffer for it.

I don't know how long I sat in the clearing. I was cold, inside and out, and shivering. My legs ached along with my heart. I could think of nothing but returning to face what my life would look like now. To accept the snubs and hard looks and cold gazes.

There had to be something more, but I couldn't think of it.

I rose, wrapping my shawl closer around my shoulders against the chill, tying the ends together. I had a moment of panic when I didn't recognize where I'd entered the clearing, and then I saw my path through the path of tall grass. I began retracing my steps.

Would I even find my way back to the farm? Were there natives still in the woods? What would they do if they caught me?

At least I was certain they wouldn't care about my past.

It was a weak jest and did nothing to ease the new fears pressing in on me. I'd never gone this far into the forest. I wasn't sure I could remember the way back.

I slowed, picking my way carefully through the underbrush, trying to make out the trail I might have taken or left behind during my flight.

What if I couldn't find my way? What if night fell? Would

Grahame be able to find me? How long might that take? Would he even try?

The thought left me even colder. What trouble it might save him, should I simply disappear. He had his use of me—the dowry. With my secret exposed, I'd be nothing but a burden, no matter what skills I'd learned. He'd be free to marry someone with an untainted past.

I clutched my shawl closer, pulling it around my neck and shoulders, but it did little to ease the chill that had buried itself deep in my heart. My shoes and stockings were soaked through, and my feet were going numb with cold. I had less to fear from phantom natives than from the cold and solitude.

I had to keep moving. Maybe if I made noise? Noise might draw something besides help. If help were even to come.

I found a scrap of fabric on a bramble bush, torn from my skirts. I was going in the right direction at least. I kept moving, slow and cautious, watching for any sign of my passage. A footprint, a scuffed pile of old fallen leaves, broken branches. Anything that might show me the way.

The shadows deepened as I moved farther into the woods. I stopped every few steps to look around and to listen for the farm. The forest was silent but for the occasional breeze through naked limbs stirring creaks out of the old trees. At first, I blessed the silence. It was easier to listen for any sounds that might lead me onward. But soon apprehension crawled up my spine, carrying with it a remembered fear. It was an echo of the sensation I'd felt that morning at the stream of being watched.

No, not watched.

Hunted.

The hair on my neck rose. I quickened my pace.

There was no other warning. No sound, nothing that might have given me a chance to prepare. A weight fell upon my back, heavy and sturdy and clawed, and I collapsed under it, pushed into the frozen mulch. Wet, hot breath stinking of decay wrapped around my neck with the blunt edge of teeth as claws dug into my shoulders. I couldn't scream, I couldn't draw breath, my face was muffled in the lump of fallen leaves. I could only choke in horror.

The thing on my back made a sound like pain and the weight dug into me, then vanished. I raised my head, stunned, only to see the creature standing in front of me. At first I took it for a mastiff, tawny and stocky, but then the shadows shifted over it and it looked smaller and more cat-like, with black-tipped ears and a black mottled coat. Its teeth were blunt and thick as it growled open-mawed at me. The eyes, though, the eyes were black holes sunken into its head and staring at me with hatred.

It reared back, raising a dog-like paw with sharp, cat claws, and I threw myself to the side with every ounce of strength, trying to protect my head and neck. The paw raked my shoulder, and I cried out as pain blossomed across my back. The claws caught my shawl, tugging it, as though trying to pull it from me, but I'd tied it around me for warmth, and it only gave when the stitches tore.

The cat-beast shrieked. I lifted my head, gasping at the pain on my shoulder, and saw the beast backing into the shadows, long tail whipping violently back and forth. The creature's eyes possessed some light of their own, and they glowed eerily green as it backed into the forest. Then even the eerie glow disappeared and I was alone.

Alone. Hurt. Cold. Terrified.

In my head, I could hear Rakes's voice repeating over and over again, "Stay in the light . . . stay in the light . . . stay in the light . . ."

I had to get up. I had to get into the light. I had to get out of these woods.

It made no sense, but it drove me to my feet. My shoulders ached with a pain deeper than any hurt I'd experienced. It stole the breath from my chest and left me gasping and afraid to move.

I had to move.

I forced myself forward, holding my tattered shawl around me with one hand and using the other to support me from tree to tree. The bark was rough and unyielding on one, then smooth and curled like paper on the next. I put one numb, sodden foot in front of the other, feeling my way forward with no other thought than "Move."

I didn't realize what I was hearing at first. A gurgling, a spitting— would the cat-beast make that sound?

No, water. It was water.

The stream.

I knew I had to get on the other side of it to be closer to the farm. I knew it flowed past the road that led to the farmhouse and then through the pasture. If I ran into any of these things, I would know where I was. I could follow the stream.

I forced my legs onward, stumbling, and reached the bank exhausted, my shoulder burning with each breath.

I had to cross it though. I could try to jump it, but it was wide enough to make leaping a challenge when I wasn't hurt and tired.

And I was starting to feel faint. My shoulder throbbed in unending waves and the ground was tilting occasionally under my feet.

I had to make it out of the forest. If I fainted here, would anyone ever find me? Would the cat-beast come back to finish the hunt?

I took a deep breath that only made my shoulder throb and plunged into the stream. I didn't think I could get any colder, but I was wrong. With a gasp, I pulled my foot out. But there was no other way. I sunk up to my ankles in the icy stream and tried to hurry before my strength failed entirely.

The water was deeper than where I'd crossed before, and I was quickly up to my knees in cold water. The current wasn't fast, but it still tugged at my skirts, trying to pull me off balance. I struggled with each step, the mud at the stream bottom sucking at my shoes, trying to trap me. Three, four, five steps, and the water receded until I was finally on the other side.

The effort had taken more out of me than I'd expected. I fell to one knee, then another, trying to fight against the urge to collapse and failing.

No, I wouldn't die out here alone, shamed, forgotten.

I crawled to the nearest tree trunk, pushing through a prickly bush to reach it. I used the trunk to climb to my feet and stood panting against it. Trembles took over, shaking through me, and I was crying in pain. Clutching what remained of my shawl, I pushed off from the tree and reached out for the next one, falling against it as my numb feet stumbled. I pushed off again and reached out for the next. And again. And again, with no other thought but the next tree and keeping my feet under me, numb with cold and my vision black-edged from the aching pain and exhaustion that shook through my limbs.

The forest opened suddenly, spilling me out onto the path to the farmhouse. I tripped to the frozen ground. The sun was still overhead, streaming a few weak beams through the empty boughs canopied over the path. After the gloom of the forest, it was as bright as a summer's day.

CHAPTER NINETEEN

I had made it out of the forest, but I wasn't home yet. I tried to raise up, but my arms were too weak and the wound too angry to let me.

Was I close to the house? I didn't know the path well enough to say, only that I couldn't see the house from where I lay.

"Help!"

My voice was weak and thin. It would never reach the house. But I tried again, taking as deep of a breath as I could.

"Help!"

I heard a rush of something large and fast, and fear woke me enough to raise partway. It was Niall's dogs, Horace and Edgar, bounding at me. They barked and skidded around me, pushing their cold noses against my face. Edgar began growling with an eerie whine. I wrapped one arm around Horace, trying to claim some of his warmth.

I turned my head and there was Marjorie's husband, Shaw, hurrying down the path toward me. He was carrying a musket.

He pushed the dogs away and went to his knees next to me, his craggy face dark with concern.

"Something . . ." I tried to tell him, but my voice wouldn't work. I forced the words out. "Something. In the woods."

He didn't answer. He looked me over, then shouldered his musket.

"I'm going to carry you, lass," he told me, and his accent, so like mine, was a balm to my fears. I managed to nod. Carefully, he threaded wiry arms under me and lifted me with a strength I wouldn't have reckoned in such a thin man. The motion brought fire to my wounds, though, and I cried out.

"I am sorry, lass," he murmured to me. And then he began to hurry down the path.

I must have fainted, for the next thing I knew I was being laid out on my bed, surrounded by a babbling of voices. One cut through the others and stabbed deep into me.

"Oh, she did it to herself. She must have! She's trying to make us all feel sorry for her so we'll forget what sort she is."

Ruthie's tone was high-pitched and cruel. I didn't have the strength to face her. Sick in body and spirit, I kept my eyes shut.

And then something shocking happened. Marjorie spoke.

"Ruthie Bright, do you think the rest of us have forgotten how you and Clay came to wed?"

Marjorie's voice was hushed, but it fell over the room like a thunderclap. I wanted to open my eyes and stare at Ruthie, but I kept still. Tension built in the room until hurried footsteps broke it, rushing out the door.

"My word, Marjorie, there was no need for that," Mrs. Giverns said.

"There was all the need in the world," Marjorie answered in her quiet way. Neither spoke again.

Another set of footsteps entered the room, familiar as my own. Cadha. A cold streak of terror cut through my pain and exhaustion.

"I've brought water and towels," she said to the others, her voice tense and focused. "We need to see how badly she's hurt. Why are Ruthie and Clay leaving?"

Silence answered her.

"So it's that way, is it?" I heard Cadha set the water bucket on the floor. "Marjorie, help me get her out of these clothes. Amelia, will you see what's salvageable and what's bound for the ragbag?"

"Good Lord, look at this shawl," Mrs. Giverns said. "Looks like something tore right through it."

"Shaw said she told him there was something in the woods."

At that, I had to open my eyes. Mrs. Giverns was holding out my shawl, and it was a tangled tatter of loose wool, gaping in the middle where the stitches were unraveling. The natural cream color was stained brown.

My blood, I realized, dried on it.

My throat caught and I choked.

"Easy, lass," Cadha soothed, laying a hand over mine. "You lie easy and let us tend you."

"The creature—" I choked on the word.

Cadha frowned. "What creature? Was that what caught you? Whyever did you go into the woods like that, Ailee?" She said my name with a mixture of exasperation and worry, but underneath, I heard doubt. Like she didn't know who I was anymore.

"A cat—" I struggled to answer. "A cat-beast." My voice was raw and hurt my throat, like I'd been screaming.

Had I been screaming?

"Big, like a dog," I added.

"I know the ones she's speaking of," said a male voice from the doorway. It was Thom. He was carrying the kettle with a thick towel. The kettle was smoking with steam. "Bobtailed cats," he said. "They sometimes attack a person."

"Best go tell the men," Cadha told him. "They're expecting natives."

I wanted to tell him that the cat-beast had a tail, but I could do nothing more than move my lips, and then even that was impossible as a sharp tremor passed through me.

"Easy, now," Cadha said to me. "You lie still and let us get you cleaned and bandaged. It might hurt," she added, but she didn't have to say it. I knew this would be unpleasant.

It was easier knowing that Ruthie had left, though. I could still guess what Mrs. Giverns might think of me, and I fretted over what Cadha thought, because her respect was important, but I took comfort knowing that Marjorie, at least, seemed not to hold anything against me. And then, I lost all thought under their ministrations.

Removing my clothing was only the beginning. I fainted again, I think, at one point, because when I came to myself, I was wrapped in a wool blanket, naked beneath it. And then Cadha began cleaning up my wounds. I had to lie on my left side, and Marjorie came around to take my hands. To help hold me in place, I thought, and then Cadha started on the wounds and the pain shot through me. Marjorie squeezed my hands, holding them tight to her, and it helped, some.

Three places on my shoulder and back burned as Cadha tended them, but a fourth flamed like hot coals touching it. It was high on my shoulder, where I'd felt the cat-beast get me when it had torn through my shawl.

"That's not good, Cadha," Mrs. Giverns said, her whisper loud enough for me to overhear.

"I know it," Cadha snapped. "Go to the root cellar and get my ointment pot."

I wanted to tell her that I had some, that it was only a few feet away, but I couldn't talk through the pain. I screwed my eyes tight, clinging to Marjorie, and tried to think of anything that would take me from it.

It was Beacham's voice that came back to me. Of the time I was sitting outside his galley in that awful ship that smelt of dead fish and vomit and old potatoes, and he was telling stories.

"All the men of his village wear them when they travel," Beacham had said, *"to protect from the wolves."*

"How?" I'd asked

"Maybe it keeps them off their neck . . ."

I wished I'd had Beacham's scarf. I wished I hadn't fled into the woods. I wished so many things, the wishing grew more painful than the wound.

Until I realized it was done, and Cadha was wrapping clean strips of cloth around my shoulder and chest to keep the wad of towels in place over the wounds. The room smelt of old blood and herbal ointment. She tucked the wool blanket around me and added a quilt to it.

"I'll sit with her," Marjorie said.

No one else spoke. I heard Cadha and Mrs. Giverns leave the room, bundling off the kettle and supplies and torn clothing. Marjorie still held my hands.

And then, unexpectedly, she began to sing.

It was an old song, a song my nanny used to sing to me when I was a child. Marjorie's voice was a tenfold better than my nanny's had been, and the purity of the song, carrying with it reminders of home and family and safety, brought tears to my eyes. I hid them, closing my eyes again, but the tears leaked free to dampen my pillow. She was still singing when I fell into an uneasy, exhausted sleep.

Voices.

"How did she sleep?"

Grahame's voice, both familiar and strange, shocked me like a plunge into cold water. A terrible longing ran through me, coupled with a horrible sense of betrayal. I couldn't resolve the two, so I stayed still. My body hurt all over, especially where the wound ripped my shoulder. It began to throb as soon as I became aware of it. I wished for sleep to take the pain away again, but the voices wouldn't still.

"Fitful." Cadha's voice, terse and tight.

"We're going back out when it's light," Grahame told her. He sounded weary to his bones.

Cadha didn't answer.

"Why was she out there?" Grahame's question was more of a demand, and I could hear the underlying rage. I hadn't heard him sound angry before. It was as horrible as the betrayal that gnawed at me.

"Now isn't the time," Cadha snapped back. "You and Thom get that beast before it comes near the farm. I'll see to your wife."

She twisted the final word, like she was twisting a dagger into Grahame. Tension flooded the room. I wanted both of them to leave and take their anger with them. I wanted sleep to claim me again and take me from the ruins of my life. Tears burned under my eyelids, and I squeezed my eyes tighter, trying to hold it all in. I ached inside and out. I'd made such a mess of everything.

I wished Elsie were here.

I could hear her in my head, like she was sitting next to my bed, speaking to me.

You're stronger than this, Ailee, she'd say to me. This isn't all your fault.

No, it wasn't. I was tired of carrying shame around me like a cloak.

I opened my eyes. The wan light of a single candle left most of the room in shadows. Cadha was standing in the doorway, and I could hear Grahame's boot steps on the stairs. My side hurt from lying on it so long, but I didn't dare move onto my back. Instead, I tried to sit up.

The pain bit deep into my back and shoulder, and I must have made a sound from it because Cadha was there in a moment.

"Don't try to move," she told me sternly, trying to get me to lay back down. She didn't seem to know where to touch me that wouldn't hurt, so I ignored her attempts and pushed myself upright with my good arm. Relenting, Cadha helped me to sit.

"A drink, please," I asked, though it took a couple of tries to get the words out. My throat was parched, my lips dry, and my mouth tasted as though it had been filled with mud and straw.

Cadha moved around the bed to the little table, and I heard water poured into a cup. It hurt to sit up, but it hurt differently than when I was laying. The darkness was oppressive, though, and I wished the sun was up. I was tired of being surrounded by shadows.

Cadha held the cup for me to drink. The water tasted of wood and iron from sitting in a bucket. Still, it was wet and soothing and I drank it all.

"Shall I fetch Grahame to you?" Cadha asked. I could hear uncertainty in her words, and she was watching me with concern.

There was no need for her to go for him, though. His frame filled the doorway.

It was like seeing him for the first time. He'd worn that same expression, a wary gentleness that seemed so out of keeping with his untamed appearance. His hair was down, falling past his shoulders, his shirt sleeves rolled up and his shirt unlaced. He looked tired.

Cadha stepped back, watching both of us. Something hung in the air, waiting, a moment about to happen, and I realized it was waiting for me. I got to decide how this moment would run.

I remembered this feeling. The last time I'd felt it, I'd been on the ship. Jacky was lying dead on his cot, and Elsie was staring at him, realizing. The moment had hung there, too, waiting for one of us to say something, to do something, only I hadn't recognized the power of it, and then it was gone, lost to Elsie's wail of grief. And I'd let myself be pushed away. I'd fled.

I'd fled. Just like yesterday, I'd fled. Just like at home, I'd fled.

I was tired of running.

I could have said a half dozen things, but there was one that was forefront in my thoughts. It had to be dealt with before I could face the rest.

"Did you find what was in the woods?" I sounded tired, worn out, aching. I wished I sounded stronger.

Grahame came forward as if my voice released him. He knelt in front of me, but he was so tall, it made him little shorter than where I sat, slumped in the bed. "We found a trail." He offered the words to me, one at a time, as if afraid I'd reject them. "We go back out at first light."

"You have to kill it." My certainty startled even me. Grahame tried to hide his surprise, and he nodded to me, one slow sturdy nod, to show he understood.

I wasn't sure he did, though. He hadn't seen it. When he saw it, then he'd understand. It wasn't like any beast I'd seen before. It was . . . wrong somehow.

Unspoken words piled up between us. He was waiting for my anger. I could see it in his eyes. I was waiting for . . . for what? For whatever else I saw in his eyes, I suppose. Something I couldn't identify, something I'd not seen in him before.

The moment was passing. I was too tired to hang on to it.

I leaned toward the head of the bed, no longer able to keep myself upright. Grahame leapt forward to catch me and helped ease me back down. He brushed the hair back from my face, like he'd done on the ship when I'd been ill. He leaned down and I felt the tickle of his beard as he brushed his lips across my cheek. His breath was warm.

He left the room without another word.

Cadha moved closer and pulled the blanket up over me. Weariness settled over me with that quilt, and I remember her sitting down next to me, and then I remembered nothing.

CHAPTER TWENTY

When I next woke, the room was lighter, but only just. I lay blinking, coming back to myself. I had been dreaming. I couldn't recall it but for an uneasiness bordering on fear and a pressing need to do something.

The room was empty. I turned my head and saw sunlight trying to peek through the cracks in the shutters. My shoulder hurt with the movement, but after the bite of pain, the ache subsided to a constant, nagging throb. The rest of me hurt, too, like I'd been tossed across a room and left lying in a heap. Under the discomfort, though, was hunger. I hadn't eaten since breakfast the day before.

Had that just been a day ago?

Carefully, I eased upright. I cautiously lifted my right arm to see if I could. It hurt, but I could raise it almost level. I didn't dare try to raise my injured one. I could already tell how that would feel.

I wanted to open the shutters. The room was cold outside the blankets, and the sunlight looked warm and inviting. I eased one leg over the edge of the bed, then the other. Everything ached in protest. I had to stop to catch my breath.

My feet were stockinged but the chill crept through the wool and into my bones. I shivered once and regretted it as my shoulder spasmed with new pain. I drew the quilt around me, awkwardly with only my one good arm, but the blanket helped ward off the worst of the chill.

I couldn't sit here all day. It felt wrong to still be abed after so many weeks of rising before the sun.

Standing wasn't as difficult as I thought. Except for the pain, it was a bit like getting to my feet after my illness on the ship, only the floor didn't try to lurch out from under me and the room smelt of herbs and chill rather than sickness and sweat.

I stood shakily, using the bed for support, before making slowly for the window. The thick glass pane opened inward on iron hinges that squealed with disuse. It was harder to open the shutter with one arm. It took longer than seemed necessary, and I was both annoyed and exhausted by the effort when the latch finally gave.

I threw open the shutter and bathed in the sunlight.

I didn't think of anything in particular, just noticed sensations. The way the cold air felt against my cheeks and stirred my hair. The sun against my eyelids when I closed them. The constant throb from my shoulder now a familiar partner in life that I could ignore if I didn't move. I could hear trees shifting when a breeze came, the far off bleat of sheep and low of cows, and the occasional outburst from a chicken.

"Ailee?"

Cadha's voice drew me from my reverie and sank me back into my life. I felt the weight of all that had happened settle over me.

I turned to find her standing in the doorway, watching me with that mixture of concern and doubt.

"We need to change that wrapping," she said. "And get a meal into you."

My stomach pinched, reminding me how hungry I was. But first I had to know where I stood with Cadha.

I just didn't know how to begin.

"Cadha—" I began, searching for the words, but she cut me off.

"We need to get you on the mend," she said, a finality in her tone. "We can speak about what happened later."

It would have been easier to let her sweep me up in her resolve, but I couldn't keep hiding and running. I didn't want to live under a shadow of speculation.

"No, I don't think we can," I said firmly. It was the first time I'd ever spoken against her.

Cadha went still. She watched me, waiting, and I realized she wasn't going to argue, but she wasn't going to help me, either. If I wanted to pursue this, I needed to do it on my own.

Fine.

But first, I needed to know what she knew.

"What did you hear about me?" I'd never asked such a bold question before. It just wasn't done. I'd never asked Mother or Father what the townsfolk said about me. I'd always assumed it was the worst imaginable. I wasn't even certain what Grahame knew, just that I'd asked Father to make sure he wasn't ignorant on the scandal surrounding me.

But, if Grahame didn't know, then how would Ruthie have known?

I braced against a wave of betrayal, but something must have shone on my face. Cadha stiffened.

"Why are you asking?" she countered. "To excuse it or to claim it never happened?"

So, she knew enough.

"No," I told her, hurt she'd think the worst of me. It was true I hadn't known her all that long, but I thought she might have learned something of my character.

But then, all this spoke so soundly against my character.

Suddenly I was weary to my bones. I circled the bed and sank into the chair set by it, wincing against the pain. It took a moment to gather myself again. Cadha had moved from the doorway to face me.

"I suppose it doesn't matter what you've heard," I confessed. "I could say it's all true, but I'm not sure what I'd be admitting to. So instead I'll just tell you that I was involved with a married man back in Lifford and it ruined me. Grahame knew when he wed me."

"For your dowry, I gather." The way Cadha said it made it sound so cruel. Mercenary.

Is that how she saw Grahame? He could be distant, even cool at times, but I'd never thought him heartless. Lately, he'd been so tender. So attentive.

And then he'd spoken of my past.

I couldn't reconcile the two feelings for him, longing and betrayal. The emotions warred under my skin, just as painful as the wound on my shoulder.

I tried to push it all away.

"Yes," I admitted, the word a whisper. "For my dowry."

Cadha straightened. I waited for the condemnation I saw gathering in her expression, her lips pursed, her eyes judging, her entire body rigid with outrage. But she hesitated.

162

"He should have known not to bring you here," she said, and while the words pelted me like stones, her tone wasn't cruel. "But what's done is done. We'll have to get by."

I stared at her, uncertain.

"We need to change that wrapping," Cadha repeated, and I knew that was all she'd say on the other matter for now. "And get a meal into you." She turned on her heels and left the room.

I stared after her. I was still poised on a knife's edge, uncertain where I stood with her even now. She didn't like what she'd learned, but she wasn't completely disregarding me, either.

I closed my eyes. It wasn't much of a start, but it was better than nothing.

Cadha left me bundled before the fire in the parlor after I'd eaten. My shoulder had finally stopped burning with pain after changing the dressing, and Cadha had seemed relieved to find it on the mend. I was fortunate, and I knew it. It all could have been so much worse. I could have been unable to return to the road. I could have been cut far worse and bled out. I could still take infection if I wasn't careful.

I could be dead.

I should be dead.

I shuddered, recalling that warm, moist, awful breath and the press of teeth. The shawl had muffled the worst of it, but I didn't understand how it had kept the beast from finishing me. I walked through the memory again and again, trying to find a different reason, but nothing else explained why the beast had left me. The shawl had done something more than just keep it from biting me. The beast should have torn through the wool and snapped my neck. Instead, it had let go. It had sounded hurt.

Mary Karney had knit that shawl from wool she'd spun from her father's flock. She'd knit it in the usual way. It wasn't like Beacham's supposedly magical scarf. It was just a knit shawl. I hadn't done anything special to it.

But I had.

I sat up a little straighter. I'd been treating it, like Cadha had said, with the wool oil. It had helped keep the wet off me when I hadn't time to put a coat on to run to the kitchen house or the hen house. It smelt of sheep afterwards, well, not quite sheep but like wool gone wet and hot. It wasn't a pleasant smell, but I'd given up pleasantry for comfort quickly enough, and I'd rather smell like soaked sheep than be drenched myself.

Was it something about the wool oil?

That didn't make sense either, though. I remembered that Thom and Niall had spoken of losing sheep to these bobtailed cats Thom suspected had attacked me.

My thoughts ran in circles as I stared at the flames and I couldn't get past them. Finally, I stopped trying. I'd been fortunate and I'd have to leave it at that. With any luck, Grahame and Thom would catch the beast, and no one else would be at risk.

Niall came into the room and stopped when he saw me.

"Where is Cadha?" His voice was cold, demanding. But he'd always spoken to me so.

"The kitchen house," I answered, trying to be polite, as I always had. He was Grahame's brother, after all.

He gave me a look and suddenly I knew. I knew it with a certainty I rarely felt. It drained the warmth out of my body and left me cold and empty.

"You told them."

The words were out of my mouth before I could think what to say.

Niall stared down at me, his nose tilted as though he smelled something rank. He didn't bother to answer.

"Why?" The hurt in my voice was thick and heavy.

"Grahame should have left you in Ireland," he said stiffly. He turned and left the room. His contempt of me lingered, tainting the small room.

I could only stare at the empty doorway in shock.

Shock, however, soon gave way to anger. Just who did he think he was? Pretending to be some grand gentleman, casting his judgment upon those less fortunate. I shook with indignation. That was the final time Niall Donaghue would talk down to me.

Cadha found me in this state not long after.

"Good heavens, girl, are you feverish?" She came to put a hand against my cheek. "Or just sitting too close to the fire? You're as flushed as a rooster's comb."

I bit my tongue to keep from speaking of it and merely shook my head.

"Well, you mind to tell me if you do feel feverish. I've something for that." She looked down at me a moment longer, then turned to leave.

"Cadha," I called to her, stopping her. "Whatever you might think of me, I hope you won't hold it against Grahame. For wedding me," I added at her look. "He's been good to me."

"Has he?"

I could hear her opinion of him clear enough in her tone. She held him to blame for my secret getting out just as much as I did.

She came over to me and drew up a chair to sit. "Ailee, we've all a past behind us. I might not think well of yours, but after some thought, I understand you've answered for it in ways you could have never guessed. You aren't made for this sort of life. It would have been kinder for Grahame to pass you by and seek his fortune elsewhere, but you're here now, and you have been trying to make the most of it. And I do admire that. So you won't hear me speak ill against you again. We just won't speak of it at all. And that's how it'll be." She leveled her gaze at me. "You take my meaning?"

I nodded, scarcely daring to draw breath.

"I can't say it won't be very hard now, with everyone knowing, but we'll get by." She stood then. "I'm finding that I'm missing your help in the kitchen house, so you mend quick. In a day or two, you can come tend the pots."

"I will."

"And hopefully by then, Grahame and Thom will have caught that beast of yours." She glanced darkly out the doorway. "Niall isn't as useful in the barns left on his own."

A thrill of victory made me smile, but I hid it quickly. Niall spoke out easily against me, but now I had something in return.

Only I would never use it. I drew a long breath as Cadha left the room. No, how useful Niall was or wasn't at his work was something I had no right to comment on. But there were other ways I might remind him of where he stood compared to where I'd come from.

It was petty and mean of me to dwell on such thoughts, but I wouldn't be taken unawares again. Niall had never had a kind word for me, and he'd stirred up trouble that would follow me 'til the end of my days. If nothing else, preparing myself for whatever he might say against me next would at least make me feel like I could hold my own.

I had little else to occupy my time. No books to read, and my shoulder too sore for spinning or knitting or stitching. All I had were my thoughts, dark as they might be.

CHAPTER TWENTY-ONE

I remembered this feeling.

My mother wouldn't speak to me. My father couldn't look at me. My brothers watched me with eyes wide with confusion and curiosity. Our two housemaids were civil, but they would fall silent if I came suddenly upon them, bending knee and bowing head until I passed and then taking up their gossip once more.

I assumed it was about me. Why wouldn't it be? I'd done the unthinkable.

The tension that laid over Cadha's farm had the same feeling. Cadha didn't seem to know what to say to me. Niall wouldn't look at me. Thom was civil but silent. And Grahame . . .

I rarely saw Grahame. He had taken to spending his nights in the barn, and his days he spent away from the farm, hunting the creature that had dared harm me.

I suppose I should have been touched at such a show of devotion. If only I didn't think it was a way for him to avoid speaking with me.

I don't know what I would have said. His betrayal still sat like a raw wound upon my heart. But I missed him. I missed his steady presence and comforting weight in the bed next to me. I missed the quiet way he would smile when our paths crossed during the day. I missed waiting to see what few words he would say in answer to me. I wanted desperately for things to be right between us again, but I didn't know how to start, or even if I should be the one to start. I couldn't help but feel wronged, yet at the same time, it was my own folly that had caused all this. The feelings warred inside of me and wouldn't give me peace.

The only time I felt truly at ease was with the dogs. On the third day after Niall had called me out, I had left the house. I was nervous, standing at the back door staring at the iron handle before finding the courage to open it. I was wearing one of Cadha's coats over my dress and had wrapped a linen kerchief around my neck. My shawl was a complete loss. What hadn't been shredded or stained had simply unraveled, and Cadha said the wool was good for nothing but nesting the chickens. Only, she said, they wouldn't go near it. Thom figured it was the smell of the cat still on it, though Cadha had thrown out the places where it had been sliced. So the entire thing was a loss. And I wasn't far enough knitting my new shawl to wear it.

When I opened the door, two tawny figures jumped to their feet. My heart leapt into my throat until I realized it was the dogs. Horace and Edgar stood lolling at me, coats flecked with frost. Horace whined, and Edgar kept licking his jowls.

I held my hand out, and they both gave me a good sniff. Then Horace sidled up against me, just barely keeping from knocking me off my feet. I stepped from the house, trying to go past the mastiff, but he moved with me, keeping close to my side. Edgar paced me a few steps away. And so with the dogs as escort, I walked to the kitchen house. I gave them both a good pat before entering the kitchen, and as I closed the door, I saw them both lay down just outside it. I smiled, unexplainably pleased.

"Goodness, are those dogs outside?" Cadha demanded as I closed the door. She was stirring something that smelled wonderfully savory in the pot hung over the coals. "They've been stretched out by the doors since Shaw brought you in. Won't even let Thom draw them away. Oddest thing I've ever seen."

For some reason, that news made me feel even lighter. "Truly? Why is that?"

"I'd say it's for you, if I thought they had the sense to realize you'd been hurt. But never seen that much sense in them before. Sit on this stool and mind this pot." She handed me the wooden spoon and pulled a stool over for me, and I took up my duties again.

I admit I felt better with their company. Horace and Edgar followed my every step in the farmyard. I talked to them as I went between out-buildings, telling them where I was going or what I'd been doing. They were attentive, as if they could understand me, staring up at me with their eyes warm and friendly. And I so much needed a friend.

I didn't know what Niall thought of his dogs attaching themselves to me. And I didn't like to think about a day coming when I might open the back door and find them gone. For now, they were my closest companions, and I treasured them.

It didn't hurt that I felt safer with them so near. Those times when we were walking the yard and they would halt, noses up and sniffing, eyes alert, ears pricked, I would stand frozen, waiting. It was always Edgar who would break off first, ready to carry on. Horace was the more cautious, giving it another moment or two before he was satisfied.

It had been almost a fortnight since I'd last gone into the woods. My back was still sore, but now with an itching that spoke of healing. The deepest wound had taken a turn with some redness and swelling, but that was now abating. There were things I couldn't do comfortably yet, but each day I was stronger and more capable. Still, it would be a long while before I'd be whole.

Mealtimes were the most uncomfortable time, with Niall and I pretending the other didn't exist and Grahame physically present but obviously elsewhere in his thoughts. He didn't offer much in the way of words, even less now than before, and there was an odd light in his eyes, like a mingling of shame and obsession. Cadha kept the talk to workings of the farm, but mostly we just rushed through the meal so we could all return to our respective chores.

That morning had been no different. When Grahame stood to leave, I wanted to say something to him, but the words wouldn't come. Instead, I watched him duck out of the room, heard him shrug into his heavy coat, take up the musket he now left by the back door, and leave the house.

After tidying the breakfast dishes, I made my way to the bake house. Cadha was inside, starting on the dough for our weekly bread-baking.

"Feeling up to throwing dough, do you?" she asked as I closed the door. The dogs had settled just outside, as had become their wont.

"Yes, I think so. I'm ready to do more than I've been doing, at the very least."

Cadha gestured with a nod toward the flour sacks. I knew how to mix the dough now without asking for the measurements, an accomplishment that usually pleased me.

"So Grahame's going back into the woods today?" Cadha asked me as we worked. The bake house smelled pleasantly of dough and wood coals, but her words chased any contentment away. She spoke in such a cautious way, as though searching for a safe subject.

"I suppose so."

"Did he not tell you?" She looked at me oddly.

"No, he made no mention of it during breakfast."

Cadha frowned. "So that's how it is. He's still sleeping in the barn?"

I flushed, and it was all the answer she needed. She threw her flour-covered hands up in disgusted. "These men! I swear, if I didn't need them to help run the place, I'd be quit of them all." She pointed a dusty finger at me. "You talk to your man, Ailee, and get this mended. I can handle fuss and bother with the neighbors, but I won't have it in my own house. Mend this between you and Grahame, and then the both of you mend it with Niall. Or I'll take matters into my own hands."

I could only nod. I had no idea how to do anything she asked, but I knew it had gone past time to settle things between us. Tonight, I resolved to do just that. I'd catch him at dinner and ask to speak with him after supper.

Which would have been perfect if Grahame had come to dinner, but only Niall joined us. It would have been another meal eaten in awkward silence if Cadha hadn't spoken of checking the barn rafters and house attic for any sign of weakness before the snows came. I tried to ignore Niall's occasional glower in my direction.

"Niall!" Cadha's sharp tone made us both jump. "Have you heard a word I've said to you?"

Niall nodded in a surly manner that Cadha did not take kindly.

"Winter is upon us. We've got to make sure the buildings are ready for it. Last year we lost the roof to the still room."

"It would be easier if Grahame weren't wasting time in the woods," Niall growled, throwing me another dark look.

"Oh, and I don't doubt that you'd like it easier, wouldn't you?" Cadha leveled at him. Niall jerked in his seat and stared at her in a stunned way that told me she didn't often speak so harshly to him. "Don't think I haven't noticed you shirking your duties since your brother's arrived. I expect everyone to pull their weight here, Niall, and I mean everyone." She stood suddenly, ending dinner. Niall left the room with a stormy expression. Cadha watched him go, her face uncharacteristically closed.

Cadha gave me a dark look before leaving the room. I was left to gather the dishes and see them washed.

It was just another example of how rough things had grown between us all. I didn't see how Niall and I could not be at odds. And I had no better idea of how to approach Grahame, if and when he gave me the chance. I still couldn't reconcile the man I thought I knew to the man who'd betrayed my trust. It was so unlikely that Grahame would gossip of my past, even to his brother—but he must have done so for Niall to spread it to the neighbors.

If only he would give me the chance to speak with him.

It was like being on the ship all over again. He seemed bent on finding ways to use work to avoid me.

I paused, holding a dripping trencher in my hand, and stared at the wall without seeing it.

He'd spent weeks aboard ship being everywhere I wasn't. It had gotten better since coming to Cadha's until I'd gotten hurt, and now he was gone all hours of the day and taking to bedding in the barn at night. Why avoid me? Was it from anger that I'd gotten hurt? But then why avoid me on the ship? I'd gotten sick, but that had been no fault of mine.

Was he ashamed? Or shamed?

I blew out a breath. It was a puzzle, and I wasn't going to piece it together standing here dripping dishwater on my boots.

I finished with the dishes and made for the bake house to check the next loaves we'd left rising. The ground was frozen between outbuildings, and my breath hovered in the air. The dogs sidled as close to me as they could as we walked. I supposed that could be another reason for Niall's glowering. His dogs had taken a liking to me, and they didn't seem to give him a second glance anymore.

Well, I couldn't help that his dogs liked me. If Niall was jealous, he could try to urge them back to him.

I froze mid-stride, an awful realization taking root inside of me.

Niall was jealous. Not of me. Of Grahame.

He didn't care a wit for me, but he wanted what Grahame had—a wife with a dowry. A young, pretty wife with breeding and a dowry.

It all made sense. I'd suspected it before, but just off-handedly as a reason for Niall's contempt of me. I'd never considered that it might have gotten in the way of the two brothers. Niall could have forced the reason for our hasty marriage out of Grahame. And then he might have shared that knowledge to spite Grahame, because surely if I was shunned by society, Grahame would feel that weight as well. It could affect anything he tried to make of himself here. It could ruin his chance to make deals and to trade and do business.

But then it would hurt the farm, too, surely. And that would in turn only damage Niall's chances at making a good match.

So Niall would only end up hurting himself by trying to hurt Grahame through me.

I leaned my head back and heaved another sigh that frosted the air. It all made my head spin, and I wasn't even certain it was the truth. It had felt right at the beginning, but now it seemed like just a foolish thing to do. And Niall had never struck me as foolish.

"Ailee!"

Cadha's shout startled me, and I froze, looking around for the danger. It took a moment for me to realize that the dogs weren't looking threatened but were watching Cadha wave from the barn.

I'd never actually gone inside the barn. It seemed a strange thing all of the sudden, to have no idea what lay on the other side of the doors. A foreboding gnawed at me. Why would she choose now to take me inside?

Had something happened? Was Grahame hurt?

My heart pounding, I hurried across the yard, the dogs trotting to keep up. Cadha shooed them back when they would have followed me inside.

The barn was dry and free of frost, which seemed odd given how cold it still was inside. Old straw was scattered over the top of the packed dirt floor. The inside was sectioned with wooden half-walls and small pens, and overhead half the ceiling was floored. I could see bags and bales stored in those upper reaches. The rest of the ceiling was bare rafters, some strung with coils of rope and leather. The place smelled of old and fresh animal droppings, hay, and dirt.

"You go with Thom," Cadha told me. I looked where she gestured to see Thom standing at the other end of the barn by a second set of doors. He had pulled on a woolen knit hat and looked to be wearing a pair of matching mittens, along with his warmest coat.

I crossed the barn to him, seeing a few sheep peer through the wooden poles from where they were penned. A couple of goats rose on their hind legs, forelegs braced on their own fence, to watch me. One of them bleated at me.

The barn was longer than I'd given credit for, with a couple opened doors set along its walls behind the pens. The ground just outside was trampled, the freezing mud ground up by many hooves. Past the pens I walked by a wooden ladder set against a half-wall leading up to the loft and wondered if that was where Grahame had been sleeping.

Where was Grahame?

If I hadn't been so worried, I might have been more curious and slowed to glance into the half-walled spaces to see the equipment and tools housed within. Or to look for where Thom slept and kept his belongings. Instead, I noted things only in passing, seeing them without realizing what I was looking at as I hurried through the barn to Thom.

Thom must have read the worry in my expression.

"He's fine," he told me. "I'll take you to him."

Breathing out in relief, I followed Thom out of the barn and under a sloping roof adjoining the barn. We passed the wagon and a plow and other odds and ends of equipment sheltering there. Open land stretched out beyond the shelter, the grasses broken and bent by frost. The pastures, I realized, and they ran to the forest's edge, halted only by more cross-rail fencing.

Beyond the fence line, I saw an open structure erected on the edge of the woods. It resembled a small gallows. A cold dread fell over me. Something was swinging from it, something smaller than one of the dogs and with thicker fur. Next to it stood Grahame and Niall.

Niall was talking, but as Thom and I neared, he fell silent. By the dark looks he was casting Grahame, I could tell it hadn't been a pleasant conversation. But what caught my gaze and held it was the pathetic creature hanging by its hind legs from the top beam of the structure. It was stout but small, only half the size of the dogs, and furred with a black mottled brown coat. It had only a short bob of a tail to speak of, big black paws, and tufted wide ears.

"I caught it on the far side of the clearing," Grahame told me. "The one past the stream."

He was watching me, that same curious light in his eyes. I could nearly feel the hum of eagerness coming off of him. He needed me to tell him this was it. This was the beast that had attacked me. He needed me to say he'd set things right between us. He needed reassurance that he'd done his duty to protect his wife.

And I dearly wanted to give it to him. I wanted to move beyond this so we could settle other matters.

But I couldn't.

It wasn't the beast.

I tried to see how maybe it was. Tried to see how the shadows of the forest might make it look stouter, how the fear would make the teeth longer and the paws wider. But I knew in my heart this poor, strange cat was not what had attacked me.

"Ailee?"

Grahame had stepped closer to me. I'd been silent too long, and I watched as his expression fell and then closed. I didn't need to say it. He saw it in my eyes.

"Are we finished here?" Niall asked sourly.

"No." Grahame reached for the musket I hadn't noticed propped against the structure's beam. He slung it over his shoulder. He would keep hunting until he found the right one, I realized. He'd hunt for it until he'd killed it because I had asked him to do so. Because it had injured me and he hadn't been there to stop it. He would not relent because that was the sort of man he was: resolute, determined, and unforgiving. Emotion swelled within me. How had I come to hold this man, this powerful, enigmatic man, in my sway?

Niall straightened, anger flashing across his face. "You killed it. It's done."

"Not yet," Grahame answered.

Niall rounded on me. "Tell him it's done."

I took a step back, startled by his sudden outrage.

"Tell him!"

"I can't." The words came out more plaintive than I'd wanted.

"This is your doing!" He took another step closer, threat in every line of him. I saw Grahame stiffen and reach to unsling his musket. Horror wrapped around me and I watched the future play out in my mind—Niall raising his hand to strike me, Grahame raising his musket to fire—and something deeper than fear snapped inside of me.

"This is your doing, Niall Donaghue." My voice was fierce and strong. "Your jealousy caused all of this."

Niall froze, shock plain on his features. He looked younger, uncertain, and weak. Then he tried to look indignant and angry, drawing himself up again, but it was a poor attempt.

"You think I fear you?" I asked before he could speak. "I've faced death and sickness and disgrace. You are nothing compared to those. I tell you, this is not what attacked me."

Niall opened his mouth to speak, but I was already turning away from him.

"Put that down," I said sharply to Grahame. He blinked, then looked at the musket in his hands. A shadow crossed his face, and he set the musket back against the beam.

"Tell me what to look for, and I'll find the right one," Grahame said, his voice hushed.

"No." My reply surprised even me. "It could take you months to find it."

"Then I'll take months—"

"We can't have you gone for that long," I interrupted. "Winter's setting in. Cadha needs you here."

Grahame looked as though he'd argue. I couldn't have that, because I'd let him convince me. I was still terrified of the beast and those black eyes and long blunt teeth and oddly shifting body. I wanted to know it was dead.

But what if it attacked him?

Cold fear knotted my stomach. I'd never considered that Grahame might be hurt by it. Grahame was all that was strong and sure. But he was vulnerable, too. He didn't have anything to protect him.

Like a shawl. Or Beacham's scarf.

I took a step toward him. "We need you here," I repeated.

Grahame was silent for a long moment, his gaze searching mine. Whatever he read there must have convinced him, for he nodded.

"Finally," Niall grumbled, and he made for the barn without giving us another glance.

An uncomfortable silence fell around us. I knew I should break it by saying words of comfort, but I didn't want to say what I didn't truly feel.

There was something, though, that I'd been meaning to ask. This was the first chance I'd gotten.

"When can we go to Germantown?"

Grahame looked startled. "Germantown?"

"You said you were going." A dark thought passed through me. "You didn't go already, did you?"

"No." Grahame still looked uncertain. "Not with you hurt."

"I'm better now. I can make the walk."

I wasn't entirely certain of that, but I wasn't going to let the chance pass by. Who knew if I'd catch Grahame in a mood where he'd consider the request?

"We'd take the wagon," Grahame told me. He looked at Thom, who was hanging back, trying to look like he hadn't overheard everything that had happened in the last several minutes. "Will the weather hold?"

Thom glanced skyward. "Should. But we'd need to leave in the next day or two."

"Tomorrow?" I turned it into a question at the last moment. I'd pushed my luck speaking out of hand so far and gotten away with it, probably because the men had all been shocked to hear a young woman speak her mind with such passion. I knew it wasn't something I could get away with often.

"I'll speak with Cadha," Grahame told me.

Relieved, I offered him a smile. The light in his eyes brightened and the tension in his shoulders eased. Things weren't completely right between us, not yet, but the foundation was laid.

CHAPTER TWENTY-TWO

I walked most of the way to Germantown the next day. Grahame tried to insist that I ride, but after a few miles, I begged to walk. The wagon's bench seat was hard, being made only of wood, and the wagon bounced over the rough wheel ruts, rattling the teeth in my head and jarring me until my sides ached. I'd never ridden in anything so uncomfortable.

It was cold but clear when we set out after first light. I was bundled in my cape, and Cadha had insisted I wear her green, hooded capelet. The extra layer did help to keep me warm, so much so that after a couple hours I pulled the hood down. I felt more protected, too, between the hood and the cape, far more so than in just a flimsy shawl.

Thom came with us, but Niall did not. He looked angry that we were going, and Cadha had seemed surprised when he refused to join us. I could only think that he didn't want to spend so much time alone in his brother's company. Or in mine. Or was he mad that the dogs were determined to go with me? Whatever his reason, it was his loss, and I stopped thinking about him as soon as we left the farm.

Thom handled the oxen, and Grahame trailed behind the wagon, his musket slung over his shoulder. Thom had the pistol stored under the wagon's bench. The wagon was only a quarter full with supplies Cadha wanted Grahame to trade in town. There were a couple bags of dried corn, an old horse harness that Grahame had mended, and a few bags of wool from the last shearing that Cadha had no use for. She'd kept the best for me to spin. She did surprise me by giving me a ball of spun wool.

"To trade," she told me, "for whatever you might need. It's from the last I'd spun. Yours is finer, so we'll keep it to use ourselves."

Both a generous gift and unexpected praise in the same breath. I had to stammer out my thanks, overwhelmed. I put the ball of wool in my satchel with the letters that I'd been writing to Elsie since arriving at the farm, hoping I'd finally have a place to send them. I hadn't written one since the attack as I wasn't ready to put all that into words yet. No need to worry her.

Unlike the last time I'd traveled with them, the dogs did not range ahead as we walked. They both stayed near me. Horace was alert with his ears lifted and his keen nose in constant motion. Edgar was more relaxed, but he'd sniff the ground often and would move back and forth on either side of me as though seeing if he could pick up a scent.

If Grahame and Thom thought it strange that we took the dogs, neither said. Both dogs had bounded over to me as we'd loaded up a few food baskets and the extra powder and cord for the muskets. They stayed next to the wagon after Grahame had handed me up. Grahame hadn't driven them back to the farm when they kept pace with us clear to the little bridge crossing the stream. It was almost as if Grahame had already made a decision about the dogs coming too.

I was happy for their company. I knew Grahame and Thom would do everything they could to keep me safe, but they couldn't hear like a dog could or smell danger coming on the wind. Even with their protection, I felt exposed on the road bordered by forest. The forest could hold any number of dangers. Leafless, the woods looked stark and dead, but bramble still choked the ground around the trunks and evergreen brushes grew in spaces between the tree trunks. Noises echoed eerily through the empty boughs. A carpet of fallen leaves covered the road, muffling the oxen's hooves and the wagon's wheels, but each creak and groan of the wagon reverberated between the trees.

I spent much of the walk wondering if I should speak and what I might say. Thom and Grahame seemed comfortable in their silence. Every topic I considered felt charged with potential disaster. In the end, I settled for the occasional word to the dogs and spent the time wondering how to approach the people of Germantown to keep my thoughts from straying toward worrying about the woods around us.

I wanted to find a letter from Elsie, but I also wanted—no, needed—to speak to someone who might teach me that odd stitch for Beacham's scarf. How to even ask? I knew I didn't have time to make an acquaintance and hope talk might turn towards stitching. I wasn't even sure I could make an acquaintance. How did one go about it without an introduction? Would Thom know someone? Would he think to introduce me? Thom probably would only know men. What would Grahame think of me speaking to a strange man?

The whole situation was rife for misunderstanding.

But I had time to set that right before it even occurred.

"Grahame," I began, uncertain what exactly to say. *I want to find someone to teach me a magical stitch to make a scarf to protect us from a strange beast roaming the forest.* It sounded ridiculous, like a story my nanny would have told me. Maybe I'd listened too well to those old stories. Maybe all this was a fool's errand.

I couldn't believe that it was. The occasional ache in my shoulder reminded me of the realness.

I glanced over to find Grahame watching me, expectant.

"Do you think," I said, trying to find the right words, "I might find someone to show me a new stitch or two while we're in town? I've only had Cadha to learn from, and I'm not complaining," I added hastily at his raised eyebrow, "but I'd hate to waste the chance to learn more."

"You miss being in town," he said, as if he'd expected it.

And there it was, swift and sudden like the bottom falling out of a bucket. I did miss being in town. I missed the people and the busyness and the goings on. I missed being surrounded by talk, even when it was of a mindless sort of gossip that did no one any good. I missed markets and fairs and shops.

I missed my life.

But at the same time, I didn't. Grahame could have taken me by the shoulders and offered to take me back to Lifford, swearing that all the scandal would be erased and I could go back to what I was before it ever happened, and tempted as I'd be, I would say no. I didn't want to go back to living like I had, ignorant of what hard work felt like and how fulfilling accomplishing a challenging task could be. I liked what I was doing at the farm, and it was shocking, in a way that a cold bed is shocking, to realize it.

"I'd like the chance to meet some of the women," I admitted at last.

"There's a man I know," Thom said, surprising me. "Works in the smithy. His wife seems kindly."

I looked at Grahame, letting him make the decision.

"I'd like to speak with the blacksmith," Grahame said, and that was that. It was decided in that way Grahame had of saying so without saying so.

I think I grinned for the rest of the walk to town.

The sun, weak wintry thing that it was, had gotten as high as it would get by the time we reached the outskirts of Germantown. The woods abated, falling away to clear cuts and fields and pasture, and the road widened as we neared.

I'd passed through the town coming to Cadha's farm, but my memory of it was spotty. It had seemed nestled in the surrounding woods, an odd little village along a strip of road on the side of a hill. It had the look of age to it, but at the same time seemed newly grown. The buildings were worn, but more from use than the passage of time. Many of the buildings were two stories, and they nestled together like a herd of sheep wary of being picked off by a wolf.

The road we were on ran straight through the middle of town with a couple of crossroads. The buildings along the main road were mainly homes. I didn't see much in the way of shops or even a post office.

"The smithy is at the end of the road," Thom told us, "near cobblers row."

"Just the one?" Grahame asked.

"Lucky to have that," Thom answered. "Hasn't been here long. Used to have to go into Clarksburg. Post office, too, but there's a little one here now."

"Can we stop there first?" I asked, eagerness buzzing through me. To have word from Elsie would make up for everything I'd gone through the past month. Well, nearly everything.

Thom gave Grahame a glance, and at my husband's nod, he steered us toward the little market square that stood mostly empty. There were a few empty wagons and a small livestock pen. A lone goat shuffled around the pen and bleated at us as we approached.

Thom tied the oxen to a post set in the ground in front of a broad brick house overlooking the square. He gave the dogs a command to stay. Horace sat on his heavy haunches, looking patient, but Edgar trotted back and forth, whining. I gave him a pat on the head and repeated the command as sternly as I could. Edgar whined again, but he dropped to the ground.

"Market days ended after the last harvest," Thom told us. "They'll pick up again come spring." He led the way up the short wood steps of the brick building. "Mr. Wigart serves as postmaster and oversees the market. He lets rooms, too, on occasion."

Thom knocked on the front door. The door had an elegant oval window set into it surrounded by fanciful carved scrollwork. It was lovely and unexpected.

A man as squat and brick-like as the house answered. He seemed to recognize Thom.

"Mr. Wigart, we've come for the Donaghue post," Thom said. "This is Grahame, Mistress Cadha's nephew."

"Ah, yes, I hear this." The man's accent was thick, and he seemed aware of it because he pronounced each word with forceful precision, and even that didn't make it easy to understand him.

Grahame half-bowed to the man, who seemed pleased by the gesture. "*Guten tag, Herr* Wigart."

I blinked. Grahame spoke another language?

Mr. Wigart brightened and grunted some indecipherable phrase in response. Grahame answered with a brief but emphatic phrase. Apparently my husband kept his speech limited even in foreign tongues.

"My wife, *Frau* Donaghue," Grahame said, introducing me. I guessed Frau must mean missus in German, if that was indeed what they were speaking.

I bent into a curtsy, the once familiar gesture feeling stiff and unpracticed. Mr. Wigart gave me an odd look.

And there it was, that sensation of hopelessness.

He knew.

Dear God, had Ruthie already come to Germantown and spewed her venom across my path? Was I never to be free of this?

Whatever eagerness I'd felt burnt away to nothing. I barely heard what remained of the exchange, only noticing that we were left to cool on the stoop while Mr. Wigart closed the door to go retrieve our post.

I tried to look unconcerned, but I caught Thom and Grahame both glancing at me, and I couldn't stop the bitterness from taking root. It was like being back in Lifford. I'd never be welcomed. I'd cause talk and looks wherever I went. Word would grow and spread. It might get all the way to Philadelphia.

Honestly, why should any of them care? What danger did I pose now? I was a married woman.

Mr. Wigart passed the small bundle of letters to Grahame and accepted payment for the post without opening the door entirely. If that didn't make it clear enough, he excused himself quickly and bid us a good day, closing the door before Grahame could finish his response.

To their credit, neither Grahame nor Thom said anything about it, but I could feel them watching me as we returned to the wagon. I was cold, colder than when we'd set out, but I did not draw up my hood. I would not hide myself from these people. I'd done nothing wrong here.

"Here's a note from Mr. Vance," Grahame said. Though much dampened, my eagerness returned. I had to bite down to keep from interrupting Grahame while he silently read the short note. I studied his expression instead, trying to guess the letter's intent. It looked like it darkened as he read, and a foreboding grew inside of me.

"He says Elsie's cousin is going to be harder to find than they'd hoped."

"What do you mean? What's happening to her?"

"He doesn't say. But he says she'll be cared for, regardless."

"We could go to her," I suggested, knowing before the words were out that it would be impossible. "We're only half a day away. We could go find her and see if she's settled."

Grahame gave me a long look. It said everything I already knew.

"What will become of her?"

"They might have found her cousin," Grahame told me. "Or Vance saw her settled, maybe even took her along."

"Elsie would have sent word. Is there another letter?"

Grahame shook his head.

"What happens next?" I asked him.

"We wait."

I didn't want to hear that.

"If we haven't heard anything by spring," Grahame told me in a gentle voice, "I'll go find her."

"You would do that?"

"Of course. She's your friend."

I warmed at his words. Spring was a long ways off, but it was something. And I trusted that Tavey wouldn't leave Elsie without some means of taking care of herself. It wasn't the news I'd wanted, but it was all I was going to get. For now, it would have to do.

"The smithy is this way," Thom told us. He untied the oxen and led the way.

In my concern for Elsie, I'd briefly forgotten my own situation, but as we walked, it came back. How word traveled so quickly, I couldn't guess. I could tell myself that it was just curiosity of the strangers coming through town that had the curtains in the windows twitching, but somehow I knew it was me. They were watching me.

I'd never be free of it.

So be it. I raised my head. I wasn't going to show shame. I didn't draw the hood back over my head, though my fingers itched to do so. The hood might protect me from the dangers of the cat-beast, but it offered no shelter against the judgment of townsfolk.

The smithy stood separated from the buildings around it, set back off the road behind a narrow paddock. Two large chestnut horses filled the paddock, and they looked up at us with placid brown eyes as Thom tied off the oxen to a fence pole. They seemed equally unconcerned by the dogs, who dropped to the ground next to the wagon at Thom's command.

The next house over, a man was working on a leather harness hanging over the porch railing. He looked up at us, curious, and I saw at once the strange knit scarf he wore looped around his neck. It looked newer than Beacham's had looked, the undyed wool still bright and creamy with a spring to it. It was all I could do not to rush over to him and demand to know who made it for him.

The blacksmith was at his bench, filing. The rasp of the file against iron set my teeth on edge, and I stayed back, letting Grahame and Thom enter the wide open doors. The stench of ever-present coals and hot metal was more of a taste than a smell, like sucking on iron filings. I listened to the conversation within but kept my eye on the man on the porch. I had the feeling he was doing the same, though he kept at his work. He was slender and young, Jacky's age, though not as tall, and his hair was longer and tied back like Grahame wore his. It was blond, lighter at the ends like it had bleached in the sun all summer and was only now growing out to its true color. He had a weathered look, too, that spoke of spending most of his days outdoors.

The voices inside had turned from greetings to explanations. The blacksmith didn't have the same thick accent as Mr. Wigart. His was more lilting, prettier somehow. I didn't think it the same language.

He'd already heard of Grahame, I realized with a sinking feeling. That he'd already heard of me, too, he confirmed by claiming his wife was ill and could not receive visitors.

So that was how it would be. Fine. I'd just have to find another way.

The paddock ended short of the building, leaving a gap wide enough to drive a cart through. I walked down the fence towards the next house and the strange man on the porch. The massive horses watched me, one of them nickering to me as I passed the paddock gate. I'd never seen horses so tall and broad and thick, like barrels with legs. Standing next to one, I'd never see over its back.

A plow rested alongside the smithy wall, looking forlorn and out of place without a field around it and an ox to pull it. Or did the horses pull it?

Was the harness for them?

I hid a slight smile. I had a way to start a conversation, at least.

I stopped at the corner of the fence and faced the horses. I could feel the man on the porch watching me.

One of the horses, the one who had nickered, moved toward me. His whole body shifted as he moved, lifting heavy hooves and plodding them down just as heavily, his large head swinging on his thick, short neck. I couldn't imagine the beast moving any faster than that slow, ponderous walk.

He breathed out onto me as he stopped at the fence, his warm, moist breaths stirring the loose bits of hair that had come out from under my mobcap. He smelled of yellow grass and hay and horse, and warmth emanated off of him. I hesitated, then reached out to stroke his nose. It was like stroking warm velvet, with whiskers that tickled my hand.

"He is Faas," a voice said from behind me. A second man had approached from around the back of the smithy. He wore a thick leather apron and a dark beard shot with gray and spoke with an accent like the man inside. "And that is Ewoud."

"They are lovely," I told him.

"You are Irish," he said, with a look of surprise.

"I am. My husband has come to talk business."

"Ah, then I should go before my son makes a deal without me." He offered me a polite nod.

"I'm wondering," I began before he could leave, "if there's a woman I might visit with. To pass the time and catch up with news," I added.

"Ailee?" Grahame had stepped out of the smithy and froze when he saw me standing at the fence with the second blacksmith.

I froze as well, and could have screamed in frustration when the blacksmith's friendly expression suddenly closed. He took a step back from me, as if I had some illness he might catch.

"Please excuse me," the blacksmith said coldly.

"If you could wait but a moment," I said, trying to stop him with words alone. "There's something I'd like to learn, a stitch. If you could but—"

But he was already striding past Grahame and into the smithy.

I stood forlorn, Faas lipping at my cape and Grahame looking at me with a stricken expression.

Then a change came over my husband. He drew up to his full height, a look of determination hardening the lines on his face. He gave me a silent command to stay with his hand raised and returned to the smithy.

He wasn't going to let the man get away with his treatment of me, I realized. He was going to confront him to defend my honor. A part of me was touched by the gesture. He was trying to make amends. But the damage had been too deeply inflicted. There was no way Grahame would be able to confront every person who rebuked me.

I turned away. How could I learn a stitch if no one would talk to me? I'd be stuck on Cadha's farm for the rest of my life, kneading dough and spinning wool and washing supper dishes and clothing. And there was nothing wrong with any of that, except I couldn't imagine it for my entire life with no change, no travel, no possibility of getting together with friends.

What friends? Elsie was lost, and I had no one else.

Not true. I had Grahame.

If I could forgive him.

Someone cleared his throat behind me. It was the young, slender man with the scarf. He was standing a few paces behind me, his hands tugging at the loop of the circle scarf.

"Forgive, *bitte*," he said in careful, broken English. "I hear."

My stomach dropped. Was he going to tell me to clear off? Or something even worse?

"I hear stitch," he continued, haltingly, searching for the words. "You, stitch?"

He plucked at his scarf.

I sucked in a breath in understanding. "Yes. No," I amended quickly. "I want to learn."

"You learn? *Frau Scheuling* stitch?" He held the scarf up. "Like this?"

"Yes! Please, do you know who might teach me?"

He glanced toward the smithy.

"If you could but introduce me," I pleaded.

The man seemed to have a little argument in his head. I knew it was over when he gave me a single nod. "Come, *bitte*."

CHAPTER TWENTY-THREE

The man led me down the space between the smithy and his house, past the plow leaning toward the wall and a wagon half-covered by a canvas tarpaulin. We went past a house standing at the back of the smithy and between two more until we were on another dirt road. It was narrow, and a few more trees grew amid the houses, with more gardens than yards, all furrowed for winter. It was quaint, with a sense of weathering but not quite age, not like Lifford. A worn-out newness, if that made any sense.

The house we came to was across the road. It was one of the older buildings with a tall tree overhanging the narrow porch. Chickens scratched freely in the yard. Two ruts led past the house to a barn beyond. The land rose behind the barn with pockets of clear-cut making way for pasture and field. The town ended beyond these homes. The forest might not be pressing in on it as it did at Cadha's, but it was there, lurking upon the hillside.

We paused on the porch before a door even lovelier than Mr. Wigart's. The man turned to face me. "Frau Scheuling, no English," he warned me. "I try."

I thanked him, too eager to fret over it. Besides, if this Frau Scheuling didn't know English, maybe she hadn't heard of me. It might be a blessing.

The man, whose name I'd not yet asked, opened the lovely carved door without knocking. The inside was dark compared to the brightness outdoors. It did not feel like a house thriving with life, either. There was a sense of loneliness, of dust and disuse that cast a pall of sadness over me. The air smelled stale, like old sweat and fermented bread. A threadbare rug covered the plank floors of the hall, and the wooden walls were bare but for a few candle sconces. Two doorways faced each other across the hall next to a set of stairs. The house for all its lack of decoration, had a more finished feel, as though it had been built all at once rather than piecemeal like Cadha's farmhouse.

The man led me into the room to the left, away from the stairs. This room was very different—warm and welcoming and lived in. Several rugs crossed over one another to cover most of the floor. Pale paper covered the walls, but I could hardly see the pattern for the items filling the space. Alongside wood carvings, small paintings, and embroidery of all designs hung elegant lanterns and sconces, several lit even this early in the day, giving off a ruddy glow and beeswax scent. It was a lifetime collection of whimsy and beauty and handcraft, and it overwhelmed me. I couldn't take it all in at once.

And then the furnishings that filled the room competed for my attention—large, heavy wooden chairs whose upholstery was buried under quilts and knitted lap blankets; small tables filled with curios and covered with elegant lace cloth; two couches thick with pillows; and a hearth burning cheerily to keep the chill at bay. Spools and balls of wool nestled in woven baskets beside several of the chairs, awaiting eager hands to knit them into useful garments. Some had projects already begun: a shawl here, a sock there, a pile of stocking caps of different sizes in another.

In the chair closest to the hearth sat a wizened old woman. Her gray hair was bound in coiled braids around her head, bare but for a thin linen cap trimmed in delicate lace. A heavy woolen shawl rested around her shoulders and a quilt blanket over her lap. She was easily the oldest person I'd ever seen, though I could not say if it was age or a hard life of toil that had wrinkled her face and hunched her shoulders. She looked frail, so frail that I wondered if she'd see another spring.

She smiled to see the man, and her expression brightened, though not enough to chase what looked to be a perpetual sorrow etched into the very lines of her face. She spoke a greeting in that odd, guttural language I'd heard at the postmaster's. The man bowed before kneeling in front of her to reply.

They spoke for a few minutes in their shared language. I tried not to fidget, standing with my hands clasped before me with a forced look of patience on my face. The old woman glanced at me once or twice, and the last time she did not look away but sat with her gaze boring holes into mine as if trying to study me from the inside out. It was a distinctive look, layered with age and experience and a wisdom gathered through years of hard living. I knew, without knowing how, that this was the only chance I'd get to convince her of my sincerity.

So I let the patience drop and put all my need and want into my own gaze, pleading with my eyes alone for her help. I could feel the desperation nipping at me, and I forced myself to recall that moist, toothy maw around my throat and the horror of being so close to death.

The old woman raised her wrinkled hand, silencing the man in mid-sentence. She beckoned me closer, and I stepped forward. She asked me a question, not unkindly.

"She asks name," the man told me.

"Ailee Donaghue," I answered, bobbing in curtsy.

"Helga Scheuling," the woman answered. She gestured to the man. "Jansen, *mein Enkel.*"

"I am grandson," Jansen explained.

Frau Scheuling asked another question, which Jansen translated for me.

"She asks you see before?" He plucked at the loop of scarf doubled around his neck.

"I have. On the crossing from Ireland. The cook wore one and said he'd had it from a German he'd met."

Jansen gave my answer to his grandmother, who nodded thoughtfully. She gestured to a nearby chair. I settled on the edge of the seat, too anxious to relax into the plush pillows.

"She asks, you know story of *Mönchskutte?*"

I tilted my head, as though that might make his words clearer. My bafflement must have been obvious, for the old woman smiled. She reached out to run her bony fingers over the edge of the capelet Cadha had lent me.

"*Mönchskutte,*" she repeated.

"I'm sorry," I said. "I don't understand."

She didn't wait for a translation but began speaking. She spoke for a time, then paused and nodded to her grandson. What followed was an old tale told to me in broken English between pauses of listening to German. I was perched on the very edge of my chair by the end of it, threatening to spill onto the floor.

In ancient days, beasts roamed the woods freely, evil beasts that stole children from their cradles and tricked travelers into straying into dangerous places. *Teufel Wölfe*, she called them with a tremble in her voice. They were deadly, and though there were many hunts for them, still they thrived. And then a priest was attacked but spared. The hood he wore, a gift from his homeland, had protected him. From that day on, the traveling priests wore the hoods and they were left unmolested. Word spread, and the women learned how to make these hoods, which wool to use—*ungewaschen Schafe*, unwashed sheep, the grandson explained—and which to avoid—she spat out the word *Ziege* with a shake of her head. "Not goat," the grandson whispered.

Over the years, the hoods changed into the looped scarf. "*Ohne Haube*," the woman said, and Jansen added, "No hood. This." He plucked once more at his scarf.

And it clicked. A cowl, I realized. A monk's cowl, without the hood.

"Were they blessed?" Did that work against the beasts? Was it like St. Patrick driving out the snakes? The divine aiding the holy? And how would that help me? I was about as far from holy as I could be.

The man frowned and repeated my question. The woman laughed, a sharp, shockingly deep sound that startled me.

"She says *alte Magie*. Old magic." Jansen looked apologetic, his back toward his grandmother. "It is old story, ja? Just old. But she . . ." He hesitated, searching for the word. "She believe. Make these— tell us to wear."

Suddenly I was angry with him. "She's right to do so," I told him heatedly. "These beasts, these *Teufel Wölfe*, I've seen one. It almost killed me."

Jansen's eyes widened, but then doubt dulled the brightness. "Just old story," he muttered again.

His grandmother prodded him, not gently, and barked a couple of words.

"She asks you will learn? She looks to teach," he added. "I promise help. You learn, she happy, ja? In peace."

Ah, now it all made sense, his bringing me here. The old woman was dying, and she wanted to pass on what she knew. If the others in town were like her grandson, no doubt she'd been unable to teach the skill she thought so necessary. Her old stories were thought just wives' tales told to frighten children in the nursery but not to heed once they'd grown.

I knew better. "Yes," I said. "Ja," I added, looking to Frau Scheuling. "Please, teach me."

She smiled. She sent her grandson on some errand with a few curt phrases, and I asked him before he left to tell Grahame where I was. He looked happy to leave us in peace. When he had left the room, she took up a basket from the floor by her chair. In it was a ball of undyed wool and a strange wooden tool. It wasn't a needle but a narrow carved hook that widened into a flat handle that fit easily into her bent and gnarled hand. She held it up for me to see.

"*Hakenstift.*" She had me repeat the word until I said it correctly.

She lifted the wool, pulling the loose strand free. It was thickly spun, almost raw in places. She ran it between her fingers, then handed me the ball and gestured. I did the same and felt the oiliness in the wool, like raw wool feels after it's sheared from the sheep.

The wool oil. I had guessed correctly. Treating my shawl had saved my life.

She took the wool from me and made a loop in the strand to insert the hook. And then, I watched as a chain grew from her steady stitching. When she was satisfied with the length, she joined the ends together. As I sat watching, she began working into each stitch in a round, and the loop grew so much more quickly than I could knit. She moved the *Hakenstift* deftly, hardly looking at her work as she stuck the tool through a stitch, grabbed up a loop of wool, and pulled it through. She worked more by feel than sight, and I sat amazed.

Suddenly, she stopped and handed the *Hakenstift*, wool, and the loop of cowl to me. I took hold of the tool, and she tutted between her teeth and changed my grip. I took hold of the wool, and she did the same. Only when she was satisfied with how I held both did she let me begin.

It was trickier than she'd made it look, and I fumbled along for several stitches while trying to get the feel of the strange new tool and how to work it into the wool. I wondered if Elsie made cheyne lace the same way, though I knew both the hook and thread would be much finer. I wished she were here to learn this with me.

My first round was a mess of oddly sized stitches. The wool was more difficult to handle than I had expected, bulky with a slight tackiness, though it left my hands soft from the oil. I feared it might loosen my grip on the *Hakenstift*, but the wood seemed to love the oil, and the tool was shaped for grasping.

By the middle of the second round, I was beginning to get the sense of holding both. The first clue I had that I was catching on was Frau Scheuling's breath of pleasure, not quite a laugh. I looked up to see her smiling at me with joy. She reached out to caress my face.

"*Danke*," she whispered to me. "*Danke schön.*"

Affection rushed through me, followed quickly by regret. I could spend days by this woman's side, listening to her stories, learning what she would teach me. But I knew I only had these precious few hours, and those were ending far too quickly.

I took her hand in mine, pressing it. "Thank you, Frau Scheuling." I tried to put all my emotion into those few words.

She blinked and offered me a sad smile, then gestured for me to return to my stitching. I knew I should excuse myself and go, that Grahame would be worried for me, but I couldn't pull myself away. Not yet. So I picked up the *Hakenstift* and continued.

The woman began talking as I worked, and while I didn't understand what she said, I could tell by the cadence in her voice that she was telling me a story. She must have been a marvelous storyteller to her children and grandchildren. Her voice was full of life, changing pitch and rhythm with the tale. I wished Jansen were here to translate for me, but even not understanding the language, I enjoyed hearing her speak. She'd correct my hold on the *Hakenstift* or the wool without pausing in her tale. When she laughed, so did I, and it was amid one of these brief outbursts that Grahame came in on us.

Jansen was with him, looking apologetic. Grahame had that worried expression he gets when he is fretting for me. I was surprised to recognize it, but I shouldn't have been. It seems in our time together, he'd spent more time worried for me than pleased. But much of that was his own doing.

I didn't rush to my feet in a wave of guilt like I might have a few months ago. Instead, I turned to Frau Scheuling. "My husband, Grahame," I told her by way of introduction.

Jansen came forward and began repeating my words in German, but his grandmother waved him off. She gestured Grahame over. He bowed in that curious, fluid way of his before approaching. He smelled of the outside, cool and crisp with undertones of smoke and hot iron. How long had he been inside the smithy before finding me missing? I pushed the question aside, not sure I wanted to know the answer.

Frau Scheuling spoke at some length to Grahame, and when Jansen began to translate, Grahame held up his hand. He answered her, much more haltingly, and I wondered if he spoke German the way Jansen spoke English.

Frau Scheuling rose stiffly to her feet, Jansen rushing to her side to offer his arm, which she ignored. She came to stand toe to toe with my husband, and Grahame towered over her.

She gave him another round of words. The color on Grahame's face deepened, and he cast me a sidelong look. And then he gave Frau Scheuling a single, steady nod.

Satisfied, though by what I had no idea, the old woman returned to her seat. I offered the wool and *Hakenstift*, along with the beginnings of the cowl, back to her. She accepted and returned them to the basket. As I stood, however, she gripped my arm.

"*Bitte*," she said, handing me the basket.

I didn't know what to say. Tears burnt my eyes and I had to blink them away. I wanted to tell her that she didn't know what this meant to me, but I could see in her face that she did. She knew exactly what it meant to me.

She gestured me closer and I leaned down, clutching the basket as if someone might try to wrest it away. She took my face in both of her hands, and they were cool and light on my cheeks.

"*Sie sind da draußen*," she said in a dark voice. I didn't know what the words meant, but I could hear the meaning behind them. She was warning me.

I nodded. She pulled me closer and kissed both of my cheeks before releasing me. I curtsied to her, though I wanted to wrap my arms around her and weep like a lost child who'd just been showed the way home.

"How do you say thank you?" I asked quietly.

Grahame answered me, and I repeated his words.

"*Danke*, Frau Scheuling."

She gave me a gentle smile and settled back in her chair with a sigh. As I stepped away, she closed her eyes. I hoped it was only sleep that fell over her. A foreboding crept over me. I suspected I would never see her alive again.

Chapter Twenty-Four

Jansen saw us out of the house. He thanked me over and over for letting his grandmother teach me and for listening to her 'old stories,' as he called them. I thanked him in return, and still clutching the basket, followed Grahame down the street.

We didn't speak as we returned to the wagon. Thom stood at the team's head, the oxen shuffling in place, ready to be underway. The load in the back had changed, though it wasn't any fuller than it had been. Barrels and bags took the place of the wool, and the harness was gone, a couple gardening tools it its place. I remembered the ball of wool Cadha had given me to trade, but I had no desire to try to find someone who would trade with me. I'd keep it and practice with it instead. The wool was washed, unfortunately, but it'd still serve, and I could treat it afterwards.

The dogs leapt up at my approach and both of them had to sniff me before they settled. Thom moved the team towards home while Grahame slung his musket over his shoulder. I thought about riding so I could practice more, but I remembered how the wagon bounced me so. I thought it best to keep my bones and teeth in one piece and practice once we'd returned. So I walked in silence with the men and dogs.

I broke the silence only when we paused to eat the meal Cadha had sent with us.

"What did Frau Scheuling say to me at the end?" I asked Grahame.

He hesitated, staring off into the woods.

"Grahame?"

"*Sie sind da draußen*," he said quietly. "They are out there."

I stared at him, the warmth leeching from me. And then I looked into the woods, already feeling the prick of a dozen hungry eyes watching me.

"She's an old woman, Ailee," Grahame said, trying to reassure me.

"And she's seen much," I said in a hushed voice.

Grahame stopped trying to reassure me. Instead, as we readied to make way again, he made a show of checking his musket.

It might have been just a show, but I felt better that he had it. I drew up my hood, called the dogs closer, and walked in silence for the rest of the journey.

We had to light the lanterns before reaching the farm. When we finally arrived, even the dogs were tired. They slunk off to the barn without complaint. Grahame and Thom followed them to unyoke the oxen and unload the wagon. I carried my precious basket into the house and took it to my room.

I had just nestled it in a safe place near the bed when Cadha came into the doorway.

"I thought I heard you about," she said. "Men gone to unload?"

"Yes."

"How was town?"

I was uncertain how to answer. It had been painful and embarrassing and wonderful.

"Fine."

Cadha gave me a dubious look. I wasn't sure what she sensed about me that suggested it had been far from fine.

"Can I do anything to help with supper?" I asked to distract her.

"The meal's done. I put some back for you. You can fetch it out for the others. In the kitchen by the hearth." She left me, and I heard her descending the stairs.

With another glance at the basket, I followed after.

I laid supper out at the table, just two places, since Thom took his meals elsewhere. It was the first time Grahame and I had sat at table together, just the two of us, since leaving Ireland. It was a strange feeling, but not unwelcomed. We needed more time together, just the two of us.

The house was quiet when Grahame and Thom came in. Thom took his meal and left with a nod in my direction. Grahame settled into his chair, looking more uneasy than I'd seen in a while.

Of course, I didn't see much of him lately.

We ate in silence. My shoulder was stiff from the long walk, with just a touch of ache to remind me that I hadn't completely healed. I tried to hide it from Grahame, but he must have noticed, for his first words to me since our return were about my shoulder.

"Does it need tending?"

There wasn't much to tend, really, though a hot compress was useful, I'd found. But I wasn't going to let the chance to keep Grahame closer slip past me.

"I think so."

"I can bring Cadha—"

"She'll be busy," I interrupted him. "I'm sure you and I can manage."

Grahame stilled, then gave a slow nod. "I'm sure we can."

It was like we'd agreed to something more than fussing with my shoulder. I hoped we were both thinking on the same matter.

Grahame helped me clear the dishes after we'd finished the meal. Cadha was in the wash room, and she must have sensed something for she sent me on my way, telling me she'd see to the washing, something she rarely·did since I had learned her way of it. I went by the kitchen house to see if there was any water left to heat. There was, and the fire hadn't been completely banked. Grahame had disappeared, but I tried not to fret. If I had to, I'd seek him out in the barn.

I poured the hot water into one of Cadha's clay mugs, the steam rising in plumes into the chilly air. I carried the mug into the house with a scrap of cloth to keep from scalding my hand. When I opened the door to our room, Grahame was inside, sitting on the bed. He stood as I entered.

"What can I do?"

"Hold this," I said, offering him the mug and cloth. I closed the door and moved to my side of the room. Self-conscious, I turned away to remove my outer garments. It was odd to still feel like such a stranger with my own husband. We'd been wed for months now, but circumstance kept nudging its way between us. I was getting tired of it.

When I was undressed to my shift, I settled on the bed. It was cold in the room, and I drew the quilt up over my lap.

"If you could soak the cloth," I suggested. Grahame stuck it into the mug. He looked out of place doing something that was akin to woman's work. It was almost comical how he was standing, holding a mug dripping water with a rag sticking out of it, watching it in great concentration. I couldn't help but chuckle.

His sharp, dark gaze found me, and I sobered.

And then smiled again.

"You don't look like yourself, standing there," I said by way of explanation.

"How should I look?" He seemed genuinely curious.

"I'm not sure. More . . . Grahame. With a knife and a piece of wood or bit of leather. Some tool to keep you busy. You always keep busy."

I watched as his shoulders relaxed and his stance eased. He moved over to the chair, still placed next to the bed, and settled into it.

"Not always."

"Always," I argued. "Especially when you're upset."

He frowned.

"I haven't seen much of you these past couple weeks," I went on, the words pouring out of me like hot water out of the kettle, all plumy smoke and heat. "You keep away from me. I don't know why. I can guess, but I don't know if I'd be wrong. You said it wouldn't be like the ship, Grahame, but it is. Only the water has become forest, and Elsie isn't here to keep me company."

Grahame looked away, but not before I caught a flash of shame crossing his face. "I did wrong by you." His words were choked.

Emotions swelled in me, and I had to struggle for a moment to find my voice. But Grahame kept speaking, surprising me.

"I shouldn't have spoken to Niall. It wasn't my place. But please believe me—" He turned to me, leaning forward with a pleading look. "I didn't know how he felt. If I had suspected he'd break faith with me, I'd never have spoken as I had."

"He's angry with you."

Grahame nodded.

"Because of me."

"It isn't you, Ailee. He'd be angry at any woman of position that I might have wed."

"But you married me, so it is because of me."

Grahame drew in a long breath, but he finally relented. "Yes."

I looked away. It was one thing to suspect it, but it was another to know it for fact. I didn't see how any of this could be mended between the brothers, not while I lived amongst them.

"That compress will get cold," I said at last. I raised my arm to draw the shift off my shoulder.

"Let me." The bed sank as Grahame moved onto it. With gentle hands, he pulled the shift away from my wound and pressed the compress against it.

It felt so good—the heat of the cloth, Grahame's warm hands on my skin, his steady, strong presence next to me. I wanted to curl up against him and forget the rift that had opened between us.

So I did. He was my husband. He was trying to make amends. Alone in our room together, curled against his strong bulk, I could forget the spitefulness of Niall and Ruthie, forget the prejudice of the townsfolk, even forget the weeks of pain and despair.

The only thing I couldn't forget was the cat-beast and its grip on my neck. I knew Grahame would try to hunt it when he could, but I feared that not even he could protect me from it should it decide to attack again.

But I knew something that could, and now I knew how to make it.

The next morning, I woke in Grahame's embrace for the first time in far too long. Pleasure rippled through me, and I snuggled closer to him, feeling rather than seeing him in the darkness of the early hours. If he was awake, he gave no sign of it, so I allowed myself several precious moments of lying in bed as if I didn't have a bevy of morning chores to rush to complete.

I wondered if I was wrong to give in to my pleasure. Should I still be angry with him? He had broken my trust and shared my secret.

A secret I'd not even have if I'd not done the unimaginable first.

And then I'd never have met Grahame. Never left home or traveled on a ship and met Elsie. Never faced a creature in the woods.

Between the events I'd never have changed and those I wished never had happened, it was no wonder I constantly felt at odds with myself. How does one reconcile such things? Was it even possible?

I should just give in and take happiness where I could. And this morning I was happy, or at least content.

I knew it wouldn't last. How could it with Niall intruding with his constant displeasure?

Grahame stirred at last in a way that told me he'd been awake for some time and had been as reluctant as I to part. But now there was no escaping it—chores awaited.

Grahame lit a candle, and we dressed in a companionable silence. I felt the beginnings of how we'd been before, with shy flirting and stolen moments. It could never return to what it had been, when my secret was silent and safe, but it was another beginning. I'd take it.

Grahame left first, giving me a slight smile as he inclined his head before leaving the room. I gathered myself and followed, taking the candle to light the way. Grahame had eyes like a cat and never seemed to need a light in the house. I wasn't quite ready for that.

Downstairs, I pulled on one of Cadha's old coats before pushing open the back door. The sight that greeted me was one that I'd always remember.

The farm had changed overnight.

Instead of defined outbuildings, hunched shapes mounded with snow greeted me. The candlelight glistened off the whiteness and reached farther than usual as the snow reflected the light. And the air—crisp and wet at once, the cold biting my cheeks and the end of my nose. The snow rose almost to my knees, and a trail broken through it showed what path the others had taken when they left the house.

Horace and Edgar raced over, and the snow parted before them like frosting. They circled before me, barking with excitement. Snow caked their backs and formed balls on their tails and belly, but they didn't seem to care.

"You dogs hush!" Cadha shouted from the kitchen house door. Light spilled from the doorway to glitter across the snow. "Oh, Ailee. Good. I need your help."

"But this . . ." I didn't know what to say. I'd never seen its like. It was beautiful and elegant and foreign. It made everything look bundled up, like a blanket had been laid over the farm.

"Give it a day and you'll be sick of it," Cadha said without enthusiasm. She retreated back into the kitchen house.

I took a tentative step forward. I sank halfway to my knee, my skirts pooling around me on top of the snow. I kept off the trail the others had made, delighting in making my own. The dogs leapt around me, breaking their own wide trails. I couldn't wait for the sun to rise, to see it all in the light of day.

It was the most amazing morning of my life. The cold tucked into every fold of my clothing, but I didn't care. I roamed the farm, admiring each building in the light of my candle, seeing them as though for the first time. And when the sun finally rose, I stood transfixed as the first light broke across the white stillness of the fields. It looked pure, untouched. Holy. And I was blessed to witness it.

When I finally forced myself to turn toward the kitchen house, I saw Grahame standing outside the barn, watching me. He offered me a smile, and I grinned in return. Before he turned away, however, I saw a shadow cross his face.

A month ago, I'd have wondered at it. I knew better now. He was looking into the days to come and to the challenges before us.

With a heavy sigh, I made my way through the snow toward the kitchen house, dragging my sodden skirts with me.

CHAPTER TWENTY-FIVE

Dearest Elsie,

I've so much to write and nearly no paper left. When I woke four days ago, there was snow. Heapings of it, covering the farm. I wonder if the same snow fell where you are.

Where are you? We went into Germantown but had next to no news of you. I am worried. If I could talk Grahame into going to Philadelphia to search for you, I would, but now that winter's come, there's little chance of it. Come the spring, if I've not had word from you, I will convince him.

For I've so much to tell you, both good and bad . . .

I paused in my writing, looking up to stare across the parlor. Cadha sat by the fire, mending a pair of Niall's breeches. Grahame was working on a bit of leather harness. Niall was smoking his pipe and staring into the fire. And there sat Thom, near Grahame, carving a new wooden trencher. It was so strange to see the quiet man in the parlor with us, but there he sat.

As winter closed around the farm, our daily life changed. The men spent time inspecting the insides of the buildings, making sure the roofs were withstanding the weather. They kept careful watch on the livestock and on the surrounding forest, wary for beasts that might come out of the woods to hunt our animals. Cadha and I still cooked and cleaned, but we didn't send Thom to the stream for water. We melted the snow by the bucketful, and for once, we had plenty of water. I was pleased that Cadha liked to keep a kettle warming on the edge of the cooking fire, because it never took long for the water to cool and for ice to try to glaze across the top, and it took so long to heat water when it was that cold.

Most of the work we finished by nightfall, which came earlier, leaving only the supper dishes to finish after we'd eaten. We spent longer hours in the parlor, gathered close to the fire. Cadha would knit and I'd spin or we'd both sew. And Thom sat with us now.

His indenture was up. He was no longer Cadha's servant, but his own man.

I turned back to my letter, finally putting into words the events of the last month. It was easier to write than I'd imagined, the pain of Ruthie's ugliness to me dampened by the joy of learning how to make Beacham's scarf.

Cowl, I corrected.

I usually went upstairs early, before Cadha could send me, both to avoid the embarrassment of being sent to bed like a child and to work secretly on the cowl. I didn't want to explain to Cadha what it was and what it meant, so for now, I kept it to myself. Grahame knew I was working on it, but I was fairly certain he wouldn't speak of it. Why would he? It was woman's work.

I finished my letter all too soon, running out of paper before I ran out of words. That was what I should have looked for in Germantown—sheets of paper. Now I'd have nothing more to write on until we could get to town again.

It was a good time to sneak off upstairs. I bid everyone good night, even Niall, though he ignored me as usual. It pleased me to seem like the forgiving one in our relationship, though, and his stubborn insistence on ignoring me only made him look more in the wrong. I could tell by the sidelong look Cadha gave him that she wasn't pleased.

I took my letter and the candle upstairs, lighting a second candle once I reached our room. I'd pulled the little table over to the bedside, and I placed both candles there. I would have thought it extravagant to have more than one candle lit before Cadha showed me the stores she had of them. Apparently the late Morley Donaghue enjoyed making them as a hobby, and he'd left his widow well set for light with tapers and pillars of all sizes and sorts. It was an odd sort of hobby, but one I was thankful for. I liked the extra light.

I undressed and snuggled deep under the blankets before pulling the precious basket up next to me. I couldn't help but think of Frau Scheuling. It had been less than a week since I'd met her, but with the snowfall and the change in our daily routine, it felt far longer. I wondered how she was.

And then I went to work.

I was pleased with my progress. The cowl was thicker by several rows and my stitches were getting more even as I progressed. I'd never taken to knitting this quickly, so I was surprised by how quickly this stitch was coming to me.

Grahame came in only a few minutes after I'd settled with my stitching. He wasn't usually this quick to come upstairs, but he looked tired. I paused in my work to look him over.

He was slowly easing out of his work clothes. His trousers were still damp around the ankles where the snow had gotten into his boots. His stockings were sodden. The shirt he'd worn under his heavy coat was sweat-stained. His black hair was also matted where it had dried salty from sweat. When he finally stood in his undershirt, he stretched with a hushed groan, shoulder muscles rippling under his shirt. I grew unaccustomedly warm at the sight.

"You work so hard," I said quietly to distract myself. "Have you always?"

"I suppose." Grahame eased into the bed, and I felt his body relax under the blankets.

"When did you learn to speak German?" My, but the questions were suddenly pouring from me. Poor man. No doubt he wished only to sleep, but it was rare to have these moments alone. And it was always thrilling to have his full attention.

"Aboard ship. A crewmate spoke it."

"This was before you took over the farm in Donegal?"

"Yes." He turned over to look at me. "I haven't told you of that time, have I?"

I gave a little shake of my head, not wanting to press him but still hoping he'd say more.

"Three years I served aboard ship. Hard years, but good ones."

"Why did you leave it?"

"I had word my father was ill."

I had no response to that, so I changed subjects. "Will Thom stay with Cadha, do you think? To help with the farm?"

"Not likely. He's waiting for spring, then he'll take his freedom dues and move on."

"Freedom dues?"

"A payment of sorts. To help get him started. Cadha offered him land, but he wants to go south."

"Why south? What's wrong with the land here?"

"Nothing, he's just heard of a place in Virginia colony. Shaw told me a handful of folks moved there two years ago and had sent back word. Shaw's planning to join them this spring, after the thaw. Thom might do the same."

Which meant Marjorie would be leaving, too. And then there would be no one but the likes of Ruthie and Mrs. Giverns for social calls. Not that I'd be invited to any.

I was being harsh towards Mrs. Giverns, who had stayed to help me after the attack, but I had also gotten the impression she'd only stayed because Cadha had wished it.

"Ailee?"

Grahame must have read my pensive look.

"I like Marjorie. I'll be sorry not to know her better."

He reached for my hand, but I was still holding the *Hakenstift* and wool.

"What's this?" Grahame touched the *Hakenstift*.

"Frau Scheuling called it a . . . hakenstiff." That wasn't quite right. "*Hakenstift*." That was it.

"May I?" He held his hand open. I pulled up the stitch I'd just worked to keep it from coming loose and shook the hook from it to hand him the tool. He turned it over, running a fingertip over the wood.

"*Hakenstift*," he said. "Do you know what it means?"

I shook my head.

"Hook-pen." He smiled and handed the hook-pen back to me. "The frau gave it to you?"

"Yes. I think she was lonely."

"When the roads clear, we could visit her again."

I gave him a smile. It was a kind offer, and I knew he made it because he'd seen my disappointment in hearing that Marjorie was leaving. But I knew in my heart that when I next went to town, Frau Scheuling would no longer be there. And there'd be no other friends to make. Not for me.

That night began a new ritual for me and Grahame, one that I looked forward to the rest of the day. I'd go up to bed early and work for a time on my stitching and after a time, Grahame would join me. And we'd lie in bed together and speak of little things while I stitched. Grahame would talk of the sheep and how they were wintering. He thought a lot about what to watch for, things like sore mouth and foot rot and wool-eating. He talked about Cadha's cow and the calf she was expecting. He even talked about the chickens.

Granted, I plied him with questions to keep his words coming. I learned a great deal during those evening talks, more than I ever thought I'd need to know about farm animals and what it took to keep them healthy. I had no idea chickens needed to eat grit or that the goats didn't care for drafts.

I asked more about Thom and his freedom dues, wondering what he might get in return for so many years in service.

"Several bushels of grain and corn," Grahame told me. "A few tools. A handful of sheep and one of the dogs. That bargain was between him and Niall, though, not on the contract. Thom helped train them."

"Which one?"

"Horace, I think he said."

"But what will Horace and Edgar do being parted? They're like brothers."

"They are brothers," Grahame corrected gently. "And they'll manage."

"But—"

"Ailee," Grahame interrupted, reaching out to stroke my cheek. He must have realized that I liked it when he did that. "Horace will have Thom. And Edgar will have you."

I pursed my lips. "He's Niall's dog."

"He's more yours now. And Niall's noticed it."

"I knew he was holding that against me. Just because his dog favors me—" I began hotly, but Grahame hushed me.

"I don't want you to fret about Niall. He's my problem."

"Grahame—"

But he sat up to look me in the eyes. "Niall's my problem."

There was no arguing when he got that look. I nodded meekly.

Satisfied, Grahame offered me one of his slow smiles. "Aren't you finished with that?" he asked, glancing at the cowl in my hands.

A warmth spread through me quite suddenly, and I wasn't quite so eager to continue my stitching. I stuffed it back into the basket and set it on the floor. Grahame leaned over me to blow the candles out.

"You're looking satisfied with yourself," Cadha said as we worked in the bake house. The room was warm, almost too warm for all the layers I wore, but it kept the dough pliant. In the last three weeks, we'd had two more snowfalls, each building upon the other to leave deep drifts against the buildings. But Cadha had been wrong. I delighted in each one.

"And you and Grahame seem more at ease," she continued.

"Do we?"

Cadha straightened from the mound of dough she'd been kneading. "Acting all innocent, are we?"

I blushed.

"The way you two are going," she said with a satisfied smile, "there'll be a bairn in the house by next harvest."

My blush deepened and a curious warmth spread through me.

"Which wouldn't bother me none," Cadha said, turning back to her dough. "I always imagined children around, but it never worked out that way for me. I'll settle for loving on yours and giving them back to you when they fuss."

I laughed, and she chuckled along with me. I couldn't imagine having a child. I'd never given it serious thought. Oh, I knew it would happen, probably, but in the distant future. Like growing old or dying—it was something that happened later, after marriage.

With a start, I realized it was later. It should be happening.

"Do you think . . ." I paused, not sure what I wanted to ask. Would it be safe? Would I die? Would the child? Bad things happened to women during childbirth, and we were far from midwives and physicians.

I felt Cadha's hand on my arm and looked to find her standing next to me, her apron dusted with flour, bits of dough still clinging to her fingers. "Don't you start fretting. When the time comes, I'll see you through it."

"Can you?"

"Birthed enough lambs. Can't see how it's much different." She gave me a wry laugh, and I knew she was jesting with me, but I felt better.

"I am glad to see you and Grahame back to rights," she told me, sobering. "Now tell him to settle things with his brother so we can move on."

"I'm not sure that will happen soon," I warned her. "Neither of them seem inclined."

"Convince Grahame. We need peace in this house."

I nodded, but I was dubious. For one, I wasn't inclined to set things 'back to rights' with Niall. Not unless he was willing to apologize and help mend some of the damage he'd done. I had no idea how he might do so, but it would be one of my conditions.

I decided to speak to Grahame about it tonight. At least then I could tell Cadha that I'd tried.

I left the bake house some time later to check for any eggs. Fewer and fewer of the hens were laying, but Grahame had told me that was natural. Still, I looked each day, hopeful. The dogs leapt up as I passed them. The latest snowfall had been packed into trails between the outbuildings, and I kept to them so my skirts wouldn't be so wet by the end of the day. The dogs didn't seem to mind getting wet, however, and they leapt into places where the snow mounded. Edgar especially loved to play in the snow.

"Horace! Edgar!"

Niall was shouting for them. He'd taken to doing so a couple times each day, though usually I was inside when he did. The dogs would disappear for a while, but I'd leave a building to find them waiting for me once again.

Niall stepped out from the barn and froze when he saw me. The dogs stilled, looking between me and Niall as though uncertain whom they should follow. I silently willed them to go to Niall. To make it easier for them, I turned away to go to the kitchen house.

The dogs hesitated, then followed me.

Oh, how I could have cursed them. The last thing I wanted was to make things worse between Niall and Grahame.

"Go," I whispered to them, making a little shooing gesture with my hand where Niall hopefully wouldn't see.

"Horace! Edgar!" Niall's shout of command was strained with anger. And it was nearly right behind me.

I stopped, hoping the dogs would slink to their master. But they hesitated again.

"You selfish, useless trollop. You think to have my dogs, too?"

The blood drained from my face, and half-turning, I stared at Niall, stunned. Niall didn't stop there but came up to stand over me, rage twisting his face into something unimaginable. I tried to step away, but he grabbed my arm in a bruising grip.

"You don't belong here," he spat out. "You're nothing but someone to warm Grahame's bed. If you died tomorrow, he'd not remember your name come summer." His grip was fearsome, and I gasped in pain, trying to twist out of it.

And then something large and fast-moving broke between us, tearing Niall away from me. I fell back, suddenly free, arm aching, and landed in the snow. The cold shocked me, but not as much as what was struggling in the snow just a little ways from me.

Grahame hunched over his brother, raining blow upon blow on the younger man. Niall had his arms raised trying to block the punches, but he grunted in pain with each pummel of those unrelenting fists.

By God, Grahame would kill him.

Struggling against my tangled skirts, I dragged myself over to the brothers.

"Grahame, stop! Stop!" I pulled at his arm, trying to halt the furious blows. It was like trying to pull against iron. "Stop now!"

And just like that, the blows stopped.

I sat back, panting. Grahame was huffing with exertion. Or was it fury still? I couldn't tell. His expression was blacker than I'd ever seen it. His knuckles were cut and bleeding, but that was nothing to Niall. Blood gushed from his nose and from a cut above his eye. He had half-curled in pain under Grahame, groaning.

"*O mo chreach* . . ." Cadha swore in the old tongue, but her voice fell away in shock. She was standing outside the kitchen house, staring with a look of utter horror.

Thom came up, halting in his steps when he saw us. His expression, usually so passive, mirrored Cadha's.

Then, almost as one, they both looked at me.

I wanted to flee. I wanted to run as far and fast as I could, anything to get away from those accusing stares. But I didn't. I stood, taking a deep breath.

"We need hot water," I said. "And clean rags. Thom, help

Grahame get Niall to his room. Cadha, we'll need your ointment." I waited, holding my breath, to see what they would do.

Slowly, Grahame stood. He stared down at his brother, his face devoid of emotion. Then he gestured to Thom. Together, the two men helped Niall rise, groaning, from the torn and blood-speckled snow.

I turned and started toward the kitchen house. Cadha stepped aside as I approached, granting me entry. I didn't wait to see what she would do. I took a heavy cloth and pulled the kettle from its place heating at the hearth. I took one of the wooden bowls and stuck it under my arm, then grabbed one of the bags of clean rags from where it hung on the wall as I left the kitchen house.

Only the dogs waited for me outside. They didn't leap about but followed me with their heads low, as if waiting for punishment.

"It wasn't your fault," I said to them before I went into the house. "You are good dogs."

Edgar wagged his tail at the sound of my voice, but Horace peered up from under a heavy brow. I could see the uncertainty and worry in his brown eyes.

I left them waiting by the back door and went straight to Niall's room.

They were all there. Grahame and Thom stood several paces back from Niall's bed, but Cadha stood over the younger man, whispering to him. She fell silent as I entered.

I set the rags down and put the bowl on the narrow table standing by the nearest wall. A linen cloth covered the top of the table, and a pair of pewter candlesticks stood at either end. It was an elegant display of sophistication in an otherwise plain room.

I poured hot water into the bowl, set the kettle on the floor, and carried the bowl and rags over to Cadha. She began cleaning Niall, dipping a clean rag into the steaming bowl to wipe the blood from his face.

I dumped the bowl three times out of the window that Thom opened for me. The bloody water melted the snow below into a red puddle.

Cadha smeared ointment onto the bruises darkening on his face. Niall lay silent, not even moaning, as she worked. I thought him unconscious until he whispered something to her through his split lips.

Cadha drew back and gestured to Grahame. "He wants you."

Grahame stepped over to the bedside. He was looking at his brother as though he didn't know him.

My chest squeezed with apprehension and guilt.

Grahame knelt by the bedside and leaned closer. Niall's broken lips moved, but I couldn't hear what he said. I watched Grahame for any sign of emotion, but nothing touched the empty darkness in his eyes.

He stood abruptly and left the room. He didn't look at me as he did.

I wanted to go after him, but I knew that now was not the time. I busied myself with cleaning up the stained rags, bundling them into the empty bowl to carry out. Cadha drew a chair over to Niall's side. Thom picked up the cool kettle and rag bag and followed me from the room.

He followed me all the way outside. The dogs whined as we left the house, slinking over to us with tucked tails.

I let the bowl fall out of my hands and fell to my knees to wrap my arms around Horace's strong neck. Sobs wracked my body.

I felt Thom's arm around my shoulders.

"Wasn't your doing," he said in a soothing voice.

I raised my face from Horace's wet coat. "I feel like it was."

"And I know it. But this is between the brothers. You just got caught in the middle."

I took a steadying breath. "You're a good man, Thom."

He looked embarrassed. "Come now. Can't let you take cold." He helped me to my feet. Together, we went to the kitchen house to refill the kettle. I went to leave the bloody rags in the wash room, but Thom stopped me. He took them, bowl and all. "Best see to dinner," he told me. "Cadha will be occupied today."

Of course. I thanked him before he left. I heard him outside, talking to the dogs, telling them the same thing he'd told me.

Numbly, I went through the motions of preparing dinner. I couldn't imagine anyone would eat it.

CHAPTER TWENTY-SIX

Grahame didn't come to bed that night. I honestly didn't expect him to. I stayed awake long into the night, the basket on the blanket next to me, but I didn't stitch. I stared, seeing over and over again Grahame hurling himself at his brother, the blows raining down on Niall, the blood speckling the snow. How could we ever come back from that?

The next morning, Cadha told me to have Thom kill a chicken to make broth. I didn't have the nerve to ask after Niall, not yet.

I found Thom starting the fire in the kitchen house. He merely nodded when I made Cadha's request.

"How are the dogs?" I asked him before he left. They hadn't been waiting for me.

"Fine. In the barn."

The rest of the day was long and silent.

When Niall finally emerged from his room the following morning, he moved as if every step pained him. His face was swollen and ugly with bruises, his nose twice its normal size and crooked. He carried one arm like his shoulder ached, something I could well understand. Cadha saw him seated at the table where I had laid out porridge and bread with jam and butter. Cadha and I both sat. She watched Niall pensively, and I watched them both, waiting for something to happen.

Grahame came into the room, Thom following. He stopped when he saw Niall sitting there, but then he continued to his seat. Thom took his helping and left. I wished I could follow after him.

Of all the meals I'd taken in that house, that breakfast was the most strained. I didn't recall the taste of the porridge or the sweetness of the jam. No one spoke. We sat long enough to choke down our meal, Niall often actually choking if he took too large a bite, and then as if reaching a silent agreement, we all rose. Grahame left the house. Cadha saw Niall to the parlor while I tidied up the remainder of the meal.

Cadha found me in the wash room, working on the laundry.

"Has Grahame spoken to you?" she asked.

I shook my head.

"What happened, Ailee?"

I stopped, elbow deep in cooling wash water. "Niall grabbed me."

"He did not!" She didn't say it in argument but as if she couldn't imagine such a thing.

Without a word, I pushed my sleeve up with a damp hand, exposing the ugly bruising on my upper arm.

Cadha drew in a sharp breath between her teeth. "Why did you not tell me?"

"Niall needed you more." I let the sleeve fall and went back to washing.

"Ailee—" Cadha began, but she was unable to continue.

"I'll see to supper again," I told her.

"No, I'll see to it. You'll be busy enough in here."

And she left me to my washing and my circling thoughts.

That night, Grahame came to our room. It was late, but I was still awake, a single candle alight. I set my stitching aside.

He sat on the edge of the bed, his back to me. I could just see his profile. His jaw was tense under the dark beard. His hands, resting on his knees, had rags wrapped over his knuckles.

I don't know how long he would have sat there if I'd not moved. I'm not certain what compelled me to move, but I couldn't sit quietly while he wrestled with the thoughts consuming him. I crawled over to him, the chill air prickling at me, and wrapped my arms around him, laying my cheek against his shoulder bone.

He reached up to grasp my clasped hands in his, then turned to wrap me in his arms. He held me so tightly.

There was nothing to be said, not now. I'd seen the best and worst side of him at one go. I knew no matter what we faced in the days to come, he would stand with me. And I would stand with him.

And somehow, I'd find a way to bridge the chasm between Grahame and Niall.

Niall healed as winter bore down upon us. At times the winds howled, and it would steal the breath out of my lungs when I walked from the house and whip loose snow like icy daggers against any exposed skin. Niall stayed near the house, doing repairs to the building, and left the animals and barn to Thom and Grahame. Honestly, I'd never seen him work much before, since he had spent most of his day away from the house, but now I got more of a sense of what he could do when he set his mind to it. He worked with a fierce determination, never asking for help, hardly sitting for a meal before he was up once more, attacking his latest project. Rather than be pleased, Cadha watched him with a growing concern.

I came into the parlor one afternoon to find where I'd laid my huswife and saw Niall shoveling ash from the hearth. It was a job Thom or I usually tended, dumping the ash into a barrel to use for soap-making. I thought about backing from the room, but Niall looked up and saw me before I could.

I ducked my head and made for the chair where I sat when sewing. My huswife was in the sewing basket next to it. I picked it up, tucked it into my apron pocket, and made to leave.

"Why did you help me?" Niall's question made me stop. I'd never heard him sound so meek. I faced him, unsure, and saw his own uncertainty. I also saw guilt, dark and full of shame.

"You needed it," I answered honestly.

"But after what I said to you—"

"You suffered enough for that."

Niall closed his eyes, turning away from me.

I left before he could ask me anything else. I could have stayed. I could have pressed the matter, tried to start healing the rift between him and Grahame, but I realized I wasn't ready for that yet. When I looked at Niall, I felt the pain of his grip on my arm. I saw my husband's bruised and bloodied knuckles. I saw blood in the snow.

No, I wasn't ready to face him yet. But at least he'd opened the door by speaking to me. It was a start.

As the days passed, Niall and I had a few more moments between us. He commented one evening on what a fine meal I'd made. When he saw me struggling with an armload of wood for the kitchen fire, he offered to take it and then stayed to help build up the flames. The dogs, who began waiting for me again, were anxious around him, but he let them be, never giving them a harsh word or command, and they slowly relaxed.

He and Grahame, however, never exchanged a word. Grahame and I began talking again, first of the sheep and then of the chickens and other goings on around the farm, but Grahame never mentioned Niall. I began to, once, and Grahame gave me such a look that the words froze on my lips.

I finished the cowl late that winter. It was a hand-span wide, from the tip of my thumb to the tip of my smallest finger. It was dense but still springy, and I could triple wrap it around my neck, or double wrap it around my neck and once around my head. It covered that unprotected part of me that my newly knitted shawl did not. I took to wearing it the next day, pinning the lowest loop in place to my shawl with Elsie's spiral shawl pin to keep it from getting in my way, and while Cadha gave me an odd look when I came into the kitchen house that morning, she didn't ask me of it until that evening.

"When did you make that scarf?" she asked after we had settled in the parlor. Niall was tying a new broom together. Thom and Grahame hadn't yet come in from the barn.

"I've worked on it for a while," I admitted. "Before sleeping."

"Learn it in Germantown?" So she recognized it.

"Frau Scheuling taught me."

"Ah." Cadha made a wry face. "She must have been pleased that you wanted to learn."

"Do you know her?"

"I know of her. She tried to teach Ruthie—" Cadha fell silent suddenly.

I tried to act as though mention of the woman who was making my life miserable didn't matter, but my breath had gone shallow. Niall stood and left the room, leaving behind the new broom he'd nearly finished.

"Well, it's a good skill to learn," Cadha said, trying to break the pall of tension that had fallen over us. "Any new stitch can be useful."

"Yes," I tried to answer, but the word stuck in my throat.

I retired to my room not long after.

Grahame was later coming to bed that night. He looked upset, his dark eyes narrowed and his color high.

"You and Cadha spoke about me," I said, guessing it at once. Grahame hesitated, but then he nodded.

"She wanted to know about town. If anyone had said anything to you."

"What did you tell her?"

"I told her the truth, Ailee. That only an old woman who spoke no English would entertain you." His words were sharp and angry.

I ducked my head, fighting against a hot burst of shame.

Grahame came over to me and lifted my face gently with his hand on my chin. "This was not your doing."

"How can you say that? It was my doing, all of it, and blaming others for it won't make it end." The anger in my own voice surprised me. Grahame drew back.

"We've settled this," he said. "Whatever came before our marriage is in the past. What is between us now is all that matters."

"To you, Grahame. The others don't see it that way."

"I don't care how they see it. They're wrong to treat you like this."

"They don't think so." But I couldn't help but feel a surge of warmth that he thought it wrong. That he wouldn't think to condemn a woman for mistakes made in her reckless youth.

Grahame stood, fists clench. "Damn Niall. He had no right."

I didn't say anything. Grahame's anger left him as quickly as it had come. He sank down onto the bed beside me. "I had no right."

I laid my hand on his shoulder. "What's done is done. I'll manage."

He took my hand in his, raising it to press to his lips before answering. "I want more than that for you."

Emotion swelled inside of me. I'd lost the respect of the people around us, but I'd gained Grahame's devotion. Was it an even trade? I didn't know, but I didn't care. I'd make the most of it.

"I have you," I told him quietly. "And Cadha and the farm and the dogs, for now. I can be content with that."

"Can you?"

"Help me find how to reach Elsie come springtime, and I can be."

I would have said more, but Grahame put a sudden end to talking.

215

Throughout the winter, the cat-beast was never far from my thoughts. Any time the dogs paused during our sojourns between buildings, I'd stop, looking around me and making sure the cowl was tight around my throat. I treated my shawl with wool oil as soon as I'd finished it. I started on a new cowl for Grahame as soon as I'd finished the first, struggling with the beginning stitches that Frau Scheuling hadn't taught me. It took two evenings to get it right, and then I had to rip the second round out three times before I got the join right so it didn't twist.

As winter began to pull away, warmer days melted the snow, only to have it freeze into an icy crust as darkness fell. It made walking outside treacherous. Late one evening when the cold had returned with ferocity, I was finishing the last of the dishes in the wash room when I heard Niall calling to Edgar with a desperate edge to his voice. I realized that I could hear fierce barking coming from far away. A chill raced through me, and I tied my shawl tighter, secured the cowl around my head and neck, and grabbed my lantern. The light spilled across the icy crust covering the snow, and my boots broke through with each step, slowing my progress. I could see Niall's lantern near the woods by the trail leading to the stream.

"Niall," I called. A shadow leaped around him, and my heart jumped into my throat before I recognized Horace.

But the barking was coming from deeper within the woods.

Heedless of the danger, I raced toward Niall. The ice caught the toe of my boot and pitched me forward, but I caught myself on one stinging knee. The lantern wasn't so fortunate, tossed from my grip and hitting the hard snow with the sound of breaking glass. The shadows swallowed me whole.

From the woods came a horrible keening wail. The sound raised the hair on my neck and arms. Edgar's barking became fearsome growling yips of outrage and fear. Horace began barking in reply, and Niall had to grab him by the scruff of the neck to keep him from bounding into the forest.

"What is it?" Grahame was suddenly next to me, a musket in his hand, the cord already smoking. He was priming it as he matched steps with me. Light spilled around us from a lantern Thom held raised high.

"Edgar's in the forest."

"Stay here."

"Grahame—"

"Thom, stay with her."

"Grahame, wait!" Something in my voice made him halt. I ripped the cowl from my head and reached up to wrap it twice around his neck. "Be careful."

Grahame gave me a quick look, the lantern light illuminating the question he didn't have time to ask, and then he hurried toward the forest.

"Stay back," I heard him tell Niall. "Let the dog go."

Niall released Horace, and together Grahame and the mastiff dove into the blackness of the forest.

Edgar's hair-raising growls twisted into a sudden, high-pitched wail that cut off suddenly.

"No!" I started forward, but Thom took me by the arm. I pulled against him once, tears burning down my cheeks.

And then Horace's barking turned savage.

We heard Grahame's shout, and the keening cry, and then the musket fired in a burst of light that blazed in the trees and then vanished into darkness.

Silence followed.

And continued for long moments.

Too long.

Niall looked back to where Thom was holding me back, and then he hurried into the forest, his lantern throwing terrifying shadows through the leafless branches. I watched the light for as long as I could until the black woods swallowed it.

"Edgar," I whispered. A sob tore through me. Thom wrapped his arm around my shoulders, and I turned into him, weeping freely.

"What's going on?" Cadha asked as she came up to us. She was out of breath from rushing across the crusty snow.

"Something in the woods," Thom told her.

"Grahame and Niall?"

"In there with the dogs."

"Was that a musket shot I heard?"

"It was."

"What's becoming of us?" she muttered worriedly.

"Edgar—" I began, but Thom interrupted me.

"They're coming."

I saw the lantern light bobbing through the trees. Niall came out first, holding the lantern high in one hand and the musket in the other. Grahame followed, carrying a heavy burden in his arms. Horace trailed after him. I could hear him whining.

I hurried forward, and as I got closer, I saw that Grahame was carrying Edgar.

He stopped and laid the dog on the crust of snow. Edgar moved lifelessly, a limp weight spreading on the hard snow. I knelt down next to him, the sight of him blurred by tears. Horace nudged against me, whining sorrowfully. He nosed his brother as if trying to wake him.

I wrapped my arms around Horace and buried my face into his warm fur.

"What was it?" I heard Cadha ask.

"Something large. Like a bobbed tail, but bigger."

"Mountain cat, come down from the hills?"

"Maybe."

"I heard the shot."

"I missed," Grahame admitted heavily.

Silence followed this pronouncement, broken only by Horace's whining and my muffled weeping.

"Take her inside," I heard Cadha say. "Take the dog with her. Thom—"

"Edgar was mine," Niall said. "I'll tend to him."

"I'll help," Thom said.

Grahame's strong hands helped me to stand. He guided me back to the house. Horace stayed by his brother, looking from Edgar's lifeless body to me.

"Go on, boy," Niall urged him.

Horace gave Edgar one last, lingering look, then followed after me. He hesitated at the door, but Grahame coaxed him to follow. Grahame paused to shed his coat, tossing it into the wood room before leading me upstairs. He helped me out of my boots, and I undressed with wooden fingers before curling into bed, weak with grief. Horace lay down on the floor beside me, whining once. I reached down to scratch around his ears, and he settled.

I felt the bed sink as Grahame sat down beside me.

"Ailee," he began, a question in his tone.

"Can we talk tomorrow?" I asked before he could continue.

Grahame went silent. He brushed my hair back from my face, then stood and left the room.

I slept fitfully, dreaming of black eyes and a whipping tail and hearing Edgar's last cry before he was killed.

CHAPTER TWENTY-SEVEN

When I woke, it was still early in the morning, closer to night than dawn. I could feel Grahame sleeping deeply next to me. I reached down and touched Horace, still stretched on the floor by the bed. Something had woken me, like a thought that hadn't fully formed in my head.

I lay in bed, listening to Grahame's breathing while I tried to recapture the thought. Or had it been a dream? I remembered uneasy ones throughout the night, of Edgar and the cat-beast and the grief that still throbbed in my chest.

Why was I in such mourning for a dog? That wasn't like me. I'd never been particularly attached to animals. The dogs had settled into my heart somehow over the past couple months, I realized, because they were the closest things I had to friends. Would probably be the only friends I'd make in this forsaken wilderness with my scandal being bandied about at every village and town. And now I'd lost one to a horrible monster who was still stalking the forest.

I reached down again to feel Horace beside me on the floor. The thought gripped me completely now. I could have helped save Edgar if I'd thought of it earlier. It had never crossed my mind that the dogs might be in danger. They were so large, so strong and able. Like Grahame, but I'd already realized the risk he faced. Why hadn't I considered the dogs?

I stole out of bed, careful not to wake Grahame or tread on Horace. It was strange to be the first one up. It must have been very early indeed, but I couldn't have slept longer. I found my clothing by feel, putting them on as quickly as I could, then felt for my basket before leaving the room. I could hear Horace's nails on the floor as he followed me. I held the door open for him, then closed it quietly.

We went to the parlor, and I spent time building up a fire. I still wasn't the cleverest at it, but I was learning. Soon it was crackling away, burning through tinder and igniting the dry wood until a cheery blaze chased the shadows back and began to warm the room.

I found a ball of wool that I hadn't started yet and pulled the hook-pen free of the cowl I'd begun. I started a new one. This one would be shorter, able to double-up around Horace's thick neck and maybe protect him from the cat-beast if it came around again.

Cadha found me there, well into the cowl. She pulled her chair closer to the fire and sat, watching me in silence for a few moments.

"Ailee?" she asked after a time.

I glanced up at her, then back to my work.

"Ailee, there was nothing anyone could have done to save that dog," she continued. "You know that, don't you, lass?"

"There was something I could do," I said, my voice tight. "And I can do it for Horace."

"A stitched collar isn't going to protect him if he gets into a fight with that cat."

"Yes, it will." I lowered my stitching to return her look. I was so utterly certain about this, I knew there was nothing she could say to sway me otherwise. But equally, I saw there was little I could do to convince her of my certainty.

Cadha heaved a sigh and rose. She gave Horace a rare pat on the head, then offered me a sad look. "You do what you need to do, then. I'll be in the kitchen house." And she left the parlor.

The sun was well into the sky before I set the stitching aside. It would take several hours of work to finish it, and I knew I couldn't spend all my time on it. There were other chores to tend. I could only indulge my grief for so long.

Breakfast was on the table, and the men were just coming in for it. Horace lay across the entryway as we took our seats, and Thom sat with us.

Niall looked haggard, as though he'd slept little. Grahame was stoic, and Thom grim.

"Any sign of it?" Cadha asked after we'd eaten for a bit in silence.

"Lost the tracks," Grahame said. "Must have taken to the trees.

But from the blood, I hurt it."

"You went after it?" I stared at him, shocked. "Why? It might have attacked you. Did you wear the scarf I made?"

"We needed to make sure it moved on," Grahame told me gently. It didn't pass my notice that he didn't answer my other question.

"Are the sheep secure?" Cadha asked.

"It won't go after the sheep," I said, and they all looked at me like I was mad. I sighed in frustration.

"They're in the barn," Thom told her.

"Let's keep them nearby," Cadha said.

And that was all that was said on the matter. I wanted to explain, to make them understand, but the men returned to work as soon as the meal was finished, and Cadha gave me a look that said she wouldn't discuss it further. I huffed in frustration, determined to at least continue making the cowls if nothing else. Maybe try to speak to Grahame that night.

It was strange to have only Horace by my side. He was subdued, walking close to me as I went to the wash room with the morning dishes. Edgar's absence was an unrelenting pain that I tried to ignore.

When I stepped into the wash room, Horace paused outside. He whined at me, looking forlorn and lost. I couldn't bear to leave him outside alone, so after glancing to see if anyone was watching, I coaxed him into the room. The laundry was hanging from lines tied to the low beams, more frozen than dry. I put the dishes on the trestle table by the wall and started a small fire in the fire pit in the center of the room before swinging the pot over it. I took up the bucket to fill with snow and left the building, walking around to the back where the snow was deeper, Horace trailing after me.

I froze. A trail of prints came within a few strides of the back of the wash house. They were larger than the dog's and shaped differently. I looked around and saw where Edgar must have charged the beast. The trail bee-lined back to the woods, a second trail aiming for it.

Horace whined again. He looked uneasy, sniffing the air.

"Ailee?" Cadha had stopped near the hen house.

I pointed.

Cadha came closer, then stopped with a hiss. "So, that's why the dog went after it. It came too close to the house."

My heart was hammering as Cadha called toward the barn. It

didn't take long for Thom and Grahame to hurry over. Grahame had his musket.

Cadha only had to point.

The men worried over the trail for a bit, following it toward the woods. Thankfully, neither entered very far before turning back. I was shivering by the time they returned, despite Horace leaning against my legs. I could feel him trembling as well.

"I don't think it'll return," Grahame said. "But we'll keep an eye out."

Cadha agreed, and she and Thom went back to their work. I absently remembered the reason I'd come out and reached for the bucket that I had dropped at some point, but Grahame beat me to it. He filled it with snow, breaking the crust with his boot heel first, then followed me back inside the wash room.

I dumped the bucket into the steaming pot and heard the sizzle of melting snow.

"I'm sorry about Edgar," Grahame said quietly.

I bowed my head, blinking back tears. "I know."

He set the musket against the wall and approached, wrapping his arms around me. I leaned against him, finding comfort. Horace leaned against us both.

"Shaw is planning to leave come spring," Grahame said quietly. "I know he'd welcome us if we joined him."

I drew back, startled. "Leave Cadha?"

"Cadha has managed the place for a long time without us. She has Niall. She'll be fine."

"But I thought—" But I wasn't sure what I thought. I never knew the full reasons for coming here, except that Grahame had been planning it for some time before he met me.

"I can't keep you here, Ailee. It wouldn't be fair. We need a new start that both of us plan for together."

I didn't know what to say. He was offering me a choice, willing to give up the life we had begun to build here for a chance at another. The thought of leaving Cadha hurt, as well as leaving what was familiar. But I'd had to start over twice already, and each time had gotten easier. And the thought of escaping Ruthie and the rumors she was spreading of me was more than just appealing. It was a blessing. I knew, should we move, Grahame would not allow that part of my past to come out again.

And then there was the cat-beast.

"Are you certain?" I asked him, my voice wavering.

"I've been considering it for a few weeks. But after last night . . . yes. I'm certain. If you are."

"I . . . I'm not sure," I admitted. "But I want to discuss it," I quickly added.

"Then we shall." Grahame pressed his lips to my forehead before leaving the wash room.

I spent the rest of the day deep in thought, a whole world of possibilities opening before me.

"Where would we go?" I asked Grahame later that night. We were curled in bed together, the room dark and quiet. Horace was stretched on the floor by my bedside. I'd laid my useless fancy cloak on the floor for him. He would need a bed of his own, made from stitched rags and stuffed with straw, but for now, the cloak would do. It was doing me little good.

"An island off the coast," Grahame answered.

"An island. Like Ireland?"

"Much smaller."

"Would we have to build a house?"

"Yes. It wouldn't be like here. We would be starting anew."

It sounded like hard work.

"What about the sheep? And your bull and cow? What about the chickens?"

"I'd make arrangements for what we'd take."

More questions kept buzzing through my head, and it was hard to catch hold of them. "What about money? Won't it cost to make the move? Would we have to travel by wagon? What if we got there late and winter set in? What if we needed help? Are there boats to use? Is there a town?"

I heard Grahame chuckling. It was a rare sound, but puzzling.

"You think I'm asking the wrong questions," I accused.

He wrapped his arm around me. "Not at all. You're asking the questions I'd expect of a wife."

I realized he was right. I was already planning how I'd manage my own kitchen, what I'd plant for a kitchen garden, how long it might take to build a bake house for making bread, and how often we'd have to go to town for supplies.

"Does this mean you want to go?" Grahame asked.

It would be hard work and a lot of it. But it would be a truly fresh start, with Grahame and I working together to make a new life. I thought about Cadha walking through her farm yard, seeing her pause and look around with a satisfied expression, knowing how far she'd come and how she'd earned everything around her. I wanted that feeling, too.

"Yes, it does."

Grahame broke the news to the others a week later. He had wanted to wait until he could speak to Shaw, and he'd taken a day of hunting to visit with him. Grahame still managed to come home with a brace of hares, too. I'd made him wear my cowl, just in case he came across the cat-beast, and I worried about him traveling on foot in the mushy snow. He came back damp and ready for dry boots, but he said the only things he'd startled during the trek was a deer and a few raccoons.

Horace and I had come in with supper, the dog wearing his newly stitched and treated collar, a smaller version of the double-wrapped cowl I'd made. I'd just finished laying out the meal when the others joined us. The talk was for farm chores as we ate, mostly Cadha listing off what was to be done the next day. After we were nearly finished eating, Grahame spoke.

"Ailee and I will be joining Shaw when he moves south." He sounded matter-of-fact, as though this should come as no surprise to anyone.

"Why?" Cadha's question burst from her, and I could hear surprise and hurt in her voice.

Grahame leveled a look at her. "I think we both know why."

Niall rose and left the room. Horace lifted his head from his paws to watch, but he didn't follow.

"We'll help get the first fields planted," Grahame continued, "and see if any early lambs come."

"Fine," Cadha said, turning from him. She stood. She looked at me with a closed expression, and I tried not to shrink back.

"So that's how it is," she said at last, facing Grahame.

"It is," was all Grahame answered.

Cadha followed after Niall.

Thom stood, but he lingered. "I wonder if we might speak later," he said to Grahame.

Grahame nodded.

When we were alone in the room, I let out a long sigh. "I don't like to hurt her."

"Cadha is tough. She knows this is best."

"I don't think she minds my past—" I began, but I saw Grahame looking darkly at Niall's chair and understood it wasn't my past that was standing between all of us. Grahame and Niall still weren't speaking. I realized they likely never would.

So that's how it is, I thought.

CHAPTER TWENTY-EIGHT

If I thought tensions were strained around the farm before, that had been nothing like they became after Grahame's announcement.

Cadha became a stoic, unapproachable force. I didn't dare ask her a question for fear of being snapped at. And I was loath to make a mistake for the same reason. She was unforgiving, driving me relentlessly. She heaped more and more chores upon me, insisting that I take over bread-making one day, then soap-making the next. She wouldn't let Thom kill a chicken for the pot—no, I had to do it, and then I had to pluck it and prepare it for the spit. I had to milk the goats, then churn the butter. I had to cook supper all that week on my own.

By the end of the week, I was exhausted, sore, and could barely keep my eyes open. When Grahame woke me getting into bed, I think I actually growled. Which made Horace growl.

"Ailee, what it is?" Grahame asked, baffled.

And so I told him what it was. And kept telling him.

"She hates me now," I finished, emotion thickening my words and tears blurring my sight. "All she's done for me, and I'm just leaving her on her own again."

Grahame chuckled and I turned on him, shocked and angry. But before I could speak, he held up his hand in peace.

"Cadha doesn't hate you," he told me quickly. "She's worried for you. She's trying to prepare you for running your own house."

I gaped at him, but suddenly it made sense. Her impatience, her handing chores over to me entirely, some that I had only just learned, was her pushing me to learn all I could.

"So this is a trial by fire," I said, calming.

"Yes. It's me she's mad at. I'm taking you away before she feels you're ready. And—" He hesitated. "Thom is coming with us."

"Thom? Surely not."

Grahame nodded. "Asked me a few days ago. He's a good man to have, so I said yes. Is that all right?"

"Of course!" I warmed, pleased that he asked me. "But won't Cadha need him here?"

"It doesn't matter if she does or not, his time is up. I overheard her talking about taking on another man. I think she means to go with us to Philadelphia to see about it."

I felt a little better about leaving. "Will she be able to keep the place running without us?"

Grahame smiled. "She managed for some time before we came."

Placated, I settled, and Grahame wrapped his arms around me. I felt closer to him than ever. I was truly a part of the planning for our new life, and having ownership in my own future was a rare and delightful sensation.

It didn't take long for sleep to claim me, and the next day, I tackled my chores with a far greater appreciation.

The days grew warmer, the snow melted into mud that stuck to everything, and our days began to change once more. The daylight came sooner and stayed later, so we ate earlier and worked longer for there was plenty to do. As Cadha entrusted more of the running of the household to me, she was able to join the men for planting once the mud began to thin. I didn't escape this new work, either, as she had me spend part of my day helping Niall plant the kitchen garden. I was surprised by how well he knew his work. He broke up the ground, digging under any stalks leftover from last harvest, then he hoed the rows as neatly as any gardener I'd seen. He gave me instructions on how to plant the seeds Cadha had held back, or how to find the starts left from the harvest. I recognized most of the names of the plants from helping in the kitchen, and it felt good to realize how much I'd learned.

Niall looked at his ease as we worked, with a peace coming over him I'd never seen before. This was what kept him on the farm, I realized. The planting and growing. This was where he belonged.

He caught me watching him and turned a wary gaze toward me.

"I didn't know how much you liked working the garden," I said.

Niall relaxed a little. "I use to help Mother. She loved her gardens."

I'd worked in those same gardens, just a little, before leaving Ireland. It was a strange thought, and one that connected me to Niall in a way I'd not considered. "I didn't know that."

He smiled a bit sadly. "Mother use to say the finest thing in life was watching it grow. Plants, lambs, us. I never cared much for the sheep, but I did enjoy the garden, and she taught me."

"She sounds like a wonderful woman."

He nodded. "You would have taken to her, I think." He paused. "She would have taken to you, too."

It was the finest compliment he could have given me.

I was working alone in the garden when Horace rose up, alert. I froze, fear trickling down my spine, and then heard a man's boot steps in the yard. I looked around to see Shaw coming toward me.

He doffed his wide-brimmed hat. "Morning, Mrs. Donaghue." He'd grown a beard over the winter, and it was more red than brown, unlike his hair. He was still just as wiry, though, and wore his breeches with a wide leather belt cinched tight.

I dusted my hands off on my apron as I stood. "Good morning." I couldn't for the life of me recall his surname. And it still felt very strange to hear my married one.

"I wondered if Mr. Donaghue was about."

"They're in the field," I told him. "Checking the sheep."

"I think I can find the way." He paused. "It is good to see you've mended from your accident," he told me. "Marjorie will be pleased to hear it."

I smiled and thanked him. I watched as he walked off, barely containing my eagerness. I'd be spending more time with Marjorie once we left. I hoped she'd fill the void Elsie had left. I desperately needed a friend. Even a quiet one.

Shaw joined us for dinner. I'd considered that he might and thought to lay an extra place for him, which please Cadha. It was a light dinner—cheese and bread with preserves Shaw brought for us from Marjorie, and pickled beets. No one spoke of our leaving but of farm work. Shaw asked questions and Cadha would answer. No one asked about his farm. I wondered what would become of it when he left.

He left after dinner, and we returned to the day's work. That night, however, Grahame told me the news Shaw had brought.

"He's hired a ship. It sails in two weeks."

It took a moment for me to process what he was saying. "We leave in two weeks?"

"Sooner. We'll need to be in Philadelphia a few days before it sails."

"Does Cadha know?"

"Yes. I told her this evening."

Two weeks. It didn't seem possible. I found that once again, I was looking into a future I couldn't imagine. Except now I had experience to measure it against.

"How long is the voyage?" I asked, thinking back on the only other ship I'd been on.

"A week at most."

"Where do we make port?"

"Norfolk."

"And you said we'd have to take a ship to the island?"

"We'll hire another in Norfolk."

"And then we'll be at the island. Three weeks."

"Or a bit more, but yes, then we'll be on the island." He took my hand in his. "Are you still sure about this?"

I wasn't completely sure about anything. But when I thought about me and Grahame making our own lives together, or of spending time with Marjorie, unburdened by my past, I was filled with warmth. I nodded. "Sure enough."

Several days later, I came downstairs to find Thom hauling wooden crates into the dining room. He had five already sitting on the table. Cadha was watching him, and when she saw me come in, she gestured me over.

"We've got to start getting you ready," she told me. "Thom put these together for you, and we're going to fill them with what you'll need to get you by until you're settled. It isn't going to be easy,

Ailee," she told me soberly. "Morley and I about starved our first winter here. We're going to help see that doesn't happen to you. Though," she added, "Grahame is a far better hunter than Morley ever was."

We started in the kitchen. The few pots and pans Grahame had brought had gone into Cadha's kitchen, but I hadn't used them enough before leaving Ireland to tell them apart from what the kitchen already held. Cadha knew each one, however. Within the hour, she had set aside everything Grahame had brought along with a few things he hadn't. I'd have enough cookware to begin my own kitchen.

I picked up one of the pots and the strangest sensation came over me. Mine. This was mine. I'd never owned a pot before, and certainly wouldn't have known what to do with it if I had. But now I could already imagine the foods I would coax from that iron pot.

I was grinning when I looked at Cadha.

"I see you feel it, lass," she said thickly. "No better feeling, putting together something that's yours and all yours. You hold onto that feeling, Ailee. It'll help get you through the hard times."

She added a rag bag and a few linens and then we went through herbs and leftover seeds. I'd have a healthy garden using them, once we put them in the ground.

"First thing," she cautioned me. "You let Grahame see to the dwelling. You get that garden in. Make a pact with Thom—offer to feed him for the use of his tools and some effort breaking ground. He'll thank you for it."

I made a note to do just that.

We went to the bake house for a bread bowl and pin. Then the wash room for a generous supply of soap and Grahame's wash tub and scrub board.

"Until you get a line hung, there's nothing wrong with tossing your washing on the bushes," Cadha told me sagely. "Just spread them out and shake them well when you pull them off. In case some wee bug tries to make a home there," she added with a knowing smile.

I didn't like to think of bugs in my clothing.

"Speaking of," she said, "you'll be troubled with them, I'm sure. Keep your food stores well sealed. Waxed cloth is best, if you can make it. I'd give you some, but I've none to spare with spring coming on. I'll send you with plenty of Morley's candles, though. And don't let the mice take over. Grahame will know what to do about them, or get yourself a couple cats."

From the smoke house, she set aside a supply of dried fish and venison. "Enough to get you out of trouble," she said. "Grahame and Thom are both good hunters. They'll keep you in meat and fish, if there's any to be had."

We moved on to the root cellar, and there she filled two crates with preserves, jams, jellies, and pickled vegetables. I was overwhelmed by her generosity and said so.

"Grahame stayed long enough to help get the planting in, and he bred his bull to my cow, and allowed for us to trade sheep to freshen my flock. And he's paid me for two of my goats. He's seen to repairs we wouldn't have gotten to in time for winter and taught his brother a few tricks. This is just fair compensation."

I had the feeling it was more than that, but I let it go.

"Now, let's see to the wool. You'll be wanting some that's already cleaned. Not much to spare you, of course, but enough to get you started before Grahame gets to shearing. It's a shame we couldn't get that done before you leave, but then you'll have wool enough once you're settled. And the sheep will have hauled it for you," she added with a laugh.

When we were finished, we'd filled all of the crates and had a fair pile of supplies besides. The crates and supplies lined the far wall of the dining room, and I stood there before laying out the evening meal, staring at it all.

Mine. I was setting up my own household. It would be far different from anything I thought I'd have when I was younger, but I had such a greater appreciation for it now than I had then. I understood all the hard work that went into it, and I felt like I was nearly ready.

There were just a few things I still wasn't certain of. I hoped Marjorie would be willing to help me learn.

Grahame came up behind me. "There's more than we brought," he observed.

"Cadha was generous."

He wrapped his arms around me. "Are you content?"

I twisted to look up at him, smiling through tears. "So very much."

The day before we were to leave for Philadelphia, I went looking for Niall. He was in the field, watching the sheep. Grahame's flock and handful Thom was taking in payment for his service had already been separated out and shared the smaller pen with the bull, cow, and two goats.

Horace was with me, and the sheep were only slightly annoyed to see the dog in their field. They moved away in protest, but Horace ignored them.

Niall watched me warily as I approached.

"I want you to have this," I told him, holding out the cowl I'd finished earlier in the week. I'd treated it with wool oil already.

Niall looked surprised. "Why?"

"To keep you safe."

He looked dubious, but I was prepared for that. "I know you don't believe me about the beast. You don't have to. But I do wish you might wear this anyway if you go into the woods. At least when it's cool outside."

Niall took the cowl, turning it over in his hands. "It's finely made," he conceded.

That concession made me ridiculously pleased. I think if we'd have stayed, Niall and I might have become friendly, if not friends. It was strange how I no longer felt so resentful towards him. I knew the feeling had ebbed after the fight, but losing Edgar had brought us together in a silent recognition of shared grief. In time, that might have become something more. He might have become more of a brother to me, even more than my own brothers had been, younger as they were and focused toward other pursuits. I couldn't imagine any of them here, working a farm like Niall.

"I wish you happy," I told him. "I hope you find a fine wife and make a good home."

Niall blinked, then offered me a nod. "I . . . I wish you happy, too."

For a moment, I thought he might apologize, but then his pride got in his way again. Wishing me joy was the closest he'd come.

"Ailee—" he called as I turned away. I stopped. "Thom and I spoke," he said, looking at the cowl in his hands as he spoke, "and we want you to have Horace."

Surprise, then gratefulness, spread through me. I reached down and put my hand on Horace's head where he stood, ever-present, at my side.

"Honestly," Niall admitted, "I don't think he'd let anyone else keep him."

"Thank you. This means everything to me."

Niall nodded, then turned his attention back to the flock. I left the field with my dog, brimming with happiness.

Cadha saw us coming from the barn. "So did he give you the dog?"

I nodded with a grin.

"Guess he'll be bringing new ones back at some point," she said with an exaggerated sigh. "Maybe I can point him towards a sheep dog. We could use one."

I called to Cadha before she went into the hen house. "I have a request, if you're willing?"

"Let's hear it," she said, waiting at the door.

"My friend, Elsie. She hasn't written to me yet, but I hope she still might. Should a letter come, could you find a way to get it to me?"

"Grahame swore to send us news on how to find him," Cadha said, considering. "I'm sure I can pass the word on and get any letters to you."

"And if I left some for her—"

"I'll see them posted as soon as I know where," she finished. She came closer to me. "I know what it is to need a friend."

I could see by her look that she did. She carried an old sorrow, coupled with an older regret. She offered me a smile and returned to her work. With relief, I returned to my room to pack my belongings once again.

CHAPTER TWENTY-NINE

Cadha and I had just finished catching the chickens and crating them when Shaw and Marjorie came around to the house.

"This bunch will be squawking half the day," Cadha said, speaking loudly above the angry clucking of the crated chickens. Their distressed was echoed by the clutch left in the hen house, turning the yard into a cacophony of squawks.

"Fine looking flock," Shaw said, looking them over. He had on his wide-brimmed hat, but he'd shaved his beard, and it made him look younger, closer to Niall's age than Grahame's. "Rooster?"

"Only one, and he's staying," Cadha said firmly.

"That's fine," Shaw told her. "I've got two."

Marjorie looked much like she had last time I'd seen her, sober and quiet. Her dark hair was pulled back and stuck under a wide-brimmed hat similar to Shaw's, this one woven from straw instead of stitched from leather. She had a knitted shawl similar to those I'd seen in Germantown, long enough to cross her chest and wrap around to tie behind her. I wondered if I could make something like it using Frau Scheuling's stitch. It would be even more protection.

Would we need the protection anymore? Would there be a cat-beast on the island?

I hoped not.

"Mrs. Donaghue," Marjorie said in greeting in her quiet voice. Once again, I had the curious sensation of homesickness and delight from hearing my accent in a woman's voice. "You look well. I'm glad for it."

"Thanks in part to you," I said. "And please, call me Ailee."

"Then you must call me Marjorie."

And so our friendship began.

Thom had the oxen already yoked, and we had loaded most everything. Grahame and Shaw added the chicken crates amid much noise and occasional poof of feathers through the wooden slats.

"I'd best go back out front," Marjorie told me as we watched. "Our flock might stray."

"I can help you," I offered.

In the front meadow, Marjorie's sheep and a couple of goats had spread out to graze. Marjorie and Shaw also had a wagon ladened with crates, barrels, and bundles, but two heavy-set horses were hitched to the front. A shaggy cow was tied to the back of the wagon, her lead long enough to allow her to graze, which she did with gusto.

"How will the horses do on the ship?" I asked Marjorie.

"They won't make it that far," she answered, moving toward the edge of the small meadow. "Shaw will sell them in Philadelphia to help cover passage, along with the cow."

"Will you miss them?"

She looked surprised by the question. Her gaze fell fondly on the horses. "Yes, I will."

"Have you been to the island?" I asked, trying to turn her thoughts away from losing the horses. I didn't think it likely that she had, but it was the first question to come to mind.

"No, but we had a letter from a friend who moved there. Edina described a paradise." There was no doubting Marjorie's eagerness. Her face brightened and she grew more animated, gesturing with her hands as she spoke. "Plenty of hunting and fishing, decent land for gardens, clean water, and no sign of natives. She said the worst things were the snakes and biting bugs, but she was making a remedy against the bugs."

"And what of the snakes?" I asked, chilled.

"The dogs were good at catching them out." She looked over to where Horace laid, not far from me. "Is he coming?"

"Yes. But I don't know how he is with snakes."

"We'll find out, I suppose."

The men came around, herding the flock of sheep and goats to the front. Marjorie's sheep began bleating excitedly and the two flocks moved in towards one another, curious. It was fun to watch them, but then a couple of the ewes started getting pushy and the men had to get involved.

"Any rams?" Grahame asked Shaw.

"No. Sold the last one. Hoping to get one in Philadelphia. You?"

"One. He's young, but he'll suit."

"That's a fine bull," Marjorie said as Thom led the oxen and wagon around from the house, the bull and cow tied to the back.

"Gentle, too," I said.

"He'll need to be," Shaw said. I figured he meant for the voyage on the ship.

Cadha came out of the house, a hat fixed onto her head and her travel cape on. She carried a walking stick in her hand and had the pistol in her belt next to a shot bag and small powder horn. I glanced to see if Niall was going to come out, but there was no sign of him.

"Daylight's wasting," she said, and not pausing, continued down the rutted lane away from the farm.

I gave the house one final look. I would miss this place, though not everything that had happened here. I hoped that one day I might see it again.

I didn't think that I would.

We reached Philadelphia as darkness was falling. The walk from the farm had been nearly uneventful. The only setback had been Shaw's wagon bogging in a muddy part of the road. It had taken everyone putting a shoulder to the wagon while Cadha urged the horses forward to get it out. The sheep had strayed while we struggled with the wagon, so it had taken a little more time to round them up again and count heads.

Otherwise, it had been a fine day for a walk. I was in far better shape for it than when I'd first arrived, and better shod for it, too. My boots had held up wonderfully. I didn't miss those useless shoes of mine at all. And my leather hat kept the sun off my face and neck and my cape kept me warm. I'd come a long way in the last several months.

I'd had a moment when we journeyed through Germantown. I wanted to ask after Frau Scheuling, but I decided against it. Did I want to hear that she'd died? It was much better to think of her as I'd last seen her, sitting in her comfortable parlor, stitching as she told stories. Besides, I didn't truly wish to face rejection from the townsfolk once more. So I passed through Germantown for the last time with my head held high.

When we reached Philadelphia, Shaw knew a place for us to stay for the night, but first we had to see the wagons and animals housed. We ended up near the wharf once again, renting space in a couple different places. I'd asked how long we would be staying and packed accordingly, so Grahame and I only had to carry a few bags between us.

Cadha had a bag as well, as she'd be staying until we emptied the wagon.

"Will Cadha be all right on her own after we leave?" I asked Grahame as we walked the shadowy streets to the inn. Horace kept pace with me, watchful but quiet. Cadha walked ahead with Marjorie, talking as they traversed the cold streets.

"She's written ahead to a family she knows," Grahame told me, "and had Thom post the letter a couple weeks ago. She'll stay with them tomorrow."

It was just like Cadha to plan ahead.

"But what about the journey home?"

"She'll travel with a supply train to Germantown and hire a man she knows there to help see her home." Grahame gave me a comforting smile. "She's done this before, Ailee. She knows what she's about."

I ducked my head. "I know. I just fret for her."

Grahame took my hand and tucked it around his arm. "Cadha wouldn't want you to worry for her," he told me gently.

I offered him a shy grin. "Then let's not tell her that I do."

He chuckled that rare, dry sound that seemed to start in his chest and end in his throat.

The inn was nowhere near as fine as the one Grahame and I had stopped in when we'd first arrived. It backed a rather noisy alehouse, and we had to share a room that had two beds and a pallet squeezed into it, with hardly any room in between. Horace squeezed between the pallet and the end of the beds, but he didn't look uncomfortable. Thom took a bed in the common room and bid us good evening.

Cadha and I took one of the beds and Grahame the pallet, with Shaw and Marjorie in the second bed. The men bought us supper and brought it to us, then returned to the alehouse to catch the latest news.

Supper was a meat pie, not nearly as good as Cadha's, who reminded us of that fact with great detail, and a cider. I hadn't tried cider yet, and it went down easily. Too easily. I hardly got my meal eaten before I was nodding off.

"Into bed with you, lass," Cadha urged me, chuckling. "You've still a long ways to go."

I don't remember if I responded before falling into a deep, dreamless sleep.

We were two days in Philadelphia before boarding the ship that would take us to Norfolk. The second night Cadha stayed with her friend. I knew I'd see her one more time, since she would need to fetch the wagon, but it felt as if our final parting was upon us as she left the next morning, and I had to hold back tears.

If Cadha noticed them, she didn't say.

We spent the morning selling livestock and equipment. Grahame sold a couple ewes and purchased a ram, and Shaw sold his horses, harness, and wagon. Marjorie and I kept back as the men bargained, Horace staying at my side. It was interesting to watch the men at their trading. The bargaining was much more subdued than I would have thought. Shaw arranged to turn over the horses and equipment on the wharf the next day after we'd unloaded supplies, but Grahame passed the sheep along and collected the ram as soon as a bargain was struck.

"If we have a moment," I asked him afterwards, "can we go to the last place Elsie was staying? To see if there is word of her?"

"I'd planned on it," he told me unexpectedly. I smiled to him, grateful.

I knew we weren't likely to find anything of her, and by Grahame's look, he thought the same. We found the place by the address Mr. Vance had given Grahame. It was another inn run by a widow woman, a threadbare place, but tidy. The widow, Mrs. Royce, was proud of it.

She remembered Elsie, but she didn't have helpful news.

"Left here with the others," she said. "Sweet girl."

"You don't happen to recall if they mentioned where they were bound?" I pressed.

"No, dearie, I do not." She seemed genuinely unhappy to disappoint me. Grahame thanked her with a coin, which brightened her spirits.

I was disappointed, though. It was frustrating to be so close, to be, perhaps, in the same town as Elsie and not be able to find her. The rest of the day I fought against my disappointment, trying without success to take interest in our last day in town. Horace was a welcomed presence by my side, and I often reached down to scratch his ears. When I got too quiet, he would gently nose my hand, reminding me that I might not have found my old friend, but I had new ones with me.

Before evening we got to see the ship. The *Mary Constance* was smaller than the *Resolution*, lacking the forecastle. I was glad she looked different. Being this close to ships brought back the memories of our crossing.

The captain was another Englishman, though he had none of Captain Dawson's bearing. He spoke more coarsely and wasn't keen with the idea of women being on his ship. Or the bull. Shaw began to apologize, but Grahame cut him off and began a spirited conversation with the captain about the ship, its crew, and where it had traveled, all aimed at flattering the man. I was surprised at how adept Grahame was at it, but I'd noticed before his knowledge of ships and crews. He seemed to know just what to say. When he was finished, the captain wasn't quite so dour. But he made it clear that Marjorie and I were not welcomed on deck.

"It will only be a handful of days," Shaw assured us both. Marjorie didn't look pleased. In fact, she was looking somewhat green.

I put my hand on her arm. "We'll manage," I said, both to her and to Shaw.

We purchased supper from a street vendor, and as darkness fell, we returned to our room. Grahame brought a few candles from his bag and lit them, and he and Shaw spoke of the animals and how they might do on the voyage while Marjorie and I got out our knitting. It was a peaceful evening, with the men sitting knee to knee on the edges of the beds and Horace stretched out on the pallet while Marjorie and I were at our stitching. It felt like a taste of my life to come.

When Cadha met us on the wharf it was just after sunrise. She looked better rested than I'd seen her in a long while.

"All set, are you?" she asked as she came up to us. We were keeping watch on the animals as the longshoremen loaded our supplies on the ship.

"The wagon is nearly empty," Grahame answered. "Waiting to load the animals."

"She's a fine looking ship," Cadha said. "You should make good time."

Grahame bowed to her. And that was as much of a goodbye as the two were going to say, apparently.

I couldn't leave it at that.

"Thank you for all you've done for me," I told her, my voice thick. "I can never repay you for your kindness."

"You can at that," Cadha rebuked. "You make a fine home and raise fine children, Ailee, and I'll consider myself repaid."

I couldn't hold back any longer. I embraced her, my tears breaking free. She stiffened, then she awkwardly returned my embrace.

"There, there, lass," she said in a low voice. "You'll do just fine."

She gave Horace a final pat, then gave Thom a curtsy, something I'd never seen her do before. He bowed in return and accepted the hand she offered to him as an equal.

"I'll miss you, Thom," she said. "May you have a long and happy life."

"And you, Mistress Cadha."

The wagon empty, Cadha took over the lead line to the oxen, and with a farewell to us all, she guided them down the bustling wharf. I thought I saw her glance back once, and then she was gone.

I had to swallow against the lump in my throat. I hope she knew how much I'd miss her and how much I owed to her.

We boarded not long after. I crossed to the deck and couldn't help but feel a sense of bewilderment at both the familiarity and strangeness of this ship. So much was similar to the *Resolution*, but then the differences kept getting in the way. It wasn't as comforting as I first though it would be. I kept expecting to see Captain Dawson nearby, or Beacham come out from a passageway. I missed the cook with a surprising pang of loss.

Marjorie and I had a small room to ourselves below decks with two cots lashed to the beams. Horace wasn't sure he liked being on the ship, and Marjorie was certain she did not. I was simply glad not to be in a berth again, surrounded by strangers, though I felt the loss of Elsie and Tavey. I even missed Iona. It reinforced that this was an entirely different sort of voyage.

Both the men checked on us before we set sail. Marjorie was looking unwell, her nervous energy subsided into queasiness. Shaw couldn't hide his concern for her.

"I'll see to her," I told him, "if need be."

He thanked me, but he left with a worried expression. Before Grahame left, he slipped a flask into my apron pocket.

"Mix that with some water," he whispered to me, "and both of you drink. I'll bring you more if it empties."

I nodded my understanding. I had a feeling it was the same concoction of grog that Beacham had made when we fell sick during the crossing.

Beacham. I wondered where he was and how he was getting on. I hadn't thought of him in some time, at least not without thinking of his scarf, too, but this time was different. Now I was remembering him—his stories, the way he instructed me and accepted me, the way he cared for us in his own, gruff way. I wondered if he knew the impact he'd had on me.

The passage was dull. Marjorie and I were forced to remain in the room. Grahame or Shaw would bring us food and help clear away the leavings, and Thom would come for Horace to take him for a stretch. I took to pacing the room when I could, just to be moving, and stitching when I wasn't pacing. Or I'd sleep. I slept more than I had in months, but even that became tiresome.

Marjorie and I would talk, a little. She would tell me about the farm she and Shaw had left behind. He'd sold the place to one of the men I had seen at the gathering at Mrs. Giverns house. He was hoping to take a wife and wanted more than a dugout to offer her for a home.

Which led us to discussing dugouts and other dwellings that could be raised quickly, and what there might be on the island to build with. Marjorie didn't want to go back to living in a dugout.

"Worst year of my life," she admitted. "Shaw was lucky I loved him, or I'd have taken the first ship back to Ireland after that."

I hoped she would speak more of her past, but she didn't. That was the only mention she made of Ireland, though I gathered she and

Shaw had met there and crossed over together.

I didn't speak much of Ireland either, but I did speak of my time with Cadha and all she'd taught me. Marjorie was curious about the stitch I was using for the cowls, too. I wasn't sure how much detail to go into, so I merely said I'd learned it recently and found it to my liking.

I was on my third cowl and pleased with how it looked. My knitting was still questionable, though I kept with it, but this stitch seemed to come more and more easily for me. I wasn't any faster at it yet, especially with the tossing ship keeping my hands unsteady, but I could feel that I might grow to be faster at it in time.

When it was too dark to work, I'd lay on my cot and turn Elsie's shawl pin over in my hands, wondering where she was and how she fared.

Thankfully, neither of us took ill, though Marjorie often turned away any food but the hard biscuits we were offered. She did accept the grog with regularity. The days ran together with monotonous slowness. By the time Grahame told us we'd be making port in another day, it felt as though months had passed. I could have cursed Grahame, though, for telling me so soon. That final day was the longest of all. Even Marjorie got to grumbling.

At long last, however, the ship docked and we were freed from our cramped room. Coming out on deck under a glancing rain, however, was not the sort of welcome I'd expected. I quickly found my leather hat and fixed it to my head. Horace whined until we were standing firmly on the wharf with Norfolk looming around us.

Norfolk was nothing like Philadelphia.

CHAPTER THIRTY

The wharf was not nearly as large as Philadelphia's, but it seemed busier even with the rain. Ships of all sizes lay at anchor, and a cacophony of languages and dialects filled the air, along with the stench of sweat and odor of fish. The town itself stretched out from the wharf in a haphazard fashion. Gone were the tidy, well-planned streets with trees and lamps. Buildings and houses were built almost wantonly, and the only bits of green were patches of weeds and clumps of grass growing where they had not yet been trampled into mud. It was a fierce, frenzied town, what I imagined London would be like.

The town spanned across a river that split in different directions. Piers stuck out from every angle. It was such a strange and convoluted place and would have been impossible for me to navigate unaided. I hoped we would not be staying long.

The captain had given Shaw the name of an inn with a pen yard for the animals, and it was, fortunately, located in the part of town where we had docked. Grahame stayed behind to see to the unloading of our belongings while Thom and Shaw escorted me and Marjorie from the ship. I was not sad to see the last of it. Marjorie looked overjoyed to be back on solid land, going so far as to whisper a prayer of thankfulness.

The streets were filled with a myriad of characters wearing styles of all kinds, from merchants in wigs and cut-breeches to sailors with open shirt-fronts and ragged pants. I even saw a few natives and a man whose skin was as dark as leather. Horace kept close to my side as we made our way down the muddy, rutted streets. I kept a close grip on my satchel, not liking the unsavory fellows around us.

The inn was called the "Fish and Kettle" and doubled as a public house. Inside, the midday meal was being served, and the place was quite crowded with sailors and travelers of all types. But it was warm and dry, so I was pleased to be inside even among the press of strangers. It was rather exciting, truly, to be in an alehouse, even one that looked so respectable. There were two rooms, one for the men and, I noticed with a little disappointment, another for women and children. All very proper, which spoke well of the innkeeper. When we were pointed to that person, the reason became clear.

The innkeeper was a woman. She was tall and robust, closer to Grahame's age than mine or Marjorie's. She wore a laced mobcap, a yellow bodice and sleeves, and a blue and yellow striped skirt, over which she had tied a spotless linen apron. She spoke in a loud voice with a British accent similar to Thom's. She swept over to us through the bustle.

"Lost doves, are we?" she asked with a laugh. "Look like the wind's just blown you in."

"Are you Bess the innkeeper?" Shaw asked.

"That I am. Irish, are you? Seen a fair few of you. Are my London cousins finally running you out?" She gave another burst of laughter and a table nearby joined in.

None of us knew quite how to respond to that.

Thom stepped forward.

"Heard you had pens to let, and lodging as well," he said, taking charge in a very un-Thom-like manner.

"Ah, so not all Irish, then," she said, eying Thom with a bold glance. When Thom didn't answer, she got a strange look that she quickly smothered. "I have both indeed. For how long?"

"Long enough to hire a ship," Thom answered vaguely.

She cocked her head. "Only just come and so ready to leave fair Norfolk?"

"We've a place to be."

"Well, then, can't have you standing here. How many pens for what beasts, and how many rooms?"

She and Thom haggled, and I watched in admiration at Thom's clever skill. Bess seemed impressed as well and at last struck hands on the bargain. "You're not new to this game," she said with a cock of her head. "Might you be from Southwark?"

Thom gave a small quirk of his lips, which might have been a smile. "I might be."

Bess laughed again, such a deep, infectious sound that I couldn't help but smile in response.

"Gone and married an Irish lass, have you?" Bess pressed.

But Thom shook his head. "Just finished my time and looking to settle."

"Don't suppose Norfolk appeals?"

Thom looked around him and then back to her. "Can't say it does."

"Pity." She did look disappointed. "Harry!" I jumped at her sudden bellow.

A boy of perhaps twelve came out from the kitchens. He had her bright blue eyes and rounded nose, along with a shock of red hair. "Yes, Mum?"

"Show these fine folk to room six, then to the pen yards."

"Yes, Mum."

The rooms were upstairs, and ours was small but tidy. Twin beds filled the space, leaving enough room to walk around them and allow Horace to stretch out. Shaw and Thom left me and Marjorie there to settle, though the last thing either of us wanted to do was to sit confined in another small room.

"I have a few coins," Marjorie confided in me. "Let's get a dish of tea."

I agreed eagerly.

The family area was clearing out as we settled at a small table near the window overlooking the street. Bess herself brought over the tea.

"And from where have you come?" she asked as she laid out the cups and teapot and two linen napkins. A plate of biscuits accompanied the tea, and they looked and smelled freshly made.

"Philadelphia," I said when Marjorie did not.

Bess cocked her head at me. "You don't say? Fine city, so I've heard. And before that?"

"Donegal," I answered vaguely.

"Been long in the new land?"

"A fair time," I said.

Bess laughed. "Oh, I see you watching the street. Not a fair long time, I'd wager. No matter. To Norfolk by ship, then, but not going north, since you've just come. South? To Charleston? Or farther?"

"Why do you ask?" Marjorie asked at last, her look suspicious.

Bess only gave a laugh. "Ah, so you've caught me out. I know a few sea captains is all. I put in a word for them, I see a bit of coin if they're hired. Nothing wrong with it now, just a bit of extra to keep me and my daughter in lace."

"Are they fine captains?" I asked.

"Well, not fine, if you're meaning manners, but they know their business and that's no lie."

"Then I'll tell my husband that he might speak with you of it," I said, feeling bold.

Bess looked pleased. "Well, then, I should look forward to it. And perhaps you'll want another plate of those biscuits." She had a twinkle in her eyes as she left us.

"Are you sure about this, Ailee?" Marjorie asked.

"No, but Thom seemed to like her, and I trust Thom. And," I added with a smile, "I rather like her, too."

Bess let us sit for as long as we would and refilled our tea pot twice and the plate once again. It was pleasant to sit and chat triflings over a cup of tea. I felt tension I didn't know I'd been carrying ease out of my shoulders and neck. I also felt a bond forming between me and Marjorie. She wasn't an easy person to get to know, but as we sat in the public house that afternoon, laughing over some of the fashions we'd seen go past on the street, I caught a glimpse of humor and spirit in her that she usually kept hidden in company.

The men found us in good spirits when they returned. I quickly told them about Bess's connections, and they were eager to speak with her. Apparently, Shaw had had no luck in the short time he'd spent in query at the wharf.

"Why is that?" I asked Grahame after Shaw had gone to find Bess.

"We need someone familiar with sailing near the islands," Grahame told me after he'd drank a cup of tea and began on a second. "Someone who knows where shoals might be hiding."

I wasn't sure what a shoal was, but it sounded ominous.

Shaw returned and pulled a chair over to join us. "I've asked that supper be brought. And gotten the name of a captain who might suit." He looked pleased. "I'll seek him out after we've eaten. Will you go, Grahame?"

"I will."

Bess and a girl who looked enough like her to be her daughter brought supper. The girl was ten or so, with hair darker than her brother's, though still red, and eyes as blue as her mother's. She wasn't a pretty thing, but she had a sweet smile for us.

"Is that handsome Southwark man not joining you?" Bess asked with a bold gleam in her eye.

"Thom keeps to himself," Grahame answered. "But you might find him taking a mug in a bit."

Bess glanced toward the doorway dividing the two areas of the public house and got a determined look. Thom would have to watch himself if this woman set her cap at him. She didn't seem like someone easily put aside.

Supper was roast chicken and dumplings with thick, crusty bread, potatoes, and greens. It was all delicious and washed down with a thick, dark ale. It was such a far cry from the fish and pea gruel we were served through most of the voyage from Philadelphia that I thought my stomach might rebel at the unexpected richness. Instead, it simply made me sleepy.

Grahame saw us up to our shared room. "We won't be late," he told me. "Put Horace by the door and lock it," he added.

I nodded and did as he said after he left.

Marjorie and I lit the candles, but I couldn't keep my eyes open long enough to knit. I woke when the men came in, unlocking the door and urging Horace to move, and then fell back to sleep listening to Shaw whisper to Marjorie that we had a ship and would sail tomorrow.

Tomorrow, we'd be home.

"Another ship," Marjorie said with a heavy sigh as we gathered our few belongings the next morning. The four of us had met Thom downstairs to eat, and afterwards the men had gone to check on the livestock.

"But only for the day," I reassured her.

Marjorie sat on the bed and brushed her hand over it. "And the last of this for a while."

"I hadn't thought of that." I sat on my own. "What will we sleep on?"

"Rush pallets work well, if we can find the right grasses." She pursed her lips, considering. "Leaves work, too, but they aren't as nice."

"Leaves or grass pallets?" I lay back on the bed, savoring it. "I'll miss this."

"It won't be so bad," Marjorie told me. "The men don't like sleeping rough, so I'm sure a bed will be one of the first things they build after shelter." We laughed together, and it helped ease some of the tension.

We met the men in the pen yards, gathering up the flocks. A heavy wagon was waiting in the yard with all the supplies and chicken crates loaded, two oxen standing placidly in the yoke. Bess's boy, Harry, stood at their heads, watching curiously. The cow and bull were tied to the rear of the wagon, looking much put upon.

"We hired Mrs. Spence's wagon yesterday," Shaw told us as we came to them, "and her boy to drive it."

"Have everything?" Grahame asked.

"I hope so," I told him. "Are we ready?"

He nodded, and with that signal, Harry whistled to his team. He led the way from the pen yard, Thom and Shaw following with the sheep and goats. Grahame kept to one side of the flocks with Marjorie and I to the other, and between us all we got them herded to the wharf. My excitement grew with each step. We were so close to the end of our long journey. And this time, I wanted it to be the end. I was ready to settle and make a home with Grahame. I was eager for that life.

The ship Shaw had hired was half the size of the last we'd taken, if that big. It looked small and set too low in the water, with the two boats lashed to the sides giving it a strange bulk. Both Marjorie and I looked at it in dismay. A wide plank had been lowered between the ship and pier just behind one of the tied boats. A handful of rough-looking men began loading our supplies as soon as the wagon stopped.

The three men helped while Marjorie and I watched from the pier. The captain came out when the supplies were nearly loaded. He was a younger man than I'd expected, close to Niall's age though much more weathered. He wore a tricorn hat with a feather cocked to one side. Niall would have envied it. He was dressed most respectably, a far cry from the open shirt-fronts and bare heads of the men loading the ship. He joined us on the pier as the final supplies were carried aboard.

"*Senhors,*" he said with a trilling accent I couldn't place. "These are many sheep to put aboard my poor ship."

"They've traveled so before," Shaw assured him. "May I introduce our wives? Captain Fonseca, Mrs. Monigal and Mrs. Donaghue."

The captain bowed low to both of us. "*Senhoras,* it is my pleasure." He straightened and gave me a sly wink. I wasn't sure how to take that and felt my cheeks begin to burn.

But he turned his attention at once back to the men. "*Senhors,* we must be off quickly. Better to make Machipongo Island before the tides turn, eh."

"And you are certain of the way?" Shaw asked cautiously.

The captain didn't take offense but grinned. "Ah, yes, I know the islands that lie just offshore. Yours is one of the largest. I hear it called Shooting Bear Island, too. You hear this?"

Shaw shook his head.

"No matter. The islands have many names. Native names, English names, Spanish names, even French names. I know them all. *Senhoras,* if you please," he said to me and Marjorie, sweeping his hand toward the plank. "Welcome to the *Senhora do Mar.*"

The ship was tidy, as tidy as the *Resolution* had been. The crew obviously took pride in their work. The brass gleamed, the yellow paint was pristine along the inside of the rails, and the deck was clean. They had roped off two sections forward and aft for the animals.

"*Senhoras,* you are welcome to the use of my cabin for the duration," Captain Fonseca told us.

"Can we watch from the deck for a bit?" I asked.

"But of course, *Senhora,*" the captain said with a wide grin. "I would never deny a lady a chance to see me at my finest."

He laughed at my blushes and strode away to watch the men herd the animals aboard.

"He's a forward sort," Marjorie said.

"He does seem it," I agreed. We smiled but smothered our grins quickly when the captain glanced our way.

We left the Norfolk wharf shortly after the animals were secure. Horace found a place near the sheep to stretch out and not be under foot. Marjorie strayed near the rail, but I caught her before she could go up to it, Beacham's warning clear in my memory.

"Best to not be too close," I explained to her. "Just in case."

It was wrong to play upon her fears, but it didn't stop me. Now more than ever I took Beacham's warnings to heart.

We watched from a few steps away from the rail as the town grew smaller. The sails caught and held the wind with a goodly measure of canvas, more than I'd have expected in such a small ship. The river current helped carry us out into the bay.

The ocean breeze was cool and tasted of salt. Seeing that stretch of blue going on endlessly was unnerving. I turned my back on the sea. I had no wish to remember those weeks spent on the open water. Instead, I watched the land break away into rocks and sandy bars, and then reform into land once more. It was a strange sort of place, with grasses riding up to the edge of the water in places, or a long stretch of beach cascading down from a sandy hill. It was soft and placid looking, not at all like the rock-strewn hills of Ireland. And not green, either, not like home. Even the green looked washed out here, tanned by the sun and stripped by the wind.

Grahame came up to us.

"I've never seen a place like it," I told him.

"Disappointed?"

"No," I said, though I was uncertain. "Not entirely. I suppose I didn't know what to expect."

"It's flatter than I'd figured," Marjorie admitted.

"It is flat," I agreed.

"There's so much sky," she added.

Grahame smiled. "It'll be different on the island. Land looks stranger from the sea. But it won't be like Philadelphia. Or like home."

"Home," I said, tasting the word. "This is home now, isn't it?"

Grahame nodded. He touched my arm, then returned to keep watch on the animals. The goats didn't like to be so close to the water, it seemed. He and Shaw had their hands full keeping them inside the rope enclosure while Thom stayed with the bull and cow.

"What did your friend call the island?" I asked Marjorie.

"She didn't," Marjorie said. "She only mentioned the foraging and hunting, and something about bears. Small ones, she said, that live near the marsh. Other animals, too. More birds than she'd ever seen. And the snakes, of course."

"And the biting bugs."

Marjorie and I exchanged looks. "It will be an adventure,"

Marjorie said, her voice firm.

"A good one, I hope."

We had sailed for some while, cutting through water with the wind pushing us northward, when the captain began giving orders. We'd passed a stretch of sandy beach, then a break where the ocean rushed past, and then another beach with the grasses coming close to the shore.

The ship banked, slowing as the sails were brought in.

"This is the best place to anchor," I heard Captain Fonseca say to the men.

"There's no pier," I said to Marjorie. She nodded, her eyes wide.

Shaw came over to us.

"We'll anchor here and offload onto the longboats. It'll take several trips," he added.

"What about the animals?"

"The sheep and goats will ride," he said, though he didn't look pleased with the idea. "The cow and bull will have to swim."

I gaped at him.

"Next to the boat," he added quickly. "Captain Fonseca assures me he's done it before."

Marjorie and I were encouraged to remain on the ship while all this transporting took place. For a short time, it was thrilling to watch. Then, as the third load of supplies was lowered into the longboats and rowed over, it grew rather dull. The captain's cabin boy, who looked suspiciously similar to the captain, brought us drinks and a light meal of bread and cheese, and we waited some more.

When the crew was finally ready to offload the animals, Grahame made them wait. He wanted us on shore first to help keep the beasts from straying too much. I was keen to try the longboat, but Marjorie looked ill at the thought. I gripped her hand before crossing to the rail.

We were lowered to the boats by a rope swing. It was breath-taking, swinging over the ocean with the small boat beneath me. It was the closest I think I'd ever come to flying.

I was laughing when Grahame caught me and handed me into the boat. He smiled to me, holding on to me longer than necessary before helping me settle. Marjorie was white as linen and wide-eyed with fright when she reached the longboat, and Horace barked madly as he was lowered in. He came to me and glued himself to my side.

The boat ride to the shore was more exciting than it had looked from the ship. The waves caught the boat, pitching it onward and upward and down again until we were riding a crest and then scraping against the sandy bottom. Horace leapt from the boat and bounded through the surf to the beach and then rolled and rolled in the sand. With a pang, I thought of how much Edgar would have enjoyed doing the same.

Grahame was determined to carry each of us to the beach so that we wouldn't be soaked through. I insisted he take Marjorie first, for she looked ready to faint. When he came for me, I was reminded again of his sheer strength. I seemed to weight nothing in his arms. With a rush of giddy delight, I pressed a kiss upon his cheek before he lowered me to my feet.

And then I was on land. Our land. Our new home. It was sandy, and covered with coarse, dense grass, and as windy as standing on the deck of a ship at sea, but it was ours.

One goat leapt from the longboat during crossing, but it made its way to shore, bedraggled and soaked. The cow and bull also made it, both of them shaking off the hands holding the ropes tied round their horns to help keep them tethered to the boats, then charging forward out of the surf as soon as they touched bottom. They didn't run off, though, but stopped as soon as they reached the grass and began lipping at it to see how palatable it was.

The sheep tried to go in all directions at once, and we had quite a time keeping them together. Horace helped, going where I pointed and barking at the sheep.

Finally, we were all gathered on the shore. I missed whatever parting words the captain had with Grahame and Shaw before they made their final crossing to the island. The ship raised anchor as soon as the longboats were secured and set sail, pointing back toward Norfolk.

The sun was getting low in the sky. I had no idea what we would do next. All of our belongings were piled in the grass. Sandy hillocks rose before us, blocking our view of the interior of the island. Not a soul had come looking to see what the commotion was. Perhaps they were too far from the beach to have heard us.

"The settlement should be this way," Shaw said, pointing up the dune. "Toward the middle of the largest part of the island, which should be this southern end. They built close to a river that runs from the marsh."

"Do you think they'll help haul our belongings?" Marjorie asked.

"I'm sure they will," Shaw said, giving her a comforting smile. "And put us up for the night."

"How many settled here?" I asked, realizing I didn't know.

"Three families and two men," Shaw answered. "Eleven in all, if there've been no births since."

Or deaths, I thought. A strange chill crept through me.

"Do they expect us?" I asked.

"I sent word last fall," Shaw told me. He didn't seem to find it strange that I asked so many questions.

"We'd best be moving," Grahame said, "before we lose the light."

Marjorie and I gathered what bags we could carry and still herd sheep, and the men took a chicken crate each. Thom tied the cow and the bull to the same lines and drew them along with him. It took some doing to get the sheep and goats pointed in the right direction, but they'd had enough of the sea and finally moved up the dunes. Horace stayed close to me, alert and curious, sniffing the air with hardly a pause.

At the top of the sandy hill, we had our first clear sight of the island. Coarse grasses changed to a meadow of sorts, and then to trees. Not the tall, ominous forest surrounding Cadha's farm, but windswept, thick, short trees used to such meager soil and salty breeze. The woods were dense but not too thick with brush. It was an odd mixture of copse and clearing.

Following the line of where forest met meadow, we saw the gleam of water that hinted at a narrow river. The first signs of cultivation was in the form of sheep, dotting the area near the river, white spots amid green. It looked idyllic and peaceful, and I let the sight settle me.

As the wind fell away behind the dunes, other noises became apparent—buzzing insects, and the rustling of the thick grass, and the far away bleat of sheep. Our own flock began to move quicker, hearing their kind.

"Let them go," Grahame told us. "They'll find the flocks and stay close."

"It's an island," Shaw added. "They can't stray far."

We laughed at that. There'd be little need for fences.

The sun was touching the tops of the trees as we neared the river. The air smelt of pine and grass and spicy scents I didn't recognize. We found a trail and followed it along the river, which cut through grasses much more to the animals' liking. The sheep had already begun to intermingle, and the goats, too, though there were no others like them. A few trees grew around us, with signs of where several more had been cut down, leaving only stumps.

The trail led to a huddle of rough wood houses far enough from the river not to be threatened by flooding. But our excitement at finding them quickly turned to bafflement.

No smoke plumed from cook fires. No dogs barked as we came up to the buildings. Garden plots grew wild, mingled with the patches of grass and weeds trying to reclaim them. A door stood open wide at one house, with no light coming from inside. There was no sound of people at a time when supper should have been cooking and evening chores finished. A handful of sheep grazed in one of the gardens, but nothing else seemed to be alive in the settlement. Only sheep.

A terror such as I'd never known crawled through me.

Only sheep.

CHAPTER THIRTY-ONE

I dropped my bundles to the ground and began digging through my satchel. The cowl was at the bottom, along with the other I'd nearly finished on the voyage from Philadelphia. The men had gone to the house, calling out, and Marjorie was chasing the sheep out of the garden. I stopped her.

"We need to get inside before it's dark," I said.

She stared at me. "Why? Did you see something?"

"I know what did this."

"Did what?"

"Killed these people." My voice was turning frantic.

"We don't know what happened here," Shaw said as he came over. "Let's not panic. I didn't see a boat on the beach. I know they had two."

"There could have been an illness," Marjorie began.

"But where are the other animals?" I pressed. "Surely they didn't just come here with sheep. Why are there no chickens or the cows? We need to get inside. We need to get the goats, the cow and bull, and the chickens and lock them inside, too."

"But not the sheep?" Shaw asked.

"They don't like sheep."

"They?"

"The cat-beasts. They're here."

Shaw and Marjorie gaped at me, and I could tell they didn't believe me. I turned away, looking for Grahame. He was heading toward the river.

Fear tore into me. "Grahame!" I screamed.

He whirled, clearly thinking we were under attack. I raced toward him and put the cowl around his neck as soon as I was close enough. "Don't go, please. You have to stay here. We have to get inside."

"Ailee—"

"I know you don't believe me, but please, I'm begging you to trust me."

Grahame looked at me, studying my face. An odd expression formed on his. I realized suddenly that he was seriously considering my words. That he might, just might, believe me.

"It's getting too late to do much else," Thom said as he came up to us. He looked worried. "We don't know what might be out there. Could be natives."

"We need to get the muskets," Grahame said.

"In the morning, please." Hot tears were burning down my cheeks.

"I'll go for them," Shaw said.

"No—" I began, but Grahame took me by the arms.

"Ailee, I know you're frightened, but we must secure this place. Thom and Shaw will go for the guns. We'll stay here, make a fire, and secure a house. We will get through this night."

I opened my mouth, but Grahame spoke before I could.

"I trust you," he said firmly. "Please trust me."

The others were already moving off to do just as he'd suggested. Aching with fear, I nodded to him.

I grabbed Thom before he could go off. I yanked the latest cowl unfinished from the ball of wool, tied a knot in the end, and thrust it at Thom. "Swear to me you'll wear this. Don't you take it off for anything."

Thom hesitated, read something of the desperation in my expression, and nodded.

I didn't have a third one to give Shaw, and he was already heading back the way we'd come. "Stay out of the trees," I called after him.

Frustrated, terrified, and desperate, I could do nothing else but as Grahame had suggested. He chose one of the homes that had a chimney, found a stack of wood, and built a fire inside. He had to clear the chimney first of a bird's nest. The whole place was dusty and smelt of disuse. It was a single room home, with a bed frame and mattress that had been torn open by some creature. Grahame dragged it outside and mice scampered from it. There were mice, at least. And birds. I'd seen birds here and there during the walk. That was something.

A rough table and stools, a few crates and a trunk, rusting cookware hanging on the wall, and scattered flour sacks and strewn herbs were all that were left in the house. Inside the crates Marjorie and I found candles that had stuck together, jars of preserves and pickles, salt, and salve. The trunk held clothing for a man and a woman, two pairs of shoes, a comb carved from bone, and a silver hairpiece. It was eerie to look upon such personal belongings left in an empty house, waiting for the owners' return.

"I'm going to see to the animals," Grahame told us. I stood up from where I was tending the fire, alarmed. He pulled at the cowl to show he still had it on, then left the house. Horace moved to the front door and laid down near it, nose pointed to the door, ears perked.

"You know something," Marjorie said quietly.

I nodded in the dim light.

"Tell me."

"I don't know that you'll believe me."

"Tell me anyway."

I looked at her. She was kneeling on the floor, the contents of the trunk spread out before her, and she was holding the hairpin.

She held it up. "This was Edina's. She had it from her mother. Edina wouldn't have left it behind without good cause."

"Did Edina ever write about wild cats on the island?" I asked, my voice trembling.

"No. Just the snakes and biting bugs. And all the birds. And the bears."

"The bears." I grabbed hold of that thought. "Would it be strange to find bears on an island like this?"

Marjorie frowned in thought. "I did think it strange at the time. Why?"

I pulled my satchel closer. Marjorie came nearer, settling on the wooden floor next to me.

"I've heard things," I said to her in a whisper. "Stories during my crossing and since. Of dangers in old places where men haven't been." I stopped with a frustrated sigh. It sounded ridiculous when I said it out loud. Like a tale told to frighten children.

"Go on," Marjorie urged.

"The thing that attacked me," I said, switching thoughts, "it wasn't a bobbed tail cat like Thom thought. It wasn't like anything I'd ever seen before. And the wool hurt it."

"Wool?"

"From my shawl. I'd treated it with wool oil not long before, and when it bit me through the shawl, it was hurt. There was nothing else about me that could have hurt it so. And then there was Frau Scheuling."

"The old woman in Germantown?" Marjorie asked. "The one who sends her grandchildren to ask if anyone will come sit with her?"

"Does she? It was her grandson who took me to her. And she told me a story about creatures in the woods that would attack travelers, but a monk's hood would protect them if it were made a certain way. She taught me." I held up the hook pen. "And she used rough wool that hadn't been washed."

"Full of wool oil," Marjorie said, catching on.

I was so relieved she understood. "And so when I saw just the sheep here . . ."

"You think it could be like the cat that attacked you." Marjorie looked into the fire. "Do you really believe this, Ailee?" Her voice was quiet.

"I have to. It's the only thing that makes sense. And I've seen and heard too much to discount it."

"But if there is no cat here?"

"Maybe it's the bears," I said. "Or another creature." I hugged my knees, growing uncertain. What did I know, really? Anything could have happened to these people. Illness, or natives, or a bad season or storm.

But then why were only sheep left behind?

Marjorie stared quietly for some time. I didn't know what she might be thinking. My heart was pounding, hoping someone, at last, would believe me even as I agonized with doubt.

"How many of those hoods have you made?"

"I made cowls," I answered. "Three of them, but I gave one to Niall before we left. Oh, and a small one for Horace, after what happened to Edgar."

"Edgar?" She looked alarmed. "Who's Edgar? What happened?"

"He was our other dog. The cat-beast came back, and Edgar

chased it. They fought. He . . . he didn't make it." I swallowed against a lump of grief, fear striking me all over again.

"And the cat-beast?"

"Grahame tried to shoot it, but it got away."

Marjorie looked surprised. "Do you think it was clever? Or just fast?"

It was a good question. I thought back to when I'd faced the beast, recalling those dark, cold eyes. They had been so terrifying. Everything about the creature had been terrifying, but the memory of those eyes had stayed with me much longer.

And now I knew why.

"Yes, I think it was clever. I think it was reasoning what had happened to it."

"Why would it come back?"

Horror spread through me all over again. "I think it was looking for me. It was nowhere near the sheep or the other animals. It was close to the house."

"It was hunting people."

We sat in cold silence, dread building up between us.

"We need to make more cowls," Marjorie said, determined. "And boil wool for oil. Spread it on our skin until we can leave the island."

I straightened, momentarily speechless. "You believe me?"

"I've heard stories, too," she admitted. "Tales about something dark and strange in the woods. Some of the stories were passed down by the natives, those friendly to us. And then there's the sheep left here. It's eerie. It could be we're wrong. It could have been illness. They might have had to eat the other beasts if the food gave out, but then why have preserves left? It could have been natives, and they left the sheep, but why leave these things behind when they could make use of them?" She gestured around the room with the hairpin in her hand. "And if it were illness, why no bodies?" She took a deep breath. "We don't know what it is for certain, but until we do, let's prepare for everything it might be."

Practical. Sensible. And yet listening to my children's story like it might be true. Marjorie astonished me.

"We need to put together a meal, somehow," Marjorie continued.

"A chicken?"

"Yes," she said reluctantly. "Seems a waste the first night, but it'll serve. We can pull whatever's growing in the garden to throw in the pot and make it a stew to share. I'll see to the chicken. You see to the garden."

"We'll need water," I said, my voice trembling again.

"Ask Grahame to fetch it."

I hesitated. Marjorie crossed to me and put her hands on my shoulders. "I know this is frightening, but we can't let the fear defeat us or we'll die before we've even begun to survive."

Her voice was firm, but her touch was gentle. I swallowed against the fear and nodded.

The sun was below the trees, and the sky was a brilliant hue of reds and purples. There was a chill in the air, but not freezing, and it was oddly damp with no sign of rain. Horace followed me as I looked for Grahame, and I was thankful for the dog's presences.

I heard Grahame before I saw him and followed the sound of his voice, but I stopped when I heard him say my name.

"Ailee is young, but she's no fool," he was saying. "She was right about the cat-beast."

I stood in shock. Grahame did believe me.

"You saw the tracks, Thom," he continued.

"I did. Never saw anything like them."

"You think there is one here on the island?" Shaw asked. He was out of breath. They must have run to the beach and back to have returned so quickly.

"I don't know what's on this island," Grahame admitted. "So let's plan for everything we can."

"All right," Shaw conceded. "What's first?"

"We need water," I said, coming out from the shadow of the building where I'd been listening. The men were standing together near a garden, muskets shared between them. "So we can cook. And we need wool."

"I found a bale in one of the houses," Grahame said. "Looks like last year's shearing. It's not been combed—"

"It'll suit," I told him. "And the animals?"

"The goats strayed," Grahame said.

"I can get them," Thom told us.

"Don't go alone," Grahame warned.

"I'll go, too," Shaw said. "See if I can find any tracks or signs."

"Come back before full dark," Grahame told them both. "I won't leave the women to look for you."

"You'd best not," Shaw told him soberly. "I'm trusting you to protect them."

"I will."

And so it went. Grahame fetched water for us from the river. Marjorie killed and plucked a chicken while I dug through the gardens. Working had a soothing effect on me, calming my fears as I focused on seeing us fed. I found leftovers from last year's potatoes, some new carrots and onions, and several types of greens. My hands were filthy afterwards, but I was pleased with the yield.

Back inside, I'd put the largest pot I could find over the fire to heat water. I used a little water to wash the vegetables. I pulled fresh candles from Grahame's bag, lit them from the fire, and set them on a tin plate on the table to see what I was doing. I found a knife, but it was far too rusty to use, so I dug through Grahame's bag once more and found one of his. It was more like working in the hold of the ship than working in Cadha's kitchen, with everything so rough and uncertain, but I had it all ready by the time Marjorie brought in the chicken. She'd already quartered it. Horace followed her in and lay across the threshold once more, alert.

Grahame had moved the bale of wool to the house. It was a bundle of five or six fleeces tied together with twine. Most where white, but two were brown, a rich color I'd not seen on Grahame's sheep.

We had the stew in the pot at last. Marjorie set aside a few jars of preserves to go with the meal, and then she eyed the fleece.

"Let's lay it over the bedframe," she suggested. "We can pick the worst of it free from there."

The bed frame was a lashing of rope strung between poles. I'd never worked with a fleece before, so it was good Marjorie was there to guide me. It was hard to see clearly in the dim light, but between us, we went over the fleece, picking out the worst of the soiled and matted parts and any debris we found. It was soothing work, and the wool was soft and easy on my hands. Marjorie had out her carders as soon as we were finished with the first fleece.

"How long did it take you to make one of those cowls?" Marjorie asked as she began carding and I started picking over the second fleece.

"A few weeks."

She grimaced. "What could make it go faster?"

I fought the urge to immediately say that I didn't know. It was strange being the one with the skill to teach. I'd not had this sensation before, and it was hard not to fall back into thinking I didn't know enough about what I was doing to be helpful. Instead, I gave the matter my full attention, hands hovering over the fleece as I considered.

The wool Frau Scheuling had used was thicker than any I'd worked with, like a few strands of twine brought together. And the hook was only so large, too, so it wouldn't be able to grasp wool much thicker. But I knew I could spin thicker wool—I'd done so when I was first learning. And a bigger hook could hold more wool for each stitch. Thicker wool would make a denser stitch. If we spun the wool thick and loose . . .

I sighed. "My spinning wheel is at the beach."

"Mine, too," Marjorie said, realizing. She straightened, setting down her carders. "I'm going to look for one here."

"It's getting dark—"

"I'll be quick," she said. She fetched a candle from the table.

I took one of the roileags of carded wool from the pile that had steadily grown at her feet. "It isn't much, but it's better than nothing," I told her, handing it to her.

She twined it carefully around her neck, a nervous laugh escaping from her. "Is this not the oddest thing you've ever done?"

"Well, I did marry a complete stranger and cross an ocean a month later."

Marjorie stared at me and then we both laughed, a high-pitched hysterical sort of sound.

"Well, then," she said, and she adjusted the roll of wool around her neck, holding it in place with one hand. "Wish me luck."

I did so, and then did one better. "Go with her, Horace," I urged. Horace didn't need any further encouragement. He followed after Marjorie into the gathering night.

I closed the door and returned to the fleece. The house was eerie with only me in it. The fire crackled, and I remembered to stir the pot. I could hear the distant roar of the surf, like a faraway breath coming over and over again. I could hear the bleating sheep far off as well. I tried not to think about my friends out in the darkness. I tried not to think about what I would do if none of them came back. I concentrated on the wool under my fingertips, the feel of it, soft and pliant and somewhat oily.

An image came to me from an engraving in a book I'd seen in Lifford. Adelle and I had been exploring her father's library, one of the largest in town. The book had engravings of kings, and some of the kings had been in armor. I remembered the armor covered the man from top to bottom, even around his neck and knees and elbows. Adelle and I had jested about what it would mean to try to sit or ride a horse or use the privy, but now I recalled the way the armor seemed to flow from head to neck to shoulders, like a mantle or a monk's cowl, but close, protective. Thick.

And an image began to form in my head about that sort of thing in wool. I'd want something that would fit close to Grahame's neck but also cover his shoulders, so it would need to be wide at the bottom and grow narrow to fit close under the chin. It wouldn't be all one piece, like the cowl, but open at the ends so that Grahame could wear it as tight or loose as he wished. But how to close it? A bit of rope, perhaps, worked through the stitches? Twine? Leather?

Leather would hold best. Maybe with a buckle, like from a harness. Did we have any harnesses left?

Marjorie did not return alone. Grahame came in with her, carrying a large spinning wheel, with Horace following after. The wheel was of a design I'd not seen before, with a larger wheel than I was accustomed to.

"Can you work it?" I asked Marjorie.

"I think so. I've seen them used in Germantown." She was going over the wheel, checking its parts. "It might take a bit to get the feel for it, but I think I can."

"Then I have an idea," I told her. "How thick can you spin the wool?"

"How thick should we?"

"Thick enough to be a mouthful." I grimaced, feeling an old ache in the scars on my shoulder. "Keep it as raw as possible. Just enough to stitch with."

Marjorie nodded. "It's certainly nothing I've tried before, but it should work up quickly. It'll take a lot of wool to make enough to stitch with," she warned.

"We'll do the best we can," I said.

Shaw and Thom returned. They'd found three of the goats and put them in a house with the cow. The bull was in another house with the chickens. "They'll foul the place well and good," Shaw said, dismayed, "but I suppose we can clean. Are you certain it's necessary?" he asked Grahame.

Grahame didn't hesitate. "Best to be safe." He caught my eye as he said it, and I couldn't have been more thankful to have him as my husband. He might not completely believe me, but he was willing to take the chance. It was enough.

We ate in silence, each of us lost in thought. The stew was decent, and the preserves yielded a fruit I'd not had before. "Figs," Grahame said.

"I believe they grow on the island," Shaw told him. "Near the marshes."

We fell silent again.

Afterwards, Marjorie and I carded together. I wasn't nearly as practiced as she, but we weren't looking for beautifully rolled roileags—just quickly made ones. Once I had the hang of it, she began to spin, getting a feel for the wheel. She had to stand to use it, and she hummed to herself as she worked at it.

"We should try to rest," Shaw told her after watching her a while. He had broken out a pipe, though he'd only smoked a little. "Can this wait 'til morning?"

Marjorie sighed and relented. "I think I've got the feel, so yes, it can wait."

We didn't have much to put together for bedding. Grahame and Thom had brought what they'd found from the other houses—a couple blankets, one mattress that hadn't been torn into by mice, and a feather pillow. Marjorie and I got the mattress and a blanket to share. Grahame offered the pillow and second blanket to Shaw. Thom had his own blanket and Grahame had his coat. Horace stretched out near the door, looking pensive. His distress disturbed me as much as anything. He knew something was wrong, or could sense what it was, but had no way to tell us. Would an illness leave traces to upset a dog? Would natives? I didn't know, but I did know that Horace had been wary of the forest back at Cadha's. I wouldn't dismiss his fears out of hand.

We banked the fire, extinguished the candles, and laid in the darkness, listening.

I don't know how long it took me to fall asleep. I will never forget how I woke.

Chapter Thirty-Two

It was a scream. A man's scream of pain and shock. And then Horace was barking madly at the door. I was upright and frozen in terror as two men hurried from the house.

"Shaw?" Marjorie rushed to the door, calling out, her voice twisted in fear and helplessness.

I found my feet and made it to the doorway.

Early morning darkness still swathed the island as the first deep colors of dawn spread from the east. The bull was kicking in his building and the chickens were going mad. Horace was standing just outside, still barking, and next to him Marjorie stood clutching the blanket around her, her dark hair spilling over her shoulders in waves of messy curls.

I heard a musket fire. Then another.

"Grahame!" I called, horrified.

"Shaw!" Marjorie shouted, her own voice just as fearful.

Nothing.

"Thom!" I tried, shouting louder.

Thom raced into view. "Blanket," he demanded.

Marjorie tore hers off and thrust it at him. He bolted back into the darkness. Her hand found mine, and we stood clutching each other in dread.

We heard the men before we saw them, rushing from the direction of the river. I could tell by their shapes that it was Grahame and Thom, and that they must be carrying Shaw between them in the blanket. Shaw was moaning in pain. The men swept past us and into the house, slowing to ease through the doorway. Marjorie and I followed.

They laid Shaw, blanket and all, onto the mattress. I lit two candles from the banked coals. Thom reached for his blanket and made to tear it into strips.

"No." Marjorie stopped him with a shaking but firm voice. She grabbed up one of the linen shifts from the clothing left behind.

Grahame was kneeling next to Shaw, tearing away the injured man's shirt. I set the candles nearby and went to the fire to stir it, adding bits of wood until it came to life. I took the last of our water, found a small pot, and put it in the coals to heat. Then I dug through my satchel for my salve.

"I've got him," Marjorie told Grahame. Grahame moved back, reaching for his musket.

"Thom?" he asked.

Thom nodded in the dim light and reached for his musket. They shared the powder horn between them, putting in shot to load, matches still smoking. Thom grabbed Shaw's powder horn and musket, then thought better and left it by the front door.

"Grahame . . ." I began, then stopped, torn. He paused by the door and I drew closer. I didn't know what to say or what I should ask. Grahame saved me from deciding.

"You stay here," he said to me, his voice grim.

"Where are you going?"

"Shooting bears."

He told Horace to stay as he followed Thom out into the early dawn.

I returned to the fire and simply stood before it, staring at the growing flames in dread and helplessness. The sound of water bubbling drew me back to the present. I pulled the pot from the coals with a folded edge of Thom's blanket. Behind me, Marjorie was talking to Shaw in a low voice, and I heard the note of desperation in it.

I didn't want to go to him. I didn't want to see. But I knew I had to.

His face was pale and twisted in pain, and blood stained much of his upper body. I could see where it oozed from punctures in his shoulder, near his neck, and from a heavy cut across his chest and one on his cheek. The dim candlelight made the blood look black, and it was hard to tell if I was seeing dirt or bruises on his face.

"Is the water hot?" Marjorie asked.

I nodded and brought the pot over. She dipped the linen into it and began washing away the blood to count the wounds. One of the punctures was deep and bleeding freely. I took another piece of torn linen to work on the ragged cut on his chest.

"This'll need stitching," I said, trying to keep my voice low and even.

"Can you?"

I wavered. "I never have. I'm not sure I—" My stomach churned at the mere thought.

"I'll see to it," she told me. "Can you . . ." She gestured to the worst of the punctures.

We were still trying to stop the bleeding and bind up the wounds when Thom and Grahame returned. If they had fired again, I hadn't noticed. My whole world had narrowed to helping Shaw. He'd fainted at some point, thankfully so, as Marjorie sewed up his gash. I had spread salve on the punctures and pressed folds of torn linen on them, and then we'd turned him to work on tying the linen down, only to find two more punctures on the back of his shoulder, the blanket clinging to them. We'd had to work the blanket free, causing them to bleed again, and we began all over.

Neither Thom nor Grahame spoke until we'd finished. I sat back, exhausted and shaking, hands bloodstained, my braid coming loose from where I kept flipping it over my shoulder to get it out of my way. Grahame had put a fresh pot of water on to heat, and I accepted a wet rag from him to wash off my hands.

He urged me to sit, but I shook my head. "We need to kill another chicken for broth," I said.

"I'll do it," Thom told us and stood, taking the musket with him.

"What was it?" Marjorie asked quietly. "What got him?"

"A bear," Grahame said. "I think."

We both looked at him.

Grahame hunched over, running his hands over his face as though to wash the images from his head. "It was dark, but the shape was right. Smaller than I've seen before."

"But you've seen them before," Marjorie pressed.

"A bear-baiting in London," he admitted. "That beast was larger. But this one . . . it's head and mouth was longer. Wider, I think. I'm not sure."

Cold fear chased away my exhaustion as I realized what he was saying. I understood all too well his confusion. I remembered how uncannily the cat-beast seemed to switch as I was watching it until I wasn't sure what I was seeing. Were they the same type of creature? How many types were there? How long could we last against them?

"What do we do?" I asked him.

"We do what you suggested," he said. He looked at me. "You were right about the cowl. The beast was going to charge us, but I took off the cowl and threw it to distract it so Thom could get a shot. The cowl landed on its muzzle, and it acted as though I'd caught it with shot. It shook it off and ran toward the river."

I only then realized he wasn't wearing it. I didn't know whether to be relieved or even more terrified.

"How did it get him?" Marjorie asked. Her voice was unnaturally steady.

"Must have come upon him and knocked him down," Grahame said. "It had a hold of his shoulder, trying to drag him off. I got a shot off. I might have hit it. It let go and backed away. By the time we got to Shaw, the beast was deciding to charge. That's when I threw the cowl."

"Did Thom hit it?"

"We're not sure. We found blood, though."

"Just like the cat," I cried. "How can it survive musket shot?"

"It was on the edge of my range," Grahame told me patiently. "If we hit it, they wouldn't have gone deep. But it might bleed out or take infection. We'll find it."

"No," Marjorie said. "It's not worth the risk."

Grahame hesitated, then he nodded. "Fine. But we need to take precautions. I'm going to scout as soon as it's full light. I'll be careful," he told me. "I need to fetch my cowl as it is." He stood and went to Shaw's side.

"It's bad," Marjorie said in a quiet voice.

"I know." He put his hand on her shoulder. "I am sorry." His expression was sincere and Marjorie gave him a tight-lipped nod. Then Grahame grabbed up his musket and left the house.

Horace sat by the door again, alert. I went to him and scratched his ears. "Good dog."

He whined, then fell silent. Marjorie sat by Shaw for a little while, and then she stood, looking determined. "We have work to do." She moved to the spinning wheel. I pulled a third fleece from the stack and laid it over the bedframe. And we worked.

I'd carded the remaining fleece, Marjorie had filled the spool with wool twice, and we'd put a chicken on to boil by the time the sun was well into the sky. Grahame had returned with his cowl around his neck once more and reported no sign of the creature. The blood trail ended at the river. Shaw was laying quiet and pale, drawing the occasional ragged breath. Marjorie sat with him.

"We're going to need a thicker hook," I told her. "But I'm not sure how to make one."

"I can carve a little," Marjorie said, "but Shaw has the better hand." She was holding his hand, stroking it. I tried not to think about how still he was lying.

"Both Grahame and Thom can work wood," I said, keeping to the matter at hand. There wasn't anything to say about Shaw that we both didn't already know.

"Do you think they'd make one?"

"I can ask."

She nodded. It was a good excuse to leave her in peace with her husband. I didn't know why he was so still and pale, but from what I'd seen of her and Grahame's reactions, it wasn't good.

I couldn't think about it. I didn't want to watch another friend die or see another wife become a widow. I had to pray that he'd pull through and do what I could to help keep this from happening again until we could leave.

I stopped outside the house, cautious, but there was no sign of threat. It was peaceful outside. Idyllic, even, if I didn't think of the man lying injured in the house behind me. Strange birds flew overhead. A few insects buzzed around me. The sky overhead was brightening into an amazing blue as the sun rose high into mid-day. I could hear the far off surf and nearer bleats of sheep. Horace relaxed beside me, lowering to sit. Thom had strung the goats, cow, and bull on a line to let them graze near the buildings. The chickens were scratching in a bare spot in the yard, clucking happily. This was the life I wanted, the life we had come here to build for ourselves. It hurt to think we had to leave.

Where would we go if we left? Back to Cadha's farm? How? Were there any boats on the island? Would we have to leave everything we'd brought, like the others had? Maybe they had all fled and not died. Maybe they had started a new life somewhere else. Or had the bear-creatures killed them all? Would they come to try to finish us off? Did they even think like that?

My thoughts kept circling until I pushed them away.

"Horace, let's find Grahame," I called to the dog. He followed after me, alert and watchful.

I found Grahame and Thom just beyond the buildings. They were inspecting a fence that someone had started not far from the last house. The fence was split wood, the rails crossed and lashed together with bark strips and a few nails to hold them in place. It was just tall enough to keep the sheep from straying, but determined ones would be able to leap over it easily.

"They started a pen?" I asked, coming to stand next to the fence.

"Looks so," Grahame answered. "There are more rails cut and stacked." He gestured toward the edge of the sparse woods. I could see wood stacked near the trees.

"Might be to circle the steading," Thom said. "Keep the sheep out of the gardens."

"That would make sense," Grahame agreed.

"Would it keep the bears out?" I asked.

"Not likely," Grahame said grimly.

"Unless we made it higher," Thom said.

"And coated it with wool oil," I said.

They both looked at me. "They don't like the sheep," I explained, "and I think it's because of the wool oil. Does any other animal have it?"

"Not like a sheep," Grahame said, thoughtful. "Are you sure about that?"

"I can't be at all sure," I told him honestly. "But so far the pieces seem to fit. My shawl had just been treated when the cat attacked me, and it didn't like it. The cowl I made you was unwashed wool and the bear didn't like it. The sheep are all alive and well. Did you find the last two goats?"

Thom shook his head with a frown. "A fence wouldn't keep the goats in," he said. "But it would the bull and the cow."

"We could build another pen for the goats," Grahame told him.

"What about a boat?" I asked. They both looked at me again. "To leave the island."

They still only looked at me and suddenly I realized. "You don't mean to leave."

Grahame came over to me. "Do you want to leave?"

"I—" But then I fell silent. Did I want to leave? This place was dangerous, yes, but so was the forest around Cadha's farm. So were lots of places, if I believed Beacham and Rakes and Frau Scheuling. Should we just pack up and run if we were scared? Or did we take a stand and try to make a home for ourselves?

I was getting so tired of fleeing. This threat was different from before. It wasn't the awful, hushed rumors destroying my name. These were creatures, animals we could outwit, maybe even kill.

Or we could keep running. Hide in a city, pretend to be safe. Hope my secret didn't come out and live with it if it did.

Grahame was watching me. He reached for my hand and drew me away from Thom.

"I'll take you away if you wish it," he said quietly.

"Where would we go?"

He shook his head. "I'm not sure."

"I'm tired of running, Grahame," I admitted to him. "I want to make a home. I want what Cadha has." I recalled all too well that sense of fulfillment when I'd thought about having a household of my own. "Is it too dangerous to make it here?"

Grahame took both of my hands in his. "Not with you to help us."

I opened my mouth to protest, but he squeezed my hands and continued. "Frau Scheuling said this moment would come. A day when I would have to choose to stand and fight or retreat. She said all I needed was to have faith in you. She knew, Ailee," he said, his voice incredulous. "She knew we'd be facing something like this. How could she know that if she hadn't faced it too? She taught you what you've been telling us for the past day, didn't she?"

"Not all of it," I told him, astonished. "I figured some out on my own."

His mouth twitched as though holding back a smile. "I knew there was something about you, Ailee Donaghue. You were so much more than what you seemed. Cadha saw it, too." He released my hands to touch my cheek tenderly. "I have faith in you, Ailee. If you are willing to stay, I know we can make a home here."

I thought my chest might burst, but I swallowed against it. "What about Marjorie?"

"Whatever she decides," Grahame said, "we'll see that it happens."

Neither of us spoke of Shaw. There was no need.

"How long to finish the fence?" I asked.

That was all the answer Grahame needed. He swept me into his arms. A wholeness came over me, so complete and absolute that there was no longer any doubt. I loved this man. How long I'd loved him or when it first came upon me, I couldn't say for certain. But I could, without doubt, say it now.

"I love you." My voice was muffled against his broad chest.

His arms tightened around me, and I felt the breath of his words against my ear.

"Not more than I love you, Ailee Donaghue."

I didn't want to let him go, but we both had work to do. "I'll tell Marjorie," I began, but Grahame stopped me.

"Not yet."

Not until Shaw died, I realized he was saying. I swallowed hard and nodded. He gave me another kiss, quickly, as though he might be caught at it, and turned to go.

"I'll need a new hook," I called after him. Grahame glanced at me. "About this wide. If you or Thom could make it."

"We'll get to it today," he said.

The day was brighter but drawn with shadows as I walked toward the house. I tried to put off going back inside for as long as I dared, giving Marjorie that time with Shaw. I checked on the animals, making sure the ropes were knotted tightly, counted chickens, and chased a few sheep out of the gardens. I found the path leading to the river, overgrown by the hardy grass but still traceable for fetching water. I thought about going for another bucketful, but hesitated. I didn't have a cowl. My hands were coated with wool oil, though. And I could get the bit of fleece Marjorie had worn the night before.

We were going to need more water. If I couldn't get even a bucketful, could I claim to try to make this place my home?

I stepped inside just long enough to find the ragged bit of roileag and tie it around my neck as best I could, then took up the bucket and paused. Marjorie was lying next to Shaw, both of them still enough to be asleep. I hoped it was only sleep. I left as quietly as I'd entered, closing the door behind me.

Horace walked next to me toward the river. Neither of us moved quickly, and I listened to the birdsong and watched Horace as he sniffed the air. We were in sight of the river when he stopped suddenly.

I stopped too, my heart leaping into my throat.

On the other side of the river sat a bear.

I think it was a bear. It was a darker shape sitting deep into the shadows of a pocket of trees and brush growing down to the edge of the water. There was no denying that it was watching me. I could see the sheen of iridescent eyes from the depth of the shadows, as though lit from an inner fire.

I clutched the bucket in one hand and got hold of the wool with the other. I could feel it regarding me, studying me, an ominous presence lurking across the slow-moving water. Neither of us moved, and the only sound was Horace's deep-throated growls next to me. Even the birds had gone silent.

Slowly, the bear stood, rising in the shadows. I clutched the fleece tighter, but the bear didn't charge. It backed away with a rustling of undergrowth. I watched as it limped away from the river with careful, strong movements. It glanced back at me just once, pausing in a spot of sunlight. Its black fur rippled, growing mottled with dark browns and sleeker, like a hound's, then turning flat black and thick once more. One shoulder was slick as though damp, and it kept that leg, at first thick and then svelte, and then thick again, off the ground. Its jaw was too long, obscenely long, then seemed shorter, as though shadows played across it.

But the eyes never changed. Dark, cautious, full of dreadful threat, but thoughtful, as if reconsidering its choice. The creature blinked at me, then it turned and disappeared into the underbrush of the stout little trees.

I understood. The line had been drawn. It knew what I knew, the threat we posed to it, and it was giving ground. As long as we did not intrude upon it, it would leave us alone.

I let out a breath I didn't know I was holding. Horace whined next to me, and I reached down to scratch between his ears. The birdsong returned, and the sense of threat faded. I went to the river, bent low to fill the bucket, and watched the clear water pool into it.

Epilogue

Shaw died four days later. Oh, Elsie, I wish I could say it was peaceful, but his breathing got worse, like he was breathing water, and after a while, it simply stopped. Shaw was a good man, like Jacky was, and we miss him. Marjorie most of all.

She's so strong, though. I know she cries when I can't see her, but otherwise, she goes about her day with us, making this place our home. It's getting close to harvest, though we'll have a meager one. Thankfully, we brought enough to keep us through the winter, and Grahame and Thom have had good luck fishing the river. We eat fish constantly. We found fig trees on both sides of the river and picked as many as we could on the side nearest us. Marjorie and I preserved as much as we had jars for, but they eat well fresh, too. We think the bears like them, because Grahame found tracks under several of the trees across the river. I was furious to learn he'd gone across, but he says he never left the water. Still, it seemed wrong to me and he agreed not to go so close to the far bank again. The bears haven't crossed the river since the attack on Shaw, at least not as we've seen. But we keep careful watch for them. It's an uneasy truce, if that is what it is and not my wishful thinking.

Bess is fitting in well. I'm surprised by her eagerness at a life outside of Norfolk. Harry and Lizzie are hard workers, and both seem fond of Thom. Harry is clever with a fishing pole, too, and Lizzie is good at spinning. I still can't tell you how shocked I was when Thom returned from Norfolk with not only supplies but also a wife and adopted family. Bess says she was ready to leave the inn, but Thom was the first man who interested her since her husband died. He seems genuinely fond of her, and we eat the best meals when she cooks. She knows many ways to cook a fish, thankfully. Fish stew gets old after a while. Thom is building her a bake house, and I think we'll have better bread than these fry cakes soon. I can't tell you how eager I am for that. She's also made a poultice out of wool oil and herbs. Thankfully, we've not had to prove its use against the bears, but it does help keep the biting flies away, for a time at least.

Marjorie stayed in the house where Shaw died. Grahame helped her fix it up and she's content, if sad. She's only alone at night, and the dog Thom brought her is a great comfort. I'm sure the dog is expecting pups. Horace was all too eager to spend time with her when she came ashore. She's a stout thing, tan colored but not a mastiff. She's closer to a hound of some sort. She's good with the sheep and with the goats, and she doesn't mind wearing the collar I made for her. Marjorie named her Ruthie. Is it wrong that we both laughed at that? Marjorie says it's time Ruthie was useful for a change. I took it as a good sign that Marjorie could find humor again. We've all lost and gained so much, and while I've the scars to show for some of my trials, many of us bear them deep inside where they can't be seen. Marjorie carries hers with grace and dignity. I think, if you were ever to meet, you would welcome her friendship as I have.

I'm nearly out of room. Thom will take these letters the next time he goes to town for supplies. I hope that we've had word from Cadha of where you are so he can send these on. The last time he went, he sent word to her on how to reach us, and he and Captain Fonseca have devised a clever way to signal when we're in need of passage. The captain is eager for any figs we can pick or preserve as payment, along with fleece. He says if we can get him a bear skin, he'd give us passage for a six-month. But that's not likely to happen. Everyone has agreed with me to stay clear of their territory, so the captain hopes in vain.

Before I close, I have a secret of my own to share. A happy secret. I wanted your blessing that, if it is a boy, I could call him Jacky. Such stories I will tell of friendships and adventures and how their mother is the most fortunate of women. And, girl or boy, I will teach my child everything I've learned, but most especially, how to stitch.

All my love,
Ailee

Beacham's Secret Stitch Cowl
Designed by Laurinda Reddig

MATERIALS: Approx. 260 yards sport weight yarn (sample on cover shown in Shaggy Bear Farms Handspun Romney Yarn in sport weight; also recommended is Cascade 220 Sport in Natural); N Hook

Tips for Working Slip Stitch
- Keep yarn loose on hook.
- Do not pull slip stitches tight.
- You may need to practice a little to get an even stitch.

Cowl Pattern:

Chain 200
Careful not to twist, join with slip stitch in back bump of first chain to form a ring.
Round 1: Slip stitch in back bump of each chain around. Use stitch marker to mark first stitch. Move up each round.
Round 2-25: Slip stitch in back loop only of each slip stitch around.
Round 26: Slip stitch in both loops of each stitch around.
Finish off and weave in ends.

For more information about Laurinda's crochet designs, please go to: www.recrochetions.com

Acknowledgements

Firstly, I am indebted to my partners in crochet, Laurinda and Monica, for encouraging me to be a part of the Ficstitches Yarns Crochet Kit Club. It has, literally and Literately, changed my life.

I am grateful for my husband, T.C., and for my kids, Kate and Liam, who supported me throughout my writing endeavors. I love how we're tackling chores together. And special thanks to Mom, who cooked for us more times than she had to and served as a much needed sounding board for story ideas.

To my lovely beta readers: Mike, Kerry, Katherine, Jeanette, Aurora, Cecillie, Laurinda, and Jane. I could not have done this without you.

Thank you to Irina of *Blizzard Yarn and Fiber* in Vancouver, WA, for being so supportive. Friendly Local Yarn Shops and the folks who run them are amazing and cannot be supported enough.

Also special thanks for my proofreader, Nancy, who caught my errors, and to my writing group, who kept me sane. See you next Thursday.

But mostly, I am overwhelmingly grateful to the women who have come before me. I can never know the full extent of your sacrifices, toils, or hardships, but I can honor you all the same. Thank you.

THE AUTHOR

C. Jane Reid's love of history began when she discovered a book about Tutankhamun's tomb in the middle school library. She's been a student of fiber arts for far less time, sadly missing the chance to learn crochet from her grandmother. By happy circumstances she was befriended by a crochet designer who insisted on teaching her. A lifelong writer, C. Jane is excited to combine her interest in history with her love of crochet in a series of stories blending romance, mystery, and a touch of the supernatural. She lives in the Pacific Northwest with her husband, daughter, son, and Kiwi, the laziest cat in the world.

To keep up-to-date with story releases and to read her ongoing serialized story published twice a month, please sign up for her newsletter at:

www.cjanereid.com

THE SOJOURN STITCH

BY C. JANE REID

That woman will bring shame down upon us . . .

The New World is no place for a penniless widow, even one as skilled at lace-making as Elsie MacClayne. Her choices are few: remain with the other Scots-Irish immigrants to become a burden on her friends or search out her cousin, Connor, who has already made Pennsylvania Colony his home. Elsie longs to make a life for herself and her unborn child, but old prejudices are still alive amongst the colonists, and she is looked upon with either pity or distrust. Can she find the courage to withstand the threats around her and claim her place in a foreign land?

The Sojourn Stitch is the second book of the *Unraveling* series, which features fiber crafts, historical detail, and a crochet pattern by designer Laurinda Reddig.

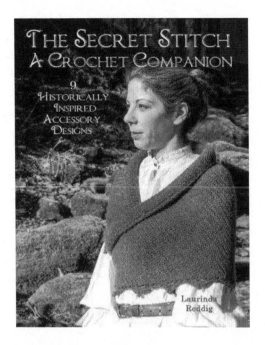

THE
SECRET STITCH
A CROCHET COMPANION
BY LAURINDA REDDIG

A Crochet Companion features nine historically inspired designs based on *The Secret Stitch*, the first novel in the new fiber fiction series by C. Jane Reid, tracing the evolution of crochet. Each design is named for a character from the story, with quotes that inspired that accessory.

Patterns feature:

- 2 shawls, 2 capes, 2 cowls, a bag, hat and mitts
- Stitch diagrams and tutorials for right- and left-handed
- Alternatives to make each one your own

Every craft lovingly handmade tells a story. Ficstitches Yarns Crochet Kit Club takes creating to another level by offering crochet patterns along with hand-dyed yarn, handmade accessories and hooks, and fictional stories, all bound together in a theme of romance, history, the coming-together of friends, and a touch of the supernatural.

Be one of the first to receive the latest book in the *Unraveling* series by C. Jane Reid, along with a crochet design from designer Laurinda Reddig and a handmade accessory, both inspired by the story, along with hand-dyed yarn from an indie yarn dyer. So much more than a yarn club, each element of these kits is an adventure, with a little bit of mystery and a whole lot of fun. Preorders open quarterly in January, April, July, and October.

For more information about the crochet kit club that inspired the writing of this novel and its companion crochet book, please go to:

www.ficstitchesyarns.com

Made in the USA
Charleston, SC
25 September 2016